IN ONE VULNERABLE MOMENT
A SAVAGE PASSION WAS IGNITED . . .

"Go away!" Jessie commanded, her eyes flashing angrily. But Morgan had no intention of leaving. He knew the girl was only pretending to be outraged. She was obviously no lady. No respectable woman would swim naked in a river.

Morgan sauntered to a mesquite tree and leaned against it, crossing his arms over his broad chest. "Nope. I don't think so. I like the view here."

Jessie began moving slowly toward the bank of the river. Morgan knew she was headed for the thick brush of evergreens, but not until she had streaked from the water into the brush did he start running.

Charging out of the brush on the other side, Morgan suddenly came to a dead halt. Instead of rushing for her clothes as Morgan expected, Jessie stood before him stark-naked, breathtakingly beautiful, aiming a Winchester rifle right at his chest.

And as he grabbed for the rifle she jumped back, saying, "Get back! Get back or—so help me God—I'll put a bullet right through your black heart!"

D1508817

Also by Joanne Redd

TO LOVE AN EAGLE
winner of the 1987 *Romantic Times* award
for Best Western Historical Romance

QUANTITY SALES

Most Dell books are available at special quantity discounts when purchased in bulk by corporations, organizations, and special-interest groups. Custom imprinting or excerpting can also be done to fit special needs. For details write: Dell Publishing, 666 Fifth Avenue, New York, NY 10103. Attn.: Special Sales Department.

INDIVIDUAL SALES

Are there any Dell books you want but cannot find in your local stores? If so, you can order them directly from us. You can get any Dell book in print. Simply include the book's title, author, and ISBN number if you have it, along with a check or money order (no cash can be accepted) for the full retail price plus $1.50 to cover shipping and handling. Mail to: Dell Readers Service, P.O. Box 5057, Des Plaines, IL 60017.

Chasing a Dream

JOANNE REDD

A DELL BOOK

Published by
Dell Publishing
a division of
The Bantam Doubleday Dell
Publishing Group, Inc.
1 Dag Hammarskjold Plaza
New York, New York 10017

Copyright © 1988 by Joanne Redd

All rights reserved. No part of this book may be reproduced or transmitted in any form or by any means, electronic or mechanical, including photocopying, recording or by any information storage and retrieval system, without the written permission of the Publisher, except where permitted by law.

The trademark Dell ® is registered in the U. S. Patent and Trademark Office.

ISBN: 0-440-20114-4

Printed in the United States of America

Published simultaneously in Canada

July 1988

10 9 8 7 6 5 4 3 2 1

KRI

Ye may know him at once, though a herd be in sight,
As he moves o'er the plain like a creature of light—
His mane streaming forth from his beautiful form
Like the drift from a wave that has burst in the storm.

Not the team of the Sun, as in fable portrayed,
Through the firmament rushing in glory arrayed,
Could match, in wild majesty, beauty and speed,
That tireless, magnificent snowy-white steed.

Much gold for his guerdon, promotion and fame,
Wait the hunter who captures that fleet-footed game;
Let them bid for his freedom, unbridled, unshod,
He will roam till he dies through these pastures of God.

—From "The White Steed of the Prairies"
by J. Barber (published in *The Democratic
Review,* April 1843)

For my sister Lawrine, a second mother to me, whose warmth, laughter, and generosity of spirit bring joy to all around her

Chapter 1

"DAMN! WHERE IN THE HELL IS THAT RANCH?"

The words were uttered by the man who sat on his horse at the top of a rise on the gently rolling Texas prairie.

At a distance, anyone watching him ride up might have mistaken him for a Comanche from the ease and skill with which he handled his spirited gelding. Even in a time and place where all men were mounted, his horsemanship was remarkable. But it was his clothing, rather than his skillful handling of his mount, that marked him as being different from one of those feared "horsemen of the prairie." No Indian wore a battered black Stetson.

At a closer look one might think the man was a cowhand. Besides the broad-brimmed Stetson, he wore a leather vest over a dark, coarse-woven shirt and a red bandanna tied around his tanned neck. The bandanna had many uses. It served as a bath towel, a sling for a broken arm, a bandage for wounds, and a sweat rag. It was used to blindfold a bronco before bridling it, to tie calves' legs together while branding them, to strain muddy water, to hold hot branding irons, to protect the mouth and nose while riding drag, to protect the neck from the sun, to tie the hat down during gales, and, finally, to place over the face of a cowhand who was being buried in the prairie without a coffin. This square of material was the flag of range country, the cowman's banner.

However, any South Texan could see this man was no local, working cowhand. Despite the lariat coiled around his saddle horn, he wore no leather leggings over his long, muscular legs, no heavy protective gloves on his hands, and there were no toe fenders on his stirrups, all absolute necessities for a cowhand in this land known as the *brasada*—the brush country of Texas.

No, this man was no "brush popper," nor was he a cowhand. His low-slung six-shooter, its handle worn shiny from use, and the dangerous gleam in his eyes marked him as a man of a much more deadly breed. Morgan West was a gunfighter, a man so skilled with his .45 that other men hired him to do jobs too dangerous for them to perform.

Morgan stood in his stirrups and looked about him with eyes the same color as finely tempered steel. From that viewpoint, he could see for miles around. On three sides of him was open prairie, the new, tender shoots of grass just beginning to poke through the browned winter stubble on the ground. Before him lay a line of trees curving to the west, trees that bordered the Nueces River, "the deadline of sheriffs," as it was called in that day.

Beyond the Nueces lay the "bloody border," a tract of

land from one to two hundred miles wide and stretching three hundred miles along the Rio Grande River. Here sat a grassland sprinkled with cactus and thick mesquite brush in which the only inhabitants for hundreds of years had been the rattlesnakes, scorpions, the longhorns and mustangs, the Lipan Apaches and the Comanches who traveled across it on their bloody forays into Mexico. Then the Mexicans had come. To this day only a few Anglos lived there. At first it had been the Apaches who kept them out, fiercely guarding that desolate land they called their own. Recently it had been the Mexican bandits who raided across the Rio Grande, burning, looting, raping, and murdering, who had kept the surge of Anglos at bay. The area hadn't been named "bloody" for nothing.

Well, Morgan thought, that was the Nueces in front of him, and Frank Gibbons had written that his ranch was just north of the river. But he couldn't see any buildings. Once again, Morgan wondered why the rancher had sent for him. Gibbons's missive had been vague. Morgan knew only that Gibbons had need of his gun.

Disgusted at being unable to spy any sign of the man's ranch, Morgan sat back down in his saddle and wiped the sweat from his brow with his forearm. Even though it was only March, the day was warm and balmy, not unusual in this part of Texas in the early spring. His horse moved restively beneath him, and Morgan knew the animal smelled water. Giving his gelding his head, Morgan allowed him to trot to the river, thinking he could use a drink of cool water himself.

As Morgan rode into the trees that bordered the river, he looked about him. The mesquites were just sprouting their new feathery leaves. A few feet from him a wild plum tree was in full bloom. He heard the drone of bees as they savored the nectar of the sweet-smelling white blossoms.

When he reached the river, Morgan reined in and dismounted. His horse immediately began to drink deeply. Dropping to one knee on the sandy bank, Morgan cupped his hand and dipped it into the water.

He felt the presence of another person before he heard the slight noise. Morgan sprang to his feet, his hand going to the gun at his hip in a lightning-fast movement, his eyes scanning both banks of the river. But the gun never cleared leather. Morgan rose to his full, imposing height, his hand still on the butt of the .45, and stared in disbelief at the sight in the river.

A girl was swimming, her long golden hair trailing behind her. Apparently she was unaware of Morgan's presence, for she swam leisurely downriver, her creamy shoulders and arms glistening in the sunlight as she moved closer and closer to where Morgan stood. And then, when she did spy him, her head shot up, her eyes wide with surprise.

For a long moment the two stared at each other across the shimmering water, the girl in surprise and Morgan in fascination. He had never seen eyes that color, a vibrant, deep green. With the water on her eyelashes glittering in the sunlight, her eyes looked like enormous emeralds surrounded by diamonds. Tearing his gaze away from the arresting sight, Morgan quickly scanned her face. Her nose was small and turned up, her mouth generous. He glanced down and realized she was nude. Straining his eyes, Morgan cursed the murky water that prevented him from viewing the rest of her clearly. All he could see was the tantalizing milky white of her body as she trod water. Morgan felt his heat rise and a stirring in his loins.

"What . . . what are you doing here?" the girl sputtered in an accusing tone of voice.

Realizing that his hand was still on his gun, Morgan felt foolish. Surely this girl presented no danger to him. Grinning sheepishly, he replied, "My horse and I were just getting a drink of water. We didn't mean to disturb your"—his gaze once again swept over the partially concealed form in the water— "your bath."

Jessie had been shocked when she looked up and saw the stranger standing on the riverbank. She had surveyed the area carefully before stripping and entering the water. Where had he come from, and how had he managed to slip up on her so quietly? She wished he would stop staring at her and wondered how much he could actually see through the water.

She realized she was in a precarious position, being caught by a strange man, all alone, without even her gun for protection. Even worse, something about the glint in this man's eyes and his alert, expectant stance told her he was dangerous. He reminded her of a tightly coiled rattler just before it struck with its deadly fangs. A shiver of fear ran through her slim body.

Jessie examined the dark-haired stranger more closely. His size alone was intimidating. He was tall, muscular, and exceptionally broad-shouldered, and he radiated power, virility, and danger the way the sun radiates heat.

Her gaze dropped to the gun that rode low on his lean hip, a lethal weapon he wore with such ease and confidence that it appeared to be an extension of the man himself. Then she saw that he was sexually aroused. Despite herself, she stared, thinking that he was as well endowed in that area as any stallion she had ever seen.

A flush came to her face at the shocking thought, while her heart raced with a mixture of fear and excitement.

Jessie tore her gaze away and glanced once more at Morgan's rugged, bronzed face. Seeing his smug smile and the taunting glitter in his silver eyes, she knew he had guessed his effect on her. Anger rose in her, completely overriding her fear.

"Go away!" she commanded.

Morgan only grinned wider at the impudence of this girl's trying to tell him what to do.

"I said go away," Jessie repeated, her eyes flashing angrily.

Morgan had no intention of leaving—not until he had satisfied that powerful ache in his body. He knew the girl was only pretending to be outraged. She was obviously no lady. No respectable woman would swim naked in a river without her underclothes. And he had seen the way she had boldly stared at his arousal. No, she was only playing games with him. Well, he didn't object to a little coy foreplay, if that was what she wanted. He'd play along—for a while.

Morgan sauntered to a mesquite tree and leaned against it, crossing his arms over his broad chest. "Nope. I don't think so. I like the view here."

For a good while it was a silent stalemate, Jessie glaring at Morgan and treading water and Morgan smiling arrogantly back at her. Then, as Jessie began to move slowly toward the bank of the river, Morgan knew she was headed for the thick brush of evergreen *coma* farther downstream and guessed that was where she had left her clothes. Not until she streaked from the water and into the brush did he show any sign that he knew what she planned. Morgan whirled and ran into the brush, swearing under his breath at the dartlike thorns that tore at his hands and arms as he pushed his way through.

But when Morgan ran out of the brush on the other side, he came to a dead halt. Instead of rushing for her clothes, as Morgan had expected her to do, Jessie stood before him stark-naked, aiming a Winchester rifle right at his chest.

"I told you to go away and I meant it!" Jessie said, relishing the look of surprise on the stranger's face.

From the corner of his eye, Morgan saw the bay standing beside the brush and the empty saddle holster on its back. He cursed himself for a fool. He should have known she'd have a gun with her. A small muscle twitched in his cheek. His silver eyes glittered angrily. "Sweetheart, you'd better put that thing down before you get hurt. I don't like anyone pointing a gun at me."

"And I don't like anyone planning to rape me!" Jessie retorted.

"Rape?" Morgan asked. "Hell, who said I was going to force you? I may have been staring, sweetheart, but you were doing a little of your own. Seems to me you were just as interested in me as I was in you."

A slow flush rose on Jessie's face.

"Look," Morgan said in a soothing voice, "I was just thinking of us passing an hour or so enjoying ourselves, but if you don't want to . . ." His voice trailed off as he shrugged indifferently.

"What in God's name made you think that? That I was one of *those* women?"

Morgan's eyes flashed. "What was I supposed to think? Hell, you were running around here stark-naked, before God and everyone. If that's not an out-and-out invitation, I've never seen one. Any woman who would do that is just asking for it."

Almost too late, Jessie realized that Morgan had been slowly inching toward her. Just as he grabbed for her rifle, she jumped away. "Get back!" she cried. "Get back—or so help me God, I'll put a bullet right through your black heart!"

Morgan glared at Jessie in silent frustration. Damn, she was as quick on her feet as a mountain lion. And God, she looked magnificent standing there stark-naked. Her body was just as beautiful as her face. Even if she was slimmer than the women he had known in the past, all of the curves were in the right places. Slowly his gaze roamed over the full, high breasts with their pert, rosy nipples, the tiny waist he could span with his hands, the gentle flair of her hips, then locked on the triangle of golden curls between her thighs. He clenched his teeth as sweat broke out on his forehead. Never had he wanted a woman as he wanted this one. And, by God, he'd have her! But it wouldn't be rape. He'd never forced a woman, nor would he ever do so. No, by the time he finished with her, she'd surrender gladly, she'd beg him for it!

Jessie was acutely aware of Morgan's staring at her. She felt his hot look almost as if his hands, and not his eyes, were roving over her. Again that strange excitement made her heart race, and she felt a warm tingle deep in her belly. Mortified at her own reaction, she felt vulnerable as she had never felt before. Yes, he was a dangerous man.

Determined not to succumb to this man's strange power over her, Jessie squared her shoulders, making her full breasts jut out even more, and tightened her grip on the gun. "You've got exactly one minute to get out of here, mister," she said, trying her best to sound calm.

Morgan tore his gaze from Jessie's body and looked her in the eye. He had been considering rushing her, but seeing her determination and the knowledgeable way she handled her weapon made him take pause. No woman was worth getting killed over.

"Now you've got half a minute," Jessie said in a hard voice.

Morgan didn't like the turn of events. The idea of this exquisite girl holding him at bay with a gun didn't sit easy with his masculine pride. She was doing what no man had ever dared and lived to tell of. Reluctantly, he backed away. Jessie followed him, still pointing her gun at his broad chest.

Jessie watched silently as Morgan mounted his horse, unable to keep herself from admiring his graceful swing into the saddle. And then, as he sat on his horse staring down at her, she felt a ridiculous urge to toss away her rifle and ask him to stay after all. She bit her lower lip, fighting down the impulse.

"Sorry things didn't work out differently, sweetheart," Morgan said in a soft voice. "I have a feeling it would have been damned good between us."

Jessie swallowed hard. What in the world was wrong with her? She should be relieved that he was leaving, glad that she would never lay eyes on him again. But as he turned his horse and rode away, she felt regret.

At the rise of the hill above the river, Morgan whirled his horse around and called out, "What's your name, sweetheart? Seems a man ought to know the name of the only woman who's ever turned him down."

The mention of other women was Morgan's undoing. A wave of raw jealousy ran through Jessie. Then, realizing if she *had* surrendered to him she would have been just one more conquest, she shouted, "None of your damned business, you bastard!"

Despite her insult, Morgan couldn't help but laugh at her angry retort. The girl looked magnificent standing there stark-naked with only her long golden hair to cover her and her beautiful eyes flashing, the living picture of defiance. Grudgingly he admitted he admired her, still amazed that she had put her defense before her modesty. That showed a presence of mind he hadn't credited a respectable woman with having.

He wheeled his horse and rode off at a gallop, promising himself he'd find out her name. Hell, there couldn't be another woman with hair like spun gold and eyes like precious jewels in this country, nor one as fiercely spirited. Yes, they'd meet again, and when they did—there wouldn't be a Winchester between them!

Chapter 2

AFTER HE LEFT JESSIE AT THE NUECES, MORGAN spent two hours searching for Frank Gibbons's ranch. However, it wasn't the sight of buildings that finally led him there. Rather, the sight of a longhorn yoked to a tame ox clued him into what direction it lay. He had been a brush popper at one time himself and knew the ox would head straight back to the ranch with its unwilling prisoner.

An hour later Morgan sat in the ranch office waiting for his future employer to appear. He hadn't really expected Gibbons to be at home. Any rancher worth a damn wouldn't be there in broad daylight when there was work to be done on the range, and apparently Gibbons was a successful one, if the ranch house and its outbuildings were anything to judge by.

Morgan was impressed with Gibbons's home and the ranch itself but had been surprised to find that the rancher's house servants weren't Mexican, as was invariably the case this close to the border. Instead, Morgan had been met at the door by a sour-faced woman who spoke with a strong Slavic accent.

The door to the office opened, and a beefy, red-faced man entered, his upper lip completely concealed by a scruffy blond mustache. Morgan knew by the broken veins in the bulbous nose that the flush on the rancher's face was caused not by the sun but by too much exposure to alcohol. Morgan rose, towering over the shorter man, and offered his hand, introducing himself.

"Frank Gibbons," the rancher replied gruffly, giving Morgan's hand a perfunctory shake.

It wasn't until then that Morgan noticed that Gibbons's left sleeve was pinned to his shirt. He wondered briefly if the rancher had lost his arm in the Civil War or from some accident on the ranch.

"I'm glad you arrived today," Gibbons said, motioning for Morgan to be seated. "I wanted to talk to you before the others got here."

Morgan sat down in the overstuffed chair Gibbons had indicated and watched Gibbons seat himself behind his battered desk. "What others?" he asked.

"I've hired several men for this job, but I want you to be in charge. You've had more experience in these matters." Gibbons took off his Stetson, revealing his thinning blond hair, and tossed it to the side before continuing. "I understand you served with the Texas Rangers under Captain McNelly, that you were with him at the old Palo Alto battleground when the rangers wiped out that band of Mexican cattle thieves."

Morgan wasn't surprised that Gibbons knew of his service with the Texas Rangers. After all, the rancher was hiring him because of his expertise with a gun, and every ranger was an expert horseman and a crack shot, requirements that came second only to bravery and disregard for hardship. It was because of his experience with the rangers that Morgan had been approached for his latest jobs, acting as a guard on stagecoaches and the wagon trains bringing silver out of Colorado, and then as one of the outriders on the King Ranch, an armed vanguard that protected Captain King from ambushes by the Mexican bandits.

"Yes," Morgan answered, "I was with McNelly at Palo Alto."

"And were you with him when he went into Mexico and thrashed those Cortinistas down at Cortina's ranch?"

"Yes, I was," Morgan answered with a casual shrug of his broad shoulders.

Gibbons's pale blue eyes glittered with excitement. Juan Nepomuceno Cortina, the "Red Robber of the Rio Grande," was the most feared, and most daring, Mexican *bandido* chieftain ever to terrorize the border country. "That was a mighty brave thing you rangers did, crossing the border against federal orders and attacking that bastard Cortina at his own headquarters.

"That's why I chose you for this job," Gibbons continued when Morgan made no comment. "You know how to deal with these Mexican bastards."

"You're having trouble with Mexican bandits," Morgan surmised.

"I'm having trouble with Mexicans, all right," Gibbons answered in a hard voice. "A bunch of mustangers. And it wouldn't surprise me one bit if they weren't spying for the Red Robber and setting me up for a raid."

"Cortina is in Mexico City now," Morgan informed the rancher. "President Díaz's *rurales* arrested him several years ago."

"Yeah, so Díaz claims," Gibbons answered with a sneer. "Hell, you know you can't trust any of them. That's why I won't allow any Mexicans on my ranch."

"If these Mexicans are trespassing on your ranch, why don't you just get the sheriff to throw them off?" Morgan suggested.

"The sheriff was killed last year by a bunch of bandits. Ain't found no one crazy enough to take the job since then. Besides, those Mexicans aren't on my ranch, at least not technically. They're camped on the open range right next to me—and I want them to get the hell out of there!"

Morgan wasn't surprised by Gibbons's words. Unless the land adjacent to theirs was claimed by someone else, all ranchers had a proprietary air about the open range around them, grazing their cattle on it as if it were their own.

"Hell," Gibbons continued, "even if those mustangers aren't spying for the *bandidos*—which I still ain't convinced of—they're making a nuisance of themselves. I'm trying to round up the cattle that wandered off into the brush during the winter to send on a trail drive up north in a couple of months, and those damned Mexicans are always getting in the way. Twice, their herds of mustangs have stampeded my cattle."

"So what do you want me to do?"

"Scare those Mexicans off. I don't care what tactics you use. Just get rid of them! For all I care, you can string up the whole damned bunch of them."

Morgan frowned. "I hardly think such drastic measures will be necessary."

"Hell, those mustangers ain't no ordinary bunch, running like scared rabbits every time a white man looks at them. They're an insolent bunch. That's why it wouldn't surprise me if they weren't in cahoots with the bandits."

"Look, Gibbons," Morgan said. "Maybe we'd better get something straight. I've killed more than a few bandits, and a few men who drew on me first because they thought they were faster than me, but I'm not a hired killer. So if you've got ideas about murdering those Mexicans, you'd better find yourself another man."

"Murder? Hell, they're nothing but varmints. Since when is killing Mexicans murder?"

Silently, Morgan rose from his chair. As he turned to walk out, Gibbons jumped to his feet, saying hastily, "All right, West. No killing. I'll leave it in your hands. I don't care what you do. Just get those damned Mexicans out of this part of the country."

Morgan turned and eyed the rancher thoughtfully for a long moment before he answered. "Okay, I'll take the job."

"There's a deserted cabin not too far from where the Mexicans are mustanging," Gibbons explained. "You can operate out of there. You can stay tonight in the bunkhouse, and tomorrow morning I'll have one of my men show it to you. When the other men I've hired arrive, I'll send them down to you."

"I prefer to work alone."

"Look, West, there's at least twenty men in that mustanging outfit. That's why I'm not doing the job myself. I can't spare the hands right now. And it ain't a one-man job."

Gibbons picked up his hat and walked around the desk. "I've gotta get back on the range. Come on, I'll show you to the bunkhouse."

Morgan followed Gibbons out of the house, and as they walked toward the bunkhouse Morgan looked

around him. "You've got a nice place here. How big a
spread do you have?"

"Not as many square miles as Kennedy or King, south
of here, have," Gibbons answered. "But my ranch will
be just as big someday," he added in a determined
voice. He pointed to a building next to the bunkhouse,
saying, "You can pick up what food supplies you think
you'll need at the cookhouse tomorrow. And if you
think you'll need more horses, you can get them from
my remuda."

After Gibbons had left him in the bunkhouse, Morgan
laid his saddlebags and Winchester on the small chest at
the foot of a bunk Gibbons had told him was unclaimed
by one of his hands. Removing his gun belt, he wrapped
it around the gun and holster and stuck it beneath the
pillow. Then he lay on the bunk and stared at the cracks
in the adobe ceiling, deep in thought.

Gibbons's job certainly hadn't turned out to be what
he had expected. Chase off a bunch of mustangers?
Hell, it didn't make good sense. Ranchers and mustangers usually had no trouble getting along. In fact,
ranchers were usually grateful to the mustangers for
clearing the area of the wild horses. Did Gibbons's insistence on getting rid of the mustangers stem from prejudice?

Morgan hadn't been particularly surprised by the
man's attitude toward Mexicans. That was as much a
part of South Texas as its mesquite trees and cactus. It
was a hatred that went all the way back to the Texas War
for Independence, to the Alamo and the massacre of
Texan prisoners by the Mexicans at Goliad.

But despite all the hard feelings, most Texas ranchers
had Mexican *vaqueros* working for them who were
loyal, trusted employees, and most Texans differenti-

ated between good and bad Mexicans. Yet Gibbons had said he wouldn't have *any* Mexicans on his ranch. Was that why he was so anxious to get rid of the mustangers?

The ranch hands were coming into the bunkhouse. Morgan watched while they hung up their gear and washed for supper, aware of the curious yet wary glances sent his way.

Finally one of the bolder men walked up to Morgan and asked, "You one of them fellas Gibbons hired to chase off those Mexicans?"

Morgan swung his feet off the bunk and rose, saying, "Yes. Names's West. Morgan West."

"Hey, I've heard of you!" one of the other hands said in an excited voice. "You were with McNelly's border rangers, weren't you?"

"Yes, I was," Morgan admitted. The men's looks of open admiration made him feel a little ridiculous. He wasn't a hero. Like the rest of the rangers, he had only been doing a job that needed doing. "But before that I was just an ordinary cowhand like you boys."

"What kind of cowhand? Range or brush?" a long-limbed, older man asked.

Morgan heard the hint of challenge in the man's voice and smiled. Brush cowhands knew they were the superior cowmen. It took a lot more skill, grit, and daring to flush a stubborn steer from the brush than just to round one up on the open prairie, and the ride the brush popper took during that task would make a broncobuster's look tame by comparison.

Morgan grinned at the man who had asked the question. "I was a brush popper first, then worked the prairie. The only thing I had to do when I changed territory was buy a longer lariat."

The men, who had crowded around Morgan while

awaiting his answer, grinned back, and Morgan knew that he had been accepted, despite their earlier wariness over his deadly skill with a gun.

After a supper of thick steaks, sourdough biscuits, and red beans, Morgan sat at the table in the bunkhouse, playing cards with some of the hands. As usual, the game was monte, as any number could play with one deck. The conversation covered the predictable topics: cows, horses, and the hands' latest trip into town.

The mention of a town caught Morgan's attention. All afternoon he had been thinking of the girl at the Nueces and wondering where she lived. "There's a town near here?" he asked.

"Well, it's not really a town," a cowhand named Charlie answered. "Only a cantina and a little general store that just opened. We ain't got any towns with hair on them anywhere close by, but it's someplace to go on Saturday night, just to get out of this stinking bunkhouse."

Morgan frowned at Charlie's answer, then asked, "What's the female situation around here?"

"Females? What's that?" one hand quipped.

"That bad, huh?" Morgan asked.

"Hell, females are as scarce as snowballs in hell in these parts," another hand commented in disgust.

"Aren't there women on any of the ranches?" Morgan asked.

"Not young ones, unless you're interested in one of those little Mexican gals," Charlie answered. "Of course, if you've just got an itch that needs scratching, there's a cathouse down in Nuecestown, about a day's ride from here."

Later that evening Morgan lay in his bunk, listening to the snores all around him and thinking. Obviously, the girl he had seen at the river wasn't from around here, because if she had been, surely the hands would have mentioned her. With her remarkable beauty she would be the main topic of conversation among the men. Who was she, and where did she live?

That night Morgan was tormented by dreams of a beautiful, green-eyed water sprite, with hair like spun gold, who enticed him deeper and deeper into the woods, only to disappear every time he reached for her.

Chapter 3

TWO DAYS LATER, MORGAN AND HIS PARTY OF HIRED guns left the small cabin on the eastern boundary of Frank Gibbons's ranch in search of the mustangers' camp.

As they rode Morgan eyed his three companions with distaste. Fess, Red, and Cole, they were called respectively, and Morgan didn't like the looks of them today any more than he had when Frank Gibbons had presented them to him the day before. These men were obviously hired killers, men who gloried in the power their guns gave them and took pleasure in killing. They were no better than the murdering bandits who terrorized this area.

Nor did Morgan trust them. He had seen the resentment in their eyes when Gibbons had told them Morgan would be giving the orders. He knew the only way he'd be able to control them was to be meaner and tougher than they were, and that he'd have to watch his back every minute. He could only hope that when they rode into the mustangers' camp and announced they'd been sent by Frank Gibbons, the Mexicans would realize they were being pitted against gunslingers and would pull out—*pronto*!

Morgan and his men didn't have far to ride before they found the Mexicans' camp. It was only a mile from their cabin and nestled in the tree line that followed yet another creek.

Reining in on a hill overlooking the Mexican camp, Morgan was surprised at what he saw. These mustangers were no amateurs out looking for a few wild horses they could capture and make some quick money on. They were a well-organized group. To one side of the camp lay the pen the mustangs were driven into, a huge enclosure made from mesquite posts lashed together with strong rawhide, making the fence somewhat elastic and yet hard to break. The figure-eight shape of the pen had two purposes: The first oval prevented the horses from rushing into a corner and breaking it down, and the second oval kept the horses from circling and rushing back out before the gate was closed. To each side of the gate, huge brush-covered wings stretched out in a V, one wing at least a mile in length, the other half as long. Driven through these camouflaged wings, the wild horses couldn't distinguish them as fences until they were well between them and it was too late to turn back.

Morgan stood in his stirrups to get a better look at the camp beyond the pen. A large herd of horses grazed at the side opposite to where the huge empty pen lay, and there were several smaller corrals between the herd and the mustangers' headquarters. Straining his eyes, Morgan could barely see the dugout, which was built

into a hillside and was half cabin and half cave, one of
the old, deserted ranch houses that had been con-
structed by the earliest settlers in this area.

Morgan sat back in his saddle and said to his companions, "Okay, let's go down there and pay them a visit."
Shooting the men a hard look, he added, "But remember, I do the talking and no gun play."

Ignoring the gunslingers' sullen glances, Morgan
kneed his mount and galloped down the hill. He passed
the huge empty pen and skirted the herd of mustangs
grazing on open range, wondering why the animals
hadn't run away, as wild horses usually did when a man
approached them. Then he saw the reason. A long rawhide strap was tied to the front ankle of each, a strap
designed to trip the animals if they tried to run away.
After a few rough tumbles, the mustangs had learned
their lesson and were now "herd-broken."

Riding closer to the headquarters, they passed the
corrals, and Morgan noted that one held only mares, an
unusually fine collection of horseflesh. As they approached the dugout Morgan deliberately slowed his
horse to a walk, wanting the Mexicans to get a good look
at them. Seeing the frightened expressions on the mustangers' faces, Morgan knew that they had recognized
them as more than just gringos—Anglos not to be
trusted—but men who were much more dangerous and
lethal. Morgan smiled. That was just the reaction he had
wanted, hoping that all it would take to scare them off
would be a show of arms.

A youth darted from the group of *mesteñeros* and ran
into the dugout. Morgan and his men came to a halt
before the crude cabin, knowing that their presence
was being announced. A small, wiry man with graying
brown hair emerged from the dugout.

Morgan's eyebrows rose in surprise. He had expected the mustanger to be a Mexican, but this man was just as Anglo as he. Quickly recovering from his surprise, Morgan asked, "Are you the boss of this outfit?"

Gabe's hazel eyes were wary as he scanned the four mounted men before him. He'd pegged them as gunfighters at first sight. But despite the mean look of the other three, it was the man who had spoken that made the hair on the back of his neck stand on end. The gleam in those cold silver eyes told him that that one was much more dangerous, a sleek, fierce *lobo* in a pack of mangy dogs.

"Nope," Gabe answered, trying hard to appear calm and composed. "The boss ain't here."

"Where is he?" Morgan asked. "I'd like to have a word with him."

Despite his fear, Gabe smiled at Morgan's words. Naturally, the gunfighter would assume the boss was a man. "Out there," he answered vaguely, motioning to the prairie.

Morgan turned in his saddle. A herd of mustangs raced across the open land, their unusually long manes and tails strung out behind them as they ran from the band of mustangers who were slowly closing in on them. Morgan watched in admiration, for there was nothing more beautiful than a herd of these wind-drinkers in full gallop, presenting every color of horseflesh in the world. This herd contained approximately one hundred horses, which meant several *manadas* had been stampeded and merged together. Looking closer, he could see the stallions nipping at the necks and flanks of his *manada*—his mares—each savagely driving their band in an effort to urge them to greater speed in order to escape.

Catching a glimpse of something gold, Morgan strained his eyes to see. When he focused on a rider racing beside the thundering herd, his expression turned to one of utter disbelief. The rider's long hair streamed out behind her like a golden banner as she bent low on her horse's back, the bay's silver mane whipping about the girl's face. Morgan recognized both the girl and the horse. He had found his water sprite.

Morgan had heard of *mesteñeras*—female mustangers—but he had never seen one. He had assumed that they were big, muscular women, almost mannish, for mustanging was strenuous work. But he knew that girl was anything but mannish, remembering only too well how her beautiful femininity had been exposed to his eyes.

He watched in fascination as she angled her horse closer and closer to the galloping herd, and reluctantly admitted that she was the best equestrienne he'd ever seen. As the racing herd rushed past him, shaking the ground with their pounding hooves, so close he could smell the overpowering odor of their sweat and feel their heat, Morgan silently cursed the choking dust that obliterated his view, loath to take his eyes off the golden-haired girl for one second. Then, as his mount moved restlessly beneath him, Morgan was too occupied to watch as he fought to control his gelding, whose instincts urged him to run with the wild ones.

Once his mount was under control, Morgan frowned in puzzlement as the mustangs rushed right past the wings of the pen. He had assumed the mustangers had meant to drive the horses into the enclosure. Then his breath caught in his throat, from both fear and disbelief, as he saw the girl gracefully leap from her horse to the back of the mustang she was racing beside, deftly throwing a loop over the horse's muzzle as she flew through the air. Landing as light as a feather, she gripped the sides of the mustang with her slender legs before she veered the animal away from the herd by its *bozal*—its nose band. Morgan could only stare as she and the wild mare raced away and, finally, disappeared over the horizon.

Morgan wondered if he only imagined what he had seen, but one glance at the three gunslingers' gaping mouths told him that they, too, had witnessed her remarkable leap. He whirled around, his eyes boring into Gabe's. "Who is she?"

There was an urgency about Morgan's voice that disturbed Gabe even more than knowing the man was a dangerous gunfighter. He didn't like the gunman's interest in Jessie one bit. Gabe raised his whiskered chin in defiance, his mouth firmly and stubbornly closed.

In a flash, Morgan flew from his saddle and caught Gabe's shirt in one fist, yanking the shorter man up until he stood on his tiptoes. "Dammit, answer me! Who is she?"

Morgan was aware of the three gunmen watching him curiously and of the frightened Mexicans around him. Even he was surprised by his violent demand, but he couldn't seem to help himself. He couldn't let her get away from him again. He *had* to know who she was.

"She is the *patrona*," a calm voice said from behind him.

Morgan released Gabe so abruptly that the older man almost fell to his knees. Morgan turned and found himself facing an elderly Mexican who stood as proud as any aristocrat, his dark eyes meeting Morgan's unflinchingly.

"Who are you?" Morgan asked.

"I am Pedro, the head *mesteñero.*"

Morgan glanced at Gabe for confirmation of the Mexican's words, and the older man nodded his head.

"What does he mean when he says she's the *patrona*?" Morgan asked Gabe.

"He means she's the boss of this outfit, and since the Mexicans work for her, she's their protector."

"That little snip of a girl runs this outfit?" Morgan asked in disbelief.

"You'd better not let Jessie hear you call her that. She considers herself a full-grown woman."

"Jessie? Is that her name?"

"Well, actually it's Jessica. Jessica Daniels. But no one has ever called her that. Just Jessie."

"And you expect me to believe she's the boss?" Morgan asked with a slight sneer.

"She sure is. Has been ever since her pa got killed in a stampede four years ago."

"But she's just a girl!" Morgan objected.

"No, she ain't *just* a girl. She's Jessie," Gabe answered stubbornly. "And let me tell you something else, mister. She's one of the best damned mustangers in the business, even better than her pa was. Why, we took more horses to San Antonio last year than any other mustanging outfit."

Morgan heard the pride in Gabe's voice. "Who are you? A relative?"

"Nope. I'm Gabe, and I just work for her, like Pedro here, except he's kinda her foreman. Her mother and brothers all died of cholera a few years before her pa got killed. But I was with Jessie's pa for years, so I'm kinda like family."

"Are there any other Anglos in this outfit?" Morgan asked, glancing around him.

"Nope. The rest of them left when Jessie took over. Said they weren't gonna work under no female. Just the Mexicans and me stayed. They're as loyal to her as I am."

Morgan didn't miss the subtle warning. Gabe was telling him that any man who harmed Jessie would have to answer to him and the Mexicans who worked for her. He scanned the camp and counted fourteen grown men, including Gabe, Pedro, and the men who had just returned from chasing the mustangs. The rest were youths and two women. Yet Gibbons had said there were at least twenty men in this camp. The rancher had lied to him, both about this outfit being entirely Mexican and about its strength, and he was damned sure going to find out why. But first he wanted to talk to this girl named Jessie.

He turned his attention back to Gabe. "How long will she be gone?"

Gabe shrugged. "Until she runs that mare down."

Fess, one of the gunslingers, scoffed and said, "Hell, she'll founder that mustang if she tries to run it down."

Gabe glared at Fess. "No, she won't! Jessie has never foundered any horse from riding it too long or too hard. She's too smart for that. No, sir, when she brings that mare back in, that mustang won't even be breathing hard, and it will be half broke!"

Morgan had to admire the feisty little man for defending Jessie to the gunfighter, but he didn't trust Fess not to pull a gun on Gabe. He stepped between the two men and said to the mounted gunslingers, "You men go on back to the cabin. I'm going to stay here to talk to . . . the boss."

Fess started to object, but Morgan gave him a hard, warning look. Reluctantly, Fess turned his horse, shot

Morgan a murderous look over his shoulder, then rode
from the Mexican camp, the other two gunslingers falling in behind him.

Morgan turned to find Gabe frowning at him. "What
do you want to talk to Jessie for, mister?"

"I guess I forgot to introduce myself. I'm Morgan
West, and me and my men work for Frank Gibbons.
Hired on yesterday."

Gabe's face turned ashen. That bastard Gibbons had
sicced a bunch of dirty gunslingers onto them! Damn,
he had tried to talk some sense into Jessie after Gibbons
had told them to get out, but the girl was as stubborn as
a mule.

Gabe glanced at Pedro and saw the Mexican was just
as worried as he. Stalling for time and hoping Jessie
would listen to reason once she heard of the new devel-
opments, Gabe said to Morgan, "Jessie might not be
back for hours. Why don't you come back tomorrow?"

"Sí, señor," Pedro chimed in. "The patrona might not
be back until nightfall."

"I don't mind waiting," Morgan said calmly. "But if
it's going to be that long, I think I'll wait inside."

Morgan walked to the dugout, leading his horse behind him, while Pedro and Gabe watched in dismay.
After tying his mount to a rail, he stepped into the dim,
musty interior, ducking his head as he passed through
the low doorway and pushing aside the blanket that
served as a door.

Morgan gazed about him at the crude building. The
only furnishings in the central room were a table and
several rickety chairs. To both sides were doors that
probably led to smaller rooms used for sleeping. The
cabin butted against a hillside, which served as its back
wall. The other three walls were made of logs, and in

one wall, off to the side, there was a half-crumbled stone fireplace.

Morgan walked across the room and peeked into one of the smaller side rooms, seeing the built-in bunk and the clothes that hung on pegs on one wall. A battered chest with a cracked mirror stood in one corner. On it sat a porcelain pitcher and a washbasin. Spying a brush beside the basin, Morgan walked over and picked it up, smiling when he saw the golden hairs in the bristles.

He turned and plucked a shirt from one of the pegs on the wall, holding it up. It was ridiculously small; two shirts this size could be made from one of his. A sweet scent drifted from it, and Morgan raised it to his nose, inhaling deeply. He had a mental vision of Jessie standing naked and defiant before him, a vision that seemed to be branded on his brain. His male body responded to both scent and vision with a swiftness that startled him. Muttering curses, he tossed the shirt down on the bunk and stalked back into the main room.

Morgan barely had time to throw his hat on the table and sit down before he heard the sound of a horse approaching the camp. He peered out the small open window and saw Jessie riding in, her long, golden hair trailing behind her and her green eyes sparkling with excitement. A surge of pure joy shot through Morgan at the sight of her, a spontaneous reaction that irritated him to no end, particularly after his body's recent unexpected arousal. What in the hell was wrong with him? he wondered in disgust. He was making an ass out of himself over her. Hell, women were a dime a dozen, and he could have his pick.

But despite his self-disgust, Morgan watched in rapt fascination, unable to take his eyes from her, as Jessie tossed the end of the rawhide rope tied around the mare's muzzle to one of the *mesteñeros* and lightly jumped from the back of the animal. Morgan noted that the horse's sleek hide was lathered with sweat from its hard ride, but surprisingly its breathing didn't look at all labored, and the only sign that the animal had been wild shortly before was the wary look in its eyes and the nervous pawing as the Mexican led it away. Gabe hadn't exaggerated, Morgan thought in amazement. Jessie had brought the mustang back half tamed.

Gabe and Pedro rushed up to Jessie. Knowing they were telling her of his and his men's visit, Morgan stepped back from the window so they couldn't see him watching. At the two men's excited words, Jessie shot a startled look toward the dugout, making Morgan grin with self-satisfaction. For several moments the two mustangers appeared to be arguing with the girl, and then Jessie started walking toward the dugout in quick, determined strides, her eyes like angry storm clouds in a look that wiped the smug smile completely from Morgan's lips and brought a scowl to his face.

The blanket at the door was pushed aside roughly. Before she even spied him in the dim interior, Jessie was saying, "See here, Mr. West, I'm not going to be intimidated by any gun—" She came to a dead halt, her face draining of color as she recognized Morgan. "You!" she exclaimed in shock.

As Jessie whirled for the door, Morgan leapt across the space that separated them and caught her arm. In the fierce, silent struggle that followed, Morgan was amazed at Jessie's wiry strength. In his cowhand days he had wrestled many a full-grown longhorn to the ground for branding, but he couldn't seem to get a hold on Jessie. She was as wild as a she-cat and as slippery as an eel, twisting and turning, kicking out with a vengeance.

When the toe of her boot slammed into his shin, Morgan cursed under his breath, "Bitch!" Then, locking his powerful arms about her in a viselike grip, he lifted her off her feet and held her against him.

Realizing it was useless to struggle against this man's superior strength, Jessie opened her mouth to scream. "Don't!" Morgan warned her in a hard voice. "Not if you value the lives of your friends."

Jessie could feel the handle of Morgan's gun biting into the tender flesh of her hip. Its presence reminded her of the grim fact that this was a professional gunman, who would have no compunctions about killing a man in cold blood. A tingle of fear ran up her spine. And then Jessie became aware of something much more disturbing. With their bodies pressed together so tightly, her breasts were flattened against his hard chest, her belly against his. His warm breath fanned her face and his heady masculine scent engulfed her. Suddenly, Jessie found it hard to breathe, and not because of the steel-like vise of Morgan's arms around her.

"If you promise not to run away until I've had my say, I'll let you go," Jessie heard Morgan say.

Anxious to get away from him, Jessie nodded. As soon as he released her she scrambled behind the table, placing a barrier between them. "You can save your breath, Mr. West," she said angrily. "I'm not pulling out. I've already told Frank Gibbons that."

"Mr. West?" Morgan asked, his dark eyebrows arching. "My, aren't we polite? But all that formality isn't necessary. Morgan's the name."

"I don't give a damn what your first name is!"

"No? Well, I think that's a shame. After all, it's not like we're complete strangers, meeting for the first time.

Why, I feel like an old friend . . . an old, *intimate* friend."

As his gaze slowly raked her body, Jessie felt the heat rising on her face. How dare he remind her that he had seen her naked. Her eyes shot daggers at him. "Get out!"

Eyes the color of cold steel locked with a pair of stormy ones in a silent contest of wills. Finally, Morgan answered, "Not until I've had my say."

"Then say it! But it won't make any difference," Jessie added in a determined voice. "I'm *not* pulling out. This is open range, and not even a bunch of low-down, dirty gunslingers is going to make me leave. You can go back and tell Gibbons it didn't work. I *won't* be intimidated."

"What makes you so sure he's only trying to intimidate you, that he's not deadly serious?"

The color drained from Jessie's face at Morgan's hard words, but she held her ground, glaring at him silently.

"Look, this is mustang country. There's wild horses all over this territory," Morgan said in exasperation. "You don't have to operate right under Gibbons's nose. Hell, if it's agitating him, just move on. That would be the smartest thing to do."

"Just move on?" Jessie asked angrily. "Do you realize it took us two months to build that pen and those corrals? And I'm just supposed to walk off and leave them because Gibbons doesn't like my outfit being here?"

"You're getting in the way of his spring roundup, stampeding his cattle chasing those mustangs," Morgan said, repeating the story Gibbons had told him.

"That's a lie! We've never stampeded his cattle. We haven't been anywhere near his cows. No, the only reason he wants me out of here is because he's afraid I'll catch—" Jessie came to an abrupt halt as she realized what she had almost blurted out.

"Catch what?" Morgan asked.

Jessie stared at him, her lips set tightly.

Morgan lunged across the table and caught her wrist. "Catch what?" he demanded.

Jessie tried to jerk her hand loose, but Morgan's hold was like iron. His eyes bored into her.

"A . . . a mustang," she answered reluctantly. "A stallion that we both want."

Surprised at her answer, Morgan released Jessie's wrist. "Are you telling me that this squabble between you two is over a damned horse?" he asked in disbelief.

Jessie glared at him sullenly, rubbing her wrist where his fingers had left their imprint. "I'm not telling you anything. I don't owe you any explanations. Now get out!"

Morgan's eyes flashed. "You know, Jessie, you have a bad habit of trying to boss me around. A habit I don't particularly like."

"I don't give a damn what you do or don't like. I said get out!"

Again the memory of Jessie standing naked and defiant in front of him flashed through Morgan's mind. A warmth flooded his loins as his body responded to the tantalizing vision. "No, I'm not leaving. Not yet," he answered in a voice that was as smooth as silk but as hard as steel. "Not until we've settled some unfinished business."

Morgan's movement was so swift, it was a blur to Jessie's eyes as he suddenly came around the end of the table and caught her shoulders. Before she could pull away from him, his mouth swooped down on hers in a hot, punishing kiss that momentarily robbed her of all

thought with its unexpectedness. When she regained
her senses and began to struggle, Morgan's hand tangled in her long hair, cupping the back of her head in a
firm grip, holding her still while his mouth devoured
hers, his tongue plunging into her mouth and ravishing
it.

Jessie moaned. She had never been kissed this way—
so intimately. And then, as Morgan's artful tongue
worked its magic, swirling around hers in an erotic
dance, a heat suffused Jessie, a weakness engulfed her,
and she went limp in his arms.

Morgan slipped both arms around her, drawing her
soft body even closer to his hard length. His lips left hers
to place fiery kisses over her face. "Oh, God, Jessie," he
muttered, "I knew you'd taste like this . . . so sweet."

His lips nibbled at her delicate earlobe, sending shivers of pleasure through her body. Then, as he lowered
his dark head, tracing the pounding pulse beat in her
throat with his tongue, Jessie unconsciously arched her
neck. Encouraged by her response, Morgan bent her
over the table, his mouth sliding over her collarbone
and across the silken skin at the V of her shirt.

Jessie had been reeling under Morgan's sensual assault, but when his hand brushed across her breast as he
started to unbutton her shirt, she finally came to her
senses. How dare he! she thought furiously as she
grabbed for the gun at Morgan's hip.

Morgan caught her hand in a hard grip and glared
down at her. "Oh, no, sweetheart. That's another bad
habit you've got. Pulling a gun on me."

Jessie was still bent backward over the table, their
hips and legs pressed together. Suddenly she became
very aware of his hardness against her lower abdomen.
Her eyes flashed in outrage.

Morgan, too, was very conscious of his arousal. He grinned. "Sorry, Jessie, but you seem to have that effect on me."

The grin infuriated Jessie. Without even thinking, she swung her hand and slapped his face—hard! Morgan's eyes flashed dangerously, and Jessie stared at the white mark on his cheek, holding her breath, realizing that he could break her in two if he chose to.

Morgan stepped back. "If you were a man, I'd kill you for that," he ground out between clenched teeth.

"If I were a man, you wouldn't have attacked me," Jessie retorted.

It was a point that Morgan couldn't argue with. He *had* kissed her to punish her—at first. But it had quickly changed to something much more. God, he wanted her. His body was still clamoring for release. But he'd never forced a woman, and he certainly wasn't going to start with Jessie, no matter how much he ached to possess her.

To Jessie's surprise, Morgan walked to the doorway. He lifted the blanket, then turned his head. "I'm going to get the answers to some questions. But let me warn you, Jessie. I'll be back." His gaze raked her body meaningfully. "We *still* have some unfinished business to settle between us."

Morgan ducked beneath the blanket hanging over the doorway, smiling smugly as he heard Jessie's outraged gasp.

Chapter 4

MORGAN WAS WAITING FOR FRANK GIBBONS WHEN the rancher and his hands rode in later that afternoon. He watched from the porch of the house as Gibbons dismounted and walked toward the house.

"What are you doing here, West?" Gibbons asked in an irritated voice as he stepped onto the porch, dusting his leggings with his hat. "Why aren't you out there harassing those Mexicans?"

Morgan nonchalantly tossed his cigarette away and turned to the rancher. "As a matter of fact, I did pay them a visit today."

"And?" Gibbons asked anxiously.

"Let's step into your office," Morgan answered, walking into the house.

After the office door had closed behind them, Gibbons whirled on Morgan. "What in the hell is this all about? I give the orders around here—not you! I don't like your insolence."

"And I don't like a man lying to me when he hires me for a job!" Morgan retorted. "You told me those mustangers were Mexican. There are two Anglos in that outfit, and the boss is an Anglo woman."

"As far as I am concerned, anyone who associates with a Mexican *is* a Mexican."

The way Gibbons said *Mexican* grated on Morgan's nerves. He said it as if Mexicans were the scum of the earth. "Then you still intend to go through with this, even though their boss is a woman?"

"I fail to see where her sex has anything to do with it. If she insists upon acting like a man, dressing like a man, doing a man's work, then I intend to treat her like a man. I see no reason to afford her any of the consideration we gentlemen usually reserve for the ladies."

Morgan's eyebrows rose at the word *gentlemen*, thinking that Gibbons was about as much a gentleman as a rattlesnake was. "All right, Gibbons, you've made yourself clear," Morgan said in a hard voice. "But there's something else I want to know. She told me the real reason you want her out of here is because you both want the same wild stallion. Is that true?"

The color drained from the rancher's usually florid face. "She told you about the White Steed?"

Morgan frowned. "Are you talking about the White Steed of the Prairie, the horse the Indians call the Ghost Horse of the Plains?"

"You're damned right I am!"

Morgan couldn't believe his ears. The famous white mustang was a legend in his own time. Claims to have seen the stallion came from as far south as the mesas of Mexico and as far north as the Badlands; from the Brazos River in East Texas to the Rocky Mountains. He was a superb stallion whose grace, beauty, endurance, speed, and intelligence were exceeded only by his passion for freedom. He was known by many names: the White Steed of the Prairie, the Pacing White Stallion, the Ghost Horse of the Plains, and, simply, the White Mustang. The stallion was a highly prized, natural "quickstep" pacer, and he could pace faster than any other horse could run, so effortlessly and gracefully that those who had seen him said he glided across the prairie. He was reputed to be a loner, some claiming he was too proud to be seen with other horses. Scores of men had spent years chasing the stallion, to no avail, and large sums of money had been offered for his capture.

"The White Steed has been seen around here?" Morgan asked, still disbelieving.

"Yes. This is one of his old territories, between the San Antonio and Nueces rivers. About every ten years he returns."

"How do you know it's him, and not some other white stallion?"

"Because I'd know that bastard anywhere!" Gibbons's eyes glittered with anger as he patted his empty sleeve. "He did this to me. Do you think I'd ever forget the horse that cost me my arm?"

"A horse did that?" Morgan asked in surprise.

"You're goddamned right he did! I chased him for two years before I could get close enough to crease him."

Morgan frowned. Creasing was one method of capturing wild horses. The animal was temporarily paralyzed by putting a bullet through the top of the horse's neck at the root of the mane a little in front of the shoulder. However, it was a haphazard method that had more to do with luck than any shooting skill. In the majority of cases the horse was accidentally killed, which was why professional mustangers never used creasing to capture horses. It was the mark of an amateur.

"But that bullet didn't stun that damned stallion long enough," Gibbons continued. "Before I could get a rope around his neck, he was up. That bastard tried to kill me!"

"All wild stallions will fight to get free when cornered," Morgan pointed out.

"He *wasn't* fighting to get free! He could have run. We were out in the open. And like I said, I hadn't even got a rope around his neck. No, he came at me with murder in his eyes. Tried his damnedest to kill me. He knocked me down and pounded on me with his hooves. I have scars all over from the battering he gave me. I kept rolling, then finally got to my knees. That's when he caught my arm in his mouth. He tossed me around like I was a rag doll, twisting and chewing on my arm until it was a bloody pulp. That's when I passed out. I would have died if my partner hadn't shown up and frightened the mustang off. That stallion's a killer!"

Morgan frowned, wondering if the stallion Gibbons had creased was really the White Steed. He'd heard a lot of stories about the famous mustang but never any about the stallion being a man-killer. But then, he'd never heard of anyone getting close enough to the mustang to crease him either.

"Well, that bastard is back, and this time I'm going to catch him," Gibbons said. "I'm going to kill that son of a bitch. And no damned female mustanger is going to get to him before I do!"

There was an unholy gleam in Gibbons's eyes. Morgan knew that the man would stop at nothing to get his revenge on the horse that had maimed him, and he began to fear for Jessie's safety.

"Now, you get back out there and get rid of those mustangers," Gibbon said angrily. "That's what I'm paying you for."

Morgan was tempted to tell the man to go to hell, but he knew if he quit the job, Gibbons would only turn it over to Fess and the other gunslingers, and there was no doubt in Morgan's mind which methods they would use.

Morgan walked to the door, then turned back to Gibbons. "Are you going to kill that stallion on sight?"

"Hell, no! I intend to take that stallion alive. That son of a bitch is going to pay for what he did to me before he dies."

Gibbons planned on torturing the stallion before he killed him? The idea sickened Morgan.

"And another thing," Gibbons added in a hard voice. "You keep your mouth shut about this. I don't want anyone knowing the White Steed has been seen in this area. Then we'll have everyone who's been chasing him for years coming in here and getting in the way. That stallion is mine!"

And that was why Jessie hadn't told him she was after the White Steed after she had blurted out the real reason Gibbons wanted her out, Morgan thought. She didn't want others coming into the area to compete for the famous stallion either.

Dammit! What have I gotten myself into? Morgan swore as he rode back to his cabin. It wasn't like him to come to the aid of a maiden in distress, like some fool knight in shining armor, particularly when that maiden didn't even want his help. His lifetime rule had always been to keep his nose out of other people's business. In this country, it was the number one rule to survival. And now he was breaking his own rule on account of that stubborn, green-eyed vixen Jessie. He couldn't very well leave her to the mercy of that madman Gibbons. Now that he knew the true story, he had to make at least one more attempt to persuade Jessie to leave. He hoped, for her and her people's sake, that she would listen to reason and clear out before something disastrous happened.

The next day Morgan left the three gunmen behind at the cabin and rode to the mustangers' camp. When he crested the hill overlooking the camp, he reined in and looked down at it, noting that more activity was going on than the day before, particularly around the big pen.

Then Morgan saw the reason for the hurried preparations. A large herd of mustangs was being driven toward the wings of the pen, leaving a thick cloud of dust in their wake. There were at least two hundred horses in the herd. Riding bareback and stripped of everything but their pants, the mustangers drove the animals from the back and sides, waving their lariats over their heads and whooping to keep the herd running. When the mustangs were about a mile from the wings, another group of mustangers drove several tame horses from the side to the front of the galloping herd. These were trained mares that would take over the mustang lead mares' positions in the different *manadas* and guide the herd into the pen.

The ground shook from hundreds of pounding hooves as the herd rushed toward the wings, their lathered coats glistening in the sunlight. They were a beautiful, inspiring sight with their necks stretched out, their ears flattened, their long manes and tails flying, and their slender legs eating up the ground, red and blue roans, sorrels, golden bays, blacks, grays, paints, even a few of the rare whites. Morgan's gaze locked on one beautiful stallion, the mustang's coat a dove-colored shade of purplish gray that the Mexicans called *palomino*. He watched in fascination as its shining irises—spots where the hair lay in different directions—changed positions as the horse moved.

As the wings narrowed and the herd neared the gate, the horses were crowded together, an immense mass of rushing animal energy. For a split second Morgan held his breath, fearing there were too many to make it though the narrow opening to the pen at one time. Then they were through the gate, fanning out again as they raced along the sides of the pen, through the narrow second opening and around the second oval.

The last horse had barely cleared the gate when two mustangers jumped down from the wings and quickly shoved the heavy wooden bars across the narrow opening, and not a minute too soon, as the rest of the herd had circled the complete eight and were rushing toward the gate to escape. It wasn't the wooden bars across it that made them suddenly veer and circle the pen again, however, but the sight of a white blanket quickly tossed over the bars. The blanket was foreign to them, a frightening unknown not to be trusted. From then on, the wild horses wouldn't go near the gate.

For several minutes the mustangs continued to mill in the pen, circling and looking for an opening to escape through. One particularly determined dove-gray stallion, the same *palomino* Morgan had admired, reared on his hind legs and struck the fence with his front hooves several times, sending its creamy mane and tail flying. Had the fence not been flexible, it would have broken beneath that powerful battering.

It took a good fifteen minutes for the herd to settle

down. Then they stood, chests heaving and muscles trembling from their long, hard run. All except one, that is. The beautiful *palomino* still circled the fence, looking for a way to escape.

The dove-colored stallion stopped before the gate, eyeing the blanket. For a moment Morgan thought the mustang would charge it, despite his instinctive fear of the blanket. Then, giving an angry, shrill snort, he turned and trotted back into the herd. Morgan smiled, silently admiring the mustang's spirit.

Drawing his eyes away from the herd, Morgan searched outside the pen for Jessie. She wasn't hard to find, even at that distance. Her golden hair stood out like a beacon. Just like the other mustangers, she had stripped down to the bare necessities, only she wasn't bare-chested. He watched while she talked to Gabe and Pedro, assuming that she was giving the two men instructions. Then she turned, walked to her horse, and mounted with a single graceful leap. As she rode off toward the river, Morgan smiled, glad she was leaving the camp. He wanted to talk to her alone. Morgan kneed his horse and followed.

When Jessie reached the river, she dismounted and looked longingly at the cool water. She was hot and dusty from driving the herd into the pen, wanting only to strip down and dive in, but she knew she would have to delay her swim until after she cared for her mount. She bent and yanked up a handful of grass, carefully wiping the sweat from her horse, then tossed the grass aside and yanked up another handful. When the mare was completely dry and cooled off from her run, Jessie led the horse to the river to drink. Only then did Jessie sink to her knees to satisfy her own thirst.

The sound of a twig snapping caught her attention.

She shot to her feet and whirled around, shocked to find Morgan standing right behind her. My God, she thought, how has he managed to sneak up on me like that again? He moved as silently as an Indian.

"I want to talk to you, Jessie."

"Talk? You're always saying that. And then, the next thing I know, you're attacking me. Now, get out of my way!"

When Morgan refused to move, Jessie sidestepped him and made for her horse, but Morgan caught her arm as she passed and turned her around. "I'm serious, Jessie."

Her body's strong response to his touch frightened her. "Let go of me!" she cried, jerking her arm away.

"For Christ's sake, Jessie," Morgan said in an exasperated voice, "calm down. All I want to do is talk to you."

Jessie backed away. "I have nothing to say to you."

"No? Well, I've got a hell of a lot to say to you. I found out from Gibbons why you two are at odds. You both want the White Steed."

Jessie was shocked that Gibbons had admitted to Morgan it was the White Steed they were both trying to capture. She had thought the rancher would want to keep the identity of the stallion as much a secret as she did. Damn Gibbons! If the rancher didn't keep his big blabbermouth shut, they'd have every mustanger within five hundred miles swooping down on them.

"Why are you so determined to have that stallion, Jessie? For the money that's being offered for him?"

"No. For the horse himself."

"As a saddle mount? Wouldn't he be a little much for you to handle? Providing you did manage to capture him."

"I don't want him for a saddle horse. I don't need one.

I have La Duquesa here. She's the best saddle horse there is."

"La Duquesa? The Duchess? Why did you name her that?"

"Because she's of royal lineage. Haven't you ever heard the old Mohammedan myth that claims the first horse God created was a golden bay with a star on its forehead? Well, La Duquesa has a star on her forehead. Besides, I wouldn't have a stallion for a saddle horse. Mares are more trustworthy and have more endurance."

Morgan laughed. "You're just prejudiced, being a female yourself."

"Being a female has nothing to do with it!" Jessie snapped, irritated that Morgan didn't think she knew what she was talking about. Why, she knew more about horses and horse breeding than most mustangers and horse breeders, thanks to Pedro. "That's an Arab belief," Jessie continued. "And they should know. The Arabs are the greatest horse breeders in the world. They believe the female is so far superior to the male that they trace lineage through her."

"All right, so the mare is superior," Morgan answered impatiently, beginning to get irritated at Jessie's condescending attitude. "Then why do you want the White Steed? He's a stallion."

"For breeding purposes, for my ranch," Jessie answered, as if Morgan's question was the most stupid she had ever heard.

"You have a ranch?" Morgan asked in surprise.

"No. But I will have one soon. I've already picked out the spot on the San Saba River."

Despite himself, Morgan had to hand it to her. The San Saba country was the best horse range in Texas, lush with curly mesquite grass that cured like hay in the winter, and plentiful with clear water. The rocks along the San Saba gave the horses good hooves and taught them to be surefooted. The Comanches knew the value of that horse country. That was why they had fought for that territory longer than for any other ground in the Southwest. Yes, if you were going to have a horse ranch, the San Saba country was the best spot for it. But . . .

"Why do you want to go to the trouble and expense of starting a ranch?" Morgan asked. "Hell, there's mustangs all over Texas you can pick up for nothing."

"No, the mustangs are disappearing. Not as fast as the longhorns and buffalo, but the herds of wild horses grow smaller every year. When I was a child, there were over a million wild horses in Texas alone, and in this area— mustang country—you'd see herds with as many as ten thousand horses in them. You don't see herds that size anymore. Even a herd of a thousand head is rare these days. In ten or twenty years they'll be virtually gone. What's left will be so picked over, they won't be worth driving to market, just like that herd yesterday."

Until Jessie mentioned it, Morgan hadn't realized it *had* been a long time since he'd seen a really large herd of mustangs. He, too, remembered them from his childhood, herds of thousands and thousands of horses that stretched from horizon to horizon, and when they ran, the whole prairie seemed to undulate, like waves on an open sea.

"Don't you see, Morgan?" Jessie asked, completely forgetting her animosity toward him and unaware that she had called him by her first name in her excitement. "If I capture the White Steed, my horse ranch is bound to be a tremendous success. Why, there's no telling what people would pay for a colt sired by the White

Steed. And they will be superior colts. I'll see to that. I'm already collecting the best mares I can find for his *manada*. I'm going to produce the best horseflesh in the Southwest."

"What if the White Steed won't produce for you? I've heard he's a loner. Maybe he won't even breed."

"No, he's not a loner. The first time I saw him, he had a *manada*. A huge one. But when we chased him by relays, the mares couldn't keep up. They dropped out, one by one. That's why people have seen him alone. He's been forced to leave his *manada* behind by being chased so much. It was the only way he could escape. No, he's a herd stallion. I can assure you of that. But I don't think he's pure mustang. He's too tall. I think he has Thoroughbred blood in him, foaled from a Thoroughbred mare some mustang stallion stole from one of the ranches."

"Maybe he has bad blood in him," Morgan said in an ominous tone. "Gibbons swears he's a man-killer, that he deliberately tried to kill him."

"No, he's not like the Black Devil up on the Brazos, the mustang stallion that the Indians claim kills men and then eats them," Jessie insisted. "No one but Gibbons has ever accused the White Steed of that. Gibbons creased him—the damned fool! That's painful and stuns a horse so badly, it's confused. The White Steed probably didn't even realize that he wasn't trapped. He was fighting for his life. Any wild stallion would do that."

"Maybe the horse you chased wasn't even the White Steed," Morgan argued, taking another approach. "Maybe he was another white stallion."

Jessie closed the distance between them and unconsciously placed her hand on his arm, anxious to convince him. "Oh, but he was, Morgan. If you ever saw him, you'd know. I've never seen a horse like him, so swift, so proud, so spirited, so perfectly formed. He's the most beautiful thing in the whole world."

At that minute, all thought of the horse fled from Morgan's mind. With Jessie standing so close to him, Morgan could smell her sweet, womanly scent, a scent that made his senses reel, and could feel the heat radiating from her, particularly where her hand lay on his arm. He gazed down at her sparkling green eyes, at her face, flushed with excitement. With the sun to her back, her golden hair was shining like a radiant halo around her animated face.

He stepped closer. "No, Jessie, *you're* the most beautiful thing in the world."

Morgan's softly spoken words and the warm look that suddenly came into his eyes took Jessie aback. Was he up to some trick? she wondered suspiciously. "Look, all this sweet talk isn't going to change my mind."

With a swiftness that momentarily stunned her, Morgan took Jessie in his arms and kissed her, his mouth coming down on hers in hot demand. Jessie struggled, trying to twist her lips away, but Morgan firmly held her chin in one hand while he crushed her to him with his other arm. As Morgan's warm tongue slid into her mouth, then swirled around hers, Jessie felt an insidious weakness creeping over her and a warmth suffusing her.

Shocked at her body's betrayal, she struggled harder, but to no avail. Morgan's arm was like a vise around her, and she seemed helpless against that sensuous male mouth. With his artful tongue sliding in and out of her mouth in a torrid, insistent kiss that went on and on, she couldn't breathe and she couldn't think. The world seemed to tilt on its axis.

When Morgan unbuttoned her shirt and his hand cupped one breast, Jessie sucked in her breath sharply as a thrill of excitement ran through her. Unconsciously, she moaned and leaned into him. Not until his fingers brushed across the tender nipple, bringing it to life, and Jessie felt a wave of heat rush to her loins, did she finally regain control of her spinning senses.

Damn him! she thought. He'd caught her off guard before, but she wouldn't let him make a fool of her again. She renewed her struggle, against both Morgan and her own response to his kiss. With a strength born of fury and desperation, she tore her mouth away and shoved him back. "Stop it!"

"Jessie," Morgan muttered in a roughened voice, his eyes imploring as he reached for her.

"Don't touch me!" Jessie said, stepping back. Then, realizing Morgan's smoldering gaze was locked on her bare breasts, she yanked her shirt closed and quickly buttoned it.

"You . . . you did it again!" Jessie accused. "You said you just wanted to talk to me, and then you . . . you . . ."

"Dammit, Jessie! Don't you dare accuse me of attacking you," Morgan said in a hard voice. "If you think what was happening between us was rape, then you've got an awful lot to learn about men and women. You weren't objecting, Jessie. At first, yes, but then you were moaning and pressing yourself against me. You loved what I was doing to you."

Jessie knew that Morgan wasn't far from the truth. She *had* come dangerously close to surrendering to him. Damn! It was humiliating the way he crumbled her defenses with just a touch. To make matters worse, he was nothing but a low-down, cold-blooded gunslinger. "You liar! You'll stoop to any trick to get what you want!"

"No, Jessie, I didn't lie to you, and I didn't deliberately trick you. I came here with every intention of just talking to you . . . except I seem to have trouble keeping my senses about me when I'm around you," he admitted with with a grin. Then his smile faded. "Jessie, give up this crazy idea of capturing the White Steed. Gibbons is a dangerous man, too dangerous for you to tangle with. He's obsessed with that stallion."

"I'm not afraid of Frank Gibbons."

"Jessie, he wouldn't hesitate to kill you to get that horse."

"He wouldn't go that far. He wouldn't dare! No, he's just threatening me. He thinks because I'm a woman I'll run like a scared rabbit."

"Jessie, please—"

"No! I won't listen!" Jessie interjected stubbornly. "You, Frank Gibbons—nobody—is going to keep me from capturing the White Steed. When that stallion circles back, I'm going to be waiting for him."

"Circles back?" Morgan asked in surprise. "Are you telling me the White Steed isn't even in this area?"

"He's in this area, but not in the immediate vicinity. I told you that we chased him but didn't catch him."

"What in the hell makes you think he'll come back?"

"You don't know very much about mustangs, do you?" Jessie commented with obvious disgust. "Every wild stallion has his territory, whether it be twenty, fifty, or a hundred miles wide. But he won't cross the boundaries of that territory when he reaches them. He'll circle back. And when the White Steed comes back, I'll be waiting for him. I know all of his watering places around here."

"And in the meanwhile, you do a little mustanging?"
And get yourself killed in the process, Morgan thought
grimly.

"Of course. Spring is the best time for mustanging,
when the horses are weak from lack of grass during the
winter. I'd be a fool to waste the time, or the opportunity."

Jessie turned, mounted her horse, and picked up the
reins. Morgan stepped forward, still intent on trying to
reason with her. The determined set of her chin and the
fierce look in her eyes brought him to an abrupt halt.
They stared at each other.

"All right, Jessie," Morgan conceded in a hard voice,
"if you won't listen to reason, then maybe I'll have to
resort to other methods of persuasion. Gibbons hired
me to get you out of here, and I fully intend to do just
that."

Jessie felt a strong sense of betrayal. He was Gibbons's
hired gun, after all! Just as she'd suspected, his concern
for her safety had been nothing but a big act. Of course,
his job would be easier if he could simply talk her out of
it, rather than have to force her out. And, like the op-
portunist he was, he hadn't been adverse to taking a
little pleasure on the side. The bastard!

Jessie glared at him. "More threats, Mr. West? Well,
I'm not afraid of you, either, despite that gun on your
hip. I only regret that I didn't blow your head off while I
had the opportunity."

Jessie galloped off. Morgan watched her ride away, a
grim, determined expression on his face. Now he'd *have*
to force her to leave. It was the only way he could
protect Jessie from Gibbons—and herself.

Chapter 5

JESSIE GAZED OUT OVER THE PRAIRIE, THEN SHOOK her head in self-disgust. For the third time that day she had caught herself doing that, gazing off and hoping to see Morgan riding over the rise toward her camp. What in the devil was wrong with her? Why hadn't she been able to get the rugged gunslinger off her mind? Visions of his handsome face flashed through her mind at the most unexpected times, distracting her from what she was doing and irritating her no end. Even worse, every time she thought of him, those strange physical yearnings plagued her. Like it or not, she had to admit that she was attracted to him.

Jessie scowled at her admission. Why, of all men, did he attract her so strongly? True, he was unusually good-looking and utterly masculine, but he was also arrogant and overbearing, the kind of man she despised. Besides, he was a gunslinger, a cold-blooded killer who hired out his gun to anyone, a low-down polecat with no compassion or scruples. Why, he'd even stooped to pretending concern for her to get what he wanted. He didn't give a damn about her!

Jessie flinched at the pain of regret the last thought brought her. Despite all his faults, she wanted him to care, or at least to take some notice of her. As intensely as she disliked him, he was the most intriguing and exciting man she had ever known. Not even the knowledge that he was dangerous could dispel her attraction to him. If anything, it enhanced it, and Jessie knew that he was much more dangerous to her on a personal level than he'd ever be with his gun, for his overpowering masculinity seemed much more threatening. His strong sensuality both frightened and excited her, a combination that perversely added to her strange fascination with him.

Jessie wished she'd had more experience with men. She had never been interested in a man romantically. Her full concentration had been on making her mustanging outfit a success and trying to prove that she was just as able and tough as any man in the business. If anything, she had been at odds with the opposite sex her entire adult life, constantly fighting their discrimination against her. She was wise to all their sneaky tricks in business matters, but totally naive when it came to dealing with them on a personal level. At twenty, she had only been kissed twice. The first had been by one of the Mexicans who worked for her, a mere touching of lips before the young man had remembered he was overstepping his bounds and quickly retreated. Her second had come from an admiring cowhand, and that hadn't impressed her in the least. She had found the wet kiss repulsive. Was it only because Morgan was older and more experienced in seduction that his kisses had such a devastating effect on her? In his arms, with his lips and tongue working their dark, devilish magic, she had become a weak female with no will of her own. Never had she felt so powerless, and she had no idea of how to cope with those strange yearnings that had plagued her since he had come into her life.

Damn, she knew everything there was to know about mating horses, but nothing about what went on between men and women. Oh, she knew about the sexual act itself. Having been around horses all her life, she wasn't that naive. But there was more to it than that with humans. They didn't just simply mate, at least not the woman, not if she was respectable. Her emotions were as involved as much as her sexual desires. Then, why was she so attracted to Morgan? She couldn't stand him. He was everything she hated in a man. What in the world was wrong with her?

Jessie turned from where she was standing on the open prairie beside her herd of mares and looked back at the camp. Seeing Maria Martinez kneeling beside the cooking fire and making tortillas, she walked toward the older woman.

Maria looked up from what she was doing as Jessie approached and smiled. *"Buenas tardes, patrona. "*

"Buenas tardes, Maria."

Maria looked at Jessie with surprise when the girl knelt beside her and spooned a handful of warm *masa* into her hand from the pot sitting to one side, then started patting the cornmeal dough into a flat cake. She had expected the *patrona* to walk by after greeting her, instead of stopping to help. While Jessie was just as good a cook as she and just as adept at the Mexican art of making tortillas, the girl rarely helped the Mexican women anymore, not since she had taken over her father's duties. Neither of the women in the camp had objected to Jessie's leaving the cooking and the washing for the group in their hands. As the *patrona*, it was to be expected. Jessie's job as their leader and protector was much more physically wearing than the chores the women performed and certainly much more demanding. Maria had been amazed at how well Jessie had performed since she had taken over the awesome burden. They had never gone hungry, and Jessie had seen that they had new clothing at least twice a year and a new warm blanket every winter, something almost unheard-of for the Mexicans. And when it came to their health, Jessie was just as particular with them as she was with her horses, sparing nothing on medical supplies and the attention she gave them. Why, she had even promised them their own cabins when she got her ranch. It was something that the two Mexican women could hardly dare to dream of—a small home of their own—but neither doubted Jessie's word. She was the most determined human being Maria had ever known.

Jessie slipped the tortilla she had been shaping into the mud oven beside the fire and sat back on her heels. "Where did you meet your husband, Maria?"

The question startled Maria. Jessie had never shown the slightest interest in men or marriage. "We were born and raised in the same small village in Mexico. As long as I can remember, I have known him."

"Then you always loved him?"

Maria laughed softly. "Oh, no, I didn't say that. When we were children, we fought like cats and dogs. Even when we were adolescents, I thought he was too *macho*."

Jessie frowned. "Too manly? How can a man be too manly?"

"Ah, *patrona*, *macho* means much more than manly. It is as much a matter of attitude as a man's physical appearance. To the *patrón* or *patrona*, the Mexican male is very careful to be respectful. He never steps out of his place. But to his women, he is very domineering. For some strange reason, he seems compelled to prove how strong, how powerful he is. While I been brought up to accept this belief that the Mexican man is lord and master, it still irritated me."

"Then if you resented his trying to dominate you, why did you marry him?"

"Because I fell in love with him." Seeing the puzzled expression on Jessie's face, Maria again laughed softly. "Ah, *patrona*, we women are strange creatures ourselves. Deep down, we want our men to be strong, to be decisive. No woman wants a man she can walk over. Besides, that is the way it has always been. The man leads and the woman follows. He commands and she obeys."

Jessie didn't like what she was hearing. Why couldn't a man be strong without being domineering, and why did a woman have to become his shadow? Had it been the way of the world so long that women no longer questioned it? And something else was puzzling her. "If he irritated you so badly, how did you know you were in love with him?"

"Because no matter how much his attitude annoyed me, he excited me. When he was away, I was miserable. I couldn't wait to see him again. All I could do is think of him. When you love someone, you can overlook his faults."

Jessie liked Maria's answer even less. It sounded too familiar. Was she beginning to care for Morgan? No, she wouldn't allow herself to do that, she vowed firmly.

Falling in love with a man was a trap for a woman. Once ensnared, she had no will of her own, no control over her life. Maria might be content with that lot, but Jessie could never accept it. She'd be damned if she'd give up her hard-earned independence for any man, let him rule her life and tell her what to do, especially one as despicable as Morgan West.

That night, after Jessie, Gabe, and Pedro had finished eating their supper in the dugout, Jessie cocked her head and listened. "Did you hear that? It sounded like thunder."

Another low rumble was heard from the distance. "Yep, that's thunder all right," Gabe agreed.

Jessie pushed her chair back from the table and rose. "If there's a storm coming, we'd better get those mares out of the open and into corrals. They're still half wild. Despite those straps on their ankles, they'll try to run."

"*Sí,* and break their necks," Pedro added grimly, coming to his feet.

"Do we have to go to all that trouble?" Gabe asked. "Maybe the storm will just pass us by. A little thunder don't mean nothing."

Jessie shot Gabe a disgusted look and hurried for the doorway, with Pedro fast on her heels. Flinging aside the blanket and stepping outside, they saw the flashes of lightning in the distance, lightning that outlined the dark thunderheads rolling over the horizon.

"That storm isn't going to pass us by," Jessie said to Pedro. "It's coming right down on us."

"*Sí,* and judging from that lightning, it's going to be a bad one."

"Get the *mesteñeros* out there," Jessie instructed him. "And send someone to the big pen to tell those men to come and help us."

"You think you ought to do that?" Gabe asked as he stepped from the dugout. "They're guarding that herd."

"No one in their right mind would be out on a night like this," Jessie countered. "Not with that big storm coming down on us. Now hurry, Pedro."

As Pedro rushed off, Jessie and Gabe hurried back into the cabin, snatched up their lariats, then ran to the herd of mares that had been hobbled in the open. When they reached them, the mustangs were already frightened, nervously pawing the ground and snorting. A crack of lightning split the heavens, leaving the strong smell of ozone in the air. The mare Jessie was trying to slip her lariat around smelled it and reared, its nostrils dilating and its eyes wild.

Jessie jumped back, dodging the mustang's flying hooves, then deftly slipped the noose in her lariat over the mare's head. Stroking the terrified animal's neck, she crooned, "Easy, easy, girl. I'm not going to let anything hurt you."

Still stroking the horse's sleek neck and talking to her in a soothing voice, Jessie led the animal to the nearby corral while her mustangers roped other mares and did the same. It was a tedious, nerve-wracking task.

By the time Jessie and her men were leading the last of the herd to the corrals, the wind that preceded the storm was gusting all around them, adding to the long rolls of thunder and cracks of lightning, and exciting the horses even more. It took all of Jessie's strength to keep the mare she was leading from breaking away from her.

Then, as the last mare was turned into the corral and the gate was slammed shut, something white went flying through the air over them. Seeing it, the mustangs reared and squealed in terror at this new ghostly specter, and for a split second, Jessie feared they would stampede and break down the wooden enclosure.

"What in the hell was that?" Gabe called over the noise the storm and horses were making.

Jessie had only seen the flying object out of the corner of her eye, but she had gotten a good enough look at it to know it was a white blanket, and the only white blanket they had, had been lashed to the gate of the big pen. Had a gust of wind torn it loose? She turned and looked toward the pen, but could see nothing in the dark.

She heard another rumble, one that somehow didn't sound like thunder. Fast on its heels, a tremendous flash of lightning lit up the sky, and Jessie saw the herd of mustangs rushing from the pen in the distance, looking as if a dam had burst and was pouring out horses.

"The horses have broken down the gate of the big pen and are stampeding!" Jessie yelled.

"*¡Madre de Dios!*" Pedro exclaimed. "What will we do now, *patrona*?"

As far as Jessie was concerned, there was only one answer. Those horses were worth a thousand dollars to her. They represented the last payment on her land on the San Saba. "We're going to catch them and turn them back."

"Have you gone plumb loco?" Gabe asked. "In this storm?"

"To hell with the storm!" Jessie retorted. "We're going to catch them and turn them back. Now mount up! Everyone!"

For a moment, the *mesteñeros* hesitated. It would be mighty dangerous to turn a herd of wild horses as terrified as those were. Then, seeing Jessie rushing off for her horse, they dutifully followed, many crossing themselves as they ran to the corral that held their remuda.

It only took a moment for Jessie and her mustangers to mount once they reached their horses. Ignoring the swirling sand that the gusting wind was kicking up, which was stinging their eyes, they quickly slipped their bridles over the horses' heads and flew on the animals' backs, knowing that a saddle would only slow them down. They tore from the camp after the stampeding herd.

Jessie and her men rode their horses harder than they ever had, urging them on with whoops and hollers. The animals didn't need any urging. They were mustangs themselves and just as excited by the storm as the herd of wild horses they were chasing. The race to catch up with the stampeding herd was a ride Jessie would remember for the rest of her life.

The noise was horrendous, thunder rolling and clapping, lightning crashing all around them. Saint Elmo's fire—balls of phosphorescent light—hung over their horses' ears and danced down their manes and tails, giving the mounts a ghostly appearance. Then the rain came—torrents of it—lashing at them with a vengeance. As she rode low over her mount's neck, the wind whipped La Duquesa's mane and Jessie's long hair about her face, half blinding her.

The rain turned to hail. It pounded down on Jessie, bruising her body painfully and bouncing off the ground, making the slippery terrain even more treacherous. Up and down the gently rolling prairie they raced, twisting and turning to avoid clumps of thorny brush, La Duquesa flying over ravines filled with rushing water. Jessie was shivering with cold, and her hands turned numb. Then, blessedly, the hail turned to rain again.

"We ain't never gonna catch that herd!" Gabe called from where he was racing his horse beside Jessie's. "They got too big a head start on us."

As much as Jessie hated to admit it, she knew Gabe spoke the truth. They were never going to be able to catch up with that herd of stampeding mustangs. If the storm had abated, they might have had a chance, but if anything, it had gotten worse. To continue the chase would be utter folly. In an electrical storm this severe, all she was accomplishing was endangering her men.

"We can't catch up with them!" she yelled. "Turn back!"

The *mesteñeros* were only too happy to obey Jessie's order to abandon the chase. They were just as fearful of the lightning crashing all around them as the horses were. They slowed their mounts and turned them.

Jessie reined in and watched the herd of mustangs rapidly disappear in the distance, feeling sick at heart. Now she'd have to capture another herd, but she'd have to look long and hard to find one that would bring as good a price as that one. Of all the rotten luck. Why did that blanket have to blow away? The mustangs would have never found the courage to charge that gate if it had been across it, even as terrified as they were.

A jagged flash of lightning rent the heavens, forking several times and resembling a giant glowing spiderweb against the dark sky. The spectacular electrical display momentarily lit up the entire landscape as if it were broad daylight, and for the first time Jessie spied the riders that were racing after the herd. She knew then that the wind hadn't blown loose the blanket on the gate of the big pen. It had been deliberately untied.

And she'd stake her life that the gate hadn't been broken down by the terrified mustangs but had been opened for them. No, that herd's escaping hadn't been an act of nature. It had been planned and executed by a man. And there was no doubt in her mind just who that man was.

A fury like none she had ever known rose in Jessie. "I'll get you for this, Morgan West. So help me God, you're going to pay for turning my herd loose. This is one piece of dirty work you're going to regret. Do you hear me, you bastard?" Jessie yelled into the wind at the top of her lungs, the pounding rain lashing at her face. "You're going to pay for this!"

Chapter 6

MORGAN HAD JUST CHANGED INTO DRY CLOTHING AF-
ter returning to his cabin, and was reclining on his bunk
when the door was suddenly slammed open. He shot to
his feet, his hand automatically going for the gun that
wasn't strapped to his hip. Then his eyes filled with
surprise as he saw Jessie standing in the doorway. Her
sodden clothes clung to her curves, and her wet hair
hung around her face and shoulders.

"You bastard!" she yelled. "You did that tonight!"

"How in the hell did you get across that flooded creek
out there?" Morgan asked in astonishment.

"Do you think I'd let a little water keep me away?"
Jessie glanced quickly around the cabin. "Where are
the others?"

"I told them to keep driving that herd. By morning,
those mustangs will be halfway across the state."

Morgan's admitting that he had turned her herd loose

and had made damned sure she couldn't recapture it only fed Jessie's anger. "I'm going to kill you for that!"

Morgan found himself looking down the barrel of a Winchester as Jessie raised her rifle and pointed it at him with deadly intent. With the spectacular storm as a backdrop, her huge, jewel-like eyes flashing even more dangerously than the lightning, and her body rigid with outrage, she looked like a magnificent, fierce avenging goddess.

Jessie had wanted to see Morgan squirm before she killed him, but all the bastard could do was stare at her. "Didn't you hear me?" she shouted. "I said I'm going to kill you!"

Jessie's voice tore Morgan from his fantasies and brought him back to cold reality. Goddess or no, Jessie was bent on killing him. "I heard you."

How could he stand there looking so cool and calm, Jessie wondered. Why wasn't he afraid? Did he think she was bluffing? "Damn you! I mean it!"

"I know you mean it, Jessie. I regret that it had to be done. But I warned you I'd do my job."

Jessie laughed scornfully. "Is that all you can say in self-defense? You did your job? Do you realize what losing that herd has cost me? I could have gotten a thousand dollars for it."

"A thousand dollars? Dammit, Jessie, what's your life worth?"

Jessie was taken aback by Morgan's sudden anger, and his question. "What does that have to do with it?"

Catching her off guard, Morgan stepped forward with lightning swiftness and yanked the rifle from her hand. Tossing it to one of the bunks, he caught her shoulders and shook her roughly. "You stubborn fool! You still refuse to admit you're playing with fire. I told you Gibbons was a madman, that he wouldn't hesitate to kill you. Driving that herd away was the only way I could force you to leave. Consider yourself lucky that all you lost was a herd of horses."

"Are you trying to tell me that you drove away a valuable herd of horses to help me?"

"Yes. It was the only way I could protect you."

"Do you really think I'm going to fall for that story?" Jessie asked in a scathing voice. "That you did it to protect me? What do you think I am? Stupid? No, you did it because Gibbons was paying you to do it. You're nothing but his lackey!"

Jessie's insult, combined with her obstinate refusal to see reason, infuriated Morgan. He crushed her against him and kissed her roughly, his mouth grinding down on hers. Furious herself, Jessie struggled, twisting and kicking out wildly. When the toe of her boot slammed into his ankle, Morgan tore his mouth away from hers, cursing beneath his breath. Seizing her opportunity, Jessie pushed away from him.

"Do you think your seductive techniques are going to persuade me to move my camp?" Jessie asked, her breasts heaving with anger. "Well, you can think again, Mr. West. I'm not leaving until the White Steed circles back. The only thing you accomplished tonight was getting yourself in debt. You owe me a thousand dollars for that herd you stole from me. And *you* can consider yourself lucky to have gotten off so lightly."

Jessie turned and snatched up her rifle. As she walked to the door Morgan caught her arm. "You're not going back out into that storm?"

"I certainly am."

"It's too dangerous, with all the flooded creeks and all

that lightning. It's a wonder you didn't get killed coming here."

"What I do is none of your concern. Now, let go of my arm."

A steely look came into Morgan's eyes. "No, Jessie, you're not leaving here."

"Like hell I'm not!"

Jessie jerked on her arm. Morgan's grip on it tightened. Then, before she could stop him, Morgan grabbed the gun from her, flung it to the bunk closest to him, and tossed Jessie over his shoulder.

With her legs held tightly against his chest, all Jessie could do while Morgan quickly walked to his bunk was pound on his broad back and scream, "Put me down! Damn you! Put me down!"

Morgan put Jessie down. She found herself flying through the air and hitting the bunk so hard, it knocked the breath from her and she saw stars. Before she could recover, Morgan was tying her hand to the top of the bunk with a rope that had been lying on the floor.

"What do you think you're doing?" Jessie asked when she had recovered her breath.

"I'm tying you to the bed so you can't leave."

"You're insane!"

"No, I'm the only sane person in this cabin. You're not leaving, Jessie, and I'll be damned if I'm going to waste my energy fighting you."

Jessie came at Morgan with the nails of her free hand bared. But before she could dig them into his face, he caught her flying arm in one hand and quickly looped the other end of the rope around her wrist. Then, straddling her to pin down her thrashing legs, he tied the other arm to the top of the bed while Jessie bucked wildly beneath him. Having firmly secured both arms,

Morgan lifted himself from her and stepped to the side of the bed. He barely had time to jump back as one of Jessie's feet kicked out at him.

Morgan glared down at her. "I was hoping you wouldn't force me to tie your feet, too, but I can see you're not going to listen to reason."

"Reason!" Jessie shrieked. "Do you call tying someone to a bed reasonable?"

"It's the only kind of reason you understand," Morgan flung back.

When Morgan picked up another rope and reached for her leg, Jessie fought with all her might, kicking out with her booted feet. With an expertise born from dodging flying hooves in his cowhand days, Morgan swiftly stripped off her boots and tied her ankles to the bottom of the bunk, but not before Jessie got in a hefty blow or two. She barely had time to savor his grunts of pain before she found herself tied spread-eagle to the bed. Then Jessie used the only weapon she had left at her disposal. Her mouth. She cursed him, calling him every foul, ugly name she had ever heard in both English and Spanish, which turned out to be a long and impressive repertoire, for Jessie had grown up among a group of tough, rough-talking mustangers who hadn't always been careful to watch their language within her hearing.

Morgan sat beside her on the bunk and chuckled. "My, my, what an unladylike vocabulary you have. Someone should wash your mouth out with soap."

Realizing that her cursing him was a wasted effort, Jessie jerked on the ropes that held her wrists and ankles.

"Stop that!" Morgan said harshly. "You'll only hurt yourself. You can't pull those knots loose."

Jessie had already found that out. Jerking on the ropes had only made them bite painfully into the tender skin. She glared at him.

"Stop looking so angry, Jessie. I'm only doing this for your own good."

Jessie was furious. First he'd driven away a valuable herd of horses, and now he'd overpowered her and tied her to the bed. And all supposedly for her own good. He was nothing but a big bully. "How long are you going to keep me here?"

"Until I decide it's safe for you to travel."

"That storm might go on all night," Jessie objected.

A slow grin spread across Morgan's handsome face. "Yes, it very well might. It looks like you're going to have to spend the night with me."

There was a strong sexual innuendo in Morgan's words, and Jessie knew it. "I'd rather spend the night with a rattlesnake than with you!"

Morgan's eyes flashed dangerously, and Jessie felt a tingle of fear. Then, as quickly as it had come, the anger in his eyes disappeared. He smiled and said in a silky voice, "Would you?" He leaned forward, so close, Jessie could feel his warm breath on her face. "How do you know that, Jessie? How do you know you wouldn't like my lovemaking?"

Jessie's heart was hammering wildly in her chest at the smoldering look she saw in Morgan's eyes. "Because you kissed me before, and I didn't like it."

"You're lying, Jessie. You loved it."

"No, I didn't! I can't stand for you to touch me."

"You mean like this?" Morgan trailed his fingertips up Jessie's throat, the long caress taking her breath away. When his hand reached her chin, she jerked her head away.

"Maybe you'd prefer the feel of my lips."

As Morgan bent his head and kissed Jessie's throat, which she had conveniently exposed to him, then licked its length, Jessie shivered. "Don't!"

"Why not?" Morgan whispered as he nibbled on her earlobe, causing another thrill to ripple through her. "How can you dislike what you've never felt? Like this."

Jessie jumped as Morgan's tongue darted into her ear. She had never felt anything so exciting. Alarmed, she jerked her head back around.

It was a mistake. Morgan's mouth hovered over hers. Then he was kissing her, not roughly as he had before, but with a sensual intensity that make her ache. His warm lips lightly brushed back and forth, back and forth across hers, his tongue flicking at the sensitive corners of her mouth until Jessie thought she would scream with frustration. She tried to turn her head away, but Morgan held her face in his hands, taking his time, taunting her until Jessie was whimpering for want of his tongue in her mouth. Then Morgan gave her what she wanted, kissing her deeply, his tongue an instrument of exquisite torture. Jessie felt that familiar warmth stealing over her and a tingling in her fingertips. Holding her prisoner, over and over Morgan kissed her, first long, sweet kisses, then hot and demanding, then sweet again, until Jessie felt an overwhelming ache between her legs.

Suddenly she became aware of Morgan caressing her bare breasts. She looked down. My God, when had he unbuttoned her shirt? She watched with something akin to horror as his fingers brushed back and forth across the rosy crest and the nipple hardened and rose expectantly to his tantalizing touch. She fought against the waves of pleasure that were washing over her. "Stop it!" she choked out.

Morgan ignored her demand and lowered his head from where he had been kissing her throat. His tongue flicked out like a wet whip across the throbbing nipple, and Jessie felt a bolt of fire rush to her loins that took her breath away. Then as his mouth closed over the nipple and he rolled it around his tongue, Jessie moaned.

"Did you like that?"

"No!" Jessie denied adamantly, too adamantly.

Morgan raised his head and gazed up at her. "I think you're still lying, Jessie. Your lips tell me one thing, but your body says another."

"Why are you doing this?" Jessie asked, her voice breaking. "Is this why you tied me up? So you could rape me?"

Morgan shook his head in disgust. "You do like to dwell on rape, don't you? You still don't know the difference between that and making love. Well, you can stop worrying about your virtue, Jessie. I've never forced myself on a woman. I've never had to."

With that, Morgan pulled her shirt over her bared breasts and rose from the cot. He looked down at her, and Jessie felt that smoldering gaze clear to her toes. Her heart raced in anticipation, for secretly she yearned for him to continue his exciting advances.

"Someday, Jessie, you're going to beg me to make love to you."

Jessie bristled. Why, the egotistical bastard knew he had a dark hold over her and was throwing it in her face. "No! Never!"

Morgan chuckled at her angry retort, then turned and walked away. From where she was tied, Jessie watched as he lay down on the bunk opposite her, then rolled to his side with his back to her.

"Good night, Jessie. Sleep tight."

Sleep was the last thing Jessie could think of. She was acutely aware of the ache between her legs and of her tingling breasts. How dare he tease and torment her like that and then leave her. The devil had deliberately used his seductive expertise to arouse her just to prove his point. Jessie fought a silent struggle with herself. A part of her longed to call him back to finish what he had started, while another told her he would think her easy and scorn her when it was over. But in the end it was her fierce pride that kept her from doing it. She wasn't going to let any man get the best of her, particularly not Morgan West.

It was a long time before Jessie slept that night. While the storm raged outside, she was left to seethe with unfulfilled desire and fury at the man who had made her so miserable.

When Jessie awoke the next morning, her hands and feet were untied and Morgan was gone from the cabin. She was still furious with him for playing her body against her the night before. She'd never been so humiliated, and she'd never forgive him. There was nothing too low for him to sink to.

Quickly, she buttoned her shirt and slipped on her boots. She was just reaching for her gun when Morgan walked back into the cabin.

Seeing her grab her Winchester and point it at him, Morgan said, "That's not necessary, Jessie. I'm not going to try to stop you. The storm has passed, and the water in the creek has gone down. It's not even raining anymore. It's safe for you to leave now."

Jessie laughed harshly. "Do you actually think I'm so

gullible I'd believe that you kept me here because you were concerned for my safety?"

"Regardless of what you think, Jessie, I did keep you here for your own good." His eyes roved slowly over her body, then locked on her breasts, and Jessie knew he was thinking of last night. The memory of his hands and mouth there made her legs turn weak. Damn him! He was doing it to her again! She wished she had the courage to shoot him, but she couldn't force herself to pull the trigger.

Morgan's eyes rose and met hers. "It's a shame we couldn't have enjoyed our night together more. I still think it would be damned good between us."

"Is that all you can think about? Your lust?"

Morgan's eyes flashed dangerously. "No, Jessie, that isn't all I can think about. Right now I'm thinking what a damn fool you are for not leaving while you still have the chance. Get out, Jessie! Get out before something happens to you or one of your people."

"I'm not afraid of Frank Gibbons. I can take care of myself and my people. And turning those horses loose last night hasn't changed anything. I'm not running. I'm going to catch the White Steed. Nothing Gibbons does is going to change my mind. That horse belongs to me!"

Morgan saw the determination in Jessie's eyes. She's just as obsessed with catching that stallion as Gibbons is, he thought grimly. The only difference between the two was their motives, Gibbons driven by revenge and Jessie by her dream.

A hard look came over Morgan's face. "All right, Jessie, if that's the way you want it. But the next time it might be that herd of mares you lose. The herd you prize so much. Think about that!"

Jessie went pale at the thought of losing her prized

brood mares. Morgan had claimed he regretted what he'd done to her herd, and now here he was, threatening her again. He lied to her at every turn.

"You just try to do something to my mares, Morgan West. The first time I see you set foot anywhere near my camp, I'll blow your head off!"

Jessie stalked from the cabin, and Morgan followed. He watched tight-lipped as she swung onto her horse's back and rode off. Then, suddenly, she turned her horse and yelled, "And you still owe me a thousand dollars for that herd you stole from me!"

Morgan laughed. "Don't hold your breath, sweetheart. Hell will freeze over before I pay you for that herd."

Jessie glared at him across the distance that separated them. If looks could kill, Morgan would have been a dead man. Then she turned her horse and raced away.

Chapter 7

JESSIE RODE LA DUQUESA OVER THE GENTLY ROLLING prairie, feeling proud of herself for standing up to Morgan. It had been a week since he had driven her herd away, and he'd done nothing more to try to convince her to leave. She guessed she'd shown him that she wasn't some weak female to be pushed around.

Jessie turned her horse toward the river. When they reached it, she dismounted while her mare drank thirstily. She looked around, seeing that the bluebonnets were blooming. They were really spectacular. The whole world seemed to be carpeted in a vibrant blue.

Spying a particularly thick clump of the wildflowers beneath a gnarled mesquite a distance away, she walked to them, thinking they would make a pretty bouquet for the table in the dugout. She knelt and started picking the flowers.

Three men suddenly came rushing at her from where they had been hidden in the trees. Dropping the flowers, she sprang to her feet and ran for the Winchester in her saddle holster. But it was too late. The men caught her long before she reached her gun. Jessie fought like a wildcat, screaming and cursing, but outnumbered three to one, it was useless. They quickly overpowered her, tied her hands in front of her, and slung her on the saddle, removing the Winchester from its holster and tossing it down on the bank for good measure.

"What's going on? Who are you?" she demanded, but all three men ignored her.

A half hour later, Jessie understood what was happening. When they rode up and reined in before Morgan West's cabin, Jessie's eyes shot daggers at her captors, something she had been doing ever since they had grabbed her at the Nueces. She was furious at herself for being caught away from her horse and her rifle—picking bluebonnets, of all the stupid things to do—and furious at Morgan. Undoubtedly this was another of his ploys to frighten and intimidate her. Well, it wasn't going to work. As soon as he untied her hands—for she suspected he was waiting in the cabin for his henchmen to deliver her—she'd scratch those damned silver eyes right out of his head!

Fess dismounted, walked to Jessie's horse, and roughly jerked her to the ground. Angrily, Jessie pushed away from him, her eyes flashing and her breasts heaving with fury.

"Damn, she's a feisty one," Cole said as he and Red walked up to them. He eyed Jessie from head to toe, and she shivered. He reminded her of a snake. "And damned pretty too. Too bad we have to kill her. Seems a waste of good woman-flesh."

Fess scratched his ragged beard, his black eyes coldly calculating. "I've been thinking the same thing. Don't know why we can't have a little fun with her first. After that fight she put up, seems we deserve a little extra reward for our trouble." He fingered the long, ugly scratch on his face that Jessie's sharp nails had placed there.

Seeing the naked lust in the two men's eyes, a tingle of fear ran through Jessie. Then she reassured herself, thinking that they wouldn't dare. Morgan wouldn't let them. He wouldn't go that far to frighten her. And surely they weren't really planning to kill her in cold blood. No, Morgan only wanted to frighten her. She glanced at the cabin, wondering why he hadn't come out. He must have heard them ride up.

At the sound of a horse approaching, all four turned as Morgan rode into the clearing. Seeing him, Cole's and Red's eyes took on a wary look. They glanced at Fess in expectation. The mean-eyed leader of the three glared at Morgan hatefully as he dismounted.

"What's going on?" Morgan asked.

"Gibbons came by this morning after you left," Fess answered in a hard voice, a gloating expression on his ugly face. "Said he was tired of playing games with this little bitch, that he wanted her gotten rid of, once and for all—permanently!"

"Yes, I know," Morgan answered calmly. "I just came from talking with him. But why did you bring her back here? Why didn't you kill her where you found her?"

Jessie stared at Morgan wide-eyed, utterly shocked that he was actually standing there and calmly discussing murdering her.

Fess faced Morgan, his black eyes narrowing dangerously. "The boys and I figured we'd have a little fun with her before we killed her." His hand moved to hover over his gun. "You got any objections to that?"

Morgan's gaze swept over Jessie coldly as he answered, "No, I don't have any objections." He turned back to face Fess. "On one condition."

"What's that?" Fess asked, eyeing Morgan suspiciously.

"That I go first."

"Why do you think you should be first?" Fess asked in a surly voice.

"Number one, I'm still the boss here. Number two, I don't like wallowing in any man's leavings."

Morgan's voice vibrated with dangerous undertones, and his eyes glittered like splintered glass. The surly gunfighter backed down with a nervous laugh. "Hell, I don't care who has her first. As long as it don't take too long. I've got a powerful itch."

Morgan turned to Cole and Red.

"That's fine with me," Cole muttered, refusing to meet Morgan's hard silver eyes.

"Me too," Red added nervously.

Jessie couldn't believe her ears. For Morgan to rape her, then turn her over to his men so they could torture and degrade her, was even worse than murdering her. A blinding anger seized her. "You bastard!" she yelled at Morgan when he turned to her.

Grimly he caught Jessie's arm in an iron grip and wheeled her around, striding rapidly to the cabin.

Jessie jerked on her arm and twisted, spitting curses and kicking out at him wildly. Morgan ignored her, dodging her blows as he dragged her to the cabin.

"God damn, she's a regular wildcat!" Fess said in an excited voice. "You need some help with her?" he called to Morgan.

"No!" Morgan answered without even looking back.

"Hell, Fess, he don't need no help," Red said, seeing

Morgan cuff Jessie. "He'll tame her for us. By the time he's finished with her, she'll be as meek as a kitten."

"Not too meek, I hope," Cole said with an ugly snarl. "I like them begging for me to stop."

When Morgan had cuffed Jessie, he had deliberately made it appear harder than it actually was, but the slap had been enough to stun her, more from shock than anything else. Taking quick advantage of her momentary stillness, Morgan swung her up in his arms and closed the distance between them and the cabin door in a few swift strides, slamming the door shut behind them with the heel of his boot.

Recovering from her shock, Jessie came to life like an erupting volcano. "Take your hands off me, you son of a bitch!" she screamed, twisting and bucking wildly in his arms.

"Be still!" Morgan whispered urgently.

"Like hell I will!" Jessie hissed, managing to get her tied hands up and to catch Morgan's hair, pulling it with all her might.

Morgan grunted in pain. He dropped her to her feet, holding her against him with one steely arm while he yanked her arm down with the other hand, grinding out between clenched teeth, "Dammit! Will you calm down? I'm not going to rape you."

Morgan could have saved his breath for all the good it did him. Jessie was beyond reasoning with as she swung her tied arms at him like a club, twisting and kicking like a wild bronco. Desperate to subdue her, Morgan caught her in a crushing bear hug, staggered to one of the bunks and threw her on it, pinning her down with his weight.

Jessie squirmed and bucked and pushed at him, but it would have been easier to move a mountain than to make Morgan budge. Glaring up at him, she struggled to breathe under his weight. And then, to her horror, she felt her body responding to the feel of him pressing against her, her breasts swelling and her nipples growing hard, a flooding heat in her loins.

"I'm not going to hurt you, Jessie," Morgan said. "I'm not going to do anything to you. I'm sorry I slapped you, but I had to get you inside the cabin so you could escape."

Jessie was too stunned to speak. She stared at Morgan, afraid to trust her ears, wondering if he was up to some trick.

Morgan rolled from her and quickly untied her hands. Then he rose from the bunk, pulling her to her feet with him.

"What's taking so long in there?" Fess called from outside the cabin.

Morgan glanced over his shoulder, then looked back at Jessie. "Scream!" he commanded.

"What?" Jessie muttered in confusion.

"Dammit, scream! You're supposed to be fighting me, remember?" Morgan turned and kicked over a chair, then tossed the table to its side with a loud bang.

Finally realizing that Morgan had been telling her the truth, Jessie opened her mouth and let out a blood-curdling scream that would have made a Comanche's war cry sound tame in comparison.

Morgan pushed Jessie toward a small window at the back of the cabin. "Climb out and run for the brush out back. Don't come out until I call the all clear. And if I don't call, get the hell out of here," he added ominously.

"But—"

"No buts! Get going!"

"Sure you don't need any help?" Fess called.

Morgan picked Jessie up and half shoved her through the window. "Dammit, get out of here!"

Whirling, Morgan walked quickly to the door, slammed it open, and stepped out. Fess, about ten feet from the cabin, came to a complete halt. Then the gunslinger's eyes narrowed as he asked in a suspicious voice, "What's going on? Where's the girl?"

"Gone," Morgan answered in a deadly calm voice. "There isn't going to be any rape, or any murder."

"Gibbons said we should kill her," Cole objected angrily, rushing up to them and stopping beside Fess.

"I don't give a damn what Gibbons said," Morgan answered.

"Why, you double-crossing bastard!" Fess cried, his hand going for his gun.

But Morgan's draw was faster, his hand a streak of lightning, his gun out of its holster and exploding before Fess's six-shooter even cleared leather. The bullet slammed into the gunslinger's chest with such force that Fess spun around several times before falling to the ground.

Morgan's second shot came a split second later, aimed at Cole, who had also drawn on him. Cole's finger was just squeezing the trigger when Morgan's bullet tore through his belly, making him grunt in pain and pitch forward, spoiling his aim as the bullet meant for Morgan hit the cabin wall behind him, then ricocheted, sending splinters flying everywhere.

Crouched low, Morgan spun, his gun pointing at Red. "Don't shoot!" the terrified man cried, holding his arms out to the side. "For Christ's sake, don't shoot!"

Morgan's eyes narrowed. His trigger finger twitched. Cold sweat broke out on Red's body as he stared down the barrel of Morgan's gun.

"I didn't really want to kill the girl," Red said nervously. "Or rape her either. That was Fess and Cole's idea. Then, when you agreed with them, I was just playing along." His eyes pleaded for mercy. "Please, don't kill me."

Morgan struggled for control, fighting down the urge to kill the man. Then he straightened, saying in a hard voice, "All right, I won't kill you. But you ride out of here like hell and head straight for the border. Then keep riding. Because if I ever lay eyes on you again— you're a dead man!"

The gunslinger's face drained of all color. He ran to his horse. It took three tries before he managed to get his foot in the stirrup, but once mounted, he wheeled his horse and tore from the clearing as if all the demons in hell were after him.

Morgan watched Red until he disappeared, then walked to Fess, lying facedown on the ground. Using the toe of his boot, Morgan rolled him over. Seeing the look of surprise frozen on the man's face, Morgan knew he was dead.

He swiveled and looked at Cole, lying on his side. The man's chest was barely moving, and Morgan knew from the blood pouring out of the wound and pooling on the ground that he wouldn't live long, the bullet having obviously hit a major blood vessel. The tension he had been living with since one of Gibbons's cowhands had told him the gunslingers had captured Jessie slowly ebbed from Morgan. He slipped his gun back into its holster.

Remembering that Jessie was hiding in the brush behind the cabin, Morgan turned and found her standing in the cabin doorway instead. Less than six inches from where she stood, there was a fresh nick in one of the logs where Cole's bullet had hit before ricocheting.

"I thought I told you to wait in the mesquite thicket out back," Morgan said angrily as he walked up to her. "Don't you know you could have been killed? A lot of good it did me to try and get you out of the way."

Jessie didn't answer. Her eyes were wide with horror as she gazed at the bodies of the two men sprawled on the ground. For the first time, Morgan realized how deathly pale her face was and that she was leaning weakly against the doorjamb. He feared she might have been hit by the ricocheting bullet.

Taking her shoulders in his hands, he turned her to face him, his gaze quickly sweeping over her from head to toe, searching for signs of blood. Seeing none, he realized that she was simply in shock from what she had witnessed. "It's all right, Jessie," he said softly. "It's all over."

It took a moment for Jessie to focus on Morgan's face. Then, finally realizing that he was standing before her unharmed, she collapsed weakly in his arms. Morgan held her as if she were the most precious thing in the world, a stark contrast to his rough handling of her earlier, and Jessie allowed herself a minute to bask in his tenderness, feeling his strength infusing her.

Then she turned her head and looked back at the bodies, a shudder running through her as she asked, "They're dead?"

Her simple question made Morgan realize that Jessie wasn't out of danger yet. "Yes, and we'd better get out of here."

He led her to her horse, saying, "Now you know I wasn't fooling when I said Gibbons wouldn't hesitate to kill you. And after today, he's going to be even angrier.

Get back to your camp and pull out, Jessie. Take that herd of mares and ride like hell."

Jessie stopped in midstride and turned to him. "What about you?"

"I'm hightailing it out of here too. Gibbons isn't going to like me double-crossing him. I wouldn't be surprised if he hired someone to kill me for fouling his plans for you and shooting up his hired guns."

"But how will he know it was you who killed them? The gunslinger you let go looked so scared, he probably won't stop until he reaches Mexico City."

"He'll know who killed them, Jessie. He's been pushing for killing you all along, and I've been putting him off, telling him I could scare you away. Today, he finally got tired of my delaying tactics and turned the job over to these men."

Jessie was reeling in a maelstrom of confusing emotions. Morgan wasn't a bastard after all. He had saved her life. Knowing that he'd been telling her the truth all along when he'd said he was trying to protect her filled her with happiness, but knowing that he would be a hunted man filled her with guilt.

Morgan wanted to take Jessie with him—willing or not. He wanted her as he had never wanted any other woman. But he knew that he couldn't. To do so would only endanger her, for he knew Gibbons would seek him out with a vengeance. But once Jessie was out of this area and no longer a threat, the rancher would forget about her.

Morgan took Jessie in his arms and kissed her long and hard, trying desperately to put his stamp of possession on her. Then, while Jessie's senses were still swimming from that hot, devouring kiss, he picked her up and placed her in her saddle.

He stood back and drank in her beauty, imprinting it on his mind. Then, before Jessie could utter a word, he said, "So long, sweetheart," and slapped her bay hard on its rump.

The startled mare lurched forward and raced across the clearing. By the time Jessie had reined in and turned her horse around, Morgan was mounted and riding off in the opposite direction.

Jessie watched as Morgan disappeared, feeling a deep regret that this stubborn, impossible man was riding out of her life forever, just when she was beginning to like him.

"Thank you for saving my life," she futilely called after him. "Your debt to me has been paid in full."

Chapter 8

MORGAN PEERED OUT OF THE DINGY WINDOW OF HIS hotel room at the dusty street below him. Today was Saturday, and Dog Town was bustling with activity. Catching a fleeting glance of a bay horse, Morgan's breath caught. Then he laughed at himself derisively. It couldn't be Jessie's horse. She'd be in San Antonio by now, or maybe even up in the San Saba country, getting her ranch started.

In the three weeks since he'd left her, Morgan had done a lot of traveling, hoping to wipe out his trail in case Gibbons had sent someone after him. He'd gone to Corpus Christi and dallied there for a day. Then, leaving Corpus, he'd traveled south, crossing the huge Kennedy and King ranches on his way to Brownsville. He'd forded the Rio Grande and spent one night at Monterrey, the monte capital of the west, before wandering all over northern Mexico. Then he'd headed back north, crossed the border, and ridden into Dog Town two days ago.

Morgan smiled wryly, thinking that it was fitting he had lighted in Dog Town. It was a haven for hunted men, and Morgan was now a hunted man. Sitting on the Frio River in the middle of no-man's-land—the brush country next to the border—it had a reputation for being as wild as Dodge City, drawing both the Mexican bandits running from Díaz's *rurales* to the south, and the murderers and thieves running from the law to the north. Gunfights and murders were a daily occurrence among the outlaws, and Dog Town had its own Boot Hill.

Looking out at the town, Morgan saw the crush of men and horses in the street below him and wondered what all the excitement was about. Then it dawned on him. Dog Town, like every town in South Texas, had its weekly Saturday afternoon horse race.

Again Morgan caught a glimpse of the bay he had seen earlier, and again it reminded him of Jessie. He had meant to put his brand on her when he had given her that last scorching kiss, but it seemed Jessie had put hers on him instead. He hadn't been able to forget her. He carried the vision of her in his mind, haunting his days and torturing his nights. Morgan had thought to rid himself of her in a bout of pure lust, but it hadn't worked. Neither the sultry, dark-eyed *señorita* south of the border, nor the voluptuous redhead Jeanette—the best Dog Town's most reputed cathouse had to offer— had been able to arouse him. After Jessie, with her golden hair, her jewel-like eyes, and her undaunted spirit, they had seemed tawdry and unbearably boring. Damn the little bitch! She had ruined him for other women. She was a fever in his blood for which there was no cure, no relief.

Morgan eyes narrowed as he looked more closely at the crowd below him. Spying the glint of golden hair, his heart slammed against his chest. Jessie! What in the hell was she doing here?

Morgan turned from the window and flew from the room, taking the steps on the rickety staircase three at a time. Once outside, he shouldered his way through the crowd until he towered above the girl about to mount her horse.

Catching her by the arm, he asked, "What in the hell are you doing here?"

Seeing Morgan, Jessie felt a burst of sheer joy. But when she noticed the look of thunder on his face, she answered coolly, "I came to buy supplies. I always buy my supplies here."

"In Dog Town? Christ, Jessie! Don't you know how dangerous this town is, particularly for a woman? Hell, every low-down polecat, outlaw, and Mexican bandit within two hundred miles is holed up in this town."

"I'm not afraid. I was born here in the *brasada*. I've been coming here since I was a child. Besides, I'm not alone. Gabe came with me."

"I thought you were heading north, to San Antonio, or the San Saba country."

Jessie knew if Morgan found out she had never left the camp on the Nueces, he would be furious. He had risked his life to save hers and made an enemy of a dangerous man in order to protect her, but the lure of catching the White Steed had been too much for her. She dropped her head, deliberately avoiding his eyes. "No, I wanted to catch more mustangs to sell before I started my ranch."

"But why in this dangerous country? Hell, Jessie, there's mustangs all over Texas. Or do you just like flirting with death?"

"The best herds are in this part of the country, and I'm not flirting with death. I told you I was born and raised here in the *brasada*. I know my way around, and I know how to take care of myself."

"Sure you do," Morgan drawled sarcastically.

The color rose on Jessie's face, knowing that he was referring to the stupid way she had let herself be captured and almost killed. Dammit, if anyone had had to come to her rescue, why did it have to be this arrogant gunfighter standing before her, Jessie thought in disgust, completely forgetting that had it been anyone else but Morgan, she could well be dead.

"Riders mount up!"

At the loud call, Jessie put her foot in the stirrup. "I've got to go."

"Wait a minute," Morgan objected.

Jessie mounted and looked down at him impatiently. "I can't talk now, Morgan. I've entered La Duquesa in the race and they're fixing to start."

"You're going to race against a bunch of men?" Morgan asked, a little shocked at her lack of decorum.

"I certainly am!" Jessie snapped, her green eyes flashing. "And don't you dare tell me I can't because I'm a woman. I've already gone through all that with the judges."

Without another word, Jessie urged her horse forward to the starting line. Morgan shook his head, thinking that she was the damnedest woman he'd ever known, wearing men's clothing, doing a man's dangerous job, and now pitting herself against men in a man's sport. No, Jessie was no lady, not in the strictest sense of the word, nor was she the other kind. She lived by her own code of rules, throwing convention to the wind. Utterly feminine on the surface, beautiful, soft and silky, she had a core as tough as hardened leather. Yes, Jessie was unique. He smiled in silent admiration.

Morgan glanced quickly around him. The crowd in the street was already thinning out, everyone seeking a perch from which to watch the race, since most of it would take place in the open countryside surrounding the town. Spying Gabe standing on the flat roof of the two-storied hotel, Morgan took a running jump, grabbed the roof of the hotel porch, and pulled himself up on it. "Hey, Gabe!" he called.

Gabe turned, a surprised expression coming over his face.

"Give me a hand up, will you?" Morgan requested.

"Sure thing," Gabe answered, holding out his hand. "After what you did for Jessie, it's the least I can do."

Morgan caught Gabe's hand and climbed to the top of the roof. He turned and looked around, seeing that this was an excellent spot from which to watch the race. There were several other two-storied buildings, but the hotel was the taller than the others. From his perch Morgan could see the gently rolling prairie all around Dog Town, the Frio River to one side of the settlement glittering like a silver streamer in the sunlight.

Unfortunately, Gabe wasn't the only one who had taken note of the hotel's height. Soon the roof was crowded with men, and the betting on the outcome of the race was going hot and heavy.

"What horse you betting on?" one rangy cowhand asked Gabe.

"The bay."

"The bay? Are you crazy? There's some fool girl riding that horse. Why, she ain't even got a regular saddle. She's riding on some sheepskin thing with stirrups attached to it."

"That ain't no fool girl!" Gabe answered hotly. "She's a friend of mine, and that sheepskin thing is her special racing saddle." He stuck his chin into the cowhand's face. "I'm betting on the bay."

Another cowhand stepped forward. "You're throwing your money away, mister. That black horse from the Circle S is gonna win."

"Like hell he is," the first hand said, shooting the second a challenging look. "That roan from the Triple T is the fastest horse in this country."

"You're both wrong," a cool voice said as a third man stepped into the circle forming around Gabe. From his natty dress and the well-manicured nails on his slender fingers, everyone recognized him as a professional gambler. "The gray will win."

Morgan stood by as the bets were placed, Gabe getting the best odds. Obviously everyone was discrediting the bay because it was being ridden by a lowly female.

The gambler turned to Morgan. "How about you, mister? You betting on the race?"

Morgan looked down at the ten horses prancing impatiently at the starting line. There were some good-looking animals among them, prime horseflesh. The gray caught Morgan's eye. The animal had the mark of a Thoroughbred, and Morgan knew the stallion would be fast. He glanced at the gray's rider, a lightweight youth whose eyes were glittering with excitement, obviously a hired rider rather than the owner of the horse. Yes, Morgan could understand why the gambler was betting on that pair. The youth wouldn't slow down the gray's speed with his weight.

Morgan turned his attention to Jessie, seeing her chin was set determinedly. He remembered her remarkable horsemanship the day he had seen her chasing down the mustang mare, and knew that it would be no contest. What Jessie's mare lacked in racing blood, Jessie more than made up with skill.

Morgan turned to the gambler and asked, "What odds are you giving on the bay?"

"The bay?" the gambler asked in surprise. Then, quickly hiding his reaction, he smiled smugly, saying, "I'll give you five to one."

"Fine. I'll lay a hundred on the bay," Morgan answered calmly.

"A hundred *dollars*?" the gambler gasped.

"That's right. A hundred dollars," Morgan replied.

The bid was unusually high for Dog Town and drew the attention of the crowd around them.

"What horse is he betting on?" one man asked another.

"The bay."

"Christ! What's wrong with him? Is he crazy or something?" was the response.

"I assume you cover my bet," Morgan said to the astonished gambler.

Quickly recovering, the gambler again smiled smugly, his eyes glittering with greedy anticipation. "I can cover it. But, mister, you'd better get your money out and kiss it good-bye. It's the last you'll see of that hundred."

The sound of a gunshot, followed by galloping hooves, quickly ended the betting. "They're off!" someone cried excitedly, and the crowd of men surged to the front of the hotel roof.

Below them, the ten horses and their riders were

already tearing down the narrow main street, the on-lookers standing on the boardwalks and roofs cheering them on. A minute later the racing horses burst into the open countryside, following a rutted road that formed a semicircle around the town.

"Look at that roan go!" one man yelled. "Why, he's like greased lightning."

"Yeah, but the black's catching up with him," another commented.

Morgan watched the race without comment as the horses galloped across the rolling prairie. The roan was in the lead, followed closely by the black and the gray. Farther back ran a pinto and Jessie's bay, and behind them, the rest of the entries. For several minutes the riders and horses were concealed as the road cut through a mesquite thicket, and the only way the on-lookers on the roof could tell how far the race had progressed was by the cloud of dust that hung over the trees. When the horses emerged from the thicket, the black and roan had changed places, and the pinto had moved up, challenging the gray for third place. Jessie's bay was left in fifth place.

As the horses raced down the road beside the river, necks out and tails streaming, Morgan was beginning to have doubts. What's wrong with her? he thought. Jessie wasn't riding anything like she had the day he'd seen her ride down the mustang mare.

Seeing Morgan's frown, Gabe whispered, "Stop worrying. Jessie knows what she's doing. We're gonna make a killing."

By now the gray was in the lead, the roan and black having fallen back, and the horses had completed the semicircle and were heading back to town, their coats glistening with sweat in the sunlight.

"Still think that bay is going to win?" the gambler asked Morgan with a smirk.

The dig irritated Morgan. "Yes, I do," he answered with a confidence he didn't feel, despite Gabe's assurance that Jessie would win. "Would you like to double those odds?"

It took a minute for the gambler to recover from Morgan's surprising answer. He glanced quickly at the racing horses, saw the gray was still in the lead, and answered, "It's a deal."

Morgan turned his attention back to the race. He watched breathlessly as Jessie's bay suddenly shot forward, passing the pinto in a flurry of dust. As Jessie leaned forward so that her cheek was almost lying on the mare's neck, the bay seemed to fly, and her long hair trailed out over the animal's back like a golden pennant.

"Jesus Christ! Look at that horse go!" someone in the crowd yelled as Jessie's bay passed the roan, then the black.

When Jessie's bay and the gray came barreling down the street to the finish line, neck and neck, hooves pounding, tails streaming, the crowd went wild, yelling and cheering loudly.

"Come on, Jessie! Come on!" Gabe yelled, jumping up and down.

Morgan thought Jessie looked absolutely magnificent as she urged her horse on. "Come on, sweetheart! You can do it!" he yelled excitedly.

Hearing Morgan's call, Gabe shot the gunfighter a piercing glance, then quickly returned his attention to the race below them. In a sudden, unbelievable burst of speed, the bay surged ahead of the gray and crossed the finish line a good length ahead of it. The crowd of on-lookers went berserk with excitement, a deafening cry ringing out and bouncing off the buildings.

"I lost fifty dollars on that gray," one man said when the noise had died down, "but I'll be goddamned if it wasn't worth it. I've never seen anyone ride like that little gal!"

Morgan beamed, feeling so proud of Jessie, he could burst. He turned to find Gabe grinning broadly at him. "Didn't I tell you?" Gabe asked. "No one can beat Jessie and her bay when that girl sets her mind to it."

As Gabe moved off into the crowd to collect on his bets, Morgan turned and glanced around for the gambler. The man had completely disappeared. Morgan wasn't particularly surprised. A thousand dollars was a lot of money. What did surprise him was he didn't really care. Jessie's winning had been enough of a reward.

Morgan pushed his way through the crush of men still milling on the rooftop and jumped down to the hotel porch, then vaulted over the railing to the ground. He watched as the judges paid Jessie. And then, when she turned, his breath caught. With her face flushed with excitement, her long golden hair falling around her shoulders, and her eyes sparkling, she was undoubtedly the most beautiful woman Morgan had ever seen, a vision that heated his blood and sent his spirit soaring.

A sudden scowl came over his face as a crowd of eager, admiring cowhands surrounded Jessie and complimented her on her ride. A rush of jealousy went through Morgan, startling him with its intensity. He stalked to where Jessie stood and roughly shouldered his way through the circle of men around her.

"Hey, watch who you're pushing, mister," one cowhand complained, then turned pale when he saw the deadly gleam in Morgan's silver eyes.

Seeing Morgan, Jessie impulsively threw herself in his arms, hugging him. "Morgan, I won!"

"I know," Morgan replied with a warm smile, hugging her back.

"Oh, excuse me," the pale cowhand quickly apologized. "I didn't know you were a personal friend of the lady, mister."

Morgan ignored the man, his full attention on Jessie's excited face. "That was some ride, sweetheart."

Morgan's simple compliment touched Jessie deeper than any of the cowhands' glowing ones, and his term of endearment sent a shiver of pleasure through her. She floated on a warm, rosy cloud, basking in Morgan's appreciative gaze. Then, hearing a snicker, she finally became aware of where she and Morgan were standing and of everyone gawking at them. She pushed away from him, her flush of embarrassment adding even more color to her face. "Thank you," she muttered.

Morgan had been very conscious of Jessie's soft body pressing against his, and when she moved away his arms ached to take her back into their embrace. The need to have her rose, hot and urgent, his loins tightening in anticipation. He took her arm, turning her toward the hotel, saying in a husky voice, "Let's find someplace more private."

Jessie pulled away, saying, "No, Morgan, I can't. I have to stable La Duquesa for the night."

"I'll stable her for you," Gabe said, stepping up to them, having finally succeeded in pushing his way through the crowd of Jessie's admirers. He beamed down at Jessie. "That was the best racing you've ever done, Jessie. Even closer than that one in San Angelo last year."

"Yes, it was a little too close for comfort," Jessie admitted. "That gray was fast."

Morgan was paying no attention to Jessie and Gabe's conversation. His full attention was still on what Jessie had said before the old mustanger walked up. "You're not returning to your camp tonight?" he asked.

"No, we arrived just before the race," Jessie answered. "And since the stores will be closing soon, I'll have to wait until Monday to buy my supplies."

Morgan didn't like the idea of Jessie's being in Dog Town on a Saturday night. It was the roughest, wildest night of the week, with innumerable fights, saloon bustings, and more than a few shoot-outs. Had there been a sheriff in the town, he would have probably found his own hole to hide in that night—if he wanted to live to see the light of day.

"How far is your camp?" Morgan asked, thinking it would be safer for Jessie to return to it and ride back into Dog Town on Monday.

Before Jessie could even open her mouth to answer, Gabe said, "About three days ride from here by wagon. Down on the Nueces."

A tingle of suspicion ran through Morgan, and then, seeing the hot look Jessie was giving Gabe, he knew. His eyes bored into Jessie. "You didn't leave, did you?"

Jessie didn't answer. She couldn't. With those silver eyes glaring and his big body hovering menacingly over her, Morgan looked very dangerous.

Morgan's hands caught her shoulders. "Answer me, dammit! You're still sitting down there in Gibbons's lap, aren't you?"

"Yes, I am!" she answered defiantly, pushing his hands away.

"Why? Why in the hell didn't you clear out? What does it take to make you see reason?"

"You don't understand, Morgan. There hasn't been any more trouble. Not since you killed those men. I think it shocked Gibbons. Made him reconsider."

"You're crazy if you think that! I told you, he's a madman. He'll hire more gunfighters. Hell, he'll probably hire a whole army of them this time."

"Then I'll arm my *mesteñeros* and fight him with my own army," Jessie answered stubbornly.

"Dammit, you *do* like flirting with death, don't you? Do you think your mustangers would be any match against professional gunslingers? Christ, Jessie, if you do, you're dim-witted. They'll mow your men down like grass under a sickle. They'll massacre your mustangers."

Jessie glared at Morgan silently, resenting his arrogant intrusion into her affairs and his slurs on her intelligence.

Frustrated beyond his control, Morgan thundered, "I ought to take you over my knee and beat some sense into you."

Despite Morgan's murderous look, a look that would have made most men tremble in fear, Jessie wasn't in the least intimidated. Instead, his threat had pushed her growing resentment over the brink. "Who in the hell do you think you are?" Jessie yelled. "Just because you did me a favor and saved my life, doesn't mean you own me —or have the right to tell me what to do. No, my life belongs to me, and I make my own decisions. What I do —or don't do—is none of your damned business, you . . . you arrogant bastard!"

With that, Jessie turned, caught her mare's reins, and started leading her horse down the street to the stables.

"Wait, Jessie!" Gabe called, trotting off after her. "I'll stable her for you."

Jessie whirled around, her eyes spitting sparks, a furious look that made Gabe come to a dead halt. "I don't need any help!" She shot Morgan a murderous glance and added, "From either of you!"

As Jessie walked angrily away, Gabe walked back to where Morgan stood and muttered, "I guess she's mad at me because I let you know where we're camped."

"Then it wasn't a slip of the tongue?" Morgan asked.

"Nope. I was hoping that you might be able to reason with her. I sure haven't had any luck. Was like talking to a stone wall. Every time she finally got fed up with me hounding her, she'd fire me. I bet I've been fired ten times this past week."

"But you haven't left," Morgan pointed out.

"Nope. And Jessie don't really want me to, either. It's just her way of telling me to shut up."

"She's the most stubborn, mule-headed woman I've ever laid eyes on," Morgan said, feeling his frustration and anger rise again. "The crazy fool is going to get herself killed yet."

"Don't be too hard on her," Gabe said protectively. "You gotta know Jessie to understand her. For years she's dreamed about having her own horse ranch. I guess it just natural for a woman to want to put down roots someplace. All females seem to have that nesting instinct, wanting their own home, and since her pa died, she's been even more anxious to get it. Leading that mustang outfit ain't been easy on her, you know. It's hard, dangerous work. And even when we get those horses to the market, Jessie's got a fight on her hands. The buyers are always trying to cheat her because she's a woman."

"I can understand her wanting a ranch and wanting to get out of mustanging," Morgan said, "but what I don't understand is her obsession with the White Steed."

"He's become a part of her dream. Hell, she's heard about him since she was knee-high to a grasshopper. That's all the mustangers talk about at night around their campfires, the famous White Steed and his exploits. She's gotten the idea in her head that her ranch won't be a success without him as her stud stallion, that it will fail. That's why she's so determined to catch him, come hell or high water."

"No dream is worth risking your life for," Morgan pointed out.

"Jessie don't look at it that way. She figures she's got to gamble something to get what she wants. And she wants that ranch and that horse something awful. It's a powerful urge that's driving her."

"Sounds to me more like a devil riding her back," Morgan commented grimly.

"Yep, that, too, I reckon," Gabe answered glumly. "Well, I reckon I'd better go. I don't like the idea of her being alone in that stable, what with all these strange men around."

As Morgan watched Gabe walk to the stable, he remembered Jessie's cutting words. What had she called his saving her life? A favor? Christ! He'd risked his life because she wouldn't listen to reason, and all she could call it was a favor!

Then she had the audacity to accuse him of sticking his nose into her business and being an arrogant bastard, all because he was concerned about her. Talk about ingratitude! Well, she'd made it clear she wanted him out of her life, and that was fine with him. He didn't need or want a woman cluttering up his life, particularly not a mule-headed, ungrateful little bitch like Jessie. To hell with her!

Morgan turned and saw the line of cowhands standing before the bathhouse, the first step in their preparations for their night on the town. He decided that was just what he needed—some lighthearted relaxation. A little poker, a little drinking, a few laughs. Why, he might even pay that redhead Jeanette another visit. After that foul-tempered Jessie, she was beginning to look mighty good.

Chapter 9

AFTER MAKING STOPS AT THE BATHHOUSE THEN AT HIS hotel to change clothes, Morgan was ready to paint the town red.

He looked into a dance hall, seeing the girls with their gaudy, knee-high dresses and painted faces and their partners moving around the crowded room. What was going on could hardly be called dancing, particularly on the part of the clumsy cowhands in their awkward high-heeled boots. It was more like stomping, with a lot of side-kicking, leg-slapping, and bumping into other couples. Between the tinny piano music, the clapping, the good-natured, boisterous hollering of the hands, the girls' shrill laughter, and the sounds of boots pounding the wooden floor, the noise was horrendous. Morgan decided to forgo that particular madness and entered the saloon next door instead.

It, too, was crowded. Here cowhands and mustangers brushed shoulders with gamblers, pickpockets, outlaws, and thieves. A blue haze of tobacco smoke hung in the air, and the smell of rotgut whiskey was overpowering. Morgan carefully studied the tables where poker was being played, wanting to avoid any game in which a professional gambler or trigger-happy cowhand was taking part.

After sitting in on a game with three relatively sane-looking men, Morgan spent three hours gambling, keeping his drinking to just enough to relax him, but not enough to dull his senses, wanting to keep his wits with all the drinking and guns about, a lethal combination. When the first fight began, one man knocking another over the bar and shattering the glasses and bottles at the back, Morgan bowed out of the game and moved on.

He didn't even go through the swinging doors of the second saloon. He could hear the wild free-for-all going on inside. He barely had time to duck as a man came flying through the air and landed in the dusty street behind him. Totally undaunted, the cowhand struggled to his feet, wiped the blood from his mouth, and, head down like an enraged bull, charged back into the melee.

Morgan walked to the third saloon, through the swinging doors, and came to a dead halt, seeing some fool cowhand had ridden his horse into the building and was swinging from the chandelier—to the roaring delight of his drinking buddies below him. Morgan backed out, and then, hearing the sound of gunshots and pounding hooves, dove to the boardwalk as a group of whooping cowhands came tearing down the street on their horses, their guns blazing. He heard the sound of bullets whizzing through the air, glass breaking, and wood splintering all around him.

After the riders had passed in a flurry of choking dust,

Morgan came to his feet, swearing angrily under his breath. Things were getting a little too wild and woolly for his taste, and he decided to visit the cathouse. The activity there might be just as wild and frenzied, but at least he wouldn't be in any danger of being killed by a stray bullet.

Turning, he bumped into another man going in the opposite direction. "Excuse me," the man mumbled.

Morgan peered into the darkness, then asked in surprise, "Gabe? What in hell are you doing here?"

"Why, I reckon the same thing you are, Morgan. We mustangers have to unwind, too, you know."

"Where's Jessie?" Morgan asked, looking about him, half expecting to see the fiercely independent lady and vowing that if he did, he *would* tan her pretty bottom— by damn!

"She's in her room at the hotel."

"The hotel? You left her alone at the hotel on Saturday night, with all this going on?" Morgan asked in a shocked voice.

"She ain't in any danger. Her door is locked."

"Hell, those locks are so flimsy, anyone could break in on her."

Gabe's eyes narrowed as he drawled, "Well, I reckon if they did, they'd quickly regret it. 'Cause they'd find themselves looking right down the barrel of Jessie's Winchester. Now, if you'll excuse me, I got some more unwinding to do."

Morgan glanced over at the hotel and saw that several of its windowpanes had been broken by the cowhands' wild shots. "Wait a minute," he said, catching the mustanger's arm. "What room is she in?"

Gabe cocked his head suspiciously. "Why you wanna know?"

"Because I'm going over there to check up on her, to make sure she's all right. For all you know, she could have been hit by one of those bullets flying around here a minute ago."

Gabe thought it unlikely. "Well, if you're so dead set on it, it's room sixteen. But you're wasting your time. Jessie's been sleeping in that hotel on Saturday nights since she was a little tyke. As soon as she heard all the racket, she probably took cover."

Morgan walked to the hotel, irritated at both Gabe and himself. Here he was, going over there and checking up on Jessie, after she had made it perfectly clear she didn't want to see him again, and if Gabe had been protecting her like he was supposed to, he could be off enjoying himself. Hell, Gabe must be crazy to leave a young, innocent girl by herself with all of these wild, dangerous men roaming about. And how could Gabe be sure she hadn't been hit by one of those flying bullets? He almost had.

The hotel itself was relatively quiet, but noise from the saloons and dance halls surrounding it infringed on its peacefulness. Morgan stopped before Jessie's door and rapped on it softly, then, when there was no response, more sharply.

"Who's there?" Jessie asked, her voice muffled and sounding sleepy.

"It's me. Morgan."

There was a long silence before Jessie called, "Go away!"

Obviously, Jessie wasn't hurt, but Morgan felt a strong urge to see her. "Open the door, Jessie. I want to talk to you."

"I have nothing to say to you. Go away!"

"Jessie, open this door—before I kick the damned thing in!" Morgan threatened.

There was another long silence before Morgan heard the faint creak of bedsprings, saw a sudden light coming from under the door, and then heard the padding of feet. As the lock snapped Morgan pushed the door open and stepped into the room, then came to an abrupt halt, his eyes widening.

"What are you gawking at?" Jessie snapped.

"You're wearing a nightgown," Morgan muttered, still staring in surprise.

"Of course I'm wearing a nightgown! It's nighttime, in case you haven't noticed. And *some* people like to sleep—instead of drinking and carousing all night."

Morgan ignored her sarcasm. "I've never seen you in women's clothing."

As Morgan's gaze slowly slid over her, from the tip of her head to her toes, Jessie suddenly felt very vulnerable. She knew he couldn't see anything. Buttoned at the neck, with long sleeves, the modest gown hid practically every inch of her, and yet she was acutely conscious of her nakedness beneath it, feeling as if Morgan's eyes had somehow slipped under the material and were viewing everything.

Jessie stepped back from him. "What do you want?"

Morgan had come to assure himself that Jessie hadn't been harmed, but the sight of her aroused him. He knew now why he hadn't been enjoying himself. He wasn't interested in painting the town red. What he wanted was Jessie.

"You," he finally replied rather softly.

"You come to my room in the middle of the night, demanding to talk to me, and then you calmly announce you want me?" Jessie said in furious tones. "What gall! Get out of here!"

"No, Jessie. I'm not leaving. You owe me. I saved your life."

"I don't owe you anything! I canceled your debt to me to pay for that."

"Oh? When?"

"That day. I told you, but you were already riding off."

"No, Jessie. The only payment I'll accept is you."

There was a fierce, determined gleam in Morgan's silver eyes as he closed the distance between them. Jessie made a grab for her gun lying on the dresser, but Morgan anticipated her move and quickly jumped between her and it. When he reached for her, Jessie ducked his hands and darted for the door. Morgan was right behind her, his boots drumming on the wooden floor as he tore after her down the dim hallway. Just before Jessie reached the stairwell, he caught her. Once again, Jessie found herself flung over his broad shoulder. She squirmed and beat on his back, to no avail.

"Gabe!" she called.

"You can save your breath, Jessie. He isn't here. I ran into him outside one of the saloons."

"You bastard!" Jessie shrieked. "You knew I was alone!"

"Sshh," Morgan commanded harshly. "Do you want to wake everyone in the hotel up and have them out here gawking at us?" he asked as he walked rapidly back down the hallway.

That was the last thing Jessie wanted. Being carried as if she were no more than a sack of flour was humiliating enough without having anyone witness it. Besides, there probably wasn't another soul in the hotel but them. Everyone was out ripping up the town.

Jessie struggled in earnest then, twisting her body wildly and managing to kick her feet, despite Morgan's hold on her legs. "Be still, you little wildcat!" he hissed, slapping her on the rump.

It was more the indignity than the stinging pain that shocked Jessie. She stiffened in outrage. Taking advantage of her momentary stillness, Morgan quickly stepped through the doorway and slammed the door shut with the heel of his boot. Taking a few swift strides across the room, he tossed her roughly on the bed and then pinned her down with his full weight before she could scramble away from him.

Furious, Jessie struggled, trying to push him from her. Seeing it was impossible, her hands went for his face, fully intending to scratch his eyes out. She had the satisfaction of raking her nails down one of Morgan's cheeks as he jerked his head back, and of seeing the ugly scratch before he caught her wrists and twisted her arms back, pinning them down by her head. Then Morgan's mouth ground down on hers with a savagery that stunned her.

Through the whirlwind of passion that engulfed him, Morgan heard Jessie whimper in pain. He hadn't meant to hurt her, or to be so rough with her. This wasn't a harlot lying beneath him, but Jessie, someone he cared for.

Deliberately, Morgan softened the kiss, easing the pressure of his mouth against hers, his tongue teasing her lips, coaxing and wooing her to respond. His sudden change from fierce possession to tender seduction confused Jessie. When he broke the kiss and started nibbling and licking her throat, she felt a languidness in-

vading her. As he shifted his weight to one side and
released her wrists, she thought to push him away; then,
feeling his hand sweep over her side in a long caress
that took her breath away, the thought flitted away. His
heady male scent surrounded her, and she became
acutely aware of his hard, muscular body pressing
against her softness, seemingly scorching her right
through their clothing. Jessie knew what was happening. She was falling under his spell again.

With a strength born of desperation, she pushed at his
shoulders, muttering, "Don't. Please, don't."

"Hush, wildcat," Morgan said softly against her lips
before his mouth closed over hers. As his masterful
tongue darted inside her mouth, swirling around hers,
Jessie felt herself tingling all over. She couldn't fight
Morgan's overwhelmingly sensuous advances and her
own passionate responses too, so she gave in to the
wonderful, exciting sensations he was arousing in her,
her arms rising and curling around his shoulders.

When Jessie embraced him and her tongue tentatively met his, Morgan recognized her surrender for
what it was. An exultation rushed through him, exciting
him even more, and he had to fight the urge to ravage
the sweetness of her mouth and unleash his full passion
on her. With an iron will, he forced himself to keep his
raging need at bay, taking his time with her, teasing and
taunting, kissing and caressing, loving her masterfully
with just the right amount of male aggressiveness and
strength, tempered with tenderness. Jessie was assailed
with new and wonderful sensations as he slowly stoked
her fires, his kisses drugging her and his feather-light
touches leaving her skin burning. Mindlessly, she
arched her body into his, thrilling at the feel of his hard

readiness pressing against her, then spinning dizzily as he kissed her deeply.

Jessie wasn't even aware when Morgan unbuttoned her gown and slipped it off her. But when his mouth closed over the rosy crest of one breast, flicking erotically while his hand stroked and massaged the other, Jessie was acutely aware of him there, feeling a stab of fire deep in her loins. She arched her back, her breath coming in tiny gasps as his tongue and fingers teased the tender nipples to hardened, throbbing points, then moaned when he tugged on her, feeling an aching building between her legs.

And just when she thought she couldn't feel any more sensation, Morgan proved her wrong. His hand trailed down her side, smoothed over her hip, and touched her between her legs. Jessie's eyes flew open in shock as she protested his intimate touch, trying to push his hand away.

"Sshh, you don't know what you're doing," he whispered in her ear.

Jessie's body was swamped with sensations as Morgan's fingers slid into her and worked their magic. Jessie's hand fell weakly away, and she moaned as wave after wave of pleasurable sensation washed over her, each more powerful than the last, leaving her weak and breathless.

Still feeling dazed, Jessie opened her eyes to see Morgan standing by the bed, stripping off his clothes, and she couldn't take her eyes off him. His bronzed muscles rippled with animal strength, and there wasn't an ounce of fat on him, every inch he revealed to her eyes radiating power and male virility. When he finished undressing, the impact of seeing him stark-naked took her breath away. She was fascinated with his raw male beauty, and her gaze roamed over his broad chest with its sprinkling of dark hair, then down over his taut belly, following the fine line of hair that pointed like an arrow to his manhood. There her gaze was riveted as she stared at the proof his masculinity, standing bold and proud before her. Jessie started to tremble, for he looked enormous. *My God, he'll rip me in two!*

Morgan was acutely aware of his blatant arousal and Jessie's shocked, fearful expression. He cursed himself for not having put out the light.

He touched her shoulder, stroking it lightly as he lay down beside her. "Don't be afraid. I won't hurt you."

Jessie gasped as she felt Morgan's bare skin against hers as he pulled her into his arms. And then the only thing she could feel, could think of, was his hard arousal trapped between their bellies. It felt even more enormous than it had looked.

"No! No, don't," she protested. "You're too big!"

"Don't worry about that," Morgan muttered against her throat. "All I want to do is kiss and touch you."

Morgan gave Jessie no time for her fear to grow, his sensual assault on her body making her aware only of what she was feeling as his hands and lips and tongue moved over her, arousing her to a feverish pitch. And then Jessie was returning his caresses, stroking his shoulders and back, thrilling to the feel of his powerful muscles quivering in response to her touch. She marveled at the firm, smooth texture of his skin and the softness of the springy curls on his chest. Then when the palm of her hand brushed over his flat male nipple and Morgan sucked in his breath sharply, she was amazed to find the tiny bud hardening just as hers had under his hands and lips earlier.

Fascinated with his beautiful muscular body, Jessie

moved her hands lower, tracing the hard planes of his taut abdomen, across his hipbones, then even lower. She hesitated.

Morgan held his breath, all too aware of Jessie's hand hovering over him. When she had explored his body, Morgan had lain perfectly still, thinking that if she familiarized herself with it, she wouldn't be frightened of him. It had been an agony for him, her soft hands exciting him unbearably, and now, knowing she was so close to taking him in her hand, he thought he would burst if she didn't touch him.

Despite her fear, Jessie felt compelled to touch him there, to feel the part of him that was the very source of his masculinity. She moved her hand.

"Oh, God, Jessie!"

Morgan's strangled cry told her of the pleasure she was giving him, replacing her apprehension with excitement. A heat flooded her, and the throbbing between her legs became unbearable.

"Morgan," she gasped. "Now. Please, do it now."

He rolled her onto her back and looked down at her, his glittering silver eyes searing her soul. "Not yet," he whispered in a husky voice.

He rained a shower of fiery kisses over her face, down her throat, then placed tiny love bites over her quivering breasts, licking the little stings away. Jessie was awash in a sea of pleasure as Morgan's dark head descended, tracing each of her ribs with his tongue, his mouth sliding lower and lower over her abdomen. He stopped to pay homage to her navel, his tongue flicking erotically and sending shivers of delight racing through her. Then as she felt him dropping light, teasing kisses over the sensitive skin on her inner thighs, Jessie's legs trembled, her breath rushing in and out of her lungs.

Morgan rose, knelt between her legs, and positioned them. As his hands slid beneath her to cup her buttocks and lift her, Jessie eagerly arched her back in anticipation of his entry, thinking the release from that terrible aching was finally at hand.

Then she stiffened, her eyes flying open in shock as Morgan lowered his head, his sideburns brushing across her soft inner thighs before he kissed her there, his tongue flicking like a fiery dart. "No!" Jessie cried out, trying to squirm away.

But Morgan was determined he wouldn't be cheated of this treasure, his need to taste her sweetness and explore her secrets there overriding all. Firmly, he held her hips, his lips nibbling and his tongue swirling over her swollen flesh. As Jessie's legs went limp, Morgan felt a surge of sheer exhilaration fill him at her surrender.

Jessie was whirling in a maelstrom of sheer sensation as Morgan mastered her with his lips and tongue, making her his willing slave. Sweet ripples of pleasure coursed through her, to be replaced with powerful undulations of ecstasy that sent her blood surging through her veins like liquid fire, her skin burning with a million tiny fires, and her nerves tingling. Jessie moaned, writhing beneath him, thinking she would go insane if he didn't stop this exquisite torture. It was too much for her to bear. She would die from pleasure.

"Stop, Morgan. Please, stop," she begged breathlessly.

But Morgan didn't stop. He couldn't. Her taste and womanly scent were driving him wild. He couldn't get enough of her. His tongue plunged into her, moving in and out, and Jessie moaned, her body arching, then shuddering in ecstasy.

Morgan knew that Jessie was as ready for him as she

would ever be. He entered her when those spasms of rapture were still rocking her body, slowly, carefully, holding his passion at bay with an iron will. He was shocked at how tight she was and remembered his promise not to hurt her. But he couldn't stop, not at this point.

Jessie opened her eyes and saw Morgan hovering over her, then became aware of his slight penetration. Seeing her eyes widen and afraid she would refuse him, Morgan bent his head and covered her mouth with his, his tongue making wild, hot forays into her mouth, an incredibly erotic preliminary to what would follow, sending Jessie's senses swimming.

Then, with one swift lunge, Morgan plunged inside her, and Jessie gave a startled cry, feeling as if a bolt of lightning had impaled her, sending shock waves shooting up her spine and exploding in her brain. Morgan wasn't unaffected by that searing joining of their bodies. The feel of Jessie's muscles clutching him like hot, greedy hands almost pushed him over the brink. He clenched his teeth, fighting for control, a sheen of perspiration covering his body and his muscles trembling with effort. He braced himself on his elbows and looked down at her, dreading what he would see when she opened her eyes. He had promised he wouldn't hurt her, and yet he had. But when those thick golden lashes swept upward to reveal her beautiful green eyes, he was astonished to find no sign of pain or accusation. Jessie's eyes were filled with wonder.

Jessie had felt the sharp, stabbing pain when Morgan had plunged in, but it had been only fleeting. She was totally unaware of his incredulous expression as he gazed down at her. Her full concentration was on the feel of him completely filling her, hot and throbbing

deep inside her. It seemed impossible that her body had
stretched to accommodate him, and yet it had. The only
discomfort she felt now was a dull aching. She remembered the exciting things he had done to her. And now,
what other wondrous things were in store for her? Tentatively she moved her hips, her breath catching as
nerve endings she had never dreamed existed tingled
and electric shocks ran up her spine.

Morgan allowed Jessie to make the first moves, then
began his own countermovements, thrusting deeply
and powerfully. The fire that had been smoldering in
Jessie burst into another blazing flame. She wrapped
her legs around his slim hips and pulled him even
deeper into her velvety heat.

Morgan drove her up that breathtaking ascent with a
tender fury, their bodies rocking in a dance as old as
time. Clinging to his broad shoulders, Jessie felt herself
spiraling higher and higher, her senses expanding, the
strange tension in her growing until she thought she
would burst. She held her breath as Morgan carried her
to the summit, her heart racing, moving with a driving
urgency that matched his, sensing that she was on the
brink of discovering something more wondrous than
she had ever known. And then she was over, soaring
free, the tension in her exploding and fragmenting into
a star burst of fiery, swirling colors and bringing a cry of
ecstasy to her lips.

She drifted back slowly, as if she were being carried
back to earth on the wings of a bird. Still dazed, she
opened her eyes to see Morgan gazing down at her.

"Did I hurt you?" he asked, his breath still coming in
ragged gasps.

"No, only for a minute," Jessie admitted.

Morgan smiled, his relief so obvious that Jessie was

touched by his concern. He rolled to his side, bringing her with him and placing her head on his shoulder. Smoothing the damp hair back on her forehead, he kissed her temple tenderly. As he continued stroking her arms and back, nuzzling her neck while he muttered endearments, Jessie was floating on a warm, rosy cloud, feeling gloriously languid and relaxed, thinking his attentions to her after the fact was the best part of it. Then she was surprised to feel him getting aroused again.

Morgan rolled her to her back and looked down at her, his eyes burning with renewed desire. "I want you again," he whispered against her lips.

If Jessie had wanted to object, it was too late. Morgan was already working his magic on her and taking her to heaven.

Chapter 10

WHEN JESSIE AWOKE THE NEXT MORNING, THE SUN was streaming through the window, bathing the room in bright sunlight. Dreamily, she watched the dust motes floating in the air, feeling a warm contentment she had never known. Then the memory of the previous night came rushing down on her, hitting her like a dash of ice water.

She bolted to a sitting position and looked beside her. Seeing Morgan sleeping there, she was struck by the full force of what she had done, and her face drained of all color. Weakly, she lay back down, staring at the ceiling in shock. My God! What in the world had gotten into her? She had let Morgan make love to her, not once but twice! Damn him and his seductive expertise, and damn her weak body for giving in to him. She had done what she had sworn she would never do, let a man get the best of her and bend her to his will. And to make matters worse, he was nothing but a rover, an arrogant gunslinger with no scruples who moved from town to town and undoubtedly left a trail of broken hearts and ruined virtue in his wake. Well, she may have lost her virtue to the devil, but she was damned if she'd be foolish enough to fall in love with him.

"Good morning," a husky voice said next to her.

Jessie jumped when she felt Morgan's warm hand on her bare shoulder. Then he was hovering over her and smiling down. As he bent his head to kiss her, Jessie jerked hers away. "No, Morgan!"

Morgan chuckled and nibbled on her earlobe. "Oh, come on, Jessie, you know you don't mean that."

His hand slipped beneath the sheet and cupped one of her breasts. Jessie shoved it away. "Stop it, Morgan! I said no, and I mean it!"

Morgan raised his head and frowned when he saw the determined expression on Jessie's face. "Why the sudden change of heart?"

"It isn't a sudden change of heart. What happened last night was a big mistake."

"Why do you think that?"

"Because nothing has changed between us. I'm still going back to my camp on the Nueces, and I'm going to capture that stallion no matter what." She saw Morgan's face darken into a scowl, but she continued anyway. "Tomorrow you'll go your way and I'll go mine. Last night was pointless, nothing but a senseless bout of lust. I can't take it back—but I'll be damned if I'll let it happen again!"

Jessie shoved away from him and sat up on the side of the bed, holding the sheet over her nakedness and putting her back to him. "Now please leave," she said coldly.

Morgan's scowl deepened. "All right, Jessie, if that's the way you want it."

Jessie sat stiffly on the side of the bed while Morgan rose and dressed. He stopped at the door, his hand on the knob, and looked back. "You're sure you won't change your mind?"

Jessie's anger rose. She whirled around, her green eyes spitting sparks. "Absolutely not!"

Morgan grinned. "Never say absolutely, sweetheart. It's too final."

With that, Morgan opened the door and stepped from the room, closing the door softly behind him, leaving Jessie glaring at it with impotent fury.

Later that morning Jessie went for a long ride, hoping the fresh air would help her unravel her tangled emotions. She still couldn't understand why she had surrendered to Morgan, and she was honest enough to admit she would never have done so if there hadn't been more there on her part than just physical attraction. They had absolutely nothing in common, and he obviously didn't think much of her as a person. Why, just the day before, he had treated her like a child, threatening to turn her over his knee and calling her dream a childish whim. Damn him! What would a low-down gunslinger know of dreams?

Jessie's dream for her own ranch was far from a childish whim. It was a deep need. For as long as she could remember, she'd moved about, following the herds of mustangs across Texas, and then some. She'd never had a home, a place where she belonged.

When she was a small child, it hadn't bothered her. The chase after the mustangs had excited her as much as it did her vagabond father, and she was just as wild and free as the horses they sought, no more concerned about where they would sleep and what they would eat than he. The only thing that mattered were the mustangs, their lifeblood. She had her horses and her Mexican playmates—the *mesteñeros'* children—and the almost day to day exhilaration of the chase. She hadn't a care in the world. She thought her life perfect.

When she was about ten, Jessie noticed a subtle change in her playmates' attitude. More and more they deferred to her, instead of treating her as an equal. She finally realized that their parents were exerting pressure on them to put her above themselves, by virtue of her father's position, following the rules of an old Mexican caste system that set the *patrón* apart from his workers. It was more her friends' unyielding attitude, than the scorn the Anglos showed when they saw her in their midst, that made Jessie come to realize she didn't belong with the Mexicans. That was her first hint of insecurity.

Finding herself alone, with no friends of her own age, Jessie turned to her family. Her much older brothers offered her nothing in the way companionship, nor did her devil-may-care father whom she had adored as a child. They lived and breathed for the chase, paying her little personal attention. For the first time Jessie took note of her passive mother. What she found was a sad, lonely woman, aged far beyond her years by her hard nomadic life, a woman who had sacrificed everything to follow the man she loved. Seeing her mother cast longing looks at the homes they passed made Jessie realize that they had nothing to call their own, not even a piece of barren ground and a mud hut like those of the Mexicans they sometimes boarded with between chasing the herds. Jessie realized then that not only did she not belong with the Mexicans, she didn't belong anyplace. She was like a ship who had slipped its moorings, drifting aimlessly through life. A deep need filled her, a need for a home and a place to put down her roots.

Hardly had she begun to know her mother and empathize with her than she and Jessie's brothers were stricken with cholera. Typically, the lethal disease struck without warning and killed with a swiftness that stunned everyone, perversely sparing Jessie and her father. When he turned to drowning his sorrow in the bottle, showing her even less attention, Jessie felt more lost.

While they were traveling to Monterrey to inform a *mesteñero*'s family that he had been killed while capturing a herd, Jessie noticed a big hacienda off to the side of the road. With its white walls gleaming in the sunlight, it looked not just to be on the land but as if it had sprouted from the ground, as if its foundations had grown roots. Jessie stared, thinking it was the most beautiful and impressive-looking house she had ever seen. Leaving the others, she trotted her horse up to the massive wooden gate and peered into the courtyard, seeing the tinkling fountain and lush vegetation. It was a place of peacefulness and strength, its thick, protective walls built to withstand anything man, nature, or time could throw at it. Jessie vowed she would have a home like it someday, and a ranch to built it on. And she knew just where she'd buy the land. On the San Saba, with its sparkling spring water and lush grass. That day, Jessie's dream was born.

From then on, all Jessie could think about and talk about was her dream, but she couldn't get her father interested in her plans. He thought them foolish and pretentious, turning more and more to his bottle for company. Only Gabe and the *mesteñeros*—who were romantics at heart—listened and encouraged her. It was while sitting around the campfire and listening to the men talk about the White Steed, a horse that inspired every mustanger's imagination, that Jessie decided she would capture him for her stud horse. The horse and the ranch blended into one dream.

When her father was killed and Jessie inherited the responsibility for the group, her plan for her ranch became more than a dream. It became an absolute necessity. She had not only her own future to plan for, but that of her *mesteñeros,* who had pledged their lifetime loyalty to her. She was their *patrona,* their protector as well as their employer, particularly in Texas, where animosity ran so high against them. Their livelihood depended on her, and as with Jessie, horses were all they knew. With the mustang herds rapidly disappearing, her ranch would be the only thing between them and starvation, and its success hinged on the White Steed. Jessie had already found out how hard it was to compete in the man's business world. She couldn't just produce good horseflesh. It had to be the very best. The buyers would be just as skeptical of her skills as a horse breeder as the Anglo mustangers who had deserted her had been of her ability to lead them. With the White Steed as her stud horse, no one, not even the most prejudiced and critical buyer, could refuse her horses. The famous white stallion's notoriety alone assured that. He was her ace in the hole, her guarantee that her ranch would be a success.

No, her dream was no childish whim, and she wasn't going to let anyone stop her from accomplishing it. And she'd never make the mistake her mother had, forsaking her own personal dreams and desires for a man. She didn't need, or want, a man in her life, and certainly not an irresponsible drifter with no ambition and no purpose.

Having firmly reset her goals, Jessie turned her horse back to Dog Town. As she rode down the main street Jessie noted that the town looked different than it had the night before. Now it was almost deserted and strangely silent.

As Jessie rounded the corner of the last building and saw Gabe and Morgan standing in front of the stable, she reined in sharply. Spying her, Gabe rushed over, while Morgan followed with the lazy, feline stride that was so much a part of him.

"Morgan and I have been talking," Gabe said in an excited voice as Jessie dismounted. "He said he's for hire and willing to go back to our camp with us—"

"I don't hire anyone but experienced mustangers," Jessie interrupted, shooting Morgan a look of pure disgust.

"Hell, he ain't gonna hire on as a mustanger. Hear me out before you start jumping to conclusions. He's willing to come along to teach us how to shoot better."

Seeing the startled expression coming over Jessie's face and afraid she would out-and-out refuse their proposal, Gabe quickly continued. "Jessie, we ain't any match for those professional gunslingers Gibbons is gonna hire to send against us. And I'm as convinced as Morgan that Gibbons ain't gonna give up that easily. He wants that stallion just as much as you do. He ain't gonna to stand by and watch you capture him without a fight. Now, if we honed up our shooting skills, we'd even up the odds a little bit."

Jessie wasn't as convinced as they were that Gibbons hadn't given up. He'd made no move against them since Morgan had shot two of his hired guns and sent the other running. But she had to admit what Gabe said made sense. Her mustangers were no match for professional killers. She seriously doubted if they could even repel a bandit attack if they had to. The most they ever used their guns for was hunting. It might not be a bad idea, just in case Gibbons still persisted in trying to stop her, and she was too good a businesswoman to let her feelings about Morgan override her good sense. Except . . .

"I'm afraid I don't have the kind of money Mr. West demands for his services, Gabe."

Gabe sliced Morgan a quick look, then said, "Well, maybe you and he could come to some agreement. I tell you what. Why don't I take La Duquesa and stable her for you while you two talk it over?"

Before Jessie could object, Gabe took the reins and led the mare away, leaving her standing with Morgan. As soon as Gabe was out of hearing, Morgan said, "My services might not come as high as you expect, Jessie. What do you say to two hundred dollars?"

"Two hundred?" Jessie exclaimed in astonishment. Then her eyes narrowed suspiciously. "You can't be serious. I know you charge much more than that."

"As a matter of fact, I do. My fees start at a flat thousand. I never accept anything less."

"Then why are you proposing less for me?" As a sudden thought occurred to her, Jessie bristled and said, "If it's because I'm a woman and you feel sorry for me, you can forget it. I don't want any favors from you!"

"I'm not doing it as a favor," Morgan said in exasperation. "I still owe you for that herd of horses I chased off." His voice dropped to a husky timbre as he added, "Remember, last night I refused to accept your canceling my debt in exchange for saving your life."

The color rose on Jessie's face, a flush that stemmed partly from anger and partly from embarrassment at how eagerly she had responded to him. "I thought you said hell would freeze over before you'd pay me for those horses," Jessie reminded him.

Morgan shrugged. "I was angry at the time. I wanted to bait you. But despite your low opinion of me, I'm a man who pays my debts."

Jessie considered what Morgan had said. He did owe her. But could she trust him? "All right, you still owe me. But before we make any agreements, I want a few things perfectly understood between us. First, our relationship will be strictly business. There will be no repeats of last night."

Jessie watched Morgan's face closely for his reaction to her dictate, but his expression was totally unreadable.

"And?" he prompted.

"And I'm the boss. I give the orders. What I say goes. I won't tolerate your trying to usurp my authority."

Jessie noticed the tightening of Morgan's lips. She wasn't surprised. He was a man. Taking orders from a woman wouldn't set easy with him. She half expected him to refuse, to turn and walk away from her. Without realizing she was doing it, she held her breath. And then, to her utter surprise, he grinned.

"Whatever you say, boss lady."

Damn him! He was making fun of her. "I'm serious, Morgan. I mean it! And don't call me boss lady. My name is Jessie."

"I didn't mean to rile you. It's just that Jessie seems such a childish name for a grown woman, particularly a woman who's going to be my . . ." Morgan hesitated.

He'd be damned if he'd call her his boss in all serious-
ness. ". . . my employer."

There he goes again, Jessie thought angrily, calling
me childish. "Well, regardless of what you think of it, it's
my name!"

When Morgan made no comment, Jessie glared at
him, then said in a hard voice, "Well? Do you accept the
job under those conditions, or not?"

There was a long pause, then Morgan looked her in
the eye and said, "I accept. You just hired yourself a
gunfighter."

A wave of relief swept over her. "Fine. We'll leave
tomorrow morning, after I've bought supplies."

As Morgan walked away, Jessie stared at his broad
back, pondering over why she had been so relieved
when he had accepted her terms and the job. It was
only because she needed his shooting expertise to improve her men's marksmanship, and not for any personal reasons, she firmly told herself. Hiring him had
simply been a shrewd business move and nothing more.

But as she walked back to the hotel, Jessie felt glad
that Morgan was going back to her camp on the Nueces
with her. Her happiness had nothing to do with Morgan
the gunfighter, but rather with Morgan the man.

Chapter 11

THE NEXT MORNING MORGAN MET JESSIE AND GABE IN front of the general store. After Jessie had purchased her supplies, Morgan helped Gabe load them on the wagon and cover them with a heavy tarpaulin. The two men had just finished lashing it down when they heard the call, "Stage coming!"

None of three dallied. Gabe and Jessie quickly climbed on the wagon and sat down, while Morgan swiftly mounted his horse. Without any further ado they rode off at a brisk speed, followed by La Duquesa tied to the back of the wagon, for the stage that serviced Dog Town was pulled by a team of half-wild Spanish mules that had only one speed—a dead run—and anyone, or anything, that got in their way was bowled over.

Once out of the town, they slowed their pace and followed the Frio River, Morgan riding his horse beside the wagon.

The weather was unseasonably warm, and by midday, the sun was beating down on them with a vengeance and wilting the tender wildflowers that were blooming all around them. There wasn't even a hint of a breeze.

Later that afternoon Jessie scanned the line of trees that followed the river in the distance, thinking how cool and inviting they looked. She could hardly wait to make camp and take a dip in the river. Pointing to one tree that towered over the lower mesquites, she said, "Let's camp under that big oak."

"Kinda early to be making camp, ain't it," Gabe objected.

"I know. But if I don't get some relief from this heat soon, I'm going to be as limp as those primroses out there," Jessie replied, wiping the sweat from her forehead with her sleeve.

"Better forget about camping under that oak," Morgan commented from his horse. "Look behind you."

Jessie glanced over her shoulder and saw the angry line of dark thunderheads coming over the horizon. Lightning flashed ominously from one dark cloud to the other.

"Now we know why it was so damned hot today," Gabe said, eyeing the sky with a frown. "And we'd better make camp in a hurry. That storm is coming as fast as a herd of stampeding mustangs."

No sooner were the words out of Gabe's mouth than the sun was completely obliterated by the clouds, edging the dark thunderheads in silver and casting a shadow over the earth.

"How about those mesquites over there?" Morgan asked, nodding his head to a cluster of trees a short distance away. "They're not tall enough to attract lightning."

Without a word Gabe turned the horses and drove the wagon beneath the low trees, the feathery leaves brushing Morgan's hat as he rode under them.

There was a flurry of activity, everyone aware that they were racing the quickly approaching storm. While Morgan unsaddled his mount and tossed the saddle beneath the wagon, Gabe unharnessed the horses and tied them securely to one of the trees.

Jessie joined him with her and Morgan's horses in tow. "It doesn't look like we're going to have time to build a fire and eat."

Morgan scanned the angry sky. "No, we certainly won't. Let's cut some brush and lay it around the wagon. That should give us some protection."

Morgan and Gabe hurried to chop down some of the underbrush, dragging it to the sides of the wagon. By this time the wind that preceded the storm had hit, the gusts whipping the mesquite brush around and kicking up the dirt, the fine particles of sand stinging their exposed skin and making their eyes water. Gabe wrestled a big mesquite limb to the wagon, then cursed when the wind lashed at the branches and he was stabbed by one of the long thorns.

Jessie busied herself first making sure the tarpaulin over the supplies was securely lashed, then gathering blankets, beef jerky, a can of tinned biscuits, and several canteens of water. She crawled beneath the wagon and spread the blankets, letting out a very unladylike oath when she bruised her knee on a large rock. Lifting the blanket, she picked up the rock and hurled it out the side with all her might.

"God damn it, Jessie!" Morgan yelled above the rolling thunder. "Watch where you're throwing things, will you?"

Jessie peered out to see him rubbing his knee where the rock had hit it, then glanced up at his face, covered with scratches. "I'm sorry."

A gigantic crash of thunder shook the earth, followed by a sharp crack of lightning. Morgan and Gabe dived for the shelter of the wagon, shimmying under it on their elbows. And not a second too soon. A few patters of rain were heard on the canvas above them, followed by a deafening pounding as the rain came down in torrents.

"Sure hope we ain't parked in some gully," Gabe mumbled, staring out at the deluge.

"Well, if we are, we'll know soon enough," Morgan remarked.

But their haven proved to be on high ground, and although the wind blew some of the rain in through the brush and they could hear the water rushing down the gullies around them, they remained relatively dry.

Jessie was small enough to crawl around under the wagon, but Morgan and Gabe had difficulty moving about. They were forced to eat their jerky and biscuits propped up on their elbows, while Jessie sat crouched over, chewing the tough food with gusto.

When she offered Gabe a canteen of water, he eyed it with distaste. "Why in the hell didn't you bring my jug of white mule with you instead of that damned thing? If I wanted a drink of water, all I'd have to do is stick my hand outside."

"I guess I didn't think of it," Jessie answered. "A swallow or two of white mule would taste good right now."

Morgan's head shot up at Jessie's answer. "You drink that rotgut?" he asked in disbelief.

"Yes, I do," Jessie answered calmly. "Not enough to

get tipsy, but just a swallow or two to warm me up when I'm chilled."

"I should have known you wouldn't drink something as mild as wine, like other women. I wouldn't be surprised if you chewed tobacco."

"As a matter of fact, I do every now and then," Jessie lied, enjoying the horrified expression that came over Morgan's face.

A short while later Morgan noticed that Jessie was shivering from the cold air the storm had brought in with it. He started to remove his vest, saying, "Here, take this to cover you."

"That's not necessary," Jessie replied, peering around in the dim light. "There's an extra blanket here someplace." Then, spying it, she said, "Lift your hip, Gabe. You're lying on it."

Gabe lifted himself with a disgusted grunt, and Jessie jerked the blanket out. "I'm willing to share it if anyone else is cold," Jessie offered.

Morgan might have shown interest in sharing the blanket with Jessie—it would have given him an opportunity to caress her out of Gabe's view and undoubtedly anger her, and he loved riling her and then watching her beautiful eyes flash—but his knee was throbbing like hell.

"What's wrong with your leg, Morgan?" Gabe asked. "That's the second time I've noticed you rubbing it."

Morgan had not even been aware of his action and pulled his hand away. "Oh, nothing, really."

"That's not true," Jessie said. "I hit him with a rock when I tossed it out from underneath the wagon. Does it hurt?"

"It's throbbing a little bit," Morgan admitted.

"You'd better have a look at it," Gabe said. "It might be cut."

Morgan rose without thinking and bumped his head on the bottom of the wagon, wincing in pain and muttering a curse.

As he rubbed his new injury Jessie said, "Better let me slip off your boot and have a look. You'll never manage it in these tight quarters."

Jessie bent and tugged on Morgan's boot, unaware of his grimace every time she pulled on his leg. Finally the stubborn boot gave way. She rolled up his pant leg and gasped. His knee was swollen, and black and blue.

"You sure you didn't break your kneecap?" Gabe asked, peering at the huge ugly bruise.

"No, I'm sure if I had broken anything, it would be much more painful," Morgan replied.

Jessie wasn't so certain about that. Obviously, it was bleeding beneath the skin, and she knew it must be much more painful than Morgan was letting on. "I'm sorry, Morgan. I had no idea I threw that rock so hard."

"That's okay, as long as it wasn't intentional." He grinned. "But you do pack a mean swing there, Jess."

Jess. He had called her Jess. She rattled the name around in her head and decided that she liked it. It didn't sound as stiff and formal as Jessica, or as childish as Jessie. Realizing that was why he had called her that, she looked him straight in the eye.

"Any objections?" Morgan asked. "I think it suits you better."

"No, I don't object," Jessie answered, determined she wouldn't let him know that she actually liked the name.

Gabe was oblivious of their soft conversation, his total attention on Morgan's knee. "Well, you may not have broken anything, but you're gonna have a stiff knee for a day or two."

Gabe's words drew Jessie's attention back to the problem at hand. She looked down at Morgan's swelling knee. "It needs to be bound," she said. "Give me your bandanna, Morgan."

Morgan slipped his bandanna from his neck and handed it to her. Jessie wrapped it tightly around his knee. "Does that help?"

"It seems to be throbbing more, but I know it's the best thing to do." Then, seeing Jessie's frown, he added, "Stop worrying, Jess. I've had much worse injuries than this, believe me."

A loud crack of lightning caught everyone's attention and their heads turned in the direction of the noise, for it had sounded awfully close. Jessie's breath caught at what she saw. The oak tree was aflame; it had been struck by the lightning bolt. As she noticed red cinders floating down to the underbrush, a twinge of fear ran through her. She could only hope the brush was water-soaked enough that the fire wouldn't catch. Otherwise it would quickly spread to where they were. She sighed in relief when the glow of the cinders disappeared, but didn't fully relax until the fire in the tree was completely extinguished by the pounding rain.

"That was too close for comfort," Gabe remarked.

"Yes, it certainly was," Jessie answered, lying down weakly between the two men.

By this time, the brunt of the storm had passed and darkness had fallen. The rain continued, however, the steady patter of the raindrops on the canvas lulling them. Soon Gabe was snoring softly. Minutes later, Jessie's eyes closed. Morgan pulled the blanket up and tucked it around her shoulders, then rolled with his back to her, removing his weight from his injured knee.

But it was a long time before Morgan slept, and not because of the throbbing in his knee. He was acutely aware of Jessie's sweet scent drifting across to him, of her thigh pressing against his buttocks, of her deep, steady breathing. He imagined her soft, full breasts rising and falling with every breath and he fervently wished that Gabe was a hundred miles away.

The next day dawned bright and sunny, as so typically happened in Texas after a springtime storm generated by a cold front passing through and meeting the warm Gulf air. The earth had a fresh-washed smell, the air a crystal clarity, and there was a cool nip in the early morning breeze.

Despite the beauty of the day, preparing breakfast that morning proved difficult. The muddy ground was slippery, particularly treacherous for Morgan with his stiff knee, and they had to search for over an hour to find enough dry wood to build a fire. But they were determined to have a hearty, hot breakfast after their meager cold meal the evening before.

After eating fried bacon, wild turkey eggs—found by Gabe while searching for wood—and sourdough biscuits, baked in a double oven placed over the hot coals, they consumed a full pot of coffee before breaking camp. When Gabe offered Morgan his place on the wagon seat, in deference to his stiff knee, Morgan stubbornly refused, gritting his teeth as he put his full weight on the injured limb to mount his horse. Jessie could only shake her head in exasperation, having noticed Morgan's efforts to hide his limp and now his grim-lipped expression. She wondered why men considered it a weakness to admit to pain. Even animals had better sense than that. Yes, men were certainly silly creatures.

Traveling that day was slower than the day before. Repeatedly, Gabe had to veer off course to avoid flooded gullies and go around large, deep mud puddles for fear of getting stuck. Most of these mud holes were old longhorn wallows, looking very similar to buffalo wallows, which were seen farther north, the shaggy beasts having seldom wandered this far south. Now the buffalo had all but become extinct at the hands of the buffalo hunters with their lethal Sharp's rifles.

The next day they reached the fork of the Frio and Nueces rivers, and followed the Nueces on its southeasterly course. Jessie felt a twinge of excitement, knowing they would reach camp before nightfall, despite all the delays of the day before.

Morgan spied a roadrunner and smiled as it streaked across the prairie. "That is undoubtedly the most peculiar-looking bird God ever made," he commented, half to himself.

Jessie knew he was referring to the roadrunner, for she, too, had been watching the bird, its long legs moving so rapidly, they seemed a mere blur. "Have you ever heard the Mexican version of why the *piasano* can't fly like other birds?"

"No, I haven't," Morgan replied.

"Well, according to Mexican legend, the *piasano* was a distant relative to pheasants and was very arrogant and vain. He considered himself much higher on the social scale than he actually was, haughtily putting himself above others. One day, when the eagle, the king of all flying creatures, was discussing important matters of state with the other nobles of the kingdom, the foolish roadrunner interrupted the meeting and dared to address them as if he were an equal. The eagle was furious at his arrogance and banished him from his kingdom, condemning the *piasano* to never be able to fly again and to feed on the most unclean things of the earth—snakes, tarantulas, and poisonous insects. Since then he has been an outcast, running among the chaparral and cactus, trying to hide his shame and disgrace."

"Well," Gabe commented, "that may be just some tale the Mexicans dreamed up about the roadrunner, but they sure got that bird pegged right. There ain't nothing that can kill a rattlesnake like a roadrunner. I've seen them peck a rattler to death before it can even raise its head to strike."

"How did you learn so much about Mexican legends?" Morgan asked Jessie.

"My childhood playmates were the children of my father's *mesteñeros*. I learned to speak Spanish long before English."

Gabe chuckled, saying, "That's true. By the time Jessie was knee-high to a grasshopper, she could rattle off that Mexican gibberish faster than me. I still have to stop and think what I'm gonna say."

Morgan nodded. He, like almost everyone in South Texas, spoke some Spanish. But obviously he wasn't as fluent in it as Jessie was if she had learned the language as a toddler.

He wondered what Jessie's childhood must have been like, constantly moving about and following the herds of wild horses all over Texas. That kind of life was all right for an adult, a wanderer like himself, but it must have been difficult for a child. She'd been through a lot of rough times, but she certainly hadn't let it get her down. She was an amazing woman, Morgan thought in silent admiration, as tough as nails yet still utterly feminine.

They rode into Jessie's mustanging camp late that afternoon, and as soon as the wagon came to a halt, they were immediately surrounded by the excited *mesteñeros*, asking Jessie questions and all speaking Spanish so rapidly that Morgan and Gabe had trouble following the conversation.

Finally, Jessie addressed Pedro, the head *mesteñero*, in English. "So there was no trouble with Gibbons while I was gone?"

"No, no trouble, *patrona*. We have not even seen any of Señor Gibbons's vaqueros," Pedro answered, sneaking Morgan a wary yet curious glance.

Jessie turned to Morgan. "Thank goodness Gibbons didn't try anything while I was away."

Morgan didn't comment, knowing that Gibbons felt threatened not by the *mesteñeros* themselves but by the *mesteñeros* led by Jessie, since it was she who was determined to capture the White Steed. Morgan wondered if Gibbons had set a spy on the camp and knew Jessie and Gabe had left. Had the rancher thought they had abandoned their Mexicans? Well, if there was someone watching the camp, Gibbons would soon hear of Jessie's return, and although there had been no trouble while Jessie was away, it would soon be brewing.

Jessie and Gabe climbed down from the wagon, and Morgan dismounted. "Tell the men to unload the wagon, Pedro, and put everything in the dugout," Jessie said, then turned and headed for the crude building. Morgan fell in beside her while Gabe followed slightly behind them.

Pedro caught Gabe's shirt and tugged on it. Gabe turned to face the head mustanger.

"What is *he* doing here?" Pedro asked in a suspicious voice, his eyes boring into Morgan's broad back.

"Jessie hired him to teach us gunfighting."

"Gunfighting?" Pedro asked in surprise. Then he rose to his full height, saying indignantly, "I am no gunfighter. I am a *mesteñero!*"

"I know, and so am I. But if Gibbons sends more gunfighters against us, like Morgan and I think he will, then I'm more than willing to learn a few shooting tricks from him if it will keep me alive. And if you Mexicans are smart, so will you!"

As Gabe turned and walked away, Pedro scowled.

In the dugout, Morgan stood to the side as the Mexicans brought in the supplies and Jessie directed them to where she wanted the barrels and sacks placed. When the last man left the cabin, Jessie said to Morgan, "I guess you can bunk in with Gabe."

Morgan grinned, and a teasing twinkle came into his eyes. "Why can't I sleep with you?"

Before Jessie had sensed his intent, Morgan stepped closer and caressed her breasts. Jessie gasped at the burning sensation his hands brought her, then slapped them away, saying angrily, "I told you our relationship would be strictly business!"

Morgan shrugged. "You can't blame a man for trying."

"The devil I can't! From now on, you keep your hands to yourself and your mind on business!"

As Jessie stalked from the cabin, Morgan smiled. She hadn't disappointed him. She had risen to the bait he threw out. Damn, she was beautiful when she was angry.

Chapter 12

THE NEXT MORNING JESSIE CALLED HER *MESTEÑEROS* together and told them that Morgan would be giving them some lessons in shooting. There was a dead silence after the announcement, and Morgan could sense the men's resentment.

Jessie knew they considered themselves adequate with their rifles and felt insulted by her proposal. "I know you all know how to shoot," she said in a tone of voice that she hoped would soothe their injured pride. "We've always shot our own game. A few of you older men have even killed Indians. But if Señor Gibbons sends hired guns after us, this time there *will* be gunplay, and none of us can shoot that fast or accurately."

The Mexicans stared at her, their expressions sullen, still unconvinced of the need.

Jessie turned to Morgan. "Perhaps you could give them a demonstration of just what kind of shooting they'd be up against."

Morgan nodded, reached for his Winchester, and pulled it from the saddle holster. Pointing to a mesquite a good distance away, he said, "Watch that tree."

The Mexicans turned their dark eyes to the tree. In a flash Morgan raised the gun to his shoulder, pumping the lever-action rifle and firing in such quick succession that the ten rifle shots seemed to blend into one tremendous explosion. The Mexicans watched in amazement as ten branches crashed to the ground, all neatly severed from the tree.

A moment of stunned silence passed before Jessie said, "Now you know what kind of marksmanship we'll be up against. Can you imagine what would happen if ten or twenty men who could shoot like that came riding down on us?"

The awed expressions on the men's faces turned to fear. They glanced at each other apprehensively.

"I know you're all good shots," Jessie said, still trying to soothe their egos, "but that won't do. You've got to be better."

Jessie knew by the expressions on the men's faces that there would be no more resistance to her plan. "Half of you will take lessons in the morning and the other half in the afternoon. Pedro will decide which time each of you will be assigned." She glanced at Morgan before continuing. "There's one more thing. Señor West tells me six-shooters are much more accurate at closer distances, so seven of you will be issued the side arms I brought back with me from Dog Town and assigned as night guards. That's when we're the most vulnerable, when they can slip up on us in the darkness. Since none of us carry six-shooters, or are familiar with them, Señor West will choose the night guards from those of you he feels have the most shooting aptitude, and will give those men special lessons on their use."

Morgan saw the sudden flare of excitement in the *mesteñeros'* eyes and knew there would be fierce competition among the men to become one of the night guards. The majority of the Mexicans in Texas owned no guns—an ancient musket, perhaps, but no decent weapons. Jessie's own men would not have rifles had Jessie not provided them. Good guns were expensive, something the ordinary Mexican could not afford. So the prospect of wearing and using a side arm, of having the prestige of becoming one of the elite, would be a tremendous incentive for the *mesteñeros* to improve their marksmanship. But Morgan was going to have to correct Jessie on one thing.

"No, Jess, there will be only six night guards. That seventh Colt is for you."

Surprised, Jessie turned to him. "Me?"

"Yes. I want you to carry a side arm at all times. And you'll learn to use it, too, just like your men."

Jessie opened her mouth to object, but before she could say a word, Morgan said, "Jess, if you had had a six-shooter that day those gunslingers sneaked up on you, there's a good possibility you wouldn't have been captured. A handgun goes with you everywhere. Even if you're mounted, its easier and faster to draw than your rifle from your saddle holster, and much less awkward to fire if your horse is moving."

Jessie could hardly disagree with Morgan's logic. As much as she disliked the heavy, cumbersome gun, it appeared she was going to have to wear one. "Oh, all right," she agreed irritably, thinking that her men would probably laugh at her awkwardness with the six-shooter.

Having guessed her thoughts, Morgan lowered his voice so the Mexicans couldn't hear. "Don't worry, Jess. I'll give you private lessons."

The husky tone of his voice and the shimmering look in his eyes told Jessie he was thinking of something much more intimate than shooting lessons. She gave him a withering look that made him chuckle.

Morgan turned to the men. "We'll practice over by the river, away from the camp. Jessie doesn't want her herd of mares upset by the noise."

For the next several days the faint sounds of gunshots could be heard in the camp, despite the distance, and there was a decided smell of burned gunpowder as the acrid smoke drifted in the air.

Jessie's lessons were always last on the agenda, after the mustangers had returned to camp. On the fourth day, she watched as the Mexicans rode off, the men looking pleased with their accomplishments.

"How are they doing?" she asked Morgan.

"Better than I thought they would," Morgan admitted. He turned to face her, then frowned. "Where's your six-shooter?"

"It's hanging on my saddle horn." Seeing the frown on his face turn to a dark scowl, Jessie quickly said, "It's too heavy to wear all the time. I'm not as big as you men are. It feels like a cannon hanging on my side. It makes my walk clumsy and mounting my horse awkward."

"You'll get used to its weight, and it won't do you any good hanging on your saddle horn. What if Gibbons's men should ride in right now? You'd be dead before you could get to your gun. Now strap it on and let's get on with your lesson."

Jessie bristled. She didn't like taking orders from him.

"I don't need any more lessons. I can shoot passably well."

"Like hell you can. If I had known what a lousy shot you are, I wouldn't have bothered disarming you all those times you pulled a gun on me."

"I'm a good shot with a Winchester!" Jessie retorted, highly insulted at his criticism of her shooting ability. "I just can't get the hang of shooting a pistol."

"That's why I'm giving you lessons. And practice makes perfect. Now get your gun."

Jessie glared at Morgan. He stared back at her, as cool as a cucumber, then repeated in a firm voice, "Get your gun, Jess. We're wasting time."

Still resenting his ordering her around, Jessie turned and walked to her horse, snatching the holster from her saddle horn and strapping it around her hips. Over the past few days she had discovered that Morgan was a hard taskmaster, determined that she would learn the use of the six-shooter, and learn it well. While he had been firm with her men, he hadn't driven them the way he did her, and she was firmly convinced he was only doing it because he enjoyed bossing her around.

Over and over Jessie fired her pistol and, to her utter disgust, missed the tin cans she was aiming at. The acrid gun smoke burned her eyes; her head pounded from the deafening noises; and her arm ached from the recoil of the heavy gun.

"Fire one more round," Morgan directed.

"No," Jessie objected. "That's enough for today. I'm tired."

"Just one more round, Jess. And try to keep your arm straight."

Jessie whirled on him like a spitting wildcat. "I said that's enough!"

"And I say it isn't," Morgan answered calmly. "Your aim hasn't improved one bit. You're still firing to your left."

"Didn't you hear me?" Jessie shouted. "I said that's enough! I'm tired!"

"One more round won't make that much difference," Morgan replied with a cool determination. "Now stop arguing and do what I told you to."

Jessie's smoldering resentment at his giving her orders surged to the surface and erupted. "I'm the boss here, not you!"

"No, Jess, when it comes to these lessons, I'm the boss. That's what you hired me for, and I intend to do my job."

"I didn't hire you to teach me," Jessie reminded him. "I hired you to teach my men."

"We've already been through that, Jess. Learning to shoot a six-shooter is just as important for you as it is for them, if not more so. And I fully intend to see that you learn."

"In that case—you're fired!"

Morgan totally ignored her words and said calmly, "Fire one more round, Jess."

"Didn't you hear me? I said you're fired!"

"One more round, Jess."

Jessie stared at him in utter disbelief. She'd never met a man as strong-willed as he. When he set his mind to something, he could be as immovable as a mountain. Jessie had dealt with men all her life, had pitted her will against theirs—and usually won the struggle—but she had never encountered a man like Morgan. That he enforced his will on her with a cool, calm determination was even more disconcerting. Why, she couldn't even get a rise out of him!

"I'm waiting, Jess."

Jessie knew it was pointless to argue any further with Morgan in the mood he was in. He'd keep her out here all night, if he had to, until she shot that damned round. As much as she hated to, she was going to have to back down. Damn him! She'd never dreamed he take his job so seriously. Exasperated almost to the point of tears, she whirled around, quickly reloaded the gun, and fired it, not even bothering to aim.

Morgan shook his head, knowing full well that Jessie wasn't aiming but just emptying her gun. God, she was a handful, with her high spirits and fierce independence, but then, without them, she wouldn't be Jessie.

When Jessie turned back to him, her gun still smoking in her hand, Morgan ignored her murderous glare and thoughtfully scanned the horizon where Gibbons's ranch lay. "I wonder what Gibbons is up to. He's bound to have someone spying on us and knows I'm giving your men shooting lessons. What do you say to us riding over there and doing a little snooping of our own?"

Despite her anger at him, Jessie was agreeable to Morgan's suggestion. She was curious herself to know what the rancher was up to.

As they rode to Gibbons's ranch, Morgan observed Jessie from the corner of his eye and knew she was still angry with him by her silence and the tight set of her mouth. Morgan had a bit of a tease in him, but when it came to guns and gunfighting, he was deadly serious, particularly when it came to teaching Jessie how to defend herself. By necessity, he had pushed her harder than the men, knowing that her life could well depend on it, and each evening when the lesson was finished and he knew he had pushed her to the limits of her physical endurance, he had fought a battle with himself.

A part of him wanted to take her in his arms and comfort her, while another part of him firmly argued he was doing what was best for her. Added to his confused emotions was his sexual tension. Each evening he had wanted her, but had fought back his urges. She had made it perfectly clear to him that their night together had been a mistake and that she only wanted a business relationship with him. Nonetheless, Morgan was determined to go slowly and make her want him as much as he wanted her.

When they reached the boundary line of the ranch, they moved more cautiously, weaving their horses through the thick, concealing brush, instead of in the open. For a while they saw no activity at all, and then, hearing the sound of cattle bawling, Morgan signaled Jessie to stop and dismount.

They crept through the brush and squatted behind a *cenizo* bush, seeing the cowhands busy with branding. They watched as several calves were flushed from the herd, wrestled down by the "flanker," then branded, their ears marked, and castrated. When released, the terrified calves ran back to their mothers, who sniffed at the burned and bloody wounds, lifted their heads, and bawled in outraged protest. Even from where they hid, Morgan and Jessie could smell the overpowering odor of man-sweat, horse-sweat, wood smoke, blood, and singed hair.

Morgan's eyes narrowed, spying Gibbons in the circle of men around the fire where the branding irons were being heated. The rancher looked just as sweaty and grimy as his hands, his normally florid complexion even more flushed from the heat of the fire. Quickly, Morgan scanned the scene before him, but could see no new faces. The only men present were obviously cowhands, busy with their work. He wasn't surprised. The rancher had kept him and the other gunfighters away from his regular workers, and Morgan thought he knew why.

"See?" Jessie whispered. "There's nothing unusual going on. I told you I thought Gibbons had reconsidered. Why, I bet he's forgotten we're even around."

"No, Jess," Morgan said in a firm voice. "Just because we haven't seen them doesn't mean there aren't gunfighters lurking about. They're probably in hiding someplace. Gibbons doesn't want his cowhands getting involved in this mess. The less they know about it, the better, just in case the law starts nosing around later and asking questions."

"Then why haven't his gunfighters attacked us?"

"Jess, Gibbons knows we're preparing for his attack, that this time he's not going to be able to send a few men to do the job. He's going need a much larger force, and it will take time for that many men to drift in from all over Texas. No, he'll bide his time until they all arrive, unless the White Steed shows up before then. Then he'll send what he's got against us. Damn, I wish that horse would hurry and show up. The sooner, the better. Every day he delays will pit another hired gun or two against us."

Jessie wished the white stallion would hurry and show up, too, but not just because it would mean fewer gunfighters for them to fight off. She was anxious to capture him.

The sun was just setting when they rode back to camp, the giant orb a red ball of fire and the western sky streaked with vivid pinks and violets, casting a rosy glow over all. As they passed the two Mexican women kneeling beside their *metate*—a flat stone used for grinding corn into *masa*—Morgan glanced over at them. Distracted, he didn't notice how close he was riding to a clump of cactus. Then he heard the distinctive rattling. Both he and his horse reacted immediately, Morgan's hand flying to his gun and the gelding rearing. But it was too late. The snake uncoiled in a flash, sinking its vicious fangs deep into the horse's leg and pumping the deadly venom into its victim.

Before the diamondback could recoil and strike again, Morgan's gun roared, the sudden loud sound reverberating through the small, serene camp like a cannon shot, and the snake's head was completely severed from its long body. Morgan flew from his saddle, caught the gelding's cheek strap, and crooned, "Easy, boy, easy," one hand stroking the horse's sleek neck while the other restrained the rearing, frightened horse.

Jessie dismounted and caught the other side of the gelding's cheek strap to help hold him still, knowing that the animal's excitement and movements were serving only to make its heart beat faster, sending the venom running through its bloodstream. Gabe and Pedro rushed up to help.

Looking down at the snake's body still slithering on the ground, Gabe exclaimed, "Jesus Christ! Look at the size of that devil! Why, he's at least nine feet long, with a body as thick as my arm. He must be the granddaddy of all diamondbacks."

Morgan glanced down at the snake and saw that Gabe hadn't exaggerated. The snake had been unusually large, and if the amount of venom it carried was anything in proportion to its size, his horse was a goner for sure. "Here, Gabe, help Jessie hold him while I take a look at that bite."

Gabe stepped forward and caught the cheek strap. Morgan bent and examined the bite, which was high on the gelding's front leg. Already the area around the fang marks was discolored and swollen. Reaching into his saddlebag and pulling out a knife, Morgan asked, "Can someone bring me some coal oil?"

"No, *señor*," Pedro said, looking at the wound over Morgan's shoulder, "coal oil will not cure snakebite."

"The ranchers use it for snakebite all the time," Morgan retorted.

"*Sí*, I know that is the Anglo's way. But how often does the animal die?"

Morgan frowned, knowing that Pedro's words were true. Pouring coal oil into the wound was no sure cure. Just as many men and animals seemed to die as lived after that particular treatment.

"*Con permiso, señor,* I will treat him in the Mexican manner. I cannot guarantee he will survive, but it will give him a better chance than your coal oil."

Seeing Morgan's frown deepen, Jessie spoke up. "Let Pedro treat him, Morgan. His method *is* more successful. We've never lost a horse from snakebite that's been treated his way."

At that point, Morgan seriously doubted that any treatment could save his horse. Already the animal was trembling with toxic shock, his eyes dulled with pain. But still Morgan wanted to give him every possible chance to survive. Reluctantly, Morgan stepped back, saying, "All right. See what you can do for him."

"Get him to lie down, *señor*," Pedro instructed.

Morgan coaxed the gelding down, laying him on his side with the wounded leg exposed.

"Give me your knife and hold him down while I scarify the wound," Pedro said.

The gelding barely moved as the old Mexican cut deep slashes over the fang marks and pressed on the flesh around them, making the wound bleed freely. The horse was in such pain that the added injury wasn't even noticeable.

Pedro rose, walked to a Spanish dagger, and cut the tips from six of the plant's swordlike leaves. As he approached the gelding, Morgan asked in alarm, "What are you going to do with those?"

"Stick them around the wound, *señor*," Pedro answered calmly.

"Are you crazy? Those things are half poisonous themselves. They'll only make him sicker."

"No, they won't," Jessie informed Morgan. "The Spanish dagger seems to have something in it that counteracts the poison of a rattler."

Morgan stared at her, his expression totally disbelieving.

"It's true, Morgan," Jessie continued. "The Mexicans have been using this treatment for hundreds of years, and they certainly know more about rattlesnake bites than we do. They've been dealing with them longer. And no one knows more about treating horses than Pedro. He's spent his entire life working with them. Please, trust us," she pleaded.

Morgan thought it was the craziest thing he'd ever heard, but then, he really didn't have much choice. He'd already given Pedro his permission. He nodded gravely for Pedro to continue.

The Mexican crouched beside the horse and stuck the tips of the daggers deeply around the wound. Again the gelding hardly noticed the new insult. Then Pedro rose, walked to a cactus, and cut several of the paddle-like leaves from it, taking care not to stick himself on the wicked thorns. These he singed over a fire, then cut the leaves open and placed them over the wound.

"We will keep these wet and cool all night," Pedro explained. "They will keep the leg from swelling so much."

Morgan looked down at his gelding, lying so still on the ground. He would have thought the horse was dead had it not been for its shallow breathing. A feeling of sadness crept over him. He knew that the poison was already doing its lethal work, that the animal was on the very threshold of death. Grimly, he wondered how long it would take and if his old friend was suffering.

Jessie touched Morgan's arm, saying in a compassionate voice, "There's nothing else you can do. Come, supper is ready. Eat something. It will make you feel better."

"I'm not hungry," Morgan muttered, hating to leave the gelding all alone.

"No, *señor*, you go ahead and eat. I will stay with him," Pedro said softly.

Reluctantly, Morgan turned, yielding to the gentle pressure Jessie was exerting on his arm, and walked to the dugout. Throughout the meal he was distracted, saying nothing, hardly able to force the food down his throat. As soon as he had finished eating, he rose from the table, walked to his room, and gathered up his bedroll. Walking to the door, he said, "I'll spend the night out with my horse."

Neither Gabe or Jessie objected. Both understood how he felt. Having worked with horses all their lives, they, too, had a soft spot in their hearts for the animals.

It was dark as Morgan walked through the camp, weaving his way through the lean-tos to where Pedro had built a fire beside his horse. As he walked up, the old Mexican was pouring water from a bucket over the cactus leaves he had placed over the wound.

"How is he?" Morgan asked.

Pedro glanced over his shoulder, then sat back on his heels, placing the bucket down before he answered. "There is no change, *señor*. But it is too soon to tell," he added in a hopeful voice.

"How long will you leave the thorns in?"

"For twenty-four hours. By then we will know if he will survive or not." Glancing at Morgan's bedroll, Pedro said, "I will stay with him tonight, *señor*. I am used to sitting up with sick horses."

"No, I'll stay with him," Morgan replied in a firm voice. Seeing the Mexican's hurt expression, Morgan said, "It's not that I don't trust you, Pedro, but I feel I owe it to him. He stayed by my side plenty of times when I was ailing."

Pedro gave the gunfighter a thoughtful look, then said, "You are very fond of him, *sí*?"

Morgan felt uncomfortable. The Mexican seemed to be peering into his soul. All his life Morgan had hidden his deeper emotions, particularly in front of other men. It was the way he had been taught. Thinking Pedro would find him foolish if he admitted to a strong fondness for his horse, he answered, "Well, you know what they say here in Texas. A man is only as good as his horse, and a man without a horse is no man at all."

Suddenly, Pedro understood Morgan's discomfiture. "Ah, *señor*, but a man's horse is much more than that. He is a companion, an old friend."

Pedro rose to his feet, the firelight playing over his swarthy features. "I will leave you now. Just wet the cactus leaves every few hours. The rest is in God's hands."

Morgan's eyes rose to meet the old man's. *"Gracias,"* he said softly.

Pedro nodded, knowing that Morgan was thanking him for his understanding as much as for treating his horse. As he walked to his lean-to, Pedro was deep in thought. Over the past days the Texan had gained the respect of the other *mesteñeros,* not just as a gunfighter with an exceptional skill, but as a man. Morgan was a born leader, gaining the men's trust with his ease of command and his self-assured approach. But what had astonished the Mexicans was that Morgan treated them as equals, something almost unheard-of in this part of Texas where prejudice toward them ran high. But still, Pedro had withheld forming his opinion of the strong, silent Texan until tonight. By admitting to his fondness for his horse, Morgan had revealed more of his true character to Pedro than in any of his other dealings with the Mexicans. Pedro knew that no hardened killer would show such concern for an animal, and although the Texan's feeling might be hidden under a tough exterior, the old *mesteñero* suspected he was a man of unusual sensitivity.

After Pedro had left, Morgan spread his blanket next to his horse and lay down. The gelding nickered weakly. Surprised that it was alert enough to know of his presence, Morgan felt encouraged.

Throughout the long night, Morgan lay beside the critically ill horse, the soft, familiar night sounds soothing both man and animal. Morgan dozed between wetting the cactus leaves, using his inner alarm clock to awaken him, as he had done to take his turn at night watch when he was a cowhand. The sun was just rising when Morgan was alerted by the slight sound of twigs being broken. From sheer habit he sprang to his feet, his hand going for his gun.

Jessie jumped back in surprise when Morgan leapt

up, her face draining of all color as she looked down the barrel of his six-shooter. Then, seeing him lowering the gun, she said in a weak voice, "My God! You scared me to death."

"Don't ever sneak up on me like that, Jess," Morgan said in a tight voice.

"I wasn't sneaking. I just didn't want to awaken you," Jessie answered defensively.

"I know, but my reaction is pure reflex," Morgan answered, shaken by how close he had come to shooting before looking. Christ, he thought, I've lived by the gun too long, too damned long.

His hand trembled as he slipped his gun back into the holster lying on the blanket. "I'm not angry at you, Jess. More at myself, I guess. That was too close a call for comfort. But like I said, my draw is sheer reflex, done without even thinking. From now on, when you think I'm asleep out in the open, make plenty of noise so I'll know it's you and not some bandit or renegade Indian trying to sneak up on me and slit my throat."

"Well, you can be sure I won't make that mistake again," Jessie answered. "The next time I'll make so damned much noise you'll think a whole mustang herd is coming down on you."

Jessie knelt beside Morgan's horse, saying, "I just wanted to see how your gelding was faring this morning." Her gaze swept over the animal before she said, "I hope it's not my imagination, but I think he looks better."

Morgan crouched down beside her, saying, "Yes, his eyes do look a little clearer—but Christ! Look at his leg. It's three times its normal size."

"The swelling is always the last thing to go away," Pedro said from behind them.

Jessie looked up, surprised to see him there, while Morgan continued to stare at his horse's leg morosely. Had the gunfighter heard Pedro's approach? she wondered. If he had, his hearing was much keener than hers.

"I think he can eat a little this morning," Pedro said as he knelt at the horse's head with a feed bag in his hands. "Now, *señor,* if you will support his neck while I hold the bag for him."

When the gelding had finished eating, Morgan lowered his neck to the ground. As he rose to his feet Pedro said, "I will take care of him today, *señor.* So you can give your lessons."

"Then you think he's going to make it?" Morgan asked.

"I will not say for sure until tonight," Pedro answered in a cautious voice. "But it does look encouraging."

Morgan turned to Jessie. "I assume I can borrow a horse from your remuda."

Jessie laughed. "Of course. Did you think I would make you walk? Come with me. You can choose whichever horse you prefer."

When they reached the small corral where Jessie kept her riding horses, Morgan wasn't particularly surprised to see that they were all mares. Apparently, Jessie's preference for the females extended to her entire remuda. Morgan always rode either stallions or geldings, thinking that mares were too well mannered and boring for his tastes, so when Jessie asked him which horse he preferred, he shrugged indifferently and pointed to a red roan, saying, "I guess that one will do."

Jessie smiled smugly, having guessed Morgan's low opinion of mares. The roan he had picked was unusually spirited, and Jessie knew he would be getting much more than he had bargained for.

Jessie could hardly wait until they finished their breakfast, anxious to see Morgan's face when he mounted the mare. As she had instructed, the roan was saddled and waiting outside the dugout when she and Morgan emerged from it.

"Gracias," Morgan said, accepting the roan's reins from the *mesteñero* holding them and mistaking the man's wide grin for simple friendliness.

Jessie and the *mesteñero* stepped back as Morgan swung onto the horse, knowing full well what was coming. Feeling the weight settling in the saddle on her back, the mare went stiff for a split second, then "sunfished" as all four hooves left the ground and the animal went straight up into the air with its back arched. The expression on Morgan's face was priceless, a mixture of surprise and total disbelief, and despite herself, Jessie laughed outright.

For a few minutes Morgan and the roan fought a fierce battle of wills as the horse bucked and twisted and Morgan dug in his heels and fought for control. While the wild ride was brief, it was bone-jarring and teeth-rattling, and Morgan wasn't in the best of moods by the time the horse settled down to a nervous prancing, still shaking its head in agitation.

Morgan brought the animal to a halt in front of Jessie and glared down at her. Despite her promise to herself to appear perfectly innocent, Jessie giggled helplessly. "God damn it, Jess!" Morgan roared. "What's the idea of giving me a half-wild horse?"

"I didn't . . . give her to you," Jessie said between giggles. "You chose her, remember? And she isn't half wild. She's broken to the saddle, only she's spirited. She does that every time someone different mounts her. She's just testing."

"I could have broken my neck!"

"No, I knew you could handle her, and now she knows it too. She won't give you any more trouble."

As Morgan continued to glare down at her, Jessie said, "Oh, Morgan, stop looking so angry. I knew you thought all mares were meek, docile animals, and I couldn't resist letting you mount her, particularly after you chose her yourself. Why, I bet if I'd suggested that she was too much for you to handle, you would have insisted on riding her."

Morgan's brow furrowed as he saw the truth of Jessie's words. His male ego would have taken it as a challenge. But he felt like a damned fool. He glanced around at the crowd of *mesteñeros* who had gathered, to see their reaction. Some were grinning with amusement, while others were laughing outright.

Seeing his embarrassment, Jessie said, "Oh, Morgan, we're not laughing at you. If anything, we're laughing at ourselves. That mare has done the same thing to all of us."

"*Sí, señor,*" one of the Mexicans said, stepping forward. "But you mastered her much quicker than any of us."

As much as Jessie hated to admit it, she nodded in confirmation of the man's words. Morgan had mastered the mare quicker than she or any of the *mesteñeros.* She wondered at it. They were professional horsemen; breaking wild horses was a part of their trade. But where had Morgan learned his remarkable horsemanship? Unlike the cowhands, he hadn't tried to pull back on the reins, biting the bit into the mare's tender mouth to bring her under control, a mistake, for the pain only angered the already excited animal. Instead he had given the mare her head, mastering her with his legs and the weight of his body.

Finally realizing that the Mexicans' grins and laughter were good-natured camaraderie, Morgan grinned himself. "All right, Jess. I've gotten through your little initiation rite and passed the test. And now I'm willing to admit that mares aren't necessarily docile animals. But do me a favor, will you? If there are any more like her around, at least warn me."

"I will," Jessie promised, allowing herself one last giggle as she remembered the surprised expression on Morgan's face.

That evening, when Morgan and Jessie returned from her shooting lesson, they were both surprised to see his gelding standing on its feet. Morgan swung from his saddle and looked the horse over. The gelding's eyes were perfectly clear, his ears standing up alertly, as Morgan stroked his neck and grinned from ear to ear.

Morgan turned to Pedro, also smiling with pleasure, and said, "He made it. I can't believe it. Last night, after it happened, I could have sworn he was a goner."

"I told you Pedro's method of treatment had never failed," Jessie reminded him.

Morgan nodded, then bent to examine the horse's leg. It was still swollen, but not nearly as much as it had been that morning.

"I would not ride him for a few days if I were you," Pedro suggested. "That leg will be stiff and sore for a while. But in a week or so, he will be as good as new. Now, *con permiso*, I will take him down to the creek and soak his leg in the cool water. Then I will stake him where he can get plenty of grass and water."

"Well, I guess after fifteen years of service, he deserves a little vacation," Morgan answered, patting the gelding's neck.

As Pedro led Morgan's horse away Jessie asked, "He's been with you that long? Fifteen years?"

"Yes, I've had him since I was a boy. He was the only thing . . ."

Morgan's voice trailed off. Abruptly, he turned and walked away, telling Jessie in no uncertain terms that the conversation had been closed. Curiously, she wondered what he had been about to say.

Running to catch up with his long strides, Jessie said, "Well, I guess you're stuck with the roan mare for a while."

Relieved that she wasn't going to ask any further questions, Morgan smiled, saying, "Oh, she's not so bad, once I discovered how to handle her. She's like another female I know. Independent and stubborn."

Jessie knew he was referring to her. "Oh? And how should she be handled?" she asked, her eyes flashing.

Morgan's smile spread; his eyes twinkled. "With a firm hand. You see, she's a strong-willed female who not only needs to be mastered—but secretly wants to be."

"Let me tell you something, Mr. West!" Jessie said hotly. "You may think you know everything there is to know about women, but you're sadly mistaken. Women aren't horses. They don't like to be pushed around and bent to a man's will."

"Come on, Jess. You'd like a man who's strong-willed, wouldn't you?"

"That's what all you men think, isn't it?" Jessie flared

out. "That pushing us women around makes you strong, more manly. Well, there are some women who don't believe in all that *macho* stuff."

"Like you?"

"Yes!"

"Tell me, Jess. What kind of man are you attracted to?"

There had only been one man that Jessie had been attracted to, and the arrogant bastard was standing right in front of her.

"What qualities do you look for in a man?" Morgan prompted.

Jessie had never considered the qualities she wanted in a man, because she had never wanted a man in her life. She thought of her father and deliberately picked every attribute that was the very opposite of his. "He should be steady, a man who takes his responsibilities seriously. And he should be thoughtful and caring."

Morgan marked Jessie's words carefully, but he couldn't resist the urge to bait her. "He sounds downright boring to me. But then, every woman to her own tastes."

"Oh? And just what are your tastes in women?" she asked in an icy voice.

"I prefer a woman who is soft-spoken and serene and has a sweet disposition. One who's charming and utterly feminine."

Jessie was acutely aware that she possessed none of the attributes Morgan had mentioned. To think that he found her lacking irritated her.

"But above all," Morgan added with a perfectly serious expression pasted on his face, "she must be submissive. There can only be one lord and master."

It was the crowning blow. Jessie's anger came rushing

to the surface. "Well, I hope you find your ideal woman, Mr. West! You're welcome to her. But personally, I don't think she sounds very exciting either!"

Jessie turned and rushed off in a huff.

Morgan grinned from ear to ear. Again, she hadn't disappointed him.

Chapter 13

THE NEXT MORNING JESSIE STEPPED FROM THE DUG-
out and came to a standstill, her attention caught by the
mockingbird in the mesquite beside the crude cabin. It
would have been impossible to ignore the drab, gray
bird. Its song was so clear, so full of joy, and so beautiful
that it commanded attention, and Jessie was fascinated
with the range of its voice, from the deepest of the deep
to the highest of the high, seemingly never hitting the
same note twice.

Morgan walked from the dugout and, seeing Jessie
standing there so perfectly still, asked, "What are you
doing?"

"Listening to the mockingbird."

Morgan cocked his head and listened for a minute,
then said, "It's always amazed me how much a little,
unimpressive-looking bird can make such glorious
sounds. Not only does the mockingbird compose its own
music, but it mimics the other songbirds. I've even

heard them mimic an owl's hoot, a cat's screech, and the squeak of a buckboard."

"Yes, their whole life seems to revolve around sound, and they seem to be all throat," Jessie commented. Then, turning to Morgan, she said, "I've been meaning to talk to you. I'd like to skip my shooting lesson today."

Morgan frowned. "Why?"

"I want to do some scouting. I've decided if Gibbons can proceed with business as usual until the White Steed returns, then why can't I? There's really no reason for me to waste this time when I could be capturing a herd of mustangs."

Morgan's frown deepened. Before he could object, Jessie added, "I needed the money from the sale of those horses you stampeded to start my ranch. I may not be paying you much, but I still need that money."

"All right, but I'm going with you."

"That's not necessary. I'll have my six-shooter with me."

Morgan didn't bother to remind her of what a lousy shot she was with a handgun. "I said I'm going with you."

Jessie's eyes went up and met cold steel. Her resentment rose and she spat, "You have a bad habit of forgetting who's boss here."

"I'm not forgetting who's boss, Jess," Morgan replied calmly. "I won't interfere—when it comes to mustanging. But when it comes to doing my job, I decide what's necessary and what isn't. And protecting you is my job."

"I don't recall hiring you to be my bodyguard."

"No, but whether you like it or not, I consider it part of the job." The steely eyes bored into hers. "Now, Jess, you decide what it's going to be. Do I do my job as I see fit, or do I leave?"

At the mention of his leaving, Jessie felt pure panic rising. Her fear stemmed from much more than losing him as a shooting instructor. She had become accustomed to having him there in the background, his strong, steadying influence. She wanted his strength and yet her independence too. But the two seemed to be at odds. Frustrated, she said, "Oh, all right, then. Come along, if you insist."

Morgan was aware of the battle Jessie had fought with herself. He grinned at his small victory.

The appealing, lopsided grin didn't make matters any easier for Jessie. It tugged at her heart. And the warm, shimmering look in his eyes made her tingle all over. Damn him! she thought. He knows his power over me, and he's taunting me. She wished she didn't need his services as an expert marksman, that she could send him on his way once and for all. Then things could go back to being normal, and she'd be in complete control of her life again. But the memory of her life before Morgan appeared on the scene seemed dull and empty.

I won't be dominated by him, despite his hold over me, Jessie thought furiously. I won't play the submissive role for any man.

Jessie hurried to walk ahead of Morgan. As she saddled her horse in icy silence, Morgan decided the best approach would be to ignore her little show of temper. Jessie had been accustomed to having her own way for too long, and learning to give and take would take time —and patience on his part. For a moment Morgan puzzled over why he was willing to give that time and patience, and then, seeing Jessie ride out, he pushed the thought aside and quickly mounted, following her.

Jessie tried very hard to hold on to her anger. It was difficult to do with the early morning breeze whisper-

ing across the prairie, the birds singing joyously, the sun
warming her skin. Besides, she was acutely aware of
Morgan riding next to her, despite her studied efforts to
ignore him. His heady masculine scent drifted across to
her, a scent that always stirred her senses, and she was
much too conscious of their legs brushing together each
time one of them veered his or her horse to avoid a
clump of cactus or mesquite brush. When she spied the
herd of mustangs in the distance, she welcomed the
distraction. Maybe now she could concentrate on business.

The herd was a large one, well over three hundred
horses. To the casual observer they appeared as a whole,
but to Jessie's trained eye they were many different
manadas grazing together, each stallion setting a careful distance between his harem of mares and the next
stallion's.

Jessie reined in on the crest of a hill a good distance
from the herd, not wanting to stampede them. Since
the prevailing wind was blowing toward her and Morgan, she knew that the mustangs wouldn't be alerted by
their scent and she could take her time to decide which
manadas would bring the better price. There was no
sense in capturing scruffy horses that would bring a
mere pittance.

Morgan reined in beside Jessie and looked down at
the herd, not with the critical, professional eye with
which Jessie studied them, but simply enjoying the
peaceful beauty of the scene before him. Then his gaze
caught on one magnificent, powerful stallion. He recognized that dove-colored horse with its beautiful irises. It
was the same stallion he'd seen in Jessie's pen many
weeks ago.

Morgan glanced over the stallion's mares, both surprised he had managed to collect so large a *manada* in that short a time and impressed by the stallion's selection. These were no ordinary mares. They were all prime horseflesh, as beautiful and magnificent as the stallion himself, appropriate consorts for a king.

Seeing the stallion invading the no-man's-land between the *manadas,* Morgan's breath caught, knowing that the mustang meant to challenge another stallion for his *manada.* He quickly glanced at the stallion being singled out, seeing that he was a large black horse whose mares were just as impressive-looking as the *palomino's.*

"Look!" Jessie cried, having also noticed the challenge. "Those two stallions are going to fight."

"I know, and I hope the *palomino* wins."

"Well, I don't," Jessie responded in a hard voice.

"Why not?" Morgan asked, shooting her a curious glance.

"Because I recognize that *palomino.* He was in the last herd we captured. If he wins, he'll have the best mares in that entire herd, and I won't be able to capture them. At least, not all of them."

"Why can't you capture them?"

"Because he's smart. Smarter than most stallions. He'll never fall again for that trick of stampeding him and his mares into the pen. As soon as he sees those wings he'll turn and take not only his *manada* with him, but probably the entire herd. Then the only way I'd be able to take his mares away from him would be to capture the mares one by one."

A shrill snort reverberated in the air, and Morgan and Jessie returned their attention to the scene on the prairie below them. Naturally, the challenge had been issued by the *palomino,* and the stallion now stood a short distance from the black, his eyes blazing with determination. For a long while the two horses glared at each other, the powerful muscles in their bodies trembling with anticipation of the battle, their tails held straight out. Alerted to the danger, the rest of the herd moved to a safer distance, a few of the stallions driving their *manadas* completely away, fearful that the bold, aggressive *palomino* might decide to issue a challenge to them next.

Morgan was beginning to wonder if the two stallions were ever going to battle. Each seemed bent on forcing the other to his will by sheer eye contact. And then, with another shrill, angry cry, a noise that could be heard half a mile away, the *palomino* reared on his hind legs. The black followed suit and the two stallions walked toward each other with ears laid back and teeth bared. They struck, the razor-sharp hooves raking the hides from each other, their mouths aimed for the vulnerable jugular vein. Then, backing away, the two stallions glared at each other with murder in their eyes.

Both horses screamed as they lunged the second time, heaving their whole bodies into the thrust, then whirling and kicking with their back legs. Two pair of hooves hit like a whiplash of lightning, sending sparks flying. Then they whirled back around and reared, hooves pounding, teeth snapping, manes and tails flying.

Morgan watched the fight grimly, noting that the black was the heavier of the two and thinking that the older stallion would probably win, being more experienced than the *palomino*. But, to Morgan's surprise, what the *palomino* lacked in size, he more than made up for in agility and ferocity. Despite being given punishing blows, the younger horse fought with the tenacity of a champion, his hooves pounding back, his sharp teeth flashing and tearing huge bits of flesh from the black's neck and shoulders.

As the deadly battle continued, the dust raised by the fighting horses was so thick that Jessie and Morgan had a hard time telling which stallion was winning, seeing only a flash of black or gray as the mustangs reared and lunged, their hides glistening with sweat in the sunlight. Even from where they sat and watched, Morgan and Jessie could smell the odor of blood, horse-sweat, and animal hate. Morgan strained his eyes, cursing the concealing cloud of dust, wishing he could see how the *palomino* was faring.

"The *palomino* was crazy to pick that black to battle with," Jessie commented.

"Why do you think that?" Morgan asked, feeling a twinge of fear for his favorite.

"Because that black has a heavy, waxy tail and mane. Blacks with that kind of tail and mane are trickier and more dangerous than any other horse."

Alarmed, Morgan glanced back down, but all he could see was the thick cloud of dust. Was the younger horse up to it? he wondered. Did he have the endurance? Or was he already weakening? Morgan fervently hoped if that were so, the *palomino* would have the sense to flee. But somehow he sensed that the fiercely determined horse would never turn tail and run. No, he would fight to the death if necessary. And it was beginning to look as if that was exactly how this battle would end. Neither stallion would be satisfied until the other was dead at his feet.

Suddenly a horse darted from the dust cloud, running as if all the demons in hell were after him. For a split second Morgan couldn't tell which horse it was, and

then, seeing it was the black, he let out a burst of relieved laughter. Jessie glanced at him curiously.

A second horse emerged from the rolling dust, chasing the black and nipping at the flesh on the stallion's
withers and flanks, screaming in a mixture of anger and
victory. Seeing their master run away, several of the
black's mares ran after him. But the *palomino* would
have none of that. He had won them in fair battle; they
belonged to him now. The young stallion whirled
around, circling the fleeing mares, nipping viciously at
their flanks and necks, snorting shrill warnings until he
finally turned them back and raced them into his
manada. Then, when they stood trembling and meek
among his harem, he gathered up the rest of the black's
mares.

Morgan smiled down at the magnificent stallion. Despite the beating he had just taken, he showed no signs
of fatigue. Instead, he stood there, his head held
proudly aloft, every muscle and tendon in his sleek
body alert, daring any one of his mares to doubt who
was lord and master, and Morgan could have sworn the
mares gazed back at him with adoration.

"You were serious when you said you wanted the
palomino to win, weren't you?" Jessie asked, puzzled
by Morgan's intense interest in the horse.

"Yes, I certainly was."

"Why? What difference did it make to you?"

"I'd come to admire him." Morgan turned in his saddle to face her. "You see, I noticed him that day you
brought the herd of mustangs in. He seemed determined to escape that pen, to regain his freedom. For a
while there I thought he was going to charge that blanket your men had thrown over the gate, despite his
natural fear of it. I admired his courage and spirit."

"He *did* attack it," Jessie informed him in a half-angry voice. "I've never seen a wild horse do that. We had to let him out right then and there, before he stampeded the rest of the herd. Six of his mares escaped with him before we could get that gate closed again."

Morgan smiled in silent appreciation, his admiration for the courageous *palomino* rising yet another notch.

Jessie glanced back down at the mustangs. "We'll come back tomorrow. By then, things should have calmed down and the herd re-formed."

As Jessie turned her horse and rode away, Morgan took one last long look at the *palomino*. Then, whirling his horse, he galloped after Jessie.

As Morgan caught up with her, he said, "We'll still have time for your shooting lesson."

She shot him a look of pure disgust. "No, I want to do some more scouting."

"Why? You've found your herd, and your pen won't hold any more than that."

Stubbornly, Jessie refused to answer, her eyes staring straight ahead.

Morgan chuckled, thinking she looked delightful with her chin set so defiantly. "I think you're stalling, Jess," he taunted softly.

Jessie reined in and spun around in her saddle. "So what if I am! Can't I have at least one day of rest?"

Morgan ignored her flashing eyes and gazed about him. It was a beautiful day, the sun just warm enough to make it lazy but not uncomfortable. Eyeing a large, spreading mesquite not far from them, he said, "I suppose I could use a day of relaxation too." Then, looking her directly in the eye, he asked, "What would you like to do?"

Jessie's breath caught. His eyes shimmered like heat

waves off the desert sand, leaving no doubt in Jessie's mind of what he was proposing. Ever since that night in Dog Town, her body had been hungry for his lovemaking. During the past week, whenever he looked at her with those smoldering gray eyes, brushed up against her accidentally, or put his arm around her during her shooting lessons, her desire for him had increased. At night, alone in her empty bed, she had ached for him. Yes, she wanted him, but she'd be damned if she'd run into his arms. If she gave in to her desire, he'd see how easily he could master her. And she wouldn't be mastered by any man!

As Jessie maintained an icy silence, Morgan shrugged, saying in an indifferent voice, "Well, if you don't have any suggestions, I think I'll go over to that mesquite and have a little nap."

Jessie watched in dismay as Morgan rode off, wondering if she could have mistaken the look in his eyes. She followed him, determined to set him straight once again about their relationship. It was business and nothing more!

When she reached the mesquite, Morgan had already dismounted and was spreading on the ground the blanket he kept rolled at the back of his saddle. She watched as he tossed his hat aside, slipped off his boots, and took off his gun belt, carefully laying it at one corner, then reclined on the blanket, his head pillowed on his arms. As his eyes closed, revealing unbelievably long, thick lashes, Jessie wondered if it was some kind of a trick. Warily, she dismounted and walked over to him, but Morgan made no move toward her.

"Morgan," she began. But he didn't respond.

How dare he! Jessie thought. How dare he lie there and pretend to be asleep when I want to talk to him.

Morgan opened one eye, asking in a lazy drawl, "Is something wrong?"

"Yes, there is. I'd like to remind you that you work for me and that our relationship is purely business. I'm the boss and you're the hired gun."

With the swiftness of a striking snake, Morgan caught her and wrestled her to the ground. He looked down at her, his desire darkening his eyes to a dusky blue-gray.

"Why do you fight it, Jess?" he asked in a soft, husky voice. "You know you want me as much as I want you. Why deny each other the pleasure of our bodies? You're hurting yourself as much as me."

"I don't want—"

Jessie's words were smothered by Morgan's mouth, and then she was lost in the drugging magic of his kiss. She had forgotten how warm his lips were as they brushed over hers, how enticing his tongue as it slid over her lips, then flicked at the corners of her mouth. His breath fanned her face as his exciting scent enveloped her. A half-tortured moan escaped her lips as she slipped her arms around his broad shoulders, her lips parting in silent surrender.

But instead of plunging his tongue in to claim his spoils as victor, Morgan continued to dally, brushing it across her lips and teeth, back and forth, back and forth, then flicking it like a fiery dart, his lips nibbling at the corners of her mouth. Jessie thought she would scream in frustration, her need to taste him overriding all. Her fingers tangled in the soft hair at the back of his head, pulling him closer while her tongue snaked out.

Both felt electric shocks course through them as their tongues met and danced.

Morgan's smoldering need turned into a blazing inferno as he kissed Jessie deeply, demandingly, determined to put his brand on her once and for all. Impatiently he untied the ribbon at the back of her neck, sliding his fingers through her long, silken hair to cup the back of her head, his tongue circling and laving hers in strong strokes that would leave no doubt in her mind that she belonged to him.

His fingers trembled as he unbuttoned Jessie's shirt and parted the material, his hand sliding up to cup one soft mound possessively, his thumb teasing the tip to a hardened point. Sliding his mouth down her throat, then across her collarbone, he lowered his head to capture the other nipple, his teeth gently grazing it before his tongue soothed and flicked teasingly. When his mouth closed over the throbbing peak, Jessie felt each tug like a dart of fire to her loins.

"Stop, Morgan, stop," she muttered weakly, her pleas contradictory to her actions as she held his head against her breast and arched her back to give him better access. When he did stop his exquisite torture, Jessie cried out softly in protest, then sighed in utter bliss as he moved to the other breast, his mouth arousing while his slender fingers massaged, making Jessie's skin tingle with a million tiny fires and her muscles quiver with delight.

A muttered oath brought Jessie back from the haze in which she had been floating as Morgan tugged impatiently at her belt. Brushing his hand aside, she undid the stubborn buckle and unbuttoned her pants, lifting her hips as Morgan slid them and her underdrawers over her hips and down her legs, the brush of his fingers against the skin sending fresh tingles through her. She watched through dazed eyes as Morgan rose and swiftly stripped. When he fell to his knees beside her, his gaze hotly devouring her, she flushed, suddenly and acutely aware that she was totally exposed to him in the naked light of day. Quickly she covered her breasts with her arms.

"Don't!" Morgan commanded softly. "I want to see all of you."

He rose to his feet, bringing her with him. Then he stood back, drinking in her beauty, admiring the sleekness of her legs, her softly rounded hips and tiny waist, her high, full breasts. With the sun turning her hair to shimmering gold around her face and creamy shoulders, she was a beautiful sun goddess—his sun goddess!

Morgan didn't have to tell Jessie she was beautiful. She could see it in his eyes. Her embarrassment fled, to be replaced with pride and a gladness that he thought her so. When he stepped forward, his hands smoothing over her long hair, then down her body until he knelt at her dainty feet, a lump formed in her throat, knowing that he was adoring her.

Morgan's eyes rose to lock on Jessie's, glowing with an inner fire as they gazed deeply into hers. His hand rose and trailed up the soft skin of her inner thigh, and Jessie trembled in anticipation. Holding her captive in that searing gaze, his fingers brushed across the golden curls before slipping into her. As his fingers slid in and out, Jessie was flooded with sensations. It was heaven. It was hell. She didn't want him to stop, and yet her legs felt so weak that she doubted she could stand it for a second longer. And then, as the waves began, her body shuddering in reaction, her knees did buckle, and she collapsed in his arms.

Dazed and reeling, she rested her head against his shoulder. It took a minute for her to recover her senses and realize that Morgan had sat back on his heels when she had fallen and her legs were straddling his thighs.

She could feel his manhood trapped between their abdomens, hot and throbbing with a life of its own. But that was not where she wanted him.

She raised her head. "Morgan, I want—"

Morgan chuckled softly, saying in a husky voice, "I know, sweetheart. That's what I want too."

He lay back on the blanket, bringing them to rest with Jessie on top and still astride him. "You take the lead this time, Jessie. Ride me like you do those wild mustangs of yours."

Jessie couldn't believe her ears. He was relinquishing the dominant position to her? Her excitement soared. Yes, she wanted to ride him, feel his powerful body between her legs, feel him writhing beneath her, master him as he had mastered her.

Eagerly she raised her hips, and as she did, his erection sprang to attention. Slowly—ever so slowly—she lowered herself over him, taking him into her inch by inch, her legs firmly grasping his hips.

Morgan ground his teeth and sucked in his breath as he felt her muscles greedily contracting around him. Jessie's long hair fell in a shimmering waterfall around them, and Morgan watched enthralled as she began her movements, first deliberately slow and seductive, rotating her hips to pull him even deeper into her velvety heat, then faster and faster, throwing her head back as the sensations of pleasure began to wash over her. A sheen of perspiration broke out on Morgan's brow as his pressing need grew to an agonizing throb, loath to take his eyes off her as she rode him hard and magnificently. His hands smoothed over her hips and thighs, then rose to cup her breasts as he began to buck beneath her, his movements in perfect counterpoint to hers, driving him even deeper into her.

Jessie gasped in shock as Morgan penetrated her deeply, sucking the breath from her lungs and sending pinpoints of light flashing behind her eyes. But rather than retreat from the intense, almost frightening sensation, she rode him harder, slamming her hips down as his came up, feeling as if she were riding on the edge of a tremendous lightning bolt, then soaring out into space as a roaring filled her ears and the dam of sensation burst in fiery explosion that seemed to shake the earth around them.

Morgan held Jessie where she had fallen weakly over him, both still trembling in the aftermath, their sweat pooling between their bodies and glistening on their skin in the sunlight. Finally, becoming aware of him caressing her back and tenderly kissing her temple, Jessie raised her head and looked down, a puzzled expression on her face.

"Why did you do that?" she asked.

Morgan stole a quick kiss, then asked, "Do what?"

"Let me be on top. Let me take the dominant role."

Morgan frowned. "That first time, in Dog Town, I wanted to possess you fully, prove that you belonged to me, totally and completely." He shrugged. "I guess that's the common male reaction, to want to be the one who dominates. Like those stallions out there, I guess all of us males have a little of the despot in us. It's just our nature."

Yes, Jessie thought, the male's desire to be absolute ruler over the female went back as far as the caveman. She had yet to meet one who didn't have a little of a tyrant in him. It was the male's nature to dominate, both in the animal and the human world, placing the female beneath them in the submissive position even when mating. Yet Morgan had allowed her, even en-

couraged her, to reverse their age-old roles, even after
he had told her he liked submissive women.

"But you didn't dominate me," Jessie reminded him.

"No. Giving and taking in lovemaking is just as important as in other male-female relationships. You see,
sweetheart, it doesn't have to be a struggle over who
will dominate who, but what the two can share together
that's important."

Then, when he had said he liked submissive women,
he had only been teasing her, Jessie realized. She
averted her eyes, asking in a voice so low, Morgan had
to strain to hear her despite their nearness, "Was that
the way it was with the other women you've known? A
sharing?"

The silence stretched uncomfortably between them.
Jessie hated herself for asking; she knew the question
was totally off-limits, but she had to know. Was she just
another casual lover passing through his life, or was she
something more? And there was no doubt in Jessie's
mind that there had been others, as skillful and artful a
lover as Morgan was. A sudden surge of raw jealousy ran
through her.

Morgan had felt Jessie's question like a blow to the
gut, and he was forced to take a closer look at his feelings. He didn't know just how deep his emotions ran,
and he wasn't a man to make a commitment of any sort
lightly.

"I'm sorry, Morgan," Jessie muttered when he didn't
answer for so long. "I shouldn't have asked that. It's
none of my business."

"No, Jess, it isn't, considering it happened before I
met you," Morgan answered in a tight voice. He rolled
to his side and leaned over her, looking her straight in

the eye. "But I'm going to answer it anyway, because I think we need to start being more open with each other. I didn't care about any of those women. I'm a normal, healthy male. They just served to satisfy a need I had." He paused, then said in a cautious voice, "I care about you, Jess. A lot. I won't say any more than that at the present time. My feelings are all new and strange to me. But because I do care, I want to protect you."

"But I'm not like other women," Jessie objected. "I've been taking care of myself for years."

"I know," Morgan replied with a wry smile. "You're the most independent woman I've ever known. But that doesn't stop me from wanting to protect you. That goes along with the caring, whether you like it or not. You can't expect one from me without the other."

Jessie frowned.

"Jess, every time I tell you something, you get angry. You think I'm trying to dominate you, that I'm threatening your independence. But I'm not. I'm only showing my caring. Now, I'm a strong-willed person, myself, and things aren't going to be easy for us, unless we can both learn to give in a little. Remember, it doesn't have to be a power struggle, who gives or takes that's important, but what we share as a result of it."

Jessie had sensed Morgan's encouraging her to take the dominant role in their lovemaking had not been a whim of the moment. No, even then he had been making a point. She tore her eyes away from his and gazed over his shoulder thoughtfully. She had hoped for something much more than an admission of caring, but then, she had to admire his honesty. How many men would have vowed love, particularly right after he had made love to her, just to get off the hook? And she couldn't blame him for being cautious. She wasn't sure just how deep her emotions went, either, nor was she anywhere near to making any kind of commitment. But learning to give it wasn't going to be easy. And that seemed to be what he expected of her if their relationship was going to continue. She didn't know if she could even do it. She valued her hard-earned independence above everything. Was any man worth relinquishing that for, even a part of it? Somewhere deep in her soul, a part of her answered, Yes, Morgan was, while another part of her still held back.

Aware that Morgan was awaiting her answer, she looked back at him, seeing the expectant expression on his face. She smiled and ran her fingers over his strong jawline before she answered. "I'll try, Morgan. That's all I can promise."

Morgan knew he couldn't expect more from Jessie. Naturally, her first step at giving up some of her fierce independence would be hesitant. He smiled back warmly, saying, "We'll both try."

Morgan kissed her long and hard, putting a seal on their bargain. But with their naked bodies pressed so closely together, it was inevitable that the kiss would turn to one of a more passionate nature.

Jessie's excitement spiraled as she felt his manhood stirring, then hardening and growing between them. When Morgan's mouth left hers to blaze a trail of searing kisses down her throat, she reached between them and took his long, full length in her hand, sliding sensuously up and down it, thrilling at Morgan's hiss of pleasure.

"Morgan?" she whispered.

Morgan lifted his head, his eyes dark with passion. A

slow, mischievous smile spread across Jessie's lips as she said, "I'll let you be on top this time."

Despite the heat of his passion, Morgan chuckled, the deep, rumbling sound in his chest exciting Jessie as much as his hands caressing her.

Chapter 14

IT WAS LATE THAT AFTERNOON WHEN JESSIE AND Morgan returned to the *real*, as the Mexicans called the camp. As soon as they had dismounted, a *mesteñero* led their horses away, saving them the trouble of having to unsaddle and rub them down, a luxury Morgan was unaccustomed to.

He turned and walked to where his gelding was staked. The horse nickered a welcome, and Morgan stroked the animal's sleek neck fondly before bending to examine its leg.

Rising, he said to Jessie, "The swelling is almost gone now."

"I'm glad," Jessie answered in a distracted voice, her attention on the herd of mares that were grazing nearby. "Pedro," she called to the head *mesteñero*, who was wandering through the herd, "what's wrong with that blue roan? She's not grazing."

Pedro wove his way through the horses and came to

stand before Jessie before he answered, *"Sí, patrona.* I am afraid she has a bad case of lampers."

Gabe strolled up to them at that minute and asked, "Did you say lampers? Well, don't you worry your pretty little head about that, Jessie. I can cure lampers in nothing flat. I'll be right back."

True to his word, Gabe was back shortly. Holding out a piece of salt bacon, he said, "This will cure it."

Morgan watched in amazement as Gabe walked up to the roan and rubbed the salt bacon on the horse's tail. He turned to Jessie, asking, "Do you really believe in that old ranch cure for lampers?"

Jessie sighed in disgust. "Of course not! How can rubbing bacon on a horse's tail take the swelling out of its gums? The only cure for lampers is to scarify the gums and then hope the swelling will go down."

"Then why aren't you doing that?"

"We will—when Gabe goes back inside. You see, Gabe has a lot of strange ideas about animal remedies, and he's very emphatic about them. Rather than get into a heated argument with him, Pedro and I just let him treat the animal his way, then we do it our way, the right way, when he's not around. As long as his treatment is harmless, like putting turpentine under a horse's navel to cure colic, or hanging a frog between its eyes to cure foundering, or tying a split lizard over a broken bone, we let him do it."

"My God! Gabe actually believes in those cures?" Morgan asked.

Jessie laughed. "He certainly does. And believe me, sometimes we have a battle on our hands when we have to disagree with him. When Gabe gets something in his head, no one can change it."

Gabe walked back to them, grinning proudly and

saying, "That horse will be as good as new by morning. You'll see."

"Thank you, Gabe," Jessie replied sweetly.

"Sure, anytime," Gabe answered, turning and walking back to the dugout, a jaunty swing in his stride.

When Gabe was out of hearing, Jessie and Morgan laughed. Pedro could only shake his head in disgust.

The next morning the camp was filled with activity as the *mesteñeros* excitedly prepared for the capture of the herd of wild horses. The sound of axes biting into hard mesquite wood rang through the crystal-clear air as fresh brush was cut and tied to the wings to conceal them. Other *mesteñeros* busied themselves shoring up the pen itself, tying the logs together with fresh rawhide where the old had broken or weakened.

After the pen had passed Jessie's critical inspection, a hush fell over the camp, all the more noticeable after the loud noises of preparation and the excited babble of the Mexicans. Morgan looked around him, baffled by the strange silence and the solemn expressions on the *mesteñeros'* faces. Then, as Pedro wove his way through the crowd of men around the pen, the Mexicans fell to their knees.

Seeing the cross made from mesquite limbs that Pedro held reverently in his hands, Morgan finally understood. He watched in silence at the back of the crowd as Pedro placed the cross on the top beam over the gate and then knelt beside the other *mesteñeros*. Morgan bowed his head in respect as the Mexicans beseeched God's blessing and protection in this day's work. Mustanging was a dangerous business, and any one of these men could be killed, knocked from his horse and trampled beneath thousands of pounding hooves, or crushed if caught between the stampeding herd and one of the wings. Morgan's eyes caught sight of a golden head bowed among all the dark ones. A bolt of anger ran through him. He couldn't let Jessie participate. It was too dangerous!

Suddenly the *mesteñeros* sprang to their feet, whooping and hollering as they ran for their mounts. Jessie turned, a wide smile on her face, her eyes sparkling with excitement. Morgan knew then that he couldn't stop her, that nothing in heaven, hell—or anything in between—could keep her from participating. Grimly, he held his silence, vowing that he'd stick as close to her as possible.

As soon as their horses were led from the corral and their bridles slipped over their heads, the Mexicans stripped down, throwing hats, shirts, and boots, even belts, in every direction, determined to increase their speed by lightening the load they carried on their mounts by every possible ounce of weight. As Jessie sat down to strip off her boots and socks, Morgan did the same.

When he tossed his hat aside and shrugged from his shirt, Jessie asked in surprise, "You're going with us?"

"I certainly am," Morgan replied in a firm voice.

Jessie frowned, not liking his answer. Morgan wasn't a professional mustanger. He might get in the way, inadvertently endangering one of her men.

Guessing her thoughts, Morgan said, "As an observer, Jess. I promise I won't be a hindrance. Besides, I'm not exactly a greenhorn, you know. I have enough sense to stay out of the way."

Remembering his speech of the day before about giving and taking, Jessie reluctantly backed down. "All right." Besides, she thought as she turned to her horse, he probably won't be able to keep up with us, not if he's loaded down with both his saddle and his heavier weight.

Seeing Jessie start to tie her lariat around her horse's neck, Morgan frowned, saying, "I thought you held your lariat in your hand."

"Only if I intend to ride down a mare. Then I do it that way so I can slip the *bozal* around her nose as I leap to her back. But today we're taking the entire herd, and I don't want to take any chances of losing my rope. We use them to drive the herd. Besides, there's always the possibility that we'll have to rope a particularly unruly horse from the herd. No one has that much strength in their hands alone. I'll need the strength of my horse."

"If you used a saddle, instead of riding bareback, you could tie it around your saddle horn," Morgan pointed out.

Jessie's eyes flashed. "The stupid cowhands' way? No, Morgan, you can break a mustang's neck that way. The saddle horn won't give, while my mount's neck is flexible. Besides that, there's no danger of snapping the rope. Once you've roped a mustang with the end of your lariat tied to your mount's neck, there's no escape for it."

"But doesn't it choke your horse?"

"We don't use a slipknot. We use a horse knot. Watch, I'll show you."

Morgan watched as Jessie tied her lariat around her mount's neck, both amazed and feeling a little foolish, realizing that he was really a novice when it came to mustanging.

After copying Jessie's horse knot on his lariat, Morgan picked up his reins and leapt on his horse's back.

Jessie looked up at him with surprise. "You're going to ride bareback?"

"Looks like I'm going to have to, if I'm going to keep up with you."

"Are you sure you won't fall off? We'll be traveling at a fast clip."

Morgan chuckled at Jessie's blunt question. "No, Jess, I won't fall off. I'll admit there are a lot of your little mustanging tricks I don't know, but riding bareback isn't one of them. No, I had enough of that as a kid."

Jessie caught the hint of bitterness in Morgan's last words. Had his family been too poor to afford saddles? she wondered. Then, noticing the gun strapped to his thigh, she said, "Well, if you're worrying about weight, you'd better take off that gun."

"No, the gun stays."

"It weighs a ton," Jessie objected.

Morgan chuckled at her exaggeration. "Hardly that much."

"It will weigh you down," she argued.

"Maybe, maybe not. But it stays. I'll be the only one armed on this little expedition, and that's what I'm here for." At Jessie's stubborn silence, Morgan grinned. "Now, if you're really worried about every ounce of weight, I could strip off my pants."

The thought of Morgan riding stark-naked with only his gun and gun belt struck Jessie as ludicrous. She laughed. "You'd strip off your pants before your gun?"

"Yep. That's how strongly I feel about it. Why, I'd feel naked without my gun."

Jessie laughed even harder. "Well, at least take off that bandanna. It looks silly up there around your neck with no shirt on."

"Nope, it stays too. That and my gun. No self-respect-ing cowhand would be caught dead without either of them."

"Cowhand?" Jessie asked in surprise. "When were you a cowhand?"

"In my younger days. You don't think I was born a gunslinger, do you?"

Jessie frowned, realizing how little she really knew about Morgan. As intimately as she knew his body, she knew nothing of his past, his beginnings. She'd been curious, but something had always warned her away. This was the first time Morgan had volunteered anything. Knowing that he was beginning to open up to her pleased her.

"I'm sorry I made that crack about cowhands a few minutes ago," she said.

"That's all right. I didn't take offense. Cowhands really don't know much about catching wild horses. I'm just beginning to realize that myself. But if there's anything you want to know about cows, just feel free to ask."

Jessie laughed. "Sorry, but I'm not the least bit interested. They're the dumbest creatures on earth."

"Well, compared to a horse, I'm afraid I'll have to agree," Morgan answered amicably.

"Pardon, *patrona*," Pedro interrupted softly, "but we are ready to leave."

Jessie glanced around her in surprise, having been so amazed at Morgan's revelation that she hadn't even noticed the *mesteñeros* were all mounted and waiting. Her heart thudded with renewed excitement as she answered, "Then let's go!"

Swinging on her horse, Jessie galloped away from the camp, Morgan and Pedro following close behind and the other *mesteñeros* bringing up the rear. About five miles from camp they found mustang sign, the huge piles of horse dung topped with fresh droppings. They slowed their speed, fanning out and moving more cautiously.

When they reached the rise of the hill that overlooked the grazing herd, Jessie brought her outfit to a halt. Quickly scanning the area, she said, "Good, we won't have to worry about cutting the *palomino* and his *manada* out of the herd. I see he's keeping a distance from the rest of them."

Morgan glanced across the prairie and saw that the *palomino* and his mares were grazing a good quarter of a mile from the rest of the herd. The magnificent stallion stood on a rise slightly away from his mares, his head raised alertly and his sharp eyes scanning the area.

"Ah, *patrona,* it is a shame we cannot take them too. The *palomino* has the finest mares."

"I know," Jessie replied irritably, "but we can't take the chance of losing the entire herd because of him. Now, this is what I want you to do . . ."

Morgan paid little attention to Jessie's words as she gave her head *mesteñero* instructions, his total attention on the gray stallion in the distance, a thoughtful look on his face.

The Mexicans spread out, seeking the concealing brush that lay to both sides of the prairie to sneak up on the herd, avoiding putting their backs to the wind until the last minute. When the *aventadores,* or starters, were positioned, Jessie gave the signal to begin, letting out a tremendous whoop that would have put a Comanche's war cry to shame and half frightening Morgan out of his wits. Stunned by the unexpected loud cry, he got a late start. Suddenly realizing that he had been left behind as the others lunged forward, he muttered, "Well, goddamn!" then kneed his horse forward.

It took all his riding skill to catch up and keep up with Jessie. Looking over his shoulder, Morgan's heart leapt to his throat as he saw the thundering herd racing straight toward them. Morgan had ridden after many a herd of stampeding longhorns, dodging their wicked, clanking horns as he veered in on the lead cows in an effort to turn the herd in on itself and make it mill, but a stampeding herd of mustangs was much more dangerous because it couldn't be turned. To him, it looked as if Jessie were deliberately placing herself in front of the herd, and thousands and thousands of pounds of wild, terrified horseflesh were rushing down on them.

"Get back to the sides!" Morgan yelled at the top of his lungs.

But Jessie either didn't hear him over the noise of the pounding hooves, or she ignored him, as did the two *mesteñeros* riding counterpoint to her and Morgan a short distance away.

Only when the herd was almost upon them and he could feel their hot breath on the back of his neck, did Morgan finally realize what Jessie and her men were doing. Instead of the herd's parting and going around them, or simply trampling them by sheer brute force— as Morgan had feared—the horses crowded in together, tightening the herd, and miraculously they were suddenly riding beside the stampeding horses instead of in front of them.

Jessie and her men whooped and hollered, waving their lariats threateningly over the frightened horses' heads to keep them running. Morgan was hard-pressed to keep up and beginning to wonder if the chase would ever end. Sweat poured off him from the tremendous heat generated by the racing animals.

The earth shook from the beating it was taking, the sound of the pounding hooves reverberating in the air until it was a pulsating, deafening roar. Morgan's head began to ache from the noise, and he had to fight for every breath. With the long manes and tails of the close-running horses whipping about, it was impossible to distinguish any individual animal. That, combined with their speed, gave the whole herd an indistinct, blurred image of flashing movement.

Morgan spied a large clump of mesquite brush in his and Jessie's path. "Watch out for that brush!" he called to Jessie as he sawed hard on his horse's reins to avoid it.

To Morgan's horror, Jessie didn't veer her horse but jumped it over the brush, her mare's hooves barely clearing the top of the mesquite. When she came down, she was so close to the herd that her leg brushed one of the racing mustangs beside her.

"Crazy damned fool!" Morgan cursed beneath his breath, knowing that if Jessie had fallen, she would have been thrown beneath the herd.

When Morgan saw two *mesteñeros* racing several mares from the sidelines into the herd, he sighed in relief, knowing that the end was near. These were the trained tame mares that would usurp the lead mustang mares' positions and take the herd into the pen.

Minutes later the wings appeared, and when they were well between them, Jessie and Morgan slowed their mounts, allowing the mustangs to surge ahead. When the end of the herd reached them, Jessie rushed her horse forward again, joining several of her mustangers who were keeping the horses stampeding as the wings narrowed. One mustang bumped into Jessie's horse, causing La Duquesa to stumble, and for one terrifying moment Morgan thought Jessie would lose her seat and be thrown.

Seeing her horse recover her stride and Jessie still on the mare's back, Morgan reined in, weak with relief that she'd survived her close brush with death. Then a fury began to build within him.

Jessie had barely come to a halt as the last horse raced into the pen, when Morgan reached up and jerked her from her horse's back, setting her on her feet in front of him so hard, it jarred her teeth. She looked up at him in surprise.

"You just had to do that last bit, didn't you?" Morgan roared, his eyes blazing with anger. "It's not bad enough that you jumped that damned mesquite brush, instead of going around it, but you just had to be in on it to the bitter end, didn't you?"

"What in the devil are you talking about?" Jessie flared back.

"I'm talking about how you almost got knocked down! Following the herd right up to the pen wasn't necessary. I may not know much about mustanging, but I know that's the most dangerous part of it. It was a risk you didn't have to take. That's what you pay your *mesteñeros* for."

"I don't ask my men to do anything I won't do. And I didn't almost get knocked down!"

"Dammit, Jess, I've got eyes in my head. You damned near got killed!"

"I did not! La Duquesa just stumbled, but she didn't fall. Do you think I'd be riding her if I wasn't positive of her surefootedness?"

Morgan didn't listen to a word Jessie said, his anger

overriding his reason. "Dammit, don't you *ever* do something that dangerous again!"

A cold rage rose in Jessie. Her green eyes glittered like splintered ice. "You promised you wouldn't inter-fere in my mustanging," she said angrily. "And how dare you take me to task in front of my men. You don't own me, and you don't tell me what to do . . . not now —not ever!"

Furious, Jessie pushed Morgan aside and walked an-grily away, yelling orders to her *mesteñeros*. Too late, Morgan realized he had made a serious mistake. Not only had he broken his word to her, he had put her in an embarrassing position in front of her men, and Jessie's fierce pride would never allow that. But dammit, he thought in self-defense, what did she expect of him? To stand by and watch the woman he loved flirt with death was too much to ask of any man.

Morgan's thought stunned him. It was the first time he had admitted to himself that he loved Jessie. But his feelings for her were something that defied reason, and even if he had wanted to, he couldn't will them away.

Suddenly aware of the Mexicans' curious glances, Morgan realized that he was in the way. He looked about, wondering if he could help, then realized that Jessie would probably resent any effort he made to be helpful. Sighing with regret, he turned, mounted his horse, and rode from the camp.

Jessie watched Morgan from the corner of her eye as he rode away. Good riddance! she thought angrily. Throughout the afternoon, she fumed silently, her *mes-teñeros* giving her a wide berth and jumping to obey her orders, none wanting to be on the receiving end of her wrath.

When night fell and Morgan still hadn't returned, her

anger turned to fear. Had he left for good? she wondered. But surely he wouldn't do that. Not without his possessions and certainly not without the gelding he was so fond of. Had Gibbons's hired guns ambushed him and killed him? The thought brought cold terror to her heart.

Jessie's face was pale and drawn as she ate her supper, listlessly pushing her food about the plate, her eyes repeatedly going to the blanket that covered the doorway. Gabe and Pedro, who were eating with her, exchanged knowing glances.

Finally, Gabe said, "Stop fretting, Jessie. He'll be back."

My God! Jessie thought. Were her feelings that obvious? Why, Pedro and Gabe must think her a complete fool, first giving Morgan hell for interfering in her business, then worrying herself sick about him, like some typical, silly female. "What makes you think I'm worried about that low-down gunslinger? I hope to God he never comes back!"

Angrily, Jessie rose from the table and hurried from the dugout. Gabe shook his head in exasperation and said to Pedro, "She's gotta be the most obstinate female on this earth."

Jessie rushed into the darkness and headed for the corral where her prized mares were kept, hoping to find some solace there. One of the mares nickered a soft greeting and stuck her nose through the railing of the corral, begging to be petted. Jessie stroked the horse's neck, muttering, "We don't need him, do we? All males are good for is breeding and bossing us females around."

The mare gave Jessie a quizzical look that made her laugh despite her misery. "You don't agree, huh? Well, I guess it's different with horses. You need a stallion to protect you. But I don't need a man. I got along without him just fine before he came into my life, and I can do it again. All I need is my ranch."

Despite her brave words, Jessie felt an emptiness filling her. Tears rose in her eyes, and she furiously brushed them away. She forced herself to concentrate on her ranch and her dream.

Suddenly she knew that Morgan was there. She sensed his presence, rather than saw or heard him. As he stepped closer the warmth from his body surrounded her, a soothing balm to her tortured soul, and she could smell his distinctive scent. A rush of joy ran through her, but perversely she kept her back to him.

"Jess, we need to talk," Morgan said softly.

His deep voice caressed her, and Jessie steeled herself to his powerful male magnetism. "We have nothing to talk about," she answered stiffly.

Morgan took her shoulders in his hands and turned her to face him, saying, "Yes, we do, Jess. We have a lot to discuss."

Stubbornly, Jessie kept her face averted. Morgan cupped her chin in his large hand and lifted her head, forcing her to look at him. Jessie tried to jerk away, but Morgan tightened his grip. "No, Jess, I want you to see my face when I tell you this."

"Then say it and get it over with!" Jessie flared out in frustration. Already, her traitorous body was responding to his nearness. The devil! He had but to touch her and she melted.

"Jess, I apologize for what I did this afternoon. When I made my promise not to interfere in your mustanging, I was sincere. But this afternoon I wasn't thinking. I was just reacting."

Jessie glared at him mutely.

Morgan released her chin and ran his hand through his thick, dark hair. "Jesus, Jess. You scared the hell out of me! I must have died a thousand deaths before your horse regained her footing."

Jessie couldn't believe her ears. Morgan had faced cold-blooded killers without a flick of an eyelash. He had nerves made of steel. But she heard the anguish in his voice. He cares that much? she thought, filled with the wonder of it. For a brief moment a part of Jessie desperately wanted Morgan to say he loved her, while another part didn't, fearing a proposal would follow, and Jessie didn't know if she wanted that. Marriage was a serious step, a lifetime commitment that would mean giving up her freedom forever. As his wife, she would have to go where he went, do what he wanted, give up her dream. She couldn't do that. But still, she wanted him for as long as she could have him without giving up her freedom.

She chose her words very carefully. "I appreciate your concern, Morgan, but what I'm doing isn't danger-ous. For another woman, yes—but not for me. I've been mustanging since I was a child. Believe me, I know what I'm doing. I don't take unnecessary risks. None of us do."

"I guess it's all so new to me," Morgan muttered. "It seems everything you do is dangerous."

"Oh, there are dangers," Jessie admitted. "But we know how to protect ourselves." She laughed. "Did you know that my *mesteñeros* are absolutely terrified of the longhorns? That they call them the devil cows? That they think cowhands are the most fearless people in the world because they take such risks? You see, it's all what you're accustomed to."

Morgan smiled, saying, "All I can promise is I'll try not to worry."

Jessie recalled that all she had promised was to try. She supposed she couldn't ask for more from Morgan. Then she remembered something else. "But don't you ever reproach me in front of my men again!"

"I won't, Jess. My fear might be understandable, but jumping on you in front of your *mesteñeros* was unforgivable. If I have anything to say, I'll keep it between us."

Jessie felt as if a tremendous load had been taken from her shoulders, and all of her senses sprang to life as she became aware of the gentle evening breeze and the moonlight bathing the landscape in a subdued white light. Above her, a million stars glittered in the dark sky and the soft night sounds filled her ears. A sheer joy in living filled her soul. "It's a beautiful night," she commented, looking about her.

"Not nearly as beautiful as you."

There was a roughened timbre in Morgan's voice that made Jessie's heart hammer wildly in her chest. She saw that his eyes were glowing with desire.

He held out his hand. "Will you come with me?"

Jessie didn't ask where. It didn't matter. At that moment he could have asked her to jump off the ends of the earth, and she would have gladly done so. She nodded and took his hand.

Spying a blanket thrown over the corral railing, Morgan picked it up and flung it over his shoulder.

Jessie laughed. "Maria will have a fit when she comes for her freshly washed blanket and discovers we've stolen it."

"She'll never know it was us." He grinned. "Let her think some night creature made off with it."

Morgan led her into the woods that ran between the camp and a creek running behind it. Patches of moonlight filtered down through the lacy mesquite leaves and dabbled the ground in a soft white. To Jessie's eyes, the world around her seemed a magical fairyland, so beautiful that words could never describe it.

Then, as Morgan bent to avoid a low-hanging limb, Jessie spied the glistening drops of water in his thick dark hair. She came to a dead halt. "You've just bathed?"

"Yes, down at the river, before I returned to camp."

For the first time since he had stepped up to her by the corral, Jessie noticed that he was wearing fresh clothing. Suddenly she was acutely aware of her dusty clothes and her grimy body. She couldn't let him make love to her tonight.

"What's the matter?" Morgan asked.

"Not tonight, Morgan."

"Why not?"

"Because I haven't bathed yet, and I'm filthy. I must smell as bad as one of my horses."

"I don't care. I'm used to the smell of horses," Morgan answered with a twinkle in his eyes.

"But I care," Jessie insisted.

"All right, if it's going to make you self-conscious, then we'll get you a bath first," Morgan answered, taking her hand firmly in his and leading her away.

When they stood beside the narrow creek, Jessie said, "I can't bathe in that. The bottom is muddy. As soon as I wade in, I'll stir it up. Why, I'd be dirtier when I got out than when I went in."

"Then you'll have to settle for a sponge bath," Morgan said calmly, unbuttoning her shirt, then deftly slipping it off her shoulders and down her arms.

When he reached for her belt buckle, Jessie said, "I'll do it."

"No, Jess, I'll do it," Morgan replied in a tone of voice that brooked no argument.

Without another word Morgan stripped Jessie of her remaining clothing. When he dipped his bandanna into the creek, Jessie realized that he intended to bathe her too.

As he rose, Jessie opened her mouth to object, but Morgan stopped her. "Sshh, Jess."

He started with her face, gently wiping the dust from it. Then he dipped the large bandanna once again into the creek. "Now lift up your hair."

Jessie obeyed, acutely conscious of her breasts jutting out as she did so. Over and over Morgan wrung the sopping-wet scarf out over her shoulders, letting the cool water run down her body until she was standing in a small puddle. Then, when he began to wash her, Jessie flushed hotly, for he didn't miss an inch, and his tending to her personal needs seemed so very intimate. As the bandanna swirled around her breasts, over her legs, and then between them, Jessie began to tingle all over. Then she realized that this bath was more than just the washing of the dirt from her body, it was a preliminary to their lovemaking.

Suddenly anxious to have the bath over with so she could touch him, too, she said breathlessly, "That's enough, Morgan."

"Hush, sweetheart. I haven't finished yet."

He tossed the bandanna aside and slipped off his shirt, drying her with it. He lingered over her breasts, the coarsely woven cotton mildly abrasive and driving her wild as he brushed it back and forth over her tender nipples. When he dropped to his knees and dried her buttocks and legs, Jessie thought she would go mad if he didn't stop tormenting her. He seemed intent on touching her everywhere except where she ached for him the most.

Finally, Morgan tossed the shirt aside and spread the blanket out on the ground. He shed his clothes quickly. As he walked toward her in all his splendid naked glory, Jessie held out her arms to him, a ragged cry of relief escaping her lips. She embraced him tightly, thrilling to the feel of their feverish bodies coming together, eagerly lifting her mouth to his.

Morgan didn't disappoint her as he kissed her passionately and deeply, making her muscles quiver and her nerves tingle. Her head spun dizzily as Morgan lifted her and curled her legs around his hips. She cried out in surprise as he thrust deeply into her. Her eyes flew open, her lips parting to object.

But Morgan didn't give her time to voice her objection as his mouth captured hers again, his artful tongue ravishing her mouth and sending her senses reeling. Nor had she any need to worry about his dropping her. Morgan was fully in control, his thrusts powerful and deep. Jessie surrendered to the firestorm that was engulfing her as she wrapped her arms around his neck, her tongue dueling erotically with his, her slender legs greedily clasping his hips and squeezing so hard, Morgan groaned in a mixture of pain and delight. Jessie's senses swelled until they seemed to burst from an excess of pleasure and she threw back her head and cried out with ecstasy, giving herself up to the dark void that claimed her.

The next thing Jessie knew, she was lying on the blanket and Morgan was hovering over her.

"What happened?" she asked, feeling dazed.

"I believe the French call it 'the *petit mort*,' the little death."

"You mean I actually lost consciousness?" Jessie asked in amazement.

Morgan laughed softly, saying, "There's a lot you don't know about lovemaking, Jess." He nibbled her earlobe, whispering in a voice that immediately rekindled Jessie's desire. "But I intend to teach you, sweetheart. Everything."

And Morgan kept his promise, loving her over and over, teaching her things Jessie had never dreamed of in her wildest fantasies. By the time they walked back to camp, there was a silver streak in the eastern sky and Jessie glowed, knowing the true meaning of being well loved.

Chapter 15

WHEN JESSIE WALKED FROM HER SMALL BEDROOM the next morning, she was disconcerted to see Gabe and Pedro sitting at the table with Morgan drinking coffee.

Gabe turned to her, saying with a mischievous glint in his eyes, "Wondered when you was gonna come out of your room. Ain't like you to sleep so late. You sick or something?"

To Jessie's horror she felt a slow flush creep up her face. Quickly she turned away, snapping over her shoulder, "Of course I'm not sick! I've never been sick a day in my life. I was just tired . . . from capturing that herd yesterday," she added, knowing full well it was a lame excuse.

Gabe chuckled. If he hadn't already been suspicious, the guilty flush on Jessie's face was a dead giveaway. He might be an old fool, but he wasn't stupid. Obviously the two had slipped off someplace last night.

Gabe felt the toe of Pedro's boot rapping on his shin.

He looked across the table to see the old *mesteñero* frowning, his look warning Gabe not to bait Jessie any further. Oh, hell, Gabe thought in disgust. That old pepper-eater ain't got no sense of humor at all.

Rising from the table, Gabe said gruffly, "Well, I reckon I got work to do." He shot Pedro a resentful look, then stomped from the dugout.

Relieved that Gabe and his all too knowing grin were gone, Jessie turned and walked to the table with her cup of coffee. Sitting down beside Pedro, she asked, "How is the herd doing?"

"Hungry and thirsty, naturally, since we have not fed or watered them."

"You starve them?" Morgan asked with a disapproving frown.

"Not really, *señor*. We only withhold water and food for a day or two. *Mesteñas* can go for days without either, so it is not really cruel. Rather, it is a matter of discipline. When we finally hobble them on the prairie and allow them to graze, it is a reward for good behavior."

"What about the stallions?" Jessie asked. "Have you turned them loose yet?"

"*Sí, patrona*. We roped and brought them out of the pen this morning."

At the mention of stallions, Morgan leaned across the table and asked Jessie, "Would you mind if I skip the shooting lessons today?"

Jessie wondered if Morgan felt too tired to give the lessons after their long night of lovemaking. She wouldn't be surprised. She had been amazed at his endurance. She herself was a little tired and just a little sore. But she didn't regret it. If given the chance, she'd do it all over again—gladly.

"No," Jessie said, "if the chase yesterday tired you out, too, I don't mind if you skip the lessons today."

Morgan's lips twitched with amusement, knowing full well Jessie meant his lovemaking and not the mustang chase. "I'm not tired. If anything, I found it exhilarating," he answered, causing Jessie's cheeks to color once again. "I just had a little business in mind."

"What business?" Jessie blurted, then, thinking that Morgan would resent her sticking *her* nose into *his* business, she said, "I'm sorry. I didn't mean to pry."

"I don't mind your asking. As a matter of fact, I was going to ask for your help."

"My help?"

"Yes. You see, I want to capture the *palomino* stallion."

"The *palomino*?" Jessie asked in surprise. "But why?"

Morgan shrugged. "I've taken a fancy to him. Despite what you say about stallions not making good saddle mounts, I'd like to try."

"Morgan, that *palomino* isn't any ordinary stallion," Jessie argued. "He's a herd stallion, and a strong one. You saw the size of his *manada* and how he fought that black horse for his mares. His herding instincts run deep. He's used to dominating, not to being dominated. You could never master him, never break him to a saddle."

"I'd still like to try," Morgan answered with an appealing grin.

When Morgan smiled at her that way, Jessie felt powerless. She would have given him the moon and stars, if it were possible. She turned to Pedro, asking, "What do you think?" hoping the old man would take the burden of having to disappoint Morgan from her.

"Ah, *señor,* what the *patrona* says is true. That one

does have powerful herding instincts." Then, to Jessie's surprise, he added, "But he is magnificent, no? A horse to inspire a man's imagination."

"Pedro, you shouldn't encourage him," Jessie rebuked the old man. "You know it's impossible."

"Pardon, *patrona*, but this time I must disagree. A challenge, *sí*. But impossible? No, I believe it can be done, with much care and time." Turning to Morgan, he said, "He will never be a workhorse, but a fine horse for riding, or even racing, perhaps. But, *señor*, you must be very careful not to break his *brío escondido*, his hidden vigor," Pedro cautioned gravely. "That is what makes him so beautiful, so magnificent."

"I know. One out of three mustangs die the first year of captivity because their spirits have been broken. That's why I'm asking your help. You're both experts."

"It is the *patrona*'s decision, *señor*," Pedro answered, throwing the ball right back in Jessie's lap.

Morgan looked at Jessie expectantly. When she continued to frown at him, chewing her bottom lip in indecision, he added a bit of enticement. "If I capture that stallion, Jess, his mares will be yours for the taking."

Morgan had to laugh at the sudden gleam that came into Jessie's eyes.

"*Sí, patrona,*" Pedro said in an excited voice. "And you could get ten dollars for each of those fine mares, instead of the usual five."

"I wouldn't sell those mares, Pedro," Jessie snapped. "I'd add them to my herd of breeding mares for my ranch." Then, realizing what she had said, Jessie flushed, and both Pedro and Morgan laughed.

"All right," Jessie conceded, "you tricked me into agreeing. But Morgan, you'll have to follow Pedro's instructions. I won't stand by and see a beautiful animal like that stallion destroyed by anyone's mishandling."

"I will, Jess. I promise. I don't want to see him destroyed either." He rose from the table in a burst of excitement. "Well, let's go!"

Now? Jessie thought in dismay. She was exhausted, and the thought of riding her horse for miles and miles didn't at all appeal to her, particularly since she was already a little sore between her legs.

She sighed in relief when Pedro said, "No, *señor,* not today. Early in the morning, after the stallion has watered, is the best time. Then his muscles will be stiff and his wind shortened. He cannot run as fast."

Morgan frowned, saying, "I don't even know where he waters."

"Ah, *señor,* mustangs are creatures of habit. They always water in the same place. And I think I know where that stallion's place is. We shall try there first."

Rising from the table, Pedro said to Jessie, *"Con permiso,* I will make the *lazo de los animales* now."

"Yes, Pedro, that will be fine," Jessie answered.

After Pedro had left, Morgan asked, "What was he talking about?"

"It's a custom of the *mesteñeros.* With every herd taken, a certain number of horses are lassoed and removed from the herd to be set aside. The money brought from their sale is paid to a priest to say mass for the souls of the *mesteñeros* who have been killed in performance of their duties. For every hundred horses captured, one *lazo,* or two horses, is set aside."

It was a sobering thought. "Maybe I shouldn't have asked for your help," Morgan said. "I wouldn't want anything to happen to any of your men just because I took a fancy to a horse."

Jessie laughed, saying, "I don't think you could stop Pedro now if your life depended on it. Didn't you see the way his eyes were glittering with excitement? No, he or any of the others wouldn't be able to turn down that challenge. But if it will make you feel better, I'll ask for volunteers."

True to her words, Jessie called her *mesteñeros* together that evening and explained what Morgan wanted to do. It was like waving a red flag in front of a bunch of bulls, for they all wanted to go on the expedition. To them, capturing a single stallion and pitting their individual strength against his power was much more challenging than taking an entire herd by stampeding it into a pen. In the end, Pedro had to choose from the volunteers, selecting the six men he knew were the best ropers. As the rejected men walked away, disappointment spread all over their faces, Morgan felt sorry for them.

After the Mexicans had left, Pedro turned to Morgan, Jessie, and Gabe, who were standing outside the dugout, saying, "I think it would be wise to retire early tonight. We will leave at four in the morning."

"So early?" Morgan asked.

"It has to be that early," Gabe answered before Pedro could open his mouth. "We have to set up the trap before that stallion brings his herd down to water at dawn."

"I was hoping you would stay here at the camp, Gabe," Jessie said. "In case something goes wrong while we're gone."

"Hell, no, I ain't staying here! I ain't about to miss out on this, even if Pedro didn't choose me as one of the ropers," Gabe answered, shooting Pedro a resentful look.

"You're going along?" Morgan asked Jessie.

Seeing the fear clouding his eyes, Jessie answered, "Don't worry. I don't intend to participate. I know I'm not strong enough to hold on to those ropes once they're around that powerful stallion's neck. Gabe and I will just observe from a safe distance."

As Gabe started to object, Jessie faced him squarely, saying in a determined voice, "It's either that, or you stay here, Gabe. Pedro is in charge of this expedition, and he's chosen the men he wants."

Noting the determined gleam in Jessie's eyes, Gabe nodded sullenly, then turned and stomped away, grumbling something about "pepper-eaters" under his breath.

After Pedro had excused himself, an embarrassed expression on his swarthy face, Morgan observed quietly, "There seems to be a problem between those two."

"It's Gabe who's the problem, not Pedro. Gabe resents Pedro's being the head *mesteñero*. He seems to think that because he was my father's best friend, he should have that position. But I can't give him the responsibility, Morgan. He doesn't begin to know as much about horses and mustanging as Pedro does. I keep trying to point out that there are other things I need his help in, like the business end, but he wants to be in on the action."

Morgan nodded. He could see her dilemma.

It was pitch-dark when the expedition rode from the camp early the next morning, everyone excited about the prospect of capturing the *palomino*. Apparently the stallion had somewhat of a reputation among the Mexicans. His fierce bid for freedom when he had attacked the blanket on his previous capture had earned the men's admiration, so much so that they spoke of him with awe. Time and time again, Morgan heard the Mexicans refer to the stallion as *el magnífico, el furioso,* or *el dragón.* He could understand the first two descriptions. The *palomino* was magnificent and fierce. But he was puzzled by the latter.

"Why do they call the *palomino* the dragon?" he asked Jessie.

"If you had seen him that day he attacked the blanket, you'd know. He seemed to grow ten times in size before our very eyes. His eyes had a red glow to them, and when he lunged for that blanket, I could have sworn he was breathing fire." She shivered. "I've never seen anything like it."

About eight miles from camp Pedro led the expedition into a break in the trees that hugged the Nueces, and reined in. Beyond them Morgan could hear the soft murmuring of the river.

"Here, *señor,*" Pedro said to Morgan. "This is where I believe your stallion waters."

Morgan glanced around for mustang sign, straining his eyes in the darkness. Finally spying the mounds of dung, he trotted his horse closer to the river, leaned from his saddle, and peered at the ground. He saw the prints of hundreds of hooves that had dried in the mud, and a big grin spread over his face. "Well, obviously this is some stallion's water hole."

"*Sí, señor,* and I am gambling that it's your *palomino*'s from the number of hoofprints. Few stallions have such large *manadas.* Most cannot control so many mares."

Morgan wondered how the stallion managed it, and thanked God it was not his problem. He had his hands full with just one female.

Pedro stood in his stirrups and carefully looked over the area. No one spoke, knowing the old man was deciding how to lay the trap. Finally he licked his forefinger and held it up, testing the direction of the wind.

Sitting back in his saddle, Pedro turned to Morgan. "This is my plan. My men will wait behind that line of brush over there." He pointed to a darkened area about a half mile away. "We will hope it is thick enough that the stallion will not see them. He will wait until all of his mares have drunk before he waters. When my men see him coming from this path from the river and into the open, they will rush forward."

"We'll wait there, too, Pedro," Jessie said, shooting Gabe a warning look that made the old man turn his head away and grumble under his breath.

"What about us?" Morgan asked the old man. "Where are you and I going to hide?"

Calmly, Pedro pointed to the top of a huge mesquite tree whose limbs overhung the pathway the mustangs would have to take to get to the river. "Up there."

"We're going to hide in a tree?" Morgan asked in disbelief.

Pedro grinned at Morgan's astonished expression and answered, *"Sí, señor."*

"But they're bound to smell us, with us sitting right on top of that pathway."

"No, *señor*. Scents drift up, not down."

"Then the *palomino* will see us," Morgan argued.

"No, *señor*, that is a peculiarity of wild horses. They look around, but never up. As many times as they are jumped by panthers hiding in trees, you would think they would have learned, but they have not. Of course, we will have to be very careful he does not spy us from a distance. That is why I choose that tree. Its limbs are thick enough to hide behind as he approaches. Besides, it is the last tree he will have to pass under before he reaches the open prairie again. Our ropes will not get tangled in the other trees."

"We're going to rope him from a tree?" Morgan gasped.

"*Sí, señor.*"

"What are we going to tie our lariats to? A limb?"

"No, *señor,* you will break the stallion's neck, or your rope, if you do that. Our lariats will be tied to our belts."

"Our belts? Why, he'll yank us right out of that tree!"

Pedro shrugged, replying calmly, "*Sí.* I am afraid you had better prepare yourself for a bit of a fall, and some dragging."

Morgan stared at Pedro as if the old man had lost his mind.

"We will not be able to stop him, *señor,* not as excited as he will be, and not alone. We will only slow him down with our weight until the others can arrive."

"Isn't there any other way we can do this?" Morgan asked, not liking the idea of being dragged by a wild horse. "Rope him in the wide open?"

"No, *señor,* he would see us coming. Then the only way you could capture him would be to run him down by relays, until he is too exhausted to run anymore. That could take days."

Morgan disliked the idea of taking days to capture the *palomino* even more than being dragged on the ground. He wanted that horse—today—even if it did mean having a little skin scraped from his hide.

"All right, Pedro, we'll do it your way. But I'm the only one who is going to rope him from that tree. I won't have another man being dragged to hell and back because I've got a fancy for him."

"No, *señor*. I am the head *mesteñero*. That is my job."

"You might break a bone!" Morgan objected.

"I am not as old and frail as I appear!" Pedro snapped back defiantly, surprising Morgan. Usually he was very deferential to Anglos, so much so that he asked permission before he did anything.

Jessie's hand closed over Morgan's arm. "Don't argue with him," she cautioned in a whisper.

Morgan glared at the old man. Pedro sat stiffly in his saddle, looking every inch the proud aristocrat and not at all the humble Mexican that Morgan had become accustomed to. Morgan hadn't meant to hurt Pedro's fierce pride. He simply didn't want anyone injured because of his whim. But he knew if he refused to let the old *mesteñero* join him now, or canceled the whole thing, Pedro would never forgive him.

Morgan sighed. "All right, Pedro, we're in this together. I just hope your men are as swift riders. I don't relish the idea of being dragged across the ground for too long, not with all those rocks lying just beneath the surface and all that cactus around."

Pedro's eyes twinkled with amusement at Morgan's candid admission. "*Sí, señor*, they are fast. Let us just hope that the *palomino* does not drag us over some devil's head."

Morgan winced at the thought. Unlike other cactus, the devil's head had a treacherous spiral thorn on it that, once embedded in the flesh, was impossible to dig out. The more you tried, the deeper it went.

Morgan and Pedro dismounted, removed their lariats from their saddle horns, and handed their reins to two of the *mesteñeros*.

"What about your gun?" Jessie asked Morgan. "Aren't you going to take it off?"

"Nope. I'll keep it on."

"You can't be serious. You know you're going to be dragged. Why, it might misfire, to say nothing of the damage it would sustain."

"I didn't say I was going to wear it when I rope the *palomino*. When I know he's coming for sure, I'll take it off."

Jessie could only shake her head in exasperation. Then she smiled and said, "Well, good luck."

Morgan grinned up at her sitting on her saddle and said, "Can't you do better than that?"

Before Jessie could guess his intent, he reached up and caught the back of her neck, bending her in the saddle and kissing her soundly. When he stepped back, Jessie was blushing in embarrassment and everyone else was grinning from ear to ear, Morgan grinning the widest.

Suddenly Morgan sobered, saying, "Now, remember your promise, Jess. You're only an observer."

Aware of the dangerous thing he was about to do, Jessie swallowed hard. "I will. And you be careful."

Seeing the worried look on her face, Morgan's dark eyebrows arched in surprise. Then he shrugged, thinking it might not be a bad idea for Jessie to get a dose of her own medicine. Then she'd know how he felt when he had to stand by and watch her risk her neck.

After Jessie and the others had ridden off, Pedro said, "We will climb into the tree now."

"Why so soon?" Morgan objected. "It's still an hour before daylight."

"*Sí*, but we want the wind to have time to dissipate our scent here on the ground."

Morgan shook his head in self-disgust, wondering why he hadn't thought of that. He walked to the big mesquite, looped his lariat over one shoulder, and jumped up. He caught a low-lying limb, but his boots kept slipping on the bark.

Sighing deeply, Pedro said, "*Con permiso,* I will go first. Then I can give you a hand up."

Morgan hung by his arms and glared down at the Mexican. His gun, strapped to his hip, felt like a rock dragging him down. Finally he muttered, "Oh, hell!" and let go, dropping to the ground.

Pedro stepped forward once Morgan was out of his way and shimmied up the trunk with ease and agility. While Morgan watched in undisguised disgust, the wiry Mexican made his way to the limb Morgan had been hanging from and crouched on it, saying, "Now, try, *señor.*"

Once again Morgan jumped and caught the limb. With Pedro's help from above, he finally managed to loop one long leg around the limb and lift himself up.

As soon as Morgan was crouched beside Pedro, the *mesteñero* pointed and said, "I will take that limb over there, and you can wait in that one. They are far enough away from each other that our ropes won't get tangled."

Morgan glanced at the branch Pedro had designated as his. It would take some tricky climbing to get to it. "What's wrong with me staying on this one?"

"No, *señor,* it is too low and too near the center of the tree. The others hang out over the prairie."

Morgan slowly made his way to his limb, cursing his slippery boots all the way.

To Morgan, it seemed they were crouched on their branches forever before the sun finally came up, and when it did rise, it took his breath away. Morgan thought there was nothing as beautiful as a sunrise over the prairie—unless it was a sunset. He watched in fascination as the sky turned from a blood red to a soft rose streaked with pinks, lavenders, oranges, and greens, as if nature were trying to display every color in her artist's palette. As the huge orb rose higher and higher, the whole prairie in front of him shimmered in the light reflected from dewdrops on the grass.

Morgan and Pedro weren't the only ones awaiting the sunrise. Suddenly the woods came alive as the mockingbirds' sweet trill and the *coo-coo* of Mexican whitewings filled the air and the other creatures ventured forth to greet the new day.

Morgan scanned the horizon anxiously and, seeing no sign of the *palomino* and his mares, muttered in a disgusted voice, "Well, everything else seems to be up and moving about."

"Patience, *señor*, he will come," Pedro said with a soft chuckle.

Morgan looked around him. The fog that had been rolling off the river was dissipating on the open prairie, but still hovered in the trees. Morgan hoped the herd would come before the sun burned that off too. They needed its concealing haze.

"Look, *señor*!"

Morgan turned so fast at Pedro's excited cry, he almost lost his footing on the limb. A grin spread across his face as he saw the herd of horses in the distance, the *palomino* in the lead. Suddenly his heart hammered wildly.

"You had better take off that bandanna and put it in your pocket, *señor*. The stallion might spy it."

Morgan didn't argue. The red scarf could be seen much easier than the muted browns and grays of their clothing. He whipped it from his neck and stuffed it in his pocket, his eyes still glued on the herd. Next he removed his gun belt and placed it carefully in the fork of two nearby branches.

"Tie your lariat to your belt now, too, *señor,* and hold your loop ready to throw," Pedro instructed.

Morgan quickly did as the old man directed, and when he looked back up, he saw the herd had moved much closer. Then, as the stallion stopped and eyed the opening to the pathway, Morgan sucked in his breath, fearing that the *palomino* had seen them.

He watched breathlessly as the stallion stared at the pathway. Then, raising his graceful neck as far as he could stretch it, the stallion gazed first one way, then the other. With a satisfied snort, the *palomino* trotted forward.

Morgan closed his eyes as the *palomino* passed beneath him, praying that Pedro knew what he was talking about when he'd said the mustang wouldn't look up and their own scent wouldn't drift down. When he opened his eyes, he saw the stallion had passed through and was standing beside the river, pawing at the water.

An overly anxious mare stepped forward and dropped her head to drink. The stallion snorted shrilly and nipped her neck. Startled, the mare whinnied and backed away while the *palomino* sniffed cautiously at the water. Finally deciding it was safe, he stepped back, allowing the mares to surge forward and satisfy their thirst.

While his harem drank their fill, the proud stallion stood back and craned his neck. His ears stood up alertly as his eyes scanned the area around them for anything that might look suspicious. One by one the mares trotted back to the prairie, water still dripping from their muzzles. Only after the last mare had finished and trotted off to feast on the lush grass in the open did the stallion finally drink. Morgan was amazed at his capacity, but glad that he drank so deeply, knowing that the water would stiffen his muscles and the weight of it would slow him down.

When the *palomino* finally lifted his head from the river, he shook it, sending his long, creamy mane flying about him. As the stallion trotted up the path, Morgan tensed with expectation, his heart drumming in his chest. Carefully he slipped his lariat from his shoulder, holding the loop with his hand, keeping one eye on Pedro as he anxiously waited for the old *mesteñero*'s signal.

When the stallion passed beneath him, Morgan felt beads of perspiration breaking out on his forehead. Suddenly his hands turned clammy and numb. He cursed silently, fearing that he wouldn't be able to throw his rope when the time came and would bungle the whole thing.

As the *palomino* cleared the last branch, Morgan saw Pedro rise and begin to twirl his lariat. Cautiously, Morgan came to his feet, fervently wishing at that minute that he had listened to the old man and removed his slippery boots. Standing on a limb and throwing a loop with any accuracy was going to take some balancing.

"Now!" Pedro yelled.

Two ropes flew from the mesquite, and hearing them whizzing through the air, the stallion let out a shrill, warning snort and lunged forward. But his leap for freedom came a split second too late—both loops had fallen over his head. The frightened stallion gave a tremendous jerk and then tore off behind his galloping mares.

Morgan hung on to his rope for dear life as he flew through the air, leaving a score of broken mesquite branches crashing to the ground in his wake. He braced himself as the ground came up at him at an alarming speed, but still the impact knocked the breath from him and sent stars dancing behind his eyes.

As the stallion raced across the prairie, Morgan clung to his rope and pulled with all his might, bouncing along the hard-packed earth like a rag doll, hearing his clothes being ripped to tatters and feeling the skin being torn from his knees and elbows. When his hip smashed into a flat rock, sending him rolling, he grunted in pain, then yelled at the top of his lungs, "You goddamned *mesteñeros!* Where in the hell are you?"

Then he heard the pounding of hooves nearby and looked to the side, seeing three Mexicans racing by him with their lariats twirling over their heads. "Well, it's about time," he muttered in disgust.

With the weight of the two men and his full belly of water dragging him down, it was impossible for the *palomino* to outrace the riders coming at him from three sides, but nevertheless the valiant animal tried. With a burst of amazing strength, he suddenly pulled forward, causing the loops the Mexicans had thrown to sail harmlessly through the air behind him. Muttering curses, the *mesteñeros* quickly gathered in their ropes, urged their horses to a greater speed, and made another throw.

One loop, then another, then another dropped over the stallion's head and landed on his outstretched neck. Violently the stallion shook his head, trying to dislodge the lariats. Gradually the Mexicans whose lariats had caught slowed their speed, and the *palomino* began to feel the increased squeeze on his neck, cutting off his breath. Through blurred eyes he saw yet another loop flying through the air and ducked his head. That loop missed, but the one fast on its heels made its mark.

Staggering now, the stallion made several last desperate attempts to break the ropes around his neck, wildly twisting it this way, then that. The sudden movements only increased the pressure and the great steed fell to his knees.

As soon as the *palomino*'s speed had slowed, Morgan and Pedro were up and running. Impulsively, Morgan ran right up to the stallion, frowning at the raw marks on the mustang's neck where the ropes had chafed his hide and at the alarming way the animal's sides heaved as he drew in great gulps of air.

"Get back, *señor!*" Pedro called. "He still has a lot of fight left in him."

At that moment the stallion struggled to his feet, shaking his head angrily and sending his creamy mane flying. Then, seeing Morgan standing before him, the *palomino* reared on his hind legs, walking toward his enemy, determined to destroy this man who had dared threaten his freedom.

Frantically the *mesteñeros* backed their horses away, once again tightening the ropes around the stallion's neck, their horses pulling with all their might and the ropes so taut, a tightrope walker could have performed on them. But still the *palomino* moved forward, his ears flattened, his teeth bared, his long tail standing straight out.

Morgan watched the *palomino* approach him, mesmerized by the sight. The animal seemed to grow until it was huge, towering over him, its eyes glowing red and shooting sparks, its nostrils flaring as its chest heaved for air, and Morgan felt each rasp of its breath like the blast of a hot furnace.

"Move back, *señor*!" Pedro called in a terrified voice. "He will kill you!"

But Morgan stubbornly refused to yield, sensing that this was the moment of truth between him and this horse. He looked the *palomino* straight in the eye, a look that seemed to infuriate the enraged horse even more. Then, with a shrill, piercing scream that raised the hair on everyone's neck, the stallion gave a tremendous jerk on the ropes that held him, bringing two of the *mesteñeros'* horses to their knees as he lunged at his enemy, his sharp hooves coming within a fraction of an inch of Morgan's head before they hit the ground and shook the earth.

"*¡Madre de Dios!*" one of the Mexicans muttered to himself.

Again the stallion collapsed on his knees, his eyes bulging from the constriction around his neck, and once again he drew in deep drafts of air. Morgan looked down at him with compassion.

Pedro ran up to Morgan, saying, "That was a crazy thing to do, *señor*. You could have been killed!"

"But I wasn't," Morgan calmly pointed out.

Pedro shook his head in exasperation. Then, seeing the wide, victorious grin spreading across Morgan's face, the old man grinned back in perfect understanding. "You are a brave man, *señor*. Foolish, but brave." He glanced down at the stallion. "Now, quickly, before he regains his strength, bend and blow in his nostrils, so he will know your scent. Then tie that bandanna of yours around his neck so your smell will stay with him."

Morgan bent and blew into each nostril. The stallion was still too weak to do any more than shake his head in agitation. However, by the time Morgan had finished tying the bandanna around his neck, the mustang had regained enough strength to snap at his hand.

Morgan jerked his hand back, saying in a stern voice, "No, boy! We'll have none of that."

Once again the *palomino* came to his feet, snorting his indignation, his muscles trembling with rage. The *mesteñeros* held him firmly with their ropes, but not tight enough to choke him.

Jessie and Gabe rode up, leading Pedro's and Morgan's horses behind them. As she jumped from her horse Jessie cried, "Oh, Morgan, he's magnificent!"

Morgan beamed with pride.

Gabe silently gazed at the stallion, then said in an awed voice, "I'll be danged if he ain't as beautiful as the White Steed."

Jessie spun around. "No horse is as beautiful as the White Steed! And none can run as fast as him, either."

"Well, by golly, this one sure comes in a close second for pure good looks," Gabe persisted. "Of course, I don't know how fast he is," he admitted. "He didn't get very far today. But he's prime horseflesh, and if I'm not mistaken, he ain't all mustang either. There's some Thoroughbred blood there."

Pedro moved closer and peered at the *palomino* critically. "*Sí,* I believe he does, *señor.*"

At that point, Morgan couldn't have cared less. With or without Thoroughbred blood, the *palomino* was magnificent—and he was his!

Jessie looked at Morgan. His face was covered with scratches and bruises, and his knuckles were bleeding. His clothes were in tatters, and she could see his scraped knees and elbows. She gave Pedro a quick glance, noting that he didn't look any better. "Are you two all right?"

"Well, I left a little skin out there on the prairie, and I feel like a train ran over me, but other than that, I'm fine," Morgan answered. He turned to Pedro, saying, "How about you?"

"A few scrapes and bruises, but nothing serious," the Mexican answered. Then, with a twinkle in his dark eyes, he said, "Ah, *señor,* but it was worth it, *sí?*"

Morgan turned his gaze back to the *palomino,* saying with pride, "It certainly was." Then, anxious to start breaking him in, he asked, "When do we take him back to camp?"

"Not until I put this rawhide strap on his front ankle," Pedro answered, pulling the strap from his saddle where he had tied it.

As the old man stepped forward Morgan held out his hand, saying, "I'll do it."

"No, *señor,* let me. It will be dangerous."

"He's my horse, Pedro. I want him to know who his master is from the very beginning."

Reluctantly the old man relinquished the strap, warning, "Watch out for his hooves."

"I guess if I can dodge a longhorn's hooves and horns while I'm branding him, I can manage this."

As Morgan walked to the stallion, approaching him from the side, Pedro turned to Jessie, a questioning look on his face.

"Morgan used to be a cowman," Jessie informed the old man.

The Mexican's eyebrows rose in surprise. "He has worked with the devil cows?"

"Yes, when he was younger."

Jessie laughed as a look of sheer awe came over Pedro's wrinkled face.

Seeing Morgan approaching him from the corner of

his eye, the *palomino* snorted a warning and twisted his back, his hind legs lashing out with a vengeance. Morgan jumped back from the razor-sharp hooves, swearing under his breath. The Mexicans tightened the ropes around the stallion's neck, again choking him. When the *palomino*'s muscles began to tremble and he fell to his knees for the third time, Morgan quickly scrambled beneath him and tied the strap to his front right ankle. Alarmed at the horrible gurgling sounds the horse was making as he struggled for breath, Morgan jumped back, yelling, "Ease up on those damned ropes! You're killing him!"

Hurriedly the *mesteñeros* did as he commanded. Morgan watched, feeling sick to his stomach, as the stallion again sucked in deep gulps of air, his eyes still dazed-looking. Running his hand through his dark hair, Morgan muttered, "Jesus! I wish there was an easier way. This seems so damned cruel."

"So do I," Pedro answered compassionately. "But unfortunately it is the only way to control these powerful animals until we have them hobbled. And with this one, as fierce as he is, it would not be wise to remove the ropes too soon. But already he is learning. See how still he stands?"

Morgan looked back at the stallion, seeing that once again the horse had come to his feet. But, despite his stillness, Morgan knew the stallion was far from being submissive. The *palomino*'s eyes glittered with defiance.

"Loosen the ropes, so he can learn the purpose of the strap," Pedro called to his men.

The *mesteñeros* moved their horses forward, giving the ropes the most slack they'd had up to then. Mistakenly thinking he was free, the stallion lunged, only to trip himself on the strap and tumble to the ground. Coming to his feet, he shook his head in bewilderment, then lunged again, taking another hard fall, the air coming from his lungs in a loud *whoosh*. He came to his feet with an angry snort, shaking his leg violently. Then, seeing the strap was still there, he bent and bit savagely at it.

"He'll tear his leg off!" Morgan cried in alarm, seeing the wounds the stallion was inflicting on his ankle.

"No, soon he will realize that he can't get the strap off," Pedro assured him.

But it wasn't soon enough for Morgan. It seemed forever before the stallion finally gave up, shaking his mane and snorting in angry frustration.

"Now we will take him to our camp," Pedro said, swinging into his saddle.

Morgan and Jessie mounted, and the *mesteñeros* moved their horses forward, pulling on the ropes around the mustang's neck. The *palòmino* was reluctant to move at all, sticking his long neck out as the ropes tightened, fearing he would fall again. Then the stallion took a tentative step, followed by another, finally realizing that he could walk with the strap on his ankle, but not run.

Morgan glanced at the herd of mares in the distance. At the stallion's first warning snort they had raced away, but now they stood watching curiously. "What about the mares?" he asked Jessie. "Aren't you afraid they'll run off?"

"No, they only scatter if the stallion is killed. They'll follow, at a distance they feel is relatively safe. When we reach camp, we'll rope them and put them into the corral I reserve for my mares." Jessie laughed. "This will be the easiest capture I've ever made."

"Maybe for you it'll be easy, but it certainly hasn't been for me," Morgan said with a wry grin. Turning to his horse, he said over his shoulder, "I'll catch up with you. I have to go back and pick up my gun."

Chapter 16

By the time Morgan reached camp, the palomino had been put into a corral by himself. Morgan was relieved to see that all the ropes had been removed from the stallion's neck except one, which served to tie him to the side of the pen.

"He looks pretty meek right now," Morgan commented to Pedro as he dismounted.

The old man laughed. "Do not be fooled, *señor.* He is only waiting for the right opportunity to make his bid for escape."

Morgan looked around. "Where is everyone?"

"Off roping the mares."

Morgan walked up to the corral, placed his foot on one of the crossbars, and pulled himself up on it, allowing himself a minute or two to admire his prize. Then he asked, "What's next on the agenda?"

"We will withhold water and food for two days."

"What if he refuses to eat?" Morgan asked, a worried

frown on his face. "I've heard of mustangs starving themselves to death rather than submit to captivity."

"*Sí*, that is true, but I do not think this one is so stupid. No, he is too fierce, too full of life, to take that way out."

"So I don't do anything for two days?"

"No, *señor,* I did not say that. You will stay with the stallion, live every minute with him, even sleep with him."

"Sleep with him? You mean, I've got to sleep out here?"

"*Sí,* and do not bathe or change your clothes, so he can familiarize himself with your scent."

"But my clothes are in tatters," Morgan objected.

"Then change your outer clothing, but keep on your underwear," the *mesteñero* conceded with a shrug of his shoulders.

Morgan glared at the old man. As ripped as his clothing was, Pedro knew damned well he wasn't wearing any underwear.

His black eyes twinkling with amusement, Pedro directed his gaze to the stallion, saying, "In the daytime, walk around the pen and talk to him. It doesn't matter what you say. Just so he becomes accustomed to your presence and your voice."

Morgan frowned, saying, "I don't know how that's going to go over with Jessie. I'm supposed to be giving shooting lessons, remember?"

"The *patrona* won't object. She knew all this before she agreed."

Morgan remembered how much Jessie hated her shooting lessons and wondered if she had taken that into account when she gave her consent.

That night as Morgan spread his bedroll out beside the corral, he muttered darkly to himself, "Dammit, I didn't know what I was getting myself into. I didn't expect to have to play nursemaid."

From inside the pen, the stallion snorted, as disgusted with the sleeping arrangements as Morgan was.

It was all Morgan could do to force himself to walk round and round the pen the next day. His battered body was even sorer and stiffer than the day before, particularly the hip that had hit the rock. That morning he had done a little peeking through the rips in his clothing. What wasn't black-and-blue on him was scraped raw.

The stallion eyed Morgan warily as he limped around the pen, for Morgan's tone of voice was hardly soothing, being mostly made up of angry curses. But as the day wore on and he worked the stiffness out of his body, Morgan began to perform the task in earnest, carrying on a steady stream of talk until the stallion started to act less jumpy.

Everyone stayed away, even Jessie, for all knew this was the critical time when the stallion had to learn to accept one man—and one man only—as his master. When Morgan built his small campfire to cook his food that night, he knew the stallion was beginning to accept him, for the horse wasn't nearly as afraid of the fire as he had been the night before. If anything, the stallion seemed curious, as if wondering how this strange two-legged creature, who insisted upon forcing himself on him, could control that frightening, dangerous element of nature.

The next night Morgan stood beside the pen, smoking a cigarette and admiring the *palomino*. The stallion watched the glowing tip of the cigarette warily, his ears perking up as Morgan asked, "Afraid of this cigarette, are you? There's no need for that, you know. Watch."

Morgan threw the cigarette down and crushed it beneath the heel of his boot, saying, "See, I destroyed the fire. It can't hurt you. I'm not going to let anything hurt you."

At that moment Morgan longed to reach between the rails and stroke the sleek neck, but Pedro had sternly cautioned him not to touch the animal until the stallion had accepted food from him.

"Tomorrow, boy," Morgan promised. "Tomorrow you eat, and we get to be real friends."

Morgan was up with the sun the next morning, gathering dew-dampened grass to feed to the stallion. He wasn't surprised when he returned to the corral and found Pedro waiting for him. The old man was just as anxious as he to see if the stallion would eat.

When Pedro opened the gate and Morgan stepped inside the corral, the stallion backed away, his eyes warning Morgan away. Then, as Morgan walked confidently toward him, the *palomino*'s look became more curious than hostile. Morgan placed the bucket of water before the mustang and carried in an armful of grass, laying it at the stallion's feet. Then he backed away, watching anxiously.

For a few moments it looked as if the stallion would refuse both, and Morgan felt heartsick. If the *palomino* refused, he would turn him loose rather than stand by and watch him starve to death, Morgan decided. Then, very cautiously, the horse bent his neck to sniff the water, pawing at it and inadvertently knocking the bucket over. As the water spilled out the stallion lapped thirstily at the small puddle on the ground.

Morgan held his breath as the mustang turned his attention to the grass. Having been picked and carried by him, every blade held his scent. When he saw the stallion take a tentative bite, it was all Morgan could do to keep from jumping up and down with joy.

Morgan and Pedro stood aside, both beaming with pleasure as the stallion ate, then drank from the bucket of water Morgan had refilled for him.

When the *palomino* had finished drinking his fill, Pedro said, "Now, *señor,* touch him, but very carefully. He is used to your voice and scent, but your touch will be something entirely new to him."

Morgan's heart pounded in anticipation as he raised his hand and cautiously touched the stallion's neck. The mustang snorted, his tail twitched, but he didn't move away, offering Morgan encouragement. Deliberately keeping his touch light, Morgan gently ran his fingers over the animal's neck, marveling at the powerful muscles there. The stallion stiffened, but still Morgan kept stroking him, then gently scratched his ear.

The ear twitched, and then, to Morgan's surprise, the stallion bent his head toward Morgan's hand, silently begging for more of this new, pleasant sensation.

Morgan chuckled, saying, "You like that, huh? Well, anytime you want your ear scratched, you just come to me."

"Here, give him this," Pedro said, handing Morgan a piece of the brown sugar candy the Mexicans ate. "No horse can resist *pilonce.* But rub your hands over it first, so he will not smell my scent."

Morgan rubbed his hands over the candy and then held it cupped in one hand under the mustang's nose. As the stallion lowered his head Morgan held his breath, realizing just how vulnerable he was at that moment. If he wanted to, the stallion could easily bite his hand off.

But the *palomino* was much more interested in the candy than in Morgan's hand. As he munched on the sweet, his tail switched back and forth, and Morgan had to bite back a laugh.

"Now, remove the rope," Pedro said.

Morgan slipped off the rope and tossed it to the side. The stallion eyed it with wonder as it lay on the ground. Then he snorted, as if to show his distaste.

"Work with him today," Pedro instructed. "Pet him, talk to him, feed him, encourage him to walk about the pen. Tomorrow we will try the bridle."

As Pedro walked away Morgan called, "Hey, can I bathe and change clothes now?"

"Change your clothes, but no bathing yet," Pedro called back over his shoulder. "You don't want to wash away your scent."

"Jesus," Morgan grumbled, "even with fresh clothes I'll still stink to high heaven." He turned to the stallion, saying, "See what I go through for you?"

The *palomino* nickered and poked his velvety-soft muzzle into Morgan's hand, looking for more candy.

Ten days later Morgan and Jessie walked to the corral where the *palomino* was kept. Jessie had to run to keep up with Morgan's long, quick strides. But then, she supposed she'd be just as anxious if it were her. Today Morgan would mount the stallion for the first time.

She had been amazed at Morgan's patience with the animal. She had come to expect that kind of patience from Pedro, but had never dreamed Morgan capable of it. The process of preparing the stallion for this day had been a slow, tedious one. Two days had been spent accustoming him to the feel of the bridle, and another two days, to the weight of the saddle blanket on his back. Then the saddle had been added, followed by baskets tied to each side in which rocks were placed, the weight steadily increased each day. Today the stallion would carry a man for the first time—or at least they all hoped so.

"Are you sure you won't let me ride him first?" Jessie asked. "My weight would be less of a shock to him."

"No," Morgan answered emphatically, "he's my horse and I'll be the first human on his back. I'm the one who will be riding him, so he might as well get used to my weight from the very beginning."

Everyone in the camp crowded around the corral as Morgan saddled the *palomino,* including the two Mexican women. When Morgan led the stallion from the pen, there were many "ohs" and "ahs" of admiration. Then the crowd moved back, giving the man and horse plenty of room.

Morgan looped the reins over the stallion's neck and placed his foot in the stirrup, crooning, "Easy, boy. It's just me."

The stallion remained unperturbed. The weight on his side was much the same as the basket filled with rocks. But as Morgan swung into the saddle and settled his full weight in, the *palomino* went stiff with shock. Knowing what was coming, everyone scrambled back, and Morgan squeezed his legs in anticipation. The mustang went straight up, and Morgan's head snapped back as he flew into the air, then forward when the horse hit the ground on all four hooves, coming down with such force that Morgan bit his tongue and every bone in his body screamed. Still feeling the weight on his back, the stallion reared, trying to shake Morgan off, then reversed the position, kicking out wildly. As the mustang twisted and turned, bucking furiously, Morgan grimly held on, giving the terrified animal his head as the landscape and faces around him spun dizzily.

The dust rolled around the man and beast, and above the stallion's angry snorts and pounding hooves, Morgan could hear the *mesteñeros* yelling encouragement. Then, just as Morgan had hoped he would, the stallion tore off in a dead run.

Morgan made no attempt to guide the *palomino*, or to use his reins in any manner, and the stallion ran like the wind, tearing across the the rolling prairie, jumping mesquite brush, clumps of cactus, and dry creek-beds. Morgan gloried in the exhilarating ride as the wind whipped past his face and the ground sped by beneath him. He seemed to be flying, the scenery a mere blur to his eyes.

"Atta boy! Go!" Morgan urged, and the stallion obeyed, as if he, too, were glorying in this wild race, stretching out his sleek neck, his creamy mane whipping in the wind and his long tail trailing behind as his powerful legs gobbled up the ground.

Morgan was amazed at the stallion's endurance as well as his speed. The horse showed absolutely no signs of tiring, despite the unaccustomed weight on his back. He flew into a herd of deer, sending the startled animals scattering in every direction. Finally, Morgan turned him back toward the camp, but the stallion still raced, loath to give up his freedom of movement and reveling in it till the last possible moment.

The *palomino* was breathing hard when he finally slowed to a trot before coming to a stop beside the corral. Sweat glistened on his gray hide and the muscles in his legs quivered from his strenuous workout. But his black eyes were gleaming with satisfaction, rivaling the gleam in the eyes of the man on his back. Followed by everyone else in the camp, Jessie rushed forward as

Morgan dismounted. "Oh, Morgan, that was absolutely splendid!"

"Did you see how fast he ran, Jess?" Morgan asked as he stroked the stallion's neck, his silver eyes glittering with excitement. "Isn't he magnificent?"

Jessie had been speaking of the rider, not of the horse. Not any more magnificent than you, she thought.

"God Almighty, that critter can run," Gabe said. "I told you he had Thoroughbred blood in him."

"*Sí*, he is a true wind-drinker," Pedro agreed.

Morgan was oblivious to their compliments. At that moment he felt he would burst with pride. Only one other time had he felt that emotion so strongly. He turned to Jessie, saying, "I can't ever remember feeling this exhilarated, this proud—except the day you won that race in Dog Town."

Jessie was deeply touched, unable to reply because of the lump in her throat.

Morgan turned to Pedro. "And I could have never done it without you. *Gracias*, Pedro."

"It was my pleasure," Pedro answered in all sincerity. "It is not often that I have the privilege of working with such a splendid animal."

"What are you going to name him?" Jessie asked.

There was no hesitation on Morgan's part. The memory of the stallion towering over him like some huge monster, his eyes glowing red and spitting sparks, his hot breath searing his face, was etched in Morgan's brain. "El Dragón."

A murmur of approval ran through the crowd. Even Jessie approved. She gazed at Morgan proudly, thinking that not many men were strong and courageous enough to tame a dragon.

That evening the Mexicans held a small fiesta to celebrate Morgan's victory. After a sumptuous meal of spicy food, the *mesteñeros* brought out their guitars. Rousing songs of victory filled the air, followed by a passionate fandango to which the two *mesteñeros* and their wives danced. As Morgan watched the couples teasing and tormenting, the women's naked legs flashing in the firelight as the music changed in rhythm from slow to quick, he felt his own passion rising.

Drawing Jessie aside, he whispered, "Let's ride to the river."

Morgan wasn't the only one affected by the dance. The throbbing music had sent Jessie's blood pounding, that and just being near the rugged, virile gunfighter standing next to her. Her heart quickened as she glanced about them.

Seeing her look, Morgan said, "No one will notice our leaving."

As he led her away into the brush, Jessie laughed. "No, I don't suppose they will. I never realized how many bottles of tequila my men had hidden away in this camp."

At Morgan's insistence they would ride double on his gelding, not trusting the *palomino* to accept Jessie's weight too. The old cow horse seemed inordinately pleased to see them, and Morgan realized he had been neglecting his old friend.

"Sorry, fella," he said softly as he stroked the gelding's neck. "I didn't mean to leave you out. I promise it won't happen again in the future."

The gelding nickered softly, almost as if he had understood and had already forgiven Morgan.

Morgan quickly saddled the horse and swung into the saddle, holding his hand down to help Jessie mount. As she started to swing up behind him, Morgan caught her waist and placed her in front of him, saying, "No, I want to hold you."

Jessie was more than willing. She straddled the saddle and leaned back, glorying in the feel of Morgan's hard body behind her. Slipping one arm around her waist to bring her even closer, Morgan kneed the horse, and the gelding trotted off.

As they rode through the dark, the whisper-soft breeze in their ears, Morgan couldn't hold back his impatience to love Jessie. He bent his head, nuzzling her soft neck, his tongue dancing over the silky flesh, his teeth nibbling gently. Jessie arched her neck, feeling a warmth creep over her. His hand rose to cup one breast, the fingers massaging. Then, unbuttoning her blouse, he slipped his hand inside and claimed one lush mound possessively. Jessie squirmed in the saddle as Morgan's fingers flicked back and forth over the throbbing peak, teasing it until it stood hard and erect.

"God, I wish I could taste you there, sweetheart," Morgan whispered against her ear, his tongue darting in and out.

Shivers ran through Jessie at the erotic sensations Morgan's fingers and tongue were evoking. She gasped in surprise as she felt her belt give way and Morgan's fingers busy at her buttons. Then, as his hand smoothed over her abdomen and his fingers slid between her legs, she flushed, feeling a wetness slip from her.

Weakly she objected. "No, Morgan, not here, not—"

Her breath caught as his fingers found the throbbing bud, circling and teasing. When he dropped the reins and his other hand caressed her breast, his fingers on both hands playing havoc on her senses, Jessie vaguely wondered who was guiding the horse. Then all thought fled as she gave herself up to the waves of intense pleasure washing over her.

Weak with fulfillment, Jessie laid her head back on Morgan's shoulder, muttering breathlessly, "That was wicked of you."

Morgan chuckled, dropping kisses over her temple and hairline, before taunting softly, "Yes, but you loved every minute of it."

Despite her recent fulfillment, Jessie felt her passion rising again. As Morgan continued to caress her, she was acutely conscious of his arousal pressing against her buttocks. Each throb of that hard flesh brought a responding one in her own loins. Her lips ached for the feel of his. Twisting in the saddle, she caught his head and pulled it down.

It was a long, torrid kiss that sent the blood surging hotly through their veins. Jessie squirmed against his rigid length, desperately wishing there was some way she could get him inside her. Morgan tore his mouth away, rasping, "Enough!"

Reining in, he jumped from the saddle and swooped Jessie from it, tearing their clothes off impatiently. Then, flinging her to the ground, he came down on her, and Jessie opened to him gladly.

Their sudden, fierce joining caused both to cry out, their bodies arching as they felt a bolt of searing heat rush up their spines and explode in their brains. Then Morgan rode her with a sweet savagery that quickly brought them to that quivering zenith.

Finally regaining some control, Morgan held them there, until Jessie was writhing beneath him, every nerve ending in her body screaming for release, sobbing, "Now, Morgan. I can't stand it any longer. Now!"

With one powerful, deep thrust he sent them over,

groaning as his release came in a white-hot explosion, his life-giving seed a scalding heat deep inside her.

When reality returned, they both gazed about them in a daze, wondering how they had come to be lying on the grass in the open. Then Morgan laughed, drawing her to her feet as he rose, saying, "I'm sorry. I couldn't wait."

"Neither could I," Jessie admitted. She looked about her, then laughed. "Look. There's the river. We almost made it."

Morgan tied his horse to a bush and lifted the rolled blanket from the back of his saddle. As he took Jessie's arm to lead her to the river, she asked, "What about our clothes?"

"Leave them. We don't need them. Besides, I've a mind for a bath." He chuckled. "You know, I had to spend five days without one."

"Was it that bad?"

"Sweetheart, it's a good thing Pedro made you keep your distance those days. I smelled so bad, I couldn't stand myself."

Jessie turned and slipped her arms around his waist. Her hunger for him was on the rise again, and she didn't want to waste their precious time together with bathing. "I don't think you smell bad. I like your manly scent."

"Oh?" Morgan asked, his dark eyebrows rising.

"Yes. It excites me," Jessie answered in a voice that throbbed with seduction, her hand stroking the muscular planes of his chest.

Then, as her hand dipped lower, Morgan tossed the blanket aside and swooped her up in his arms. As he carried her toward the river, Jessie purred in satisfaction and looked up at his face. Then, seeing his wide grin and the almost diabolical gleam in his eyes, she asked in alarm, "What are you doing?"

"I think you need some cooling off, sweetheart. You're just a little too hot for me to handle right now."

Too late, Jessie realized his intent. A squeal of outrage sprang from her throat as she flew through the air. The cool water on her heated senses was like a dash of ice water, taking her breath away as she sank beneath the dark surface.

She came up sputtering and fighting to untangle the hair around her face. She heard Morgan's splash as he dived into the river, then shrieked as he caught her legs and pulled her under.

She came up the second time, her eyes blazing with fury, looking around her wildly. Morgan surfaced behind her with a loud splash, frightening her half out of her wits. She turned to see him shaking the water from his hair, a wide grin on his face.

"You . . . you . . ." she sputtered impotently, then lunged for him. But Morgan darted away, splashing water in her face.

She dived, swimming underwater until she spied the murky form of his legs. Smiling smugly, she reached for them, only to discover Morgan had disappeared in a flash and she was left with a handful of water. Feeling as if her lungs would burst, she surfaced, drawing in great gulps of air.

Morgan waited a short distance away, then taunted, "Can't catch me, can you? What happened to my little water sprite?"

The taunt was too much for Jessie. She'd catch him if it killed her! she vowed. Again she dived, but to her frustration Morgan was as slippery as an eel, and as adept at swimming. Finally giving up, she swam for the shore, calling over her shoulder, "I give up. You must be half fish."

Morgan's laughter boomed out over the water as Jessie waded to the shore. Finding the blanket Morgan had tossed down, she picked it up and dried herself, then spread it on the ground and sat on it, hearing the sound of Morgan still splashing in the river behind her.

She glanced up, seeing the moon was just rising, edging the dark shadows of trees in silver and turning the river into a glittering ribbon as it reflected the light. Then, aware that the splashing was much closer, she turned her head and saw Morgan wading from the river.

Her breath caught as his magnificent male beauty was revealed to her in the moonlight. To her, he looked like a primeval god, hewed in silver. But this god was living and breathing, his muscles rippling with unleashed power, every inch of him radiating strength and virility. Despite the knowing smile on Morgan's face as she devoured him with her gaze, Jessie couldn't take her eyes from him, thinking that he was a magnificent specimen of manhood.

And then, as he towered over her, she caught sight of the discolored area on his hip. She came to her knees, touching it, asking in a concerned voice, "How did that happen?"

"That's where my hip hit a rock when El Dragón dragged me," he answered, sitting beside her.

"Does it hurt?"

"Not anymore," Morgan answered in a distracted tone of voice as he bent and kissed one of Jessie's rosy nipples.

Jessie gasped at the delightful sensation. Morgan

watched in fascination as the nipple puckered, then bent to capture it in his mouth.

"No!" Jessie cried, and pushed him to his back.

Morgan looked up at her in surprise as she knelt over him. She bent to kiss the bruise on his hip tenderly, saying, "Let me soothe your hurts."

Morgan lay while Jessie ran her tongue over his hip. Then, discovering small scars from older wounds, she kissed and licked them, one below his left nipple, another on his shoulder, yet another on his forearm. Then, spying one on his thigh, she moved for it, her long hair trailing over his body, and Morgan sucked in his breath at the sensation.

Then, as Jessie kissed him, Morgan stiffened with surprise. He raised his head and looked down, seeing her sitting on her heels and gazing at him, a seductive smile on her lips.

"This time, it's my turn to love you," she whispered. "Just lie back and enjoy it."

"Jess, I don't think—"

"Sshh! You had your way with me earlier. Driving me out of my mind while we were still on your horse. Now it's my turn."

Morgan groaned and lay his head back down as Jessie took him in her hand, stroking erotically. Placing herself full-length over Morgan's body and holding him firmly between her thighs, she bent and dropped feather-like kisses over his face, down his throat and across his chest, licking away each drop of water she found.

Spying the small pool of water in his navel, she lapped at it, smiling smugly as she saw Morgan's muscles contract. Slipping lower, she followed the fine line of dark hair until it flared, her lips brushing tantalizingly across his groin before she placed a trail of fiery kisses down his hair-roughened leg, then back up again, dallying at his thighs, her tongue a flame of fire against the already feverish flesh.

Morgan was quivering all over when Jessie bent and kissed the tip of him, her touch as light as a butterfly's. Then, as she slid her tongue down the rigid length and back up again, a fine sheen of perspiration broke out on him. When her tongue circled him, his passion flared to a white-hot inferno. He uttered a strangled cry and reached up for her.

But Jessie wasn't about to give up her captive. Loving him in this most intimate way was both exciting her and giving her immense pleasure. She pushed his hands away, whispering, "No!"

Then as her teeth gently grazed him before taking him in her mouth, Morgan was too weak to object, her tongue driving him wild. He arched his back, his breath coming in ragged gasps as she worked her magic on him, pleasuring him beyond belief, taking him to heights he had never dreamed possible. Then, feeling the unbearable pressure building inside him and knowing the end was near, an urgency seized him. He caught her shoulders, pulling her up as he rolled and brought her beneath him, plunging into her tight, moist depths, his body jerking convulsively as he exploded and fireworks went off in his brain.

He was still spinning when he raised his head and looked down at Jessie with dazed eyes. "I'm sorry," he muttered hoarsely. "I couldn't wait any longer, and I wanted to be inside you when it happened." His eyes searched her face. "Did I hurt you?"

"No. I was ready for you. Loving you that way excited me as much as your loving me."

"But what about you? You weren't satisfied."

"Did I please you?"

Morgan laughed shakily. "My God, yes."

"Then that's all the satisfaction I need."

Jessie meant every word she'd said. She cuddled up to him, content to be in his arms.

Morgan held her, rubbing his chin over the soft hair on the top of her head, filled with wonder. "I would have never asked that of you, Jess. It wasn't something you had to do."

"I know, and that's why it pleased me so much. It was a gift of love."

Morgan's heart thudded even faster than it had at the height of his passion. He tightened his grip around her, whispering, "I love you."

Jessie turned her face into the warm crook of his neck, hoping to hide the tears of happiness that had sprung to her eyes at Morgan's words and were now trickling down her cheeks. "I love you too," she muttered.

"I—"

"No, Morgan, don't say anything else. I don't expect or want anything more right now."

In a way, Morgan was relieved. He really had nothing more to offer Jessie. He was a gunfighter by trade, a wanderer. It was certainly no life for a woman, and Jessie deserved much more.

They lay for a long time staring up at the brilliant stars glittering above them. Finally, Morgan said, "According to *el reloj de los Yaquis,* it's two o'clock. We'd better go."

Jessie raised her head, asking, "How did you know about the clock of the Yaquis? The Yaquis are Mexican Indians."

"The Mexican vaqueros always referred to the Big Dipper that way. We used the stars to tell us when it was time to change the night watch when we were on the trail."

"And if it was cloudy?"

Morgan shrugged. "Then we just guessed at the time." He chuckled. "But somehow the last man always got stuck with the longest watch."

Jessie didn't want to leave. She could lie here forever with Morgan's strong arms around her, with the stars as their only blanket, and listening to the murmuring of the river and the whisper-soft breeze. She had never known such utter contentment, such peace.

She laid her head back down on Morgan's shoulder and snuggled against him. "Do we have to leave right now?"

Morgan could feel her soft breasts brushing against his chest each time she inhaled. Her sweet scent filled his senses, and his manhood stirred in anticipation. Rolling her to her back, he placed soft kisses over her face, muttering between them, "No . . . we won't leave . . . not yet."

Chapter 17

TWO DAYS LATER JESSIE AND MORGAN WERE AGAIN beside the river. But to Jessie's utter dismay, their purpose for being there held none of the excitement and delight of their last visit. Morgan had reinstated his shooting lessons.

"I don't know why you insist upon continuing these stupid lessons," Jessie grumbled as she loaded her six-shooter. She gave Morgan a hopeful look. "There're much more enjoyable things we could be doing."

"There's a time and a place for everything—including that. Right now I'm more concerned about your being able to protect yourself." He grinned, his gray eyes shimmering with promise. "The other will come later."

Despite his promise of sensual delights, Jessie continued her tirade. "I don't need any more lessons. I can shoot a pistol much better now. After all, I'm not planning to be a gunfighter, like you."

Morgan chuckled. "I should hope not. Your aim is still lousy."

Jessie glared at him.

"Come on, Jess, stop stalling," Morgan said in a firm voice. "Get that gun reloaded and give that target another try."

Giving a very unladylike snort of disgust, Jessie returned her attention to the gun in her hand. Morgan chuckled and turned to gaze at El Dragón. He was pleased at how well the stallion was adjusting to the sound of gunfire. At first he had reared in terror and tried to bolt, but after two days of being exposed to the loud noises both morning and afternoon, his only reaction now to the roar of a gun was a slight trembling of his muscles. Considering Morgan's trade, that had been a prime requirement for a mount. A gunfighter could hardly ride a horse that stampeded every time he heard a gun go off.

Morgan's eyes narrowed as he spied a line of dust hovering over the mesquite brush to his right.

"Look!" Jessie cried. "Someone's coming!"

"Yes, and whoever he is, he's riding hell for leather," Morgan said, putting himself between Jessie and the intruder and drawing his gun.

As the rider's horse burst from the brush, Jessie cried, "Don't shoot, Morgan! That's Manuel!"

Morgan had never seen the man in his life. "Who in the hell is he?"

"The *mesteñero* I've had out watching for the White Steed. And there's only one reason he'd be riding that way. He's back, Morgan! The White Steed has returned!"

Tossing her six-shooter to the ground, Jessie ran toward the rider, her empty holster slapping at her thigh.

Morgan looked down at the gun lying at his feet, shaking his head in exasperation. How many times had he cautioned Jessie not to toss her gun around so carelessly, particularly with the hammer still resting on a loaded chamber. Dammit, it was a wonder it hadn't misfired and blown his foot off!

Morgan slipped his six-shooter back into his holster and picked Jessie's gun up, rotating the cylinder until the hammer rested on an empty chamber. Then, carrying the gun, he followed Jessie, a deep scowl on his face.

"He's back! He's back, isn't he?" Jessie cried in excitement as the rider reined in, his horse rearing on his hind legs and pawing the air at the sudden stop.

Jumping to the ground, Manuel answered, *"Sí, patrona!* I sighted him this morning."

"Where?"

"Twenty miles upriver." The Mexican's eyes danced with excitement. "Ah, *patrona,* he is as beautiful as ever. So magnificent!"

"Come on. Let's get back to camp," Jessie said, her voice breathless with anticipation.

As she started for her horse Morgan caught her arm and swung her around, saying in a stern voice, "Just a minute, young lady."

The Mexican's eyes widened, wondering who this man was who dared to speak to the *patrona* in such an arrogant manner. Seeing the gun in Morgan's hand, the Mexican's face turned ashen.

Aware of the man's startled expression, Morgan slipped the gun into Jessie's holster, saying, "I believe this belongs to you."

Laughing at the look of relief on Manuel's face, Jessie said, "Manuel, this is Señor West. He's joined our outfit since you were last here."

"My pleasure, *señor*," the Mexican answered, studying Morgan curiously.

Morgan gave the Mexican a curt nod in acknowledgment of the introduction, then turned to Jessie, saying in barely suppressed anger, "How many times have I told you not to toss your gun around like that?"

Jessie ignored his thunderous look and pushed his hand aside. "Oh, Morgan, I don't have time to be bothered with a gun. The White Steed is back."

Jessie rushed away and mounted. As she and Manuel rode away Morgan watched them for a moment, his scowl deepening. "Crazy woman," he muttered, then strode to El Dragón, mounted, and followed them.

When Morgan rode into camp, Jessie was calling out orders and the *mesteñeros* were scattering in every direction to obey. Morgan dismounted and walked up to Jessie, once again catching her arm and whirling her around to face him. "I want to talk to you. Alone!"

"Not now, Morgan. I'm busy. We've got a lot to do, if we're going to be ready to go after that stallion by daybreak."

"Jess, this is important!" Morgan said forcefully.

"And so is what I'm doing!" she replied, then turned her back on him.

Morgan caught her by the shoulder and swung her around, shaking her lightly. "Dammit, listen to me!"

Suddenly aware that every man had stopped what he was doing and was staring at them, Jessie hissed, "Take your hands off me."

Morgan tightened his grip. "No, I won't."

Jessie's eyes flashed angrily. "You promised you'd never confront me again in front of my men."

"Jess, I did ask to speak to you privately, remember? And I'm not taking you to task. I'm just trying to get you to stop and think. If you know that stallion is back, you can count on Gibbons knowing it too. I'm sure he's had scouts out watching for him, just like you. And right now he's probably making plans to—"

"I don't care what kind of plans he's making," Jessie interjected. "We'll get to the White Steed first."

Exasperated, Morgan shook her again. "Dammit, you're not listening to me! I'm not talking about plans to capture the stallion. I'm talking about plans to annihilate this whole camp!"

Finally comprehending what Morgan had been trying to tell her, Jessie frowned. Then her expression lightened as she said, "But we haven't seen any signs of gunfighters."

"I told you that they're probably in hiding, that Gibbons doesn't want his hands to know what's going on. No, Jess, they're around here someplace. I can sense it."

"You'd better listen to him, Jessie," Gabe said in an ominous voice as he stepped forward. "He knows more about that kinda thing than you do."

"All right, then, we'll pull out completely. We'll be gone by daybreak."

"And get caught in the open, with no protection at all?" Morgan asked in a biting voice. "Besides, daybreak will be too late. They'll probably attack tonight."

"Tonight?" Jessie gasped.

"Yes, if I was running the show, that's what I'd do."

"Then we'll move the mares to the corral, post the men around them and the pen—"

"Jess, you still don't get the picture," Morgan said, exasperated. "It's not your horses that are in danger, unless they happen to catch a stray bullet. Gibbons doesn't give a damn about them. It's *you* he wants out of the way. My guess is, his hired guns will come riding straight into this camp with all guns blazing. What you need to be doing is fortifying this place."

Jessie finally understood the imminent danger. "But . . . but how?"

"Will you let me handle it?"

Jessie was reluctant to turn control of her outfit over to Morgan—even briefly. Her men's acceptance of her as their leader had been hard-earned, and she guarded her position jealously. But this was a crisis she had never faced before, and she had no idea of where to begin. Aware of all eyes watching her expectantly, she nodded her head in mute consent.

Morgan turned to Pedro. "Have your men pull down some sections of those wings and drag them over to the front of the dugout."

"Sí, señor," Pedro answered, then hurried off, barking orders in Spanish.

"The dugout?" Gabe asked. "Won't we be trapped in there?"

"No, it's our best line of defense. With that earthen roof, they can't set it on fire, especially not if we wet down the walls."

"But they can come down that hill and attack us from the rear," Gabe argued.

"I think they'll try a frontal attack first. With our campfires burning and our lean-tos still standing, they'll probably think we weren't expecting them. Let's hope they won't notice those wings in the darkness and we can catch them in a cross fire. Then they might try sneaking up on us from the rear, but I'm hoping the men I place in those trees behind the cabin can foul their plans."

Gabe cocked his head and studied Morgan for a moment. "You've given this quite a bit of thought, ain't you?"

"I have," Morgan answered in a grim voice.

The old man grinned in approval, then asked, "What do you want me to do?"

"Find as many shovels and axes as you can."

As Gabe rushed off, Jessie asked, "And me? What can I do to help?"

"When Gabe returns, round up all the horses and corral them. Then have some of the men cut and pile brush around the corrals. That should stop any stray bullets."

"What about the pen? Shouldn't we pile brush around it too?"

"No, it's too far away from where I expect the fighting to take place. Those mustangs aren't in any danger."

At that moment Pedro and his men returned, dragging the sections of the wings behind their horses. Morgan directed them to erect the wings so that they ran out at right angles from each corner of the dugout. The whole camp became a beehive of activity as Morgan called out orders, his deep voice resounding through the air.

Jessie felt a twinge of resentment as the men jumped to obey Morgan's orders, some digging trenches behind the wings, others cutting brush and dragging it to the wings and the corrals, still others scurrying to load buckets with water from the creek and dashing it against the walls of the dugout to wet them down. Jessie reminded herself that she had given Morgan his authority, but she was dismayed at how eagerly her men obeyed, not once glancing in her direction to see if she approved or not. No, instead all eyes were on the tall Texan, and the Mexicans' looks of profound admiration and respect cut

Jessie to the quick. When Morgan called to the two Mexican women to speed up their preparations for the evening meal and they hurried to obey, it was all Jessie could do to keep from reminding him that this was her outfit and not his.

Then, as Morgan stopped two *mesteñeros* who were carrying grass and water to the corraled horses, Jessie couldn't keep her mouth shut for one more minute.

She rushed up just as Morgan was saying, "Don't bother with that tonight."

"No, Morgan," Jessie said in a tight voice, "I won't have my horses neglected."

"Jess, there are more important things to do," Morgan countered. "Those horses won't starve to death if they miss one meal."

"I want my horses fed!" Jessie ground out between clenched teeth.

Morgan studied Jessie, wondering why she was being so adamant. What in the hell was wrong with her, putting her horses before the safety of her people. Besides that, she looked furious, her jewel-like eyes flashing and her mouth set tight. Then, suddenly, he understood. She felt he was usurping her authority over her men.

"Jess, you gave me permission to fortify this place," Morgan reminded her patiently.

"And that's *all* I gave you permission to do! The animals are still my responsibility. And I want them fed!"

Her and her goddamned fierce independence, Morgan thought, fighting to keep his own temper down. For a moment the two waged a silent battle of wills as green and gray eyes clashed. Then, becoming aware of the bewildered looks on the Mexicans' faces as they glanced uneasily from him to Jessie, Morgan realized that there was more at stake here than Jessie's attempt to hold some of her authority over her men. Her pride. If he insisted, overrode her objection, she would never forgive him. No, she would feel she had lost the Mexicans' high esteem, something she had earned through years of struggle to prove herself capable of being their leader and protector. For Jessie's sake, he was going to have to back down.

Straightening to his imposing height, Morgan stepped back, saying to the *mesteñeros,* "My mistake, *compadres.* Sorry I interrupted you while you were performing your duties."

As Morgan walked away and the two Mexicans hurried to do her bidding, Jessie let out a ragged sigh of relief. If Morgan had insisted that things be done his way and the Mexicans had obeyed him and not her, she would have been crushed. She watched as Morgan threaded his way through the busy men, stopping here or there to give directions, calmly acting as if nothing had happened, as if Jessie had never challenged him. Strangely, the confrontation Jessie had forced on him hadn't seemed to affect the Mexicans' respect for him in the least. To the contrary. The Mexicans' eyes shone with a new admiration as they hurried to obey his orders. Suddenly, Jessie realized that Morgan's deferring to her had been done with such dignity and grace that the Mexicans didn't consider it a sign of weakness, but rather a testimony to his unusual strength. Tears sprang to her eyes as a mixture of emotions came to the surface: disgust at her own behavior, admiration for Morgan's strength of character, and a profound love for this man who had placed her pride before his.

As soon as the trenches behind the wings were dug, the men throwing the dirt to the back to give protection from that direction, Morgan said, "Find everything you can to pile behind those wings. Saddles, boxes, sacks of supplies, limbs, anything that can stop a bullet. And pile more brush in front of those wings to conceal them. We don't want the gunslingers spying them before we have them in our trap."

Then, as the light was rapidly fading, he directed the placement of the campfires.

When the fires were burning brightly, Morgan looked around him with satisfaction, seeing that the wings were hidden in the shadows. He studied the lean-tos thoughtfully, then said, "Pedro, have a few men drag some of that cut brush over here."

"What are you gonna do with that?" Gabe asked in puzzlement. "I thought we were gonna hide behind the wings."

"We are. But if they come riding in here and find all those lean-tos empty, they'll get suspicious."

"But—"

"If you'll just be patient a minute, Gabe, I'll show you what I have in mind," Morgan interjected, taking the limb that Pedro had pulled forward. Spreading a blanket out on the ground, he broke the limb into smaller pieces and laid it on the blanket. Then he rolled the blanket up, adjusting it this way and that before he came to his feet and stepped back.

"*Sí, señor!*" Pedro cried from where he was standing a short distance away. "It looks like a man is rolled up in the blanket and is sleeping there."

Morgan grinned. "That's what I was hoping it would look like. And when they come galloping in with all guns blazing, that man will be their first victim."

Then the Mexicans ran off to place more dummies beneath the lean-tos.

After they had hurriedly eaten their evening meal,

Jessie glanced about the camp, looking for Morgan. Not seeing him anywhere, she asked Gabe, "Where did Morgan disappear to?"

"He's posting those six night guards in the trees at the back of the cabin. I gotta hand it to him. He's thought of everything. With those men back there, those polecats can't sneak up on us from behind. Dammit, I can't wait to see the looks on those bastards' faces when we catch them in our cross fire. With our bullets coming at them from all sides, we'll massacre them."

"Don't be overconfident," Morgan said in a low, ominous voice as he stepped out of the darkness. Both Jessie and Gabe jumped at his sudden appearance, neither having heard his approach. That damn silent walk of his, Jessie thought, her heart still pounding in fright.

"Pedro," Morgan called out, "get the men divided up and behind those wings."

As Gabe started toward one of the wings, Morgan caught his arm. "No, not you, Gabe. I want you in the dugout with the women."

"Dammit, I ain't gonna hide in there with the women!"

"I wasn't suggesting that you hide. I was thinking more in the line of your protecting them. You can shoot from that window."

"And I'll take the other window," Jessie said.

Morgan frowned; he hadn't planned on Jessie taking part in the fight. "No, Jess. I don't want to take any chances of your being hit."

"Don't you tell me no! This is my outfit, and I told you I don't ask my men to do anything I don't do."

Seeing the determined gleam in her eyes, Morgan knew that he had no recourse, short of tying her to the furniture. "All right," he conceded with a frustrated

sigh. "But dammit, you be careful!" His eyes flicked up
to her head. "And tie something around your hair. It
stands out like a candle in this darkness."

Morgan turned and started to walk away. Jessie
stopped him, calling softly, "Morgan?"

He turned, running a hand wearily through his dark
hair. "What now?"

Jessie winced, both at his hard tone of voice and the
look of exhaustion on his face. The entire burden of the
preparations had been on his shoulders, and Jessie knew
he was worried about the outcome. She really hated to
bother him further, but she had to be assured her herd
of mustangs was safe. She swallowed hard before asking,
"Can't you put a few men around the pen?"

"Jess, I told you I don't think they're going to bother
the horses."

"But you can't be sure," Jessie argued. "That herd is
worth over a thousand dollars to me. I can't afford to
lose it."

Morgan let out a deep sigh. "All right. I'll send two
men over there."

"Just two men?"

"Dammit, Jess. I really can't afford to lose even them.
Despite what Gabe thinks, there's a good possibility we
won't win this fight. Remember, those are seasoned
gunfighters coming in after us. We may surprise them,
but we aren't going to massacre them."

Morgan turned to one of the wings and called, "Ra-
fael! Juan! Come out here."

The two men scurried out from behind the wings and
ran to where Morgan stood. "You two go over and guard
the pen," Morgan said.

The two men exchanged apprehensive looks. Finally,
Juan asked, "Alone, *señor*?"

Morgan knew both men were terrified. There was
safety in numbers. "If you think the gunfighters are
going to attack the pen, too, fire three shots in quick
succession. Then I'll know what's happening and send
some men to help you."

Knowing that they weren't being completely left on
their own, the two men nodded and trotted off in the
direction of the pen.

Morgan watched the men until the darkness swallowed them and then turned to Jessie and said, "Does
that suit you?"

"Yes," Jessie answered, knowing in all fairness that
she couldn't ask for more. Twice, Morgan had bowed to
her wishes, both times against his better judgment, and
she loved him all the more for it. As he started to turn
away she caught his arm, saying softly, "And Morgan,
thank you."

Morgan turned his head and saw Jessie smiling at
him, her heart in her eyes. He fought back the urge to
take her in his arms and kiss her until she was breathless, desperately wishing he could make love to her, for
tomorrow, one or the other—or both—of them might
be dead. He forced a smile and cupped her chin with his
hand, whispering huskily, "You'd better stop looking at
me like that, sweetheart, or I can't be held responsible
for what I might do."

At that moment, under Morgan's warm gaze, Jessie
desperately wanted it too. The realization shocked her.
She wondered how she could think of something like
that at a time like this, yet their danger seemed to
sharpen her passion, a passion that seethed just below
the surface anytime she was around this man. She
briefly considered suggesting they slip away for a while,
but she knew Morgan would never consent. His obliga-

tions at the present were to her people as well as to her. She ducked her head and averted her eyes, mumbling, "I guess I'd better get inside."

Morgan dropped his hand and took a ragged breath. "Yes, I think you'd better."

Morgan watched as Jessie walked to the dugout, thinking that she looked so small and defenseless. I won't let anything happen to her, he vowed fiercely. I won't!

He turned and walked to one of the wings, inspecting it carefully, then cautioning the men behind it, "I don't care how close they come, don't fire until I say so. Pick your man out and keep him in the sights of your gun, but don't shoot until you hear from me. And whatever you do, don't fire at random. Remember the men behind the wings across from you."

When Morgan had finished inspecting the opposite wing and repeated his lecture, he jumped into the trench and sat down beside Pedro.

For a long while there was silence in the trench, the only sounds the usual soft night noises and the steady breathing of the men. Then the *mesteñeros* began to whisper among themselves. Morgan didn't object. He knew the Mexicans had had time to contemplate fully what they were about to do and were beginning to feel edgy. Talking relieved their nervousness while they waited.

"There will be no moon tonight," Pedro commented.

"Thank God for that," Morgan replied.

"What time do you think they will come?"

"Late. When they think we're asleep."

The old man gazed up at the stars. "It is already midnight."

Morgan shrugged, casting a glance in the direction of

the dugout. He knew it was silly, but he just had to see Jessie one more time before the fight began. He rose, muttering, "Guess I'll check and see how everyone in the dugout is doing."

"Sí señor," Pedro replied with a knowing smile.

Morgan walked the short distance to the dugout and ducked beneath the blanket at the doorway, stepping in.

It was pitch-black in the dugout, and Morgan strained his eyes to see. Stepping forward a few paces, he bumped into the corner of the table, the sharp jab against his thigh making him mutter an ugly oath beneath his breath.

"Jessie? Where are you?" he whispered.

"Over here," Jessie whispered back.

Morgan followed the sound of her voice, his hands groping in the dark before him. Touching something soft that could only be a woman's breast, he smiled and cupped it intimately, then heard a startled gasp.

"You have the wrong woman, *señor,"* a female voice whispered.

Morgan jerked his hand back as if it had been burned. "Pardon me, *señora."*

The woman's only answer was a giggle, followed by another from the Mexican woman standing next to her.

"I'm here," Jessie said, catching his arm and pulling him to the side of the dugout by one of the windows. When they had settled down, she asked, "What did you apologize for? Did you bump into Señora Mendoza?"

"No," Morgan whispered. "Something much more embarrassing than that. I'll tell you about it later."

"Well, whatever it was, it served as a diversion. This waiting has all our nerves crawling."

"They'll be here soon enough," Morgan answered in an ominous voice.

He leaned back against the wall and put his arm around Jessie, taking advantage of the darkness to quickly kiss the top of her head. Jessie snuggled closer, grateful for his presence. His strength seemed to be flowing into her, easing the terrifying fear that had been plaguing her. She laid her head against his broad chest. The steady beat of his heart was reassuring, the warmth from his body soothing. She could feel the tension leaving her.

Then, feeling his body stiffen, she asked, "What's wrong?"

"Sshh! I heard something."

Jessie sat up and strained her ears, but she couldn't hear anything unusual.

Morgan rose and peeked through the window. "Yes. Here they come."

Jessie crouched beside him and peered out past the fires. "I don't see anything."

"They're there, all right. Checking the place over before they ride in."

Jessie wondered if he was hallucinating, hearing and seeing things that weren't there. Then Morgan pulled her into his arms and gave her a long, fierce kiss.

He groaned in frustration as his lips slid from her mouth to her ear. Then he whispered huskily, "We'll finish this later, sweetheart. I promise you."

Before Jessie could recover her senses, Morgan was gone, the only hint of his departure the rustling of the blanket as he ducked beneath it. Jessie wondered if the others had seen. Surely, with their bodies silhouetted against the firelight from the outside, they must have. Then, hearing Gabe's soft chuckle and the two women's giggles, she knew that they had not only seen, but had probably heard Morgan's passionate promise as well. An embarrassed flush rose on her face, but then she quickly tossed the feeling aside. He had promised, and she knew Morgan would do everything in his power to see that they lived through this night and that he kept his promise.

Her spirits buoyed by his words, she whispered in a stern voice, "Hush, now. All of you. And get ready. They're coming."

Chapter 18

MORGAN HAD BARELY SLIPPED BACK INTO THE trench when the silence was broken by the sound of pounding hoofbeats. The gunslingers rode into the camp whooping and hollering like a bunch of demented Indians with all guns blazing—just as Morgan had predicted. As they tore through the camp, riding their horses around the campfires, they fired at the "sleeping men" in the lean-tos.

Seeing a raider empty his gun into one of the dummies, which sent the blanket-shrouded brush dancing from the impact of the bullets, Pedro whispered, "*Dios!* That could have been me."

Pedro glanced at Morgan's face. The flickering firelight was reflected in his silver eyes, giving them a diabolical red glow and making them look as if they were spitting fire. A shiver ran through Pedro, and he quickly crossed himself.

"Those bastards," Morgan hissed. "They didn't come here to fight. They came to murder—in cold blood!"

"Sí, señor," Pedro answered grimly. "And, *Madre de Dios,* there are so many of them. Why, there must be at least thirty-five or forty."

With the raiders wildly weaving their horses around the scattered campfires and lean-tos, darting in and out of the shadows cast by the light, it was impossible for Morgan to get an accurate count, but he didn't think Pedro had exaggerated. The *mesteñeros* were going into this fight not only handicapped by their lack of skill with firearms, but grossly outnumbered too.

"Do you think we can repel them?" Pedro asked.

Morgan heard the fear in the old man's voice and knew every Mexican in the trench was breathlessly awaiting his answer. In truth, Morgan didn't feel at all confident of the outcome, but he knew they would lose for sure if he didn't give the men the encouragement they so desperately needed to bolster their courage. "As long as we've got these guns in our hands, we've got a fighting chance. We *are* going to repel them. We don't have any choice. Just concentrate on everything I've taught you. You can do it!"

A smile broke out on Pedro's face at Morgan's words. *"Sí, señor,* we can do it. And remember, *compadres,* God is with us."

I hope so, Morgan thought grimly, because we're sure as hell going to need His help.

At that moment, one of the hired killers yelled above the noise, "Let's get the rest of those greasers and get the hell out of here!"

As the raiders boldly rode toward the dugout with smug smiles on their faces, Morgan let out a silent sigh of relief. Apparently the gunslingers thought they had wiped out the better part of what resistance they would meet when they had murdered the "sleeping men" in the lean-tos. Now, overconfident of their victory, they had put caution aside, not one of them even glancing toward the side where the wings sat, their eyes glittering with blood lust and glued on the crude cabin they were riding toward.

When the raiders rode into the area between the wings, Morgan whispered to the *mesteñeros,* "Pick out your man and keep him in your gun sights."

Without hesitation the Mexicans obeyed, positioning the barrels of their Winchesters in the brush in front of them, but being very careful not to poke them out too far lest the metal be exposed.

"Kinda quiet, ain't it?" one raider asked the man riding beside him. "I mean, how come those greasers in that cabin ain't shooting at us?"

"Because they're scared shitless," his companion answered contemptuously. "Hell, when did you ever see a Mexican that fought back? No, they're all yellow-bellied cowards. They're probably in there on their knees, praying with those heathen beads they all carry."

Morgan had known the Mexicans in the trench were terrified. He could smell the distinctive, pungent odor of their fear. But when they heard the raider's contemptuous remarks, every man stiffened with outrage at the insults, and Morgan knew the time to attack had come.

"Fire!" he yelled, his deep voice echoing through the camp.

A deafening roar filled the night air as the *mesteñeros* fired their rifles almost simultaneously. The sharp cracks reverberated in the woods around them and made it sound as if hundreds of guns had been shot.

With surprised grunts of pain, four raiders fell from their horses to the ground, their bodies riddled with bullets.

Terrified at the sudden gunshots and the bullets whizzing all around them, the frightened horses reared on their hind legs, screaming in fear and pawing the air. The raiders desperately fought to control their mounts, glancing around them in disbelief.

As the second volley of gunshots followed close on the first, one raider yelled, "God damn, it's a trap! Let's get the hell out of here!"

Finally realizing what was happening, the raiders tried to turn their horses and retreat. The result was chaos, a confusing, crushing, milling mass of cursing men and terrified, rearing horses. One man was knocked from his saddle by the hooves of another's horse, and a raider was thrown forward when his horse's front legs became entangled with another rearing horse's legs and the animal fell to his knees. The first man managed to regain his feet, dodging the flying hooves and mounting behind a comrade. The second was not so fortunate. He was trampled to death beneath the hooves of the terrified animals. Not until the men in the rear had successfully turned their mounts and raced away were those in front afforded any space in which to maneuver their horses. But for those men it was too late. The gunslingers were caught in a murderous cross fire as the Winchesters roared for the third time, their bodies flying out of the saddles from the impact as the bullets of the power rifles hit them.

Inside the cabin, Jessie carefully aimed her gun at the back of one of the retreating raiders, determined not to miss this time. Her first shot had been ruined when the horse of the man she was aiming at had suddenly reared. She squeezed the trigger and the gun in her hand exploded, the loud noise leaving her ears ringing. Peering through the smoke, she saw the man tumble from his saddle, the circle of blood spreading on the back of his shirt even as he fell. She felt a surge of satisfaction.

Then suddenly the full impact of what she had done hit her. She had killed a man. Shot him in the back. Bile rose in her throat, and she turned from the window, weakly sliding down the wall of the cabin to sit on the earthen floor, her eyes wide with horror, the hand that still held the lethal weapon lying limply in her lap.

Instantly, Gabe was at her side, shaking her shoulder and saying gruffly, "Don't think about it, Jessie."

"I just killed a man," Jessie muttered, shudders running through her small body. "I shot him—in the back, no less!"

"And ain't that just what those murdering polecats would have done to your men if they'd been in their lean-tos? Cold-bloodedly shot them in the back? Those bastards started this, Jessie. Just remember that. Now, come on," Gabe said, bringing her to her feet. "This thing ain't over yet. We still got a fight on our hands."

Jessie looked out the window and saw that the ground was littered with at least a dozen bodies. Several horses also lay there, inadvertently killed in the cross fire. The sight of the carnage did nothing to settle her stomach, and again the bile rose. She clamped her hand over her mouth, desperately fighting it down. Then her eyes widened in disbelief as she saw that the raiders had regrouped and were rushing the wings.

Morgan was stunned when he saw the gunfighters racing toward them. "The goddamned fools," he muttered. "They really are gluttons for punishment."

"Get down!" Morgan yelled to the Mexicans, bringing Pedro down in the trench with him. "Don't even try to shoot back until they've emptied their guns. Then catch them when they ride back out."

The *mesteñeros* bit the dust as a hail of bullets whizzed over their heads, sending mesquite brush flying everywhere. Again and again the Mexicans heard the dull thud as bullets hit the saddles, boxes, and logs they had piled behind the wings. Sweat broke out on their foreheads as the barrage continued, and they thanked God that Morgan had had the foresight to build this trench.

Jessie was baffled when there was no answering fire from the wings. "What's wrong with them?" she asked Gabe. "Are they too scared to shoot back?"

"Danged if I know," Gabe answered. Then, as a sudden thought entered his head, his eyes flashed with anger as he spat, "If those damned pepper-eaters have turned and run, I'll kill them with my bare hands."

There was no time for Jessie to react to Gabe's words. A split second later he yelled, "Get down! They're coming at us!"

Jessie was thrown to the earthen floor as Gabe pushed her down, her face buried in the dust. She squirmed to raise her head so she could breathe, but Gabe had thrown his arm around her neck when he fell, and he held her down with a strength she would have never dreamed the old man possessed. She sputtered impotently, spitting out dirt as her ears rang with the sound of guns roaring, wood splintering, glass breaking, and the Mexican women's terrified screams.

Morgan had been content to follow his own orders and crouch in the safety of the trench—until he saw several of the raiders riding toward the dugout with their guns blazing. Jessie was in there! For a brief moment he was paralyzed. Then, as a rage filled him, he came to life and sprang from the trench, racing around the end of the wing and into the open, his Winchester spewing bullets as he pumped the lever with a vengeance.

The men attacking the crude cabin suddenly found themselves face-to-face with an apparition they weren't sure was animal, or man—or a combination of both. His body was that of a man, but his silver eyes glittered with the fury of a rabid *lobo*, and there was a feral snarl on his face, while the angry scream coming from his throat was the unholiest they had ever heard. But the startled men didn't have time to ponder this terrifying sight for long. They died with that surprised expression frozen on their faces.

At the same time, the other raiders turned and raced away. The *mesteñeros* in the trenches let go with a scathing fire that sent several gunslingers flying from their saddles. Morgan tossed aside his empty rifle and drew his side arm, shooting at the retreating men with a deadly aim as he ran for the dugout.

He crouched at the dugout door and once again took aim. Then, realizing that the raiders were out of his gun range, he slipped his gun in his holster, firmly vowing that if they had hurt Jessie in any way, he'd seek them out and kill them, even if he had to search to the ends of the earth and it took a lifetime.

As Morgan lifted the blanket at the doorway, he knew that someone must be alive in the bullet-riddled dugout, and they were female, judging from their shrill, hysterical screams.

Then, when he stepped into the cabin, he heard Gabe yelling over the noise, "Will you pepper-eaters cut out that damned caterwauling? It's getting on my nerves. Besides, they're gone."

Standing in the total darkness, Morgan knew that Gabe and the Mexican women had survived the murderous barrage of bullets. But Jessie? He peered around him, his mouth dry with fear. He opened his mouth, and the single word that came out was a hoarse croak. "Jess?"

Morgan heard several sharp intakes of breath. No one in the cabin had realized he was present. Then he heard a muffled sound.

"God damn it, Jess, answer me!"

"I will if this jackass on top of me will let me up!"

"Oh, sorry, Jessie," Gabe muttered, rolling from her. "I forgot you were there."

Following the sounds of their voices, Morgan walked toward them, groping in the dark. Jessie had scrambled to her feet as soon as Gabe had rolled from her, and was searching blindly for Morgan. Morgan felt a soft hand brush his, caught her wrist, and yanked her forward. Their bodies came together with such force, it took her breath away.

There was no doubt in Morgan's mind that the woman in his arms was Jessie. He recognized each curve of her body, and her scent filled his nostrils. Convulsively he tightened his arms in a fierce embrace that threatened to crush Jessie's ribs.

"Morgan, let go of me. I can't breathe," she muttered.

His brain heard the breathless words, but his body refused to respond to her plea. He wanted to absorb her into himself, carry her with him where he could be assured of her safety. Jessie began to squirm, and finally her desperate message got through to him as he loos-

ened his hold, leaving her drawing in ragged breaths of
air.

"I'm sorry, sweetheart," Morgan muttered, "but I
was afraid you'd been shot."

Deeply touched, Jessie marveled at the depths of
Morgan's love. A lump rose in her throat. "I'm not
hurt."

"You're sure?" Morgan asked, his hands running over
her.

"I'm sure," Jessie answered. "But what about you?"
Now she was running her hands over Morgan's body.

"Well," Gabe said dryly, "in case anybody is interested, I ain't hurt either."

Both Morgan and Jessie stiffened at Gabe's words.
They had completely forgotten the others were there.
A flush rose on Jessie's face as she realized that after
tonight, her relationship with Morgan would no longer
be a secret. Yes, by tomorrow the two women would
have spread the news all over the camp. Then Jessie
realized that she didn't care. She wanted their love to
be out in the open. It was too wonderful and beautiful to
hide away from the others any longer.

Morgan chuckled, and Jessie felt the sound as a deep
rumble in his chest, for he still held her tightly against
him. "I'm glad you're not hurt, Gabe," he said over
Jessie's head.

"Well, you could have fooled me," Gabe grumbled.
"The way you two lovebirds were acting, I could've
sworn you'd completely forgotten we were here."

Morgan chuckled again. "To be honest with you, we
did forget for a moment there. But not because we
aren't concerned about you too." He gazed down at
Jessie, his voice dropping an octave. "It's just that Jessie
and I have a more profound concern for each other."

Jessie's heart leapt. Morgan had declared his love openly. Tears of happiness glistened in her eyes.

"*Señoras,* are you all right?" Morgan asked perfunctorily, out of politeness. Morgan seriously doubted that anyone who had screamed as loud as the two women could have been wounded, at least not seriously.

"*Sí, señor,* we are fine," one woman answered for them both. "We turned the table over and hid behind it."

There was a brief silence before the other woman spoke up timidly. "Forgive us, Señor Gabe. We did not mean to scream so loud. But it did seem to relieve our fright."

Morgan's eyes had adjusted to the darkness, and he saw Gabe shaking his head in mute disgust before he surprised everyone with his gallant answer. "That's all right, ladies, I understand."

"We'd better see if anyone outside was injured," Jessie said.

"*I'll* see if we have any casualties," Morgan said in a firm voice. "You're not stepping out of this cabin."

"But—"

Morgan put his finger over Jessie's mouth, silencing her. "The battle isn't over, Jess. This is just a lull in the fighting. If anyone is injured out there, we'll bring them in here, where the women can tend to them."

"In the dark, *señor?*" one of the women asked.

"No, I'm afraid you'll need light for that. But whatever you do, stay away from the windows and the door when you have a light burning. For all I know, those men out there could be carrying a Sharps or two."

"What is that, *señor?* A Sharps?"

"A powerful rifle with an unusually long range. The

buffalo hunters use them. With those rifles, a man could pick you off from a good distance away."

"We'll be careful," Jessie promised.

"The lamp is broken, *patrona.* I heard a bullet hit it."

"There's another one in my room," Jessie said, turning to grope in the dark. "I hope it survived."

"I'll find it," Morgan said, pulling her back.

"You can't see any better in this darkness than I can," Jessie pointed out.

Morgan chuckled and fumbled in his shirt pocket for something. Jessie heard a scratch, then jumped as the match flared to life.

She looked up to see Morgan grinning down at her. "If you had them all along, why didn't you use them earlier?" she asked in irritation. "Instead of groping around here in the dark and stumbling all over everybody."

"Because the first time, I was afraid the raiders might see the light and get suspicious, and the second time, I was just too damned scared something had happened to you to even remember I had them," Morgan answered calmly before he passed her, the meager light cupped in his hand.

When a sudden glow came from the bedroom doorway, everyone knew that Morgan had found the lamp still intact. As he walked back into the main room carrying the lamp, Jessie was already giving orders.

"*Señoras,* one of you get a broom and sweep up the broken glass, while the other starts a fire so we can have hot water. Gabe, go into the bedrooms and bring back all the blankets and linens you can find."

As Gabe rushed off, Jessie called, "And bring back my medicine kit too."

"God damn it," Gabe grumbled, "how many arms do you think I've got?"

Morgan darted beneath the blanket before Jessie could start shooting orders at him, too, and darted to the side of the building. Crouching there, he peered out at the darkness beyond the camp. Then, seeing something from the corner of his eye, he swung around, his hand going for his gun.

"Don't shoot, *señor*!" Pedro cried, walking up to Morgan.

As the old man passed the window Morgan grabbed him, saying, "Get down!" and pulling Pedro down beside him.

"But *señor*, we are out of their gun range," Pedro objected.

"Not if they're carrying Sharps, we aren't. How many injured do we have?" Morgan asked.

"Two men were shot, but neither is injured seriously. One in the arm, the other in the shoulder."

Morgan could hardly force the next question from his mouth. "How many dead?"

The old man's face broke into a wide smile. "None, *señor*."

"None?" Morgan asked in disbelief. "We didn't lose a single man?"

"No, not one man."

Morgan couldn't believe it. He quickly counted twenty-four bodies sprawled on the ground between the wings. With his six best shooters hidden in the trees behind the cabin and the two men he had sent to guard the herd, there had been only eleven armed in the camp, including Jessie, Gabe, and himself. "It's a miracle," he muttered.

"*Sí*, God played his part. He sent us you."

Morgan's head shot up. "No, Pedro, I can't take credit for all of those dead men."

"No, *señor*, but you can a good dozen of them." Then Pedro beamed, his chest expanding with pride. "The rest we killed. Not bad shooting for a bunch of poor Mexicans, *sí, señor?*"

And these were the men who hadn't even shown any particular shooting skills, Morgan thought in amazement. "You're damned right it's not bad shooting. That's one man apiece. I'm proud of all of you."

"Ah, but if it had not been for you, we would have been massacred in our sleep, or many of us killed in that last rush. We owe you a great debt."

"You don't owe me anything, Pedro. None of you do. Besides, it's not over yet," Morgan added in a grim voice.

"*Sí*, but we survived the first two waves, and the odds are much more in our favor now."

Morgan had been so caught up in his anger that he hadn't even noticed how many raiders had ridden away. "How many do you figure are left?"

"I would guess about a dozen men. You see, now we have them outnumbered."

Outnumbered, but not outgunned, Morgan thought. "Don't get overconfident, Pedro. That was the gunslingers' first mistake. The second was letting their anger get the best of them and rushing back in. But they've learned their lesson now, and they'll be much more cautious," and he added ominously, "and much more dangerous."

Chapter 19

WHEN MORGAN AND PEDRO SETTLED BACK DOWN IN the trench, there was a dampness in the air as a gray ground fog slowly crept from the prairie and into the camp.

"We could have done without this damned fog tonight," Morgan said. "With it to conceal their approach, it will be all the easier for them to sneak up on us, and even so they know exactly where we are."

"*Sí, señor*," Pedro agreed gravely.

"*Señor?*" Morgan asked, his dark eyebrows rising. "I thought I asked you to call me Morgan."

Pedro grinned sheepishly. "I am sorry . . . Morgan. But old habits are hard to break." The old man chuckled, adding, "Besides, your Anglo name seems strange to my Mexican tongue. It is difficult for me to say. Perhaps just *amigo* would suffice?"

Morgan laughed. "Anything but that damned *señor*. Christ, it makes me feel ancient when you call me that."

The next thirty minutes seemed like a lifetime to the men in the trenches. The tension was even worse than before, for then they'd had a good idea from which direction the raiders would attack. Now they had to watch both sides, and their backs, too, relying more on their hearing than on their sight because of the fog that shrouded everything in a ghostly mist.

Hearing a rustle in the brush behind them, the Mexicans tensed, then whirled around, their eyes nervously searching the mesquite.

Morgan caught sight of what had caused the noise and chuckled softly. "Relax. It's just a possum."

"It has been well over an hour since they rode away. Perhaps, they have left," Pedro said hopefully.

"No, I don't think they'd give up that quickly. Undoubtedly they're mad as a bunch of hornets over the way we drove them away so effectively. I imagine being beaten by a bunch of Mexican mustangers has sorely injured their pride. After all, they're professional gunmen. No, I'm afraid we've made this a much more personal fight now. They're out for revenge."

Pedro shuddered, knowing that there was nothing more dangerous than a man seeking vengeance.

"But come to think of it," Morgan continued, "it has been a while since they rode out of here." He glanced over his shoulder, saying, "Long enough for them to circle that hill behind us."

As Morgan rose and stepped from the trench, he said, "Keep the men alert, Pedro. I'm going back there and make sure the men in those trees aren't catnapping."

"Be careful, *amigo.* They may mistake you for one of the raiders in this fog."

Morgan nodded and crept away.

The fog in the woods was even thicker, giving the

whole area an eerie, ghostly appearance. Cautiously, walking in a half crouch, Morgan approached the tree he had assigned to one of the night guards, calling softly, "Carlos?"

The man in the tree turned so quickly, he almost lost his balance and tumbled from it.

Seeing the man fanning his gun wildly, Morgan called, "Don't shoot! It's me, Morgan."

As Morgan straightened and the Mexican could distinguish his tall form in the swirling fog, the man let out the breath he had been holding and said in a shaky voice, "Oh, *señor*, you frightened me. I'm afraid I would have shot—if I could have seen you."

"Give me a hand up, will you?"

Slipping his gun into his holster, Carlos caught hold of a limb next to him and held out his hand to Morgan. When Morgan was crouched on the limb next to the Mexican, he asked, "Have you seen anything?"

"How can I in this thick fog?" Carlos shivered, saying, "It's . . ."

"Spooky?" Morgan asked when the man seemed to be searching for the right word.

"*Sí, señor.*"

"Don't let it unnerve you. Remember, they don't know you're here. And the fog is just as thick in these trees as it is down there."

"Señor West, we have been wondering," a *mesteñero* from a nearby tree said softly. "What happened back at the camp? We could hear shooting but couldn't see anything because of the trees."

"We beat the hell out of them." Sensing the men's disappointment in missing out on the fight, Morgan quickly added, "But now it's your turn. Now, no more talking. You don't want to give away your positions."

The moments passed agonizingly slowly, the silence in the woods all the more profound for the men listening so hard. Then Morgan's sharp hearing caught the faint rustling of a branch. He nudged Carlos and pointed to the mesquite brush to their right. The Mexican strained his eyes, peering into the dense fog, then nodded, having finally seen the dark form of a man creeping around it.

Morgan spied a shrouded movement to his left. As the murky form became more distinct, he swung his gun in that direction. The man sneaking though the curling tendrils of fog below him was totally unaware that he was in the sights of Morgan's gun.

From his peripheral vision, Morgan saw the *mesteñero* in the nearby tree aim his gun very carefully and knew that he, too, had found a target. Hoping that the other *mesteñeros* had done the same, Morgan squeezed his trigger.

Gunshots rang out throughout the woods, followed by grunts and cries of pain.

"I got him, *señor*!" Carlos yelled excitedly.

"Sshh!" Morgan cautioned sternly.

"Son of a bitch! They're in that tree!" one of the raiders yelled.

Morgan pushed Carlos down until the man was bent double as a furious barrage of bullets whizzed all around them, one so close to Morgan's head that he felt the rush of wind as it passed. Broken mesquite branches flew everywhere. Seeing the flashes from the raiders' guns, the Mexicans in the other trees let go with a barrage of their own.

"Christ! They're all over the place, Joe!" one terrified man on the ground yelled.

There was a brief moment of silence.

"Joe?"

Then, "God damn it, they got Joe!"

Furious, the hired gun came running from behind the mesquite bush where he had been hiding and into the open, emptying his six-shooter into the tree above him. Even as he ran the man was riddled, his body jerking this way then that from the impact of the bullets. When the echoes from the gunshots died away, the foolishly impulsive gunslinger lay sprawled in a pool of blood.

"Stupid son of a bitch," another raider muttered, and then the bush from which the voice had come was blasted to pieces as a hail of bullets from the *mesteñeros'* guns tore through it.

Morgan grinned, pleased at how quickly the *mesteñeros* had caught on to the finer points of night fighting, aiming their guns at the spots where they had seen the flashes of light and where the voices had come from.

Apparently the gunfighters realized their mistake, for there was total silence around them now. Morgan's nerves crawled as he peered out into the darkness, his ears straining for any sound.

A gun roared from one of the trees, and the man below screamed out in pain as the bullets tore through him.

"God damn it, I'm getting the hell out of here," one of the raiders yelled.

A sudden rustling of bushes was followed by more rustling as the raiders ran through the brush up the hill, shooting wildly into the trees as they fled. The *mesteñeros* fired back, but the men on the ground zigzagged in and out of the bushes as they ran, and the bullets missed their mark.

Finally, Morgan called out, "Cease fire! They're out of your gun range."

The sudden brief silence was broken as the Mexicans began to whisper back and forth in elated voices. The acrid smell of gun smoke drifted around them. Morgan allowed the men a few moments to savor their victory, then jumped down from the tree and, looking up around him, called out, "Okay, cut the talk for a moment and call out your names."

When Morgan got six hearty returns to his order, he sighed in relief, then asked, "Anyone wounded?"

There was a long silence.

Morgan walked up to one tree whose broken branches were dangling at crazy angles and looked up, asking, "What about you, Fernando? This tree of yours took quite a blasting when that fool emptied his gun into it. You sure you didn't catch a bullet?"

"No, *señor*. Just a scratch."

"Come down here," Morgan commanded in a firm voice.

"But *señor*, it is just a scratch."

Morgan shook his head in exasperation. He was beginning to see where Jessie got her fierce pride. He had never realized what a proud people the Mexicans were.

"Dammit, I said get down here!" Morgan roared.

Morgan heard a rustling in the tree, and a moment later Fernando dropped down from the tree. Seeing the bloodstain on the youth's pants, Morgan said, "Pull up your pant leg. I want to see what you call a scratch."

The Mexican leaned forward and complied. Morgan bent and peered at the youth's calf, seeing that it was only grazed, although the wound was bleeding freely. Morgan rose, saying, "Okay, you can stay. But you'd better tie something around that wound before you bleed to death."

Fernando's face lit up with relief. "*Sí, señor*, I will."

"And later, when this is over, I want you to have it attended to, understand?"

"*Sí*, Señor West."

Morgan turned and called softly to the other men, "If they get their courage back, they might attempt another attack. Just to be safe, find yourself new trees in case they remember which ones they saw the shots coming from."

As the men dropped to the ground all around him, Morgan turned and walked to the dugout. When he neared the trench, he crouched behind one of the trees and called out, "Don't shoot. It's me, Morgan."

"*Sí, amigo,*" Pedro called back.

Morgan rose and walked toward the trench. Two figures emerged from the fog in front of him. Seeing Jessie, he frowned and said, "I thought I told you to stay in the dugout."

"Don't scold me, Morgan. We heard all the gunshots out back and then nothing. We've been worried sick. What happened?"

"They tried to sneak up on us from behind."

"And?"

Morgan grinned and threw his arm around her shoulders. "And those *mesteñeros* of yours gave them hell. The last I saw of those gunslingers they were running over the hill with their tails between their legs."

Jessie and Pedro laughed. Then Jessie asked, "Do you think it's over?"

"I can't say. Just to be safe, I think we'd better stay where we are until daylight, and then I'll take a look around."

All three heads snapped up at the sudden sounds of excited cries coming from the camp. Morgan whirled, saying, "What in the hell's going on back there?"

As Morgan tore off at a dead run, Jessie and Pedro followed. Morgan reached the camp first, scowling deeply as he passed the trench and saw it was empty. When he came into the clearing before the dugout, he came to an abrupt halt. The Mexicans had gathered between the wings, shouting with joy, clapping each other on the back, two dancing a merry jig.

"You crazy fools!" Morgan roared. "Get back under cover!"

A man near Morgan turned, a grin stretching from one ear to the other. "No, *señor*. It is over. We have won."

"What in the hell makes you think that?" Morgan snapped.

"We saw them leaving, *señor*."

Morgan turned to the man who had spoken. Recognizing him, he asked, "What are you doing here, Juan? You're supposed to be guarding the pen."

"*Sí*, but when we saw the *pistoleros* riding toward the *rancho*, we knew it was over."

"And how did you know that?" Morgan demanded.

"From the way they were riding, *señor*. Like all the *diablos* in hell were after them."

"It must be true," Jessie said, stepping forward from where she had been listening. "Why would they ride in that direction if they hadn't given up?"

Morgan frowned, then asked Raul, "Did you see how many there were?"

"*Sí*, there were seven. But two were wounded. We could tell by the way they were slumped in their saddles. Ah, *señor*, they rode right by the pen and didn't even notice us."

Morgan did a quick mental head count, wishing he

knew how many they had killed in the woods behind the cabin.

"Ah, *señor,* when we saw them riding in this direction earlier, we were *mucho* afraid for our *compadres* here. We didn't dream they could fight off thirty-seven gringos." The man flushed, realizing that he had used the term for Anglo that Mexicans used with just as much contempt as Anglos used the term *greasers.* "Forgive me, *señor,* I did not mean to insult you."

Morgan waved his apology away impatiently, saying, "You said thirty-seven. Are you sure of that?"

"*Sí,* we both counted them. For a while we considered coming back to camp so we could help, but then we remembered your orders."

Morgan could tell by the tone of the man's voice that he was disappointed at having missed out on the action. "Yes, and you two did a good job. Guarding that herd was important too. It's very valuable to the *patrona,* here."

Mollified by Morgan's praise in front of the others, Juan smiled, saying, "*Gracias,*" then turned and walked away.

Morgan turned to find Jessie laughing softly. "What's so funny?" he asked.

"You. If I remember correctly, you didn't like the idea of sending those men to guard my herd one bit. Now you're praising them for it."

"I was serious, Jess. I assigned them a job to do, and they stuck to it. I'm proud of the way all your people acted tonight."

"So am I," Jessie answered, suddenly serious. "Do you think the danger is over?"

Once again Morgan did a quick head count, then answered, "For tonight, yes."

"What now?"

"Well, first I'd better send someone to get those men out back down from their roosts, then form a burial party."

Jessie refused to look at the dead bodies scattered all around her. The sight unnerved her. "Can't that wait until morning? Everyone is exhausted."

"No, Jess, there isn't going to be any time for resting today. You've got a range war on your hands. As soon as we get these men buried, we've got to get out of here."

"Pull out? Now?"

"Jess, this isn't the end. It's just the beginning."

"But there are only seven of them left, and two are wounded. They wouldn't dare attack again!"

"I'm not talking about an out-and-out attack like to-night. I'm talking about ambushing us, picking us off a few at a time. Hell, Jess, those men are sharpshooters. They can hide in the brush and pick us off like a bunch of sitting ducks in the daylight."

"But where can we go?"

"I'd like to say clean out of this area, but I know you'd never agree to it, not since the White Steed has returned."

"I should say not!"

Morgan nodded his head grimly. "I thought not." Then, taking her arm, he said, "Come on, let's go inside and sit down. We've got some planning to do."

When Jessie and Morgan entered the cabin, Pedro and Gabe were sitting at the table. Morgan glanced across Gabe's shoulder at the cup sitting before the old mustanger. "Is that coffee?"

Gabe looked over his shoulder and grinned. "Nope, it's white mule. You wanna join us?"

"No, thanks. I'll have enough trouble staying awake without that."

Jessie crossed her arms over her breasts and said firmly, "All right, you two. One cupful, and one cup only."

"One cup?" Gabe asked in disbelief. "Hell, we won't even get a buzz out of that."

"I don't want you to get a buzz," Jessie retorted.

"Christ! Who put a bee in your bonnet? We deserve a little celebrating after tonight."

Pedro's gaze had been shifting from Jessie's to Morgan's face. Pushing his cup away, he said, "I think they have something important to say, *compadre.*"

"Yes, I do," Jessie answered. "Morgan thinks we should pull out, that the gunfighters will be back."

"After the whipping we gave them?" Gabe asked in disbelief. "Hell, those yellowbellies will be too scared to come nosing around here anymore."

"Morgan, tell them what you told me while I start a pot of coffee." She gave Gabe a hard look, adding, "Strong coffee."

Morgan explained that he feared the gunslingers would try to ambush them in small groups, or pick them off from a distance. When he finished, Gabe snorted. "I still say they're too scared to come back. "Why, they're probably halfway to the border by now."

"No, the men at the pen saw them riding toward the ranch," Morgan reminded him. "If they were going to skip out on Gibbons, they would have been headed in the opposite direction. Remember, these men are hired killers. Gibbons is paying them for this, and they don't get paid until the job is done. They may demand a higher price now, but Gibbons can afford it, considering

he doesn't have to pay the men that got killed here
tonight."

"*Sí*, the only thing that will change, will be their tactics," Pedro said in a solemn voice.

"That's right," Morgan agreed.

"What do you want me do, *amigo*?" Pedro asked.

"First, send someone to call in the men out back. But
tell them to keep their distance and yell loud, or they're
liable to get their heads blown off."

Pedro nodded and asked, "And after that?"

"Round up the wounded and then get those dead
men out there buried."

"Hell, why do we have to do that?" Gabe spat. "Let
Gibbons bury them!"

"If I know Gibbons, he couldn't care less. He'd let
them lie there and rot before he'd bury them."

"Then let them rot!" Gabe retorted. "They ain't nothing but a bunch of murdering polecats."

"No, *compadre*," Pedro said, coming to his feet.
"They were human beings, and we will give them a
decent burial. It is our Christian duty."

As the old man walked to the door, Morgan said,
"Bury them in the trenches, Pedro. We don't have time
to dig individual graves."

After Pedro had left, Jessie returned to the table and
poured coffee into two empty cups sitting on it. "Where
will we go?" she asked Morgan. "Even if we leave, they
can follow our tracks."

"There are ways of covering tracks, Jess. At least
enough to keep them busy doing more tracking than
trailing. We'll have to stay on the move, never make
camp in the same place. But Jess, you can't take your
herds with you. There's no way we can cover that many
tracks."

"I know. I had planned to send them on to San Antonio with half of my men, while I took the other half to help capture the White Steed, but now I hate to split up the outfit."

"Jess, if it's your mustangs you're worrying about, forget it. Those men won't be going after them. It's us they'll be following. And with fewer people in our party, we'll be able to move faster."

"What about the wounded?"

"Put them in your wagon and let them travel with the group that's going to San Antonio. Once they're out of the immediate vicinity, they can take their time. As for us, we're going to travel as light and fast as we can."

"When do you think we should leave?"

"This morning, if possible. Do you think you can manage that?"

"We'll have to," Jessie answered glumly.

Jessie took another sip of coffee, then took a deep breath. She turned to Gabe. "I want you to take the herds to San Antonio."

"Me?" Gabe asked in a shocked voice. "Why me? Why don't you send Pedro?"

Because I'm going to need Pedro's expertise to capture the White Steed, Jessie thought, but said instead, "Gabe, you know I can't send Pedro. Señor Rodriguez might let me graze my herd of mares on his range, but he'll never let me graze that big herd of mustangs. No, that herd is going to have to be sold as soon as it reaches San Antonio, and Pedro would never be able to deal with those buyers. You know how low their opinion of Mexicans is. Besides that, Pedro doesn't even understand our monetary system. You know yourself that he can hardly add and subtract. Why, they'd cheat him coming and going, and laugh behind his back the whole time they were doing it."

"But, Jessie," Gabe argued, "if I take your herds to San Antonio, I'll miss out on the capture of the White Steed."

"I know, and I'm truly sorry about that."

"I ain't gonna do it!" Gabe said angrily, coming to his feet. "You find someone else to take those herds to San Antonio. I'm going with you!"

"There isn't anyone else! They're all Mexicans, and they'll all get cheated!"

"Dammit, I ain't gonna do it! That's all there is to it. I ain't gonna do it!"

With that, Gabe stomped angrily out of the cabin.

Jessie folded her arms on the table and laid her head on them, muttering, "Oh, God, what am I going to do now?"

Morgan rose, squeezed her shoulder gently, then said, "Don't despair, Jess." He turned and walked from the dugout.

When he stepped outside, Gabe was pacing angrily before the cabin. Seeing Morgan, the old man came to an abrupt halt, saying belligerently, "If you came out here to try and talk me into it—forget it!"

"Whoa, back off," Morgan drawled lazily. "That's between you and Jessie. My job is protecting this outfit. Nothing more. I just came out for a quiet smoke."

Gabe glared at Morgan's broad back as he smoked. "You think I'm a selfish bastard, don't you?"

"I told you, it's none of my business," Morgan replied.

"Yeah, but you're still thinking. And I bet you think I'm wrong."

Morgan turned, leaning against the railing. "No, as a matter of fact, I don't. I'm glad you stood up to her."

"You are?" Gabe gasped in surprise.

"Damned right! You know," Morgan said, dropping his voice to a confidential tone, "it makes me sick the way women try to take advantage of us men. Once they get it into their heads that they can depend on you, they come running to you every time they find themselves in a tight spot, wanting to unload their problems on your strong shoulders."

Gabe's expression turned thoughtful. "Yeah, Jessie does kinda depend upon me."

"You're damned right she depends upon you. Too much! Hell, you don't owe her nothing. It's not like you're family, or something. You just work for her."

Gabe frowned, his bushy eyebrows meeting over the arch of his nose.

"Now, there's no reason why she can't send Pedro," Morgan continued. "All that talk about him not being as smart or capable as you is just a bunch of hogwash to get you to do what she wants you to. That's another female trick."

"Nope, she's right about that," Gabe admitted. "That old pepper-eater don't know nothing about selling horses. They'd cheat the pants off him."

Morgan shrugged, saying, "So they'd pull the wool over his eyes. Jessie would just have to take the loss."

"But she needs that money to buy her land."

"Then she can take the herd and sell in San Antonio herself."

"But if she did that, the White Steed might be gone by the time she got back. She'd be awful disappointed."

"Not any more disappointed than you'd be if you missed out on his capture," Morgan countered. "But that didn't stop her from asking you, did it?"

Gabe's frown turned to a deep scowl. He'd be disappointed, but Jessie would be absolutely heartbroken.

Morgan tossed his cigarette away, pushed himself from the railing, and peeked in the window, saying in a disgusted voice, "Now, isn't that just like a woman? As soon as she doesn't get her way, she starts crying."

"Jessie ain't never cried a day in her life," Gabe said defensively. "Not even the day we put her pa in the ground."

"Well, she looks like she's going to start crying any minute. Hell, from the look on her face, you'd think she'd lost her best friend."

Gabe shot Morgan a sharp look, then leaned over to peer in the window. What Morgan had said was true. Jessie was staring out into space, her eyes glittering with unshed tears, the picture of abject despair.

Gabe felt a pang of deep shame. He turned to Morgan, saying defiantly, "I'm going in there an' tell Jessie I'm gonna take those herds to San Antonio, just like she wants me to."

Morgan shrugged. "Like I said, it's none of my business. It's between you and Jessie."

"You're damned right it is!" Gabe spat as he turned and walked back into the dugout. Outside, Morgan choked back a laugh.

Gabe walked over to Jessie and said, "I'm sorry, Jessie, gal. I didn't mean to blow up like that. I ain't gonna let you down. I'll take those herds to San Antonio for you."

Jessie turned, an astonished look on her face. Then she shot to her feet. "You will?"

"Sure will. And I'll get you a good price for them too."

"Oh, thank you, Gabe," Jessie cried, throwing her arms about him and hugging him tightly. "And I know you'll get a good price for them. Why, I bet you'll get the best price I've ever gotten."

"Damn right I will! Those buyers ain't gonna pull the wool over my eyes. They're gonna find I'm a hard man to deal with."

Jessie stepped back and asked, "Would you do me one more favor?"

"What's that?" Gabe asked, a suspicious gleam coming into his eyes.

"Stay at the Rodriguez *rancho* and keep an eye on my mares until I can join you?"

Gabe frowned.

"I'd hate for anything to happen to them, and I know I can trust you."

Gabe looked into Jessie's pleading eyes. "Okay," he agreed reluctantly, then, seeing the happy smile spreading across Jessie's face, repeated more enthusiastically, "Okay, I'll do it."

"Thank you, Gabe. I knew I could depend on you. You're always there when I need you."

Gabe beamed at her praise, then turned and saw Morgan standing just inside the door. He glared at the tall Texan as he walked from the cabin, then hissed as he passed, "You ought to be ashamed of yourself. Talking about poor little defenseless women like that."

It was all Morgan could do to keep a straight face while Gabe pushed the blanket back and stepped outside.

As Morgan walked over to Jessie, chuckling softly, she asked, "You talked Gabe into it, didn't you?"

"No, I can honestly say he talked himself into it. All I did was give him a little nudge in the right direction."

Morgan poured himself a cup of coffee and took a sip. His silver eyes bored into Jessie's. "Why did you ask him to watch over your mares? I thought you didn't trust him with them."

A guilty flush came over Jessie's face. "I don't. But I was afraid he'd get the notion to come looking for us after he'd sold the herd and get lost—or worse, inadvertently run right into Gibbons's hired guns."

"And so you used your womanly wiles on him?"

Jessie's flush deepened, then she retorted, "Yes, I did! And stop looking at me so accusingly. I wouldn't have done it if it hadn't been for his own good." She chewed her lower lip, a worried expression coming over her face. "Oh, God," she groaned, "I hope those mares stay healthy. The thought of Gabe using any of his remedies on them makes me shudder."

Morgan laughed, emptied his cup and set it back down on the table, and said, "I'm going out there and help with the digging."

"I'll start dividing up the supplies."

"Remember, we're traveling light," Morgan reminded her.

"I know. But we still have to eat!" Jessie retorted.

Chapter 20

WHEN EVERYONE WAS IN THEIR SADDLES AND READY to leave, Gabe yelled to the *mesteñeros* surrounding the two herds, "Move 'em out!"

As the herds of mustangs ambled away, Gabe turned in his saddle and said to Jessie, "Don't you worry about nothing on this end."

"I won't," Jessie lied gracefully, sneaking a last worried look at her prize mares. "And we'll see you in San Antonio in a few weeks."

Riding off, Gabe called over his shoulder, "And I'm gonna want to hear everything about the White Steed's capture, so you be sure and remember."

"I will," Jessie called back.

When the wagon with the wounded and supplies in it rolled off after the mustangs, Morgan said, "Let's get out of here too."

Jessie glanced up, seeing the buzzards circling overhead, the scavengers awaiting the humans' departure so they could feast on the dead horses. She shivered at the gruesome thought and kneed her horse forward.

Morgan and Jessie rode at the head of the column, Pedro slightly behind at their right, followed by the four *mesteñeros.* Behind them, the two *mesteñeros* serving as *remuderos* led the remuda of ten horses, including Morgan's gelding.

When they reached the river, Morgan guided his horse down the bank and into the water. Jessie reined in, asking, "Why are you crossing? The White Steed was sighted upriver on this side."

Morgan pivoted El Dragón and faced Jessie. "Yes, and that's the first place Gibbons's hired guns will look for us, on this side of the river."

"Oh," Jessie muttered lamely, then kneed her mount forward to follow Morgan.

The river at that point was both wide and deep, and everyone dropped their reins when they reached deep water, for pulling back on them would cause their mounts to sink. Jessie wasn't surprised when the remuda passed them, the freed horses unhampered by the weight of saddles and humans. The animals climbed up the opposite bank and vigorously shook the water from their hides, sending a shower of glittering droplets as the others emerged from the river.

Through the mesquites Morgan caught sight of a herd of mustangs grazing on the open prairie just beyond the tree line. Looking about him on the ground, he saw the hundreds of hoofprints from where they had just recently watered. El Dragón began to rear and snort shrilly. Morgan fought him down, pulling on his reins to make him circle. "What in the hell's wrong with you?" he muttered as the stallion reared again, shaking his head wildly and sending his mane flying.

"It's simple," Jessie said with a smug smile. "He sees that herd of mustangs and wants loose so he can challenge one of the stallions for his mares. I told you mares were more manageable mounts."

"Are you telling me every time he sees a *manada* he takes a liking to, I'm going to have to go through this?" Morgan asked in dismay as he forced the frustrated stallion to circle round and round.

"He's a herd stallion. It's all he's ever known. Old habits are hard to break," Jessie answered.

At the sound of El Dragón's shrill snort, the herd had stampeded. Seeing them disappear in the distance, the stallion finally settled down, pawing at the ground and snorting at what Morgan guessed must be disgust at his master's lack of cooperation.

Morgan leaned over and patted the *palomino*'s neck. "Sorry about that, fella. But you're going to have to stop chasing every female you take a fancy to."

He looked up to see the amused looks on everyone's faces, then said, "Well, I guess I'd better put him back in the remuda and ride my old gelding."

"And have him get the notion that my remuda horses are his mares and run off with them?" Jessie countered. "Oh, no, we've kept him away from my mares all this time and we'll continue to. He's your problem."

"Would he really do that?" Morgan asked Pedro. "Try to steal Jessie's mares?"

"*Sí, amigo,* he might. The desire to be free is still as strong as his herding instincts. It will take time, and mastering."

"How come he didn't cut up like this back at camp?"

"Because we don't have any stallions," Jessie answered. "It was the sight of them that set him off."

"Well, in that case I hope we don't run into too many

herds." Morgan gazed off in the direction the herd had disappeared, then said, "However, running into that herd is the best thing that could have happened to us. If we follow their trail, the men tracking us are going to have a hard time figuring out which direction we went after they cross the river. When they see all these hoof-prints, hundreds more than went into the river on the opposite side, they'll know a mustang herd watered here. Then they might figure we swam our horses up- or downstream and go looking there. By the time they realize we followed the herd, they could be half a day behind us."

"I'd feel better if we could put more time and distance than that between us," Jessie said with a worried frown.

"We will. This is just the first of several plans I have," Morgan answered.

"There is only one problem, *amigo*," Pedro said. "Your gelding is shod. Our horses and the mustangs are not, and his print stands out."

Morgan looked down and saw the clear prints of horseshoes. Grimly he dismounted, pulled his knife from his saddlebag, and walked to the gelding, saying, "Sorry, boy, but this is where you lose your shoes. Better for you to have sore feet for a few days, than us get killed."

Ten minutes later Morgan tossed the last shoe into the river and remounted El Dragón. "Run the remuda back and forth over this area until these shod hoofprints have been obliterated," he told the *remuderos*.

Morgan led them over the trail the stampeding herd had taken, noting with satisfaction that their hoofprints blended in with the others so well that no one could tell two separate groups of horses had passed.

As they rode one mile, then two, Jessie began to glance back over her shoulder. Finally she asked, "Can't we double back to the river now? At this rate we'll never catch sight of the White Steed today."

"Not yet," Morgan answered in a firm voice, his eyes scanning the area in front of them. "We're not leaving this mustang trail until I can find the right spot to do it." Turning his attention to Jessie, he said, "And Jess, forget about the White Steed for today. Today we concentrate on shaking those men back there."

About two miles farther on, Morgan spied a dry creek bed before them. The ravine was deep but not wide, and for that reason the mustangs that had passed earlier had simply jumped it, rather than contend with the cactus and brush that grew on its steep sides.

Morgan reined in and studied the creek bed thoughtfully, then stood in his stirrups and followed its twisting course through the prairie. Sitting back in the saddle, he said to the others, "We'll follow this creek bed north. It looks like it runs pretty much parallel to the river. Farther up-country we'll cut back to the Nueces."

Jessie looked down at the creek bed. "It looks awfully narrow. We'll have to ride our horses in single file."

"Yes, and that will make covering their tracks all that much easier," Morgan responded.

"Those rocks and that gravel are going to be hard on your gelding's tender feet," Jessie observed. "He's already limping."

Morgan glanced back at the unfortunate animal, saying, "I know, but it can't be helped. If we wipe out our tracks where we descend into the ravine, and then behind us, those men will never figure out where we left the trail. At least not for a long time. This is the ideal spot."

"Ah, *amigo,* I have been pondering over your gelding's problem and think I have a solution," Pedro said, moving his horse forward. He reached into his *morral* and brought out a piece of sheepskin, saying, "We can cut this up and tie it around his hooves to cushion them."

The relief on Morgan's face was obvious to all. Taking the sheepskin from Pedro, he said, *"Gracias,"* then, "Pedro, you go first so I can bring up the rear. Follow the creek as far north as you can before you cut back to the river."

Pedro guided his horse down the steep bank into the ravine and turned north, the others following. Morgan held his gelding back until the last, then led the animal into the creek bed, dismounted, cut the sheepskin into strips, and tied them around his hooves. Giving the horse a small slap on his rump, he said, "Go on, boy," and the gelding obediently trotted off behind the others.

Morgan cut a small limb from one of the mesquites that hung over the ravine and brushed all signs of their hoofprints from the steep bank of the creek bed. Mounting, he urged El Dragón forward, dragging the limb across the sand and gravel behind him, watching carefully over his shoulder to see that not one hoof mark remained to give away where they had left the trail.

While the dry creek did run parallel to the river, it meandered a lot through the countryside, twisting and turning as it cut across the prairie. In some places it traveled through thick brush, looking like a long, dark tunnel. Finally, when it made a wide loop into the woods that fringed the river, Pedro judged it time they leave the ravine and urged his horse up the steep incline. There he, Jessie, and the others waited for Morgan.

Jessie wiped the perspiration from her forehead with the sleeve of her shirt, relieved to be in the shade of the trees. For the most part they had been exposed to the hot sun on their seemingly endless ride through the ravine. "How far north do you think we traveled?" she asked Pedro.

"It is hard to say. I would guess about ten or eleven miles."

"And it's already four o'clock," Jessie muttered to herself. Then, seeing Morgan emerging from the ravine, her eyes brightened.

"We'll travel upstream a little farther and make camp," Morgan announced.

"So early?" Jessie objected. "There's still a few hours of daylight left."

"Jess, everyone is exhausted."

"But—"

"I know," Morgan interjected. "You're *still* hoping to catch sight of the White Steed today. But Jess, even if we sighted him, we're too exhausted to do anything about it. Better to get a good night's sleep and start out bright and early tomorrow morning."

Jessie really couldn't argue with the wisdom of Morgan's plan. The *mesteñeros* looked as if they were going to fall from their saddles, their eyes red-rimmed from lack of sleep. But despite her own exhaustion, she could hardly wait to lay eyes on the magnificent stallion again and seriously doubted that she'd be able to sleep a wink. Seeing Morgan patiently awaiting her answer, she sighed in disappointment and said, "Oh, all right."

They made their camp by the river under a rustling cottonwood. By the time the horses had been watered

and fed and the evening meal prepared and eaten, it
was dusk.

Having returned from the river, where he had
washed his eating utensils, Morgan sat them down
where the others were stacked by the fire, saying, "I'll
take first watch."

Jessie looked up from where she sat across the fire and
got a really good look at Morgan for the first time that
day. His face was deeply lined with fatigue, and his eyes
were bloodshot. Even his shoulders, which he always
held so erect, were slumped, all testimony to the long,
hard hours he had put in and the mental strain he had
been under for the past two days. Remembering how
she had wanted to push even farther, Jessie felt a strong
pang of self-reproach. "Can't we skip that tonight?"

"No. Even though I feel fairly sure those hired killers
haven't picked up our trail yet, I don't want to take any
chances." He picked up his Winchester and walked to a
tree a distance away, sitting down and leaning against
the trunk, placing the rifle on his lap.

Pedro and the other *mesteñeros* wearily spread their
blankets and lay down. None had offered to take first
watch instead, Pedro because he knew Morgan would
firmly refuse him, and the others because they could
hardly keep their eyes open. Soon the camp was filled
with the soft snores of the men.

Mostly out of boredom, Jessie spread her blanket and
lay down, absently watching the dancing flames in the
fire and thinking she would never go to sleep, she was so
excited about what tomorrow would bring. But it was
inevitable that her exhausted body would eventually
make its need known. Lulled by the sounds of the murmuring river beside her and the softly rustling tree
above, her eyelids fluttered down.

As the night passed, Morgan found himself nodding more and more often. Finally he rose and walked to the river, washing his face in hopes the cool water would stimulate him. Then he forced himself to pace back and forth, thinking that as long as he could stay on his feet, he could stay awake. But his exhaustion was bone-deep, and several times he staggered and had to shake his head.

Hearing a slight noise, he whirled and saw Pedro walking toward him.

"I will keep watch now," the old man said softly.

Morgan glanced at the stars, then said, "You only slept five hours. Go on back for a little longer. I'll wake you."

"No, *amigo*. I have recuperated. That is one of the advantages of growing old. My body does not require as much sleep as when I was younger."

"You're sure?"

"*Sí*. Now go lie down, *amigo*. Before you fall down."

Knowing rest was finally at hand, Morgan's body almost refused to obey one more command from his brain. It was all he could do to force himself to stagger to the fire and spread his blanket beside it. Then he fell on it, facedown, asleep before his head even hit the ground.

Morgan was still in that same sprawled position when the rest of the camp awoke the next morning. Seeing he had fallen asleep with his gun belt still on, and thinking that the gun digging into his hip must be uncomfortable, Jessie crept to his side and reached for it. She gasped as Morgan's hand flew to his gun and he rolled over and sat up, all in one smooth, lightning-quick movement. Jessie found herself once again looking down the barrel of his six-shooter.

Morgan lowered his gun, saying, "Jesus Christ! I've told you never to sneak up on me like that!"

"I forgot. Besides, you looked like you were dead to the world."

Morgan shook his head to clear the cobwebs from it, muttering, "I was." He looked about the camp and saw that breakfast was already being prepared and the horses watered and fed. "What time is it?"

"Eight o'clock."

"Eight o'clock?" Morgan repeated in surprise. "God, I must have been tired. I never sleep this late."

Rising, Jessie said, "I'll bring you some breakfast."

When she returned carrying a tin plate of food and a cup of fresh coffee, Morgan accepted them, saying, "This is the life. First sleeping late, and now breakfast in bed. You'll spoil me."

Jessie laughed. "Oh, no. Don't expect this treatment every morning."

She walked back to the fire and returned with her own plate and cup, dropping down on the blanket beside Morgan. As they ate Morgan took note of the sparkle in her eyes and the excited flush on her face. "You seem to be very excited about something this morning," he teased.

"Oh, Morgan, I can hardly wait to be off. It seems like I've been waiting for this day for years, instead of months."

"Well, I hope I'll at least have time for a shave," Morgan said, rubbing the dark, two-day stubble on his chin.

"Do you really have to?"

Morgan laughed and set his plate aside. "You don't want to ride all day beside a man who looks like a desperado, do you? I promise I won't take long."

Jessie watched as he picked up his saddlebags and

strolled down to the river, thinking that he had the most graceful walk she had ever seen on a man. Her eyes drifted admiringly over his tall, muscular physique. Then, realizing she must look like a child hungrily eyeing a piece of candy, she flushed, jumped to her feet, and started calling orders to her *mesteñeros*.

By the time Morgan returned from the river, the camp had been completely cleared, and everyone was in their saddle and waiting. He looked about him in amazement, saying, "That must have been a world's record for breaking camp."

"*Sí, amigo*," Pedro said with a twinkle in his eyes, handing Morgan the reins to El Dragón, "the *patrona* is in a bit of a hurry this morning."

"Well, thanks for saddling my horse for me, Pedro. Otherwise I might have been left behind."

Morgan glanced up at Jessie, fidgeting impatiently in her saddle. She's as excited as a kid on Christmas morning, he thought in amusement as he swung onto his horse.

Morgan had hardly hit leather when Jessie was off, racing La Duquesa across the prairie with her long golden hair flying out behind her.

"Ah, *amigo*, we are going to have some hard riding to do today if we are going to keep up with her," Pedro said, kneeing his horse.

It took some looking to find the famous stallion. They crisscrossed the area over and over with no success, until Morgan began to wonder if the Mexican who had sighted the horse had only imagined he had seen the mustang. As the day wore on and Jessie became more and more frantic, Morgan began to doubt their sanity. Maybe the horse *was* just a legend, nonexistent except in the minds of men, and they'd never find him, no matter how far or how long they searched.

Then, at sundown, when they crested a small rise, Jessie reined in and called out, "There he is!"

Morgan had lived among the mustangs in Texas all his life. More times than he could count, he had admired their beauty and grace, either singularly or in groups. But the impact of seeing the White Steed for the first time took his breath away. It was a vision that would be imprinted on his memory in vivid clarity for the rest of his life.

The snowy-white stallion stood poised majestically at the top of a hill in the distance. Behind him, the setting sun was a huge ball of fire that sent golden beams of light radiating into a rosy sky, a fitting backdrop for this animal of extraordinary beauty.

And *beautiful* was the only word that could possibly describe him. His head was raised proudly, revealing the sleek lines of his slender neck, his ears standing at attention as he surveyed the prairie around him. Perfectly proportioned, the stallion's powerful muscles rippled beneath his gleaming coat, and his silky white mane cascaded to his knees, while his long tail swept the ground, both shimmering in the light and tinged with gold, then rose, then gold again.

Spying the group, the stallion lifted his head even higher and stared at them, and Morgan could feel the defiance in that steady, piercing gaze even across the distance that separated them. Then, shaking his head and giving a shrill snort, the mustang sprang forward and raced across the prairie, as if daring them to try to catch him.

Morgan had always thought that the speed of the White Steed must have been exaggerated by those who claimed to have seen him, for surely no creature of flesh and bone could run that fast. But now he knew those men had spoken the truth. Never in his life had he seen anything as swift as this stallion, nor as graceful. He was beauty in fluid motion, a natural pacer whose gait was so smooth and effortless that he seemed to float through the air. As the mustang sped across the prairie, the wind blew his long white mane out to both sides, making him look as if he had sprouted wings and was now flying, a huge, beautiful white bird with the head of a horse, a mythological creature that sailed across the panorama of a sky filled with the brilliant colors cast by the setting sun.

Long after the magnificent stallion had disappeared over the horizon, Morgan and the others sat in total silence, awed expressions on their faces. "Now I know why you're so determined to have him, Jess," he said softly.

Morgan's voice brought Jessie back from the strange spell the stallion had cast over all of them. Still feeling dazed, she asked, "Have you ever seen anything so beautiful?"

"No, I can't say I have, and I've seen some beautiful things in this country," Morgan answered. Then, feeling an excitement rising in him, he asked, "How will you try to capture him? Set up a trap for him at his watering place, like we did for El Dragón?"

"No, he'd never fall for a trap like that. He's much too smart."

Although Jessie hadn't realized it, there had been a sharp edge to her words. Thinking that Morgan might feel El Dragón's intelligence was being slurred and take offense in behalf of his horse, Pedro quickly said, "The White Steed is not only an animal of rare beauty, grace, and speed, but unusually intelligent, too. He has to be, to have escaped capture after all these years of being pursued by so many. Somewhere in the past, someone apparently tried to trap him at his watering hole, for he is very cautious. He will only water in the open and, unlike other mustangs, looks up before he passes beneath a tree."

"Yes, I suppose he *has* become a master at escape by necessity," Morgan agreed. "So how will you try to capture him?"

"By wearing him down with relays," Jessie answered. "It's the only way. Keep him moving, both day and night, until he's so exhausted he can't flee, or his speed is so drastically reduced we can catch him."

"*Sí, amigo,* we tried that before. When we finally closed in on the fourth day, we thought he was too worn down to run anymore. We had totally underestimated him. He ran clear out of this area."

"And now he's back. But this time we won't underestimate him," Jessie said in a determined voice.

They returned to the river to make camp. While they were eating, Jessie gave instructions to the *mesteñeros* on where to set up their relay stations the next day. Morgan insisted on participating, just as excited at the prospect of capturing the famous white mustang as the others were.

After the night guard had left for his post and the other Mexicans had retired, Jessie and Morgan sat and talked beside the campfire. Not until he heard the men snoring softly did Morgan take Jessie's hand and rise, pulling her up with him.

He looked down at her, the firelight playing over his rugged features and reflected in his eyes, eyes that were dark with desire. As he led her from the camp Jessie didn't ask where they were going. She knew. He was taking her down to the river to fulfill the passionate promise he had made her the night they had been attacked by the raiders. "Later" had arrived.

Morgan stopped to pick up a blanket, tossing it over his shoulder. No sooner had they stepped into the shadows of the trees than Morgan crushed her to him, his mouth covering hers in a hot, searching kiss, his tongue making deep forays into her mouth and bringing Jessie to her tiptoes. She strained against him, not caring that one of the *mesteñeros* might stumble upon them on his way to the woods for a call of nature, too intoxicated by Morgan's kiss to be aware of anything but the blood pounding in her ears, her breasts swelling against his chest, and his hard arousal pressing against her lower abdomen.

Their breath rasping in their throats, they parted, took a few steps, then fell into each other's arms again, their mouths fusing in yet another deep, passionate kiss. Morgan slipped Jessie's shirt from her, and bent, kissing and laving her breasts with his tongue. Jessie cried out softly, arching her back and holding him to her, feeling a scalding heat rush to her loins.

Again they parted, took a few steps, and came together. This time it was Morgan's shirt that fell to the ground, Jessie's hands running over his shoulders and back feverishly as their tongues danced erotically.

Finally, Morgan drew back, muttering, "At this rate we'll never reach the river."

Scooping her up in his arms, he carried with quick, purposeful strides through the moon-dabbled woods, and Jessie snuggled closer, burying her head in the crook of his neck, loving the feeling of being cradled in his strong arms and his powerful heart pounding against her breast. She drank in his exciting scent, then, unable to resist the temptation, her tongue flicked out against the tanned skin of his throat.

Morgan stiffened and missed a step. "Dammit, Jess," he rasped, "don't do that. I'm already so damned excited I can hardly walk."

Jessie giggled, then attacked his ear, her tongue gently ravishing it. Morgan clenched his teeth, grinding out in a warning voice, "Jess!"

But Jessie couldn't stop. She was hungry for the taste of him and, if truth be known, she enjoyed tormenting him. She nuzzled his soft sideburns and kissed the length of his strong jawline. Morgan fought to endure her sensual assault, his aroused male flesh straining at the restrictive material of his pants and making it uncomfortable to walk. Then, when Jessie deliberately brushed her breasts against his naked chest and he felt her nipples stabbing him like fiery darts, he sucked in his breath, hissing, "Little witch!"

Morgan's mouth captured Jessie's in a kiss that scorched her clear down to her toes and quickly reduced her to a quivering mass of sheer need in his arms. When he reached the river and set her on her feet, Jessie was so weak, she could barely stand, and everything was spinning around her, the trees, the moon, the stars.

Morgan made quick work of the rest of their clothing, impatiently popping a button on his pants in his haste. He pulled Jessie to the blanket with him, his mouth locking on hers in yet another fiery kiss that played havoc with her already reeling senses, his body covering hers like a warm blanket. Frenziedly, Jessie ran her hands over him, kissing him back with wild abandon, twisting her hips so his legs were between hers and his manhood lay between their bellies, immense and searing her sensitive flesh.

Then Morgan was sliding down her body, the crisp hairs on his chest abrading her throbbing nipples, his lips dropping erotic love bites over her shoulders and across her breasts. Jessie moaned, a guttural sound at the back of her throat, her fingers twining mindlessly in his hair as his tongue laved one soft mound before he took the nipple in his mouth. As he worked his magic every nerve ending in Jessie's body seemed suddenly to come to life, tingling and burning, especially in her hidden, secret woman's place.

She uttered a strangled protest when Morgan lifted his hips and lay to one side of her, then sucked in her breath as his hand slid between her thighs and into her dewiness. As his slender fingers teased and tantalized, driving her wild with mindless excitement, hot spirals of sensation shot through her loins. She reached for him, her hand folding around his fiery hardness, needing him inside her, knowing that only he could quench the fire that was consuming her.

"Christ!" Morgan ground out between clenched teeth, feeling as if he would explode. Urgently, he pried her hand loose, rose over her, and lifted her hips, then drove deeply into her welcoming moist heat.

Jessie gave a glad cry and wrapped her legs around his slim hips, pulling him deeper and holding him there with a fierce tenacity, her muscles contracting greedily around him and driving him wild—driving them both wild.

Frenzied with need, they rode that hot crest, feverish bodies straining, hearts pounding, breath rasping, their excitement reaching an unbearable, almost painful, pitch, the pressure building and building until it burst in a powerful release of blinding, searing light.

For a long time they lay with Morgan collapsed over Jessie, both too weak to move and still feeling dazed, their bodies trembling with aftershocks. Finally, Morgan started to rise.

But Jessie didn't want to give him up. "No," she whispered fiercely. "Stay where you are."

"I'm too heavy," Morgan objected.

"I don't mind. I just want to hold you a while longer."

Resting his upper weight on his elbows, Morgan slipped his arms around her, his head nestled in the soft crook of her neck. Jessie reveled in the feel of his warm skin pressed against hers, his lips against her throat, his breath fanning her ear. She ran her hands over him, starting at the back of his neck, then over the smooth skin of his shoulders, wanting to commit every tendon, every powerful muscle, every inch of him, to memory so she could carry him with her always.

As her fingers moved down his back she felt a ridge of hard skin that could only be a scar. Trailing its length, she wondered how she could have missed it before. "When did you get this?" she asked softly.

Morgan stiffened in her arms, and for a moment she thought he wouldn't answer. When he did speak, his voice was full of bitterness. "It's my legacy from the Comanches."

Jessie pushed on his shoulders and when he raised his head, she asked, "You were captured by the Comanches and survived?"

"Yes."

"When?"

Morgan rolled from her and lay on his back, staring at

the stars. Jessie's question had brought back memories, painful memories.

Jessie turned on her side and raised up on one elbow, looking down at Morgan. The expression on his face tore at her heart. "You don't have to tell me about it if you don't want to," she said softly.

Morgan had never revealed his past to anyone. The memories of his childhood and youth had been buried deep inside him, and those who had been curious enough to ask had always wished they hadn't, suddenly finding themselves facing a man with a hard, warning look in his eyes, a man as silent, as inexorable, as stone. But now, with Jessie's love-filled eyes looking down at him, Morgan found that, for the first time in his life, he wanted to talk about it.

"My mother and I were abducted by Comanches from the ranch we lived on in West Texas. My father and older brothers were out working on the range that day. Since I was only five years old, I was left behind to help my mother. We were out in the yard in back of the house, gathering up the dried laundry my mother had washed that day. Suddenly we were surrounded by Indians. They seemed to come at us from behind every tree and bush. We were both terrified and fought and screamed, but it was useless. She was thrown on a horse in front of one Indian and I, in front of another.

"It turned out that the Indians who had captured us were part of a large party of Comanches returning from a raid into Mexico. Besides the thousands of horses and other booty they had stolen, they had captives, Mexican women and children. The next morning my mother and I were stripped naked like the other captives, the first of the rites of humiliation the Indians would inflict on us. I was too young to know real shame, but my mother was mortified. Then our hands were tied behind our backs and we were forced to run behind our captors' horses with rawhide tethers tied around our necks. It was fall, warm enough in the daytime to get sunburned, yet cool enough at night for us to be cold with no protective clothing."

There was a faraway look in Morgan's eyes, and Jessie knew he was no longer telling his story, but reliving it.

"I learned early on that long trek back to *Comancheria* that the Comanches had no compassion for their captives. Every time we stumbled or fell, we were beaten. I also discovered the Indians had no patience for weakness or cowardice. After seeing a woman killed in cold blood by her captor because he had become disgusted with her weakness, and a Mexican boy only a year or two older than me castrated because he was crying, I learned to hide my fear, to endure the whippings and hunger, to force myself to keep up despite my cut, swollen feet and my aching muscles. Survival was my only goal.

"When we reached the Indians' main camp, my mother and I were both put to work. After all, we were slaves. I was sent to tend the horses, while she was put to the backbreaking labor of hauling water, digging for roots, scraping hides, and collecting buffalo chips for the fires. In many ways we were more fortunate than some of the other captives, though. Buffalo Horn, our captor, was harsh, but not cruel, nor did he allow his wives to get overzealous in their punishments. We were never burned with hot sticks or cut with knives, like some other captives. However, my mother didn't escape being raped, yet another of the Comanches' rites of humiliation. Since we slept in the tepee with our captor and his wives, I was present at those times, although I was still too young to realize what was happening and it was too dark to see. But I heard my mother sobbing and pleading, and that alone was enough to upset me."

Horrified by what she was hearing, Jessie wisely kept her silence, somehow sensing that these were things Morgan had never told anyone. These ugly, terrifying memories had been locked deep inside him for many years, and now, as they poured from him in a rush of words, he was cleansing his soul.

"So you see, all in all I fared better in our captivity than my mother did. I was young enough to adjust to the hard, rigorous Indian way of life. As the memories of my previous life faded, the hardships of the new life forced on me no longer bothered me. I was content to run around half naked, eat stringy, half-raw buffalo meat, sleep on the hard ground with only a stinking, lice-invested buffalo pallet, go for months without bathing, endure the endless taunts and jeers of the Indian children. I became as brown and lean and tough as the Indian boys my age, as adept at riding a horse bareback as they were. I looked like an Indian, acted like an Indian, was even beginning to think like an Indian. I'm sure if my mother hadn't insisted we converse in English, I would have completely forgotten my native tongue.

"When we had been at the Indian camp for four years, a *Comanchero* came from Santa Fe to trade with the Indians and discovered us. He was a white man, not a half-breed, and took compassion on us. He approached Buffalo Horn about releasing us for a ransom. Buffalo Horn was willing to let my mother go for a price, but wanted to keep me. I think he was considering adopting me. I have that *Comanchero* to thank for my return to civilization. He insisted it would be either both—or neither—of us, and Buffalo Horn finally agreed.

"While the *Comanchero* was away collecting the ransom from my father and buying the trading goods Buffalo Horn had demanded, all my mother could talk about was how wonderful it would be to get back to civilization, how happy we would be when were back at the ranch with my father and brothers. She was totally unprepared for the reception we received."

Morgan was silent for a long while and Jessie didn't push him. When he finally spoke, there was a hard glitter in his eyes and a bitterness in his voice. "I don't know why my father even bothered to ransom us. I suppose he felt it was something he had to do to keep the neighboring ranchers' respect, but it was clear from the very beginning that he didn't really want us back. Everyone around knew that my mother had been raped. They pitied and scorned her at the same time. She had been a plaything for an animal and was considered dirty and disgraced. It was bad enough that she was scorned and ostracized by everyone else, but my father scorned her too. He seemed to blame her for her disgrace, as if she, and not the Indian, had committed the crime. Oh, he accepted her into his house for propriety's sake, but he simply tolerated her, and my brothers followed his example. My mother's position in her own home was one of a lowly servant, instead of a wife and mother.

"Things were no better between my father and me. I was an acute embarrassment to him in public and an irritation in the privacy of our home. As I said, I looked and acted like a Comanche. I refused to wear the white man's clothes, ride on a saddle, sleep in a bed, or eat with a knife and fork—not out of stubbornness, as my father thought, but because they were uncomfortable to me. The boots pinched my feet and the clothes felt restrictive. The saddle was too hard and the bed too soft. And eating with a knife and fork felt awkward. I had to be forced to bathe, and my father and brothers had to wrestle me down to cut my long hair. Of all the things my father forced on me, I think that was the most traumatic. To a Comanche, his long hair is a part of his masculinity, second only to his sexual organs. I felt I had been emasculated.

"Eventually I made the transition back to the white man's way, but more for my mother's sake than anything my father did. He blamed my savage ways on her, saying it had been her responsibility to keep me from turning wild. He had no idea how little contact I'd had with my mother those years with the Indians, or how little say she had over me. Knowing that she was being punished for my behavior, I tried to change my ways, but it was never good enough or fast enough to suit my father. We were both outcasts in our own home."

By this time, silent tears were streaming down Jessie's face for the woman and boy who had suffered so much, so needlessly. She ached for Morgan.

Morgan was unaware of Jessie's tears. He was still reliving those years. "My mother died when I was eleven. She had survived four years of hard labor and humiliation at the hands of the Indians and only two enduring the cruelty of her own people. I blamed my father for her death. Even though she had been ostracized by the others, if he had shown any kindness, any compassion at all, I think she could have overcome her shame and lived a reasonably contented life. But he put his pride before her feelings. She grieved herself to death."

An angry tone came into Morgan's voice. "I was determined to punish my father for the way he had treated my mother, for the added misery and suffering he had caused her. I took every opportunity to embarrass him in public, behaving just like the wild savage he had accused me of being, and did anything and everything to agitate him. My brothers came to his defense, and I declared open war on them too. Hardly a day went by when I didn't have a fight with one or the other of them. When I was thirteen, I decided I'd had enough. I took my horse, my saddle, and the clothes on my back and simply rode out. My father and brothers saw me leaving, but not one of them said a word. They were as glad to see me leave as I was to go."

"But you were so young to be on your own," Jessie objected. "Still just a boy."

"No, my time with the Indians had matured me beyond my years and prepared me for taking care of myself. Comanches become self-sufficient early in life. And to give the devil his due, my father did teach me a lot about cattle ranching during those years. I left West Texas and headed for the *brasada*. I had no trouble hiring on as a cowhand, particularly since I was large for my age."

"And when did you become a gunfighter?"

"After my stint with the Texas Rangers. I acquired somewhat of a reputation as a fast gun while I was with them." Morgan shrugged. "Hiring out my gun was more lucrative than running cows."

"And more dangerous too," Jessie pointed out.

Morgan laughed. "Not necessarily. Sometimes I think I'd rather face a man with a gun than an angry longhorn."

Jessie was lying on her back beside Morgan. He

glanced to the side to see her reaction to his last words and, for the first time, saw the tears trickling down her temple and into her hair.

He rolled to his side and looked down at her. "You're crying," he muttered in astonishment, remembering Gabe had said that Jessie never cried.

"I . . . I can't help it."

"Don't pity me, Jess," Morgan said in a hard voice. "Dammit, don't you dare pity me!"

"It's not pity! I'm crying because I love you. Because I can't bear to see you hurt."

Morgan wiped a tear from Jessie's cheek with his thumb. "I'm not hurting anymore, Jess. It's over now—finally. I shouldn't have held it in so long. It just sat in there and festered. But I could never open up to anyone, until you, until tonight. I shouldn't have burdened you with it."

"No! I'm glad you told me," Jessie cried out fiercely. "That's what loving someone is all about. Sharing your pain as well as your joy."

"Yes, I suppose it is," Morgan agreed, then bent and tenderly kissed her mouth.

Jessie smoothed her hand over his dark sideburns and strong jawline. "You must hate the Comanches for what they did to you. They robbed you of your childhood, ruined your mother's life, turned your father and brothers against you, changed your whole life."

Morgan gazed off thoughtfully for a moment, then said, "No, strangely I don't. It was the whites, who claimed to be civilized and such good Christians, who hurt me the most. The Comanches were only doing what they had been doing for thousands of years. Raiding and taking captives is their way of life. It was the white man who betrayed me."

Sitting up, Morgan glanced at the sky, saying, "We'd better get back to the camp if you're to get any sleep tonight. Tomorrow is a big day for you."

"No, not yet. We can stay here and sleep until it's time for your watch."

She pulled Morgan down and cradled his dark head on her breasts, both wanting and needing to comfort him further. Morgan nuzzled the warm, soft mounds and stretched out his long legs beside hers, lying half over her as he slipped his hands under her shoulders.

After a few moments he muttered, "We can't sleep like this. It's much too uncomfortable for you."

"No, stay where you are. Your head isn't heavy."

In truth, Morgan didn't want to move. His head pillowed on her soft breast seemed the most natural thing in the world. He closed his eyes, and Jessie held him close to her heart while he slept.

Chapter 21

JESSIE WAS SHAKEN FROM HER SLEEP THE NEXT MORN-
ing by the sound of the horses' shrill, frightened neighing. Alarmed, she and the others threw back their blankets, grabbed their Winchesters, and ran to the edge of
the woods, where the remuda had been placed in a
small roped-off corral the night before. When they arrived on the scene, Morgan was already there, trying to
calm the nervous animals.

"What is it? What frightened them?" Jessie asked as
she ran up to him. She glanced up at the trees, scanning
their branches. "Did they see a panther?"

"No, I'm afraid that's what got them upset," Morgan
replied, motioning to the open prairie beside them.

Jessie whirled and saw the two huge longhorns standing not more than a hundred feet away. The bulls were
facing each other, pawing at the ground and snorting
angrily, with murder in their eyes.

"Take the horses down to the river," Jessie told the

mesteñeros. "Quickly, before those bulls start fighting and stampede them."

After the Mexicans had rushed the horses away, Jessie and Morgan turned their attention back to the bulls. Roaring their challenge, they dropped their massive heads and charged. Skull met skull with a retort that shattered the air, their horns clattering like huge sabers. Horns locked, they shoved against each other, their huge neck thews rising as they strained, bellowing in rage. Neither gave ground. Shaking their heads to disengage their horns, they stepped back, each trying to gore the other with its master horn as it broke away. Again their horns clashed, sending sparks flying. Over and over they charged, head smashing against head, the impact shaking the ground. The dust rolled about them as their tongues lolled and their bloodshot eyes bulged. Still, neither would retreat.

Disgusted, Jessie turned and walked swiftly back to camp. Morgan fell in beside her. "Stupid animals," Jessie spat. "They'll stay out there, beating their brains out, until one kills the other. And for what?"

"Stallions fight too," Morgan pointed out.

"Yes, for mares or territory. But bulls don't fight for females, not even in the mating season. No, they only fight out of pure dumb orneriness. At least a stallion knows what he's fighting for, and if it's for mares, he's constant. Unlike the bull, he doesn't run off as soon as the mating is over. He stays with his females and protects them."

Morgan chuckled. "You sure don't like cows."

"No, I don't. They're dumb, clumsy creatures. They have none of the intelligence, beauty, grace, or nobility that the horse has. I don't see how you could stand to work with them all those years."

"Oh, they're not so bad. After a while you get used to them. They kinda grow on you."

When Jessie and Morgan entered the camp, the *mesteñeros* who were to begin the relays were already preparing to leave. Jessie walked up to them and gave last-minute instructions. After they had ridden away, Morgan expected everyone to rush to break camp, but to his surprise their breakfast was leisurely. Even when it was finished, no one seemed to be in a hurry to get started.

Finally, Morgan asked, "Shouldn't we be getting to our relay stations?"

"No, it will take a while for the men to find the stallion and get him headed in this direction. He may have wandered fifteen or twenty miles since we saw him last night."

At midmorning, they broke camp and left. The relays were set up five miles apart. At each end of the run, there were two *mesteñeros* stationed to turn the stallion and get him started back down the run.

When Jessie left Morgan at his station, she cautioned him. "Now, remember, don't crowd him. If you do, he'll take off cross-country instead of the direction we want him to run. Then we'll have to chase him down and start all over."

After Jessie had left, Morgan kept his eyes peeled on the horizon. The sun climbed higher and higher in the sky, until his eyes began to ache from watching so hard. Just when he had decided something must have gone wrong, the white stallion streaked over the horizon, skimming across the softly waving sea of grass like some giant ocean bird.

As the stallion came closer and closer Morgan had to strain his eyes to see the horseman who was chasing him, for the fleet mustang had left the *mesteñero* far behind.

When the White Steed passed them, Morgan kneed El Dragón. The stallion shot forward, needing no further urging, anxious as always for an exhilarating run. Morgan gave the *palomino* his head and El Dragón stretched out his neck as his powerful legs ate up the ground and they flew across the prairie, the wind rushing past Morgan and whipping El Dragón's creamy mane around him. Morgan kept his eyes on the white mustang before him. Was it his imagination, or was El Dragón actually gaining on him? He was—to Morgan's utter amazement.

El Dragón gave a shrill snort, and Morgan realized then that the stallion was challenging the famous steed, determined to outrun him. Accepting the challenge, the white mustang snorted back, then leapt forward like a shot out of a cannon. Valiantly, El Dragón strained to keep up with the grueling pace the white mustang had set, stretching his legs as far as he could, his chest heaving until Morgan feared his lungs would burst with his magnificent effort. Seeing the *mesteñero* on the next relay swinging in behind the White Steed, Morgan pulled back on his reins, but El Dragón fought the bit, refusing to give up the chase.

Cursing, Morgan pulled back harder, the bit cutting into the stallion's tender mouth. Neighing sharply in pain, El Dragón slowed and finally came to a standstill, shaking his head and pawing the ground in frustration.

Morgan dismounted and walked to El Dragón's head. The stallion glared at him angrily. "Sorry, fella," Morgan said softly. "I didn't want to hurt you, but I couldn't let you kill yourself just to prove a point."

Morgan patted the stallion's neck, soothing him until

he had calmed down, then looked in his mouth. Just as he had feared, the bit had torn the tender flesh in several places. "Well," Morgan said in a mixture of self-disgust and irritation at the horse for having forced him to do it, "it looks like you're going to have a sore mouth for a while and we're out of the relays for today."

The White Steed raced past them from the opposite direction an hour later, and El Dragón went wild when he saw the stallion. It was all Morgan could do to hold the *palomino* back by his cheek strap as the other horse whizzed by.

Pedro, who had been chasing the white stallion on that part of the relay, rode up to Morgan and asked, "Is something wrong, *amigo*?"

"Can you take my relay until I go back to camp and pick up a horse from the remuda?" Then Morgan told the old man what had happened, ending with "His mouth is tore up pretty bad, and I don't want to ride him any more today for fear I'll do more damage."

"*Sí*, I can take your run until you get back. But I do not think you should let El Dragón run any more relays. I saw how hard it was for you to control him when the White Steed passed. I'm afraid every time he sees that mustang racing, El Dragón will be even more determined to beat him. The next time he races against him, El Dragón could well kill himself before he would admit defeat. This one has a gallant heart and a stubborn spirit," Pedro ended, reaching across and patting the *palomino* on the neck.

As Pedro raced off, he called over his shoulder, "Remind me tonight to give you something to take the soreness out of his mouth."

Morgan turned to El Dragón, saying, "You don't like

being beat, huh? Well, I can't say I blame you. I don't like being defeated either."

For the next four days the relays were continued, running the White Steed back and forth, back and forth, over a twenty-mile area. Even at night the white horse was given no peace. One of the *mesteñeros* always stayed close enough to prevent him from sleeping, moving in as if he were going to resume the chase every time the stallion nodded his head. Morgan was amazed at the mustang's stamina and endurance. Finally, on the sixth day, the White Steed showed definite signs of tiring, and Jessie judged the time right to move in for the capture.

There was a full moon, and Jessie decided to attempt the capture that night, hoping the stallion's reflexes would be slower then, because horses were not by nature nocturnal animals. As soon as the moon rose, they left their camp by the river and rode back out on the prairie, slowly and cautiously circling the stallion, riding closer and closer. The mustang seemed to be totally unaware of their approach, looking as if he were in a deep sleep. Jessie motioned to the *mesteñeros* to ready their lariats. Then, when she gave the signal, everyone rushed in, hearts pounding with anticipation and ropes whirling in the air.

The White Steed came to life with a sudden, shrill snort and shot between the horses racing toward him, ducking his head to avoid the lassos flying everywhere, and breaking free.

Stunned, everyone watched as the stallion raced away cross-country, and Morgan knew then why the Indians called him the "Ghost Horse of the Plains." With his white coat reflecting the light of the moon, his long mane stretched out like arms, and his gliding gait, he did resemble a mysterious, ethereal apparition.

"Dammit," Jessie cursed, her eyes filled with tears of frustration, "he's done it to us again."

"*Sí*, he has bolted, and he will run clear out of this area again," Pedro said glumly.

"Well, I'm not going to wait for him to come back this time," Jessie said angrily. "I'm following him—even if I have to chase him to the ends of the earth!"

Turning in her saddle, she said to the *mesteñeros* behind her, "We'll go back to camp and pick up our supplies and the remuda."

"You plan on leaving tonight?" Morgan asked in surprise.

"Yes, tonight! I'm not letting him get out of my sight."

Since the moon was full, they had no difficulty in following the White Steed all night. At daybreak they mounted fresh horses from the remuda and tried to get in front of the stallion. But the White Steed would have none of that. Every time they attempted to race ahead, he would pull forward with a burst of speed that amazed them.

After the fourth unsuccessful try, Pedro said, "Ah, *patrona*, you will never be able to run him down by relays again. He is wise to that trick now."

"I'm afraid you're right, Pedro," Jessie answered wearily. She gazed off to where the white stallion was standing and watching them from a distance, ready to bolt at the first sign of their resuming the chase. Turning to the *mesteñero* beside her, she said, "Manuel, you stay here and see that he doesn't sleep. After Raul has had a few hours of sleep, I'll send him to relieve you."

As Manuel's horse trotted off the others turned and rode back to the river. Dismounting, Pedro and Morgan began to unsaddle their horses, and Morgan said to the old *mesteñero,* "As disappointed as we all were about not catching the White Steed last night, I'm glad to be out of that area and on the move. Let's hope that this way we won't be sitting ducks for Gibbons's hired killers."

"I suspected you were worrying about that," Pedro answered. "Over the past few days, I have seen you scanning the prairie all around us more than once. Do you think they have finally picked up our trail?"

Morgan pulled his saddle off and tossed it on the ground before answering. "Even if they didn't, they knew we were coming after the White Steed and that he was somewhere in the vicinity. All they had to do was keep searching the area until they eventually found us."

"Perhaps now that the White Steed is on the run again and out of Gibbons's territory, he will call off his *pistoleros,*" Pedro said hopefully.

"I don't think there's any chance of that. He wants that horse, and as soon as he learns we're on the stallion's trail, he'll follow. I just hope we can keep far enough ahead of him and his killers."

They were stalking the mustang and being stalked themselves, Pedro thought. If the stallion got caught, he lost his freedom; if they got caught, they lost their lives. Despite the warmth of the afternoon, the old man shivered and said, "We will have to watch our backs."

"Yes, we certainly will," Morgan answered grimly.

For the next three days they followed the White Steed, chasing him during the day and hounding him at night. The stallion followed the river up-country and crossed it just below where the Frio flowed into it, then followed the Nueces westward. The terrain became more hilly and rocky, the grass and vegetation sparse. The only trees of any size at all hugged the river.

On the afternoon of the third day they pitched their camp under an unusually thick copse of trees. Everyone welcomed the coolness of the shade, for even in May temperatures often rose to the nineties in this country, and the sun could be blistering hot in the open.

But soon after they had settled down, Morgan discovered another irritant besides the heat. The trees were full of cicadas, and they were making a horrendous noise, their shrill, loud calls grinding on his nerves.

"Christ! Don't they ever shut up?" Morgan complained to Jessie.

Jessie looked up from where she was sitting on the ground, mending a bridle. "The cicadas?" she asked in surprise, not even having noticed the noise. Then she laughed. "Just be glad it's not midsummer. The hotter it gets, the louder they get." A mischievous twinkle came into her eyes. "Besides, don't complain to me. It was a male that brought that particular misery down on us."

"What in the hell are you talking about? What male?"

"The male cicada. It's another Mexican legend."

Morgan waited for Jessie to continue, but she remained silent and turned her attention back to the bridle in her lap.

Finally he asked, "Well, now that you've got my curiosity aroused, aren't you even going to tell me the legend?"

"I thought maybe you were getting tired of my stories."

Morgan glared at her, and Jessie laughed at his irritation, then said, "Well, if you insist. In the beginning, the cicada was a beautiful insect, and the male, La Cigarra, was a merry person, too lively to suit his wife. Every spring he became so excited with the perfumed air and the joy of living that he forgot to be a faithful husband and made love to all the butterflies and hummingbirds. His wife was jealous and went to King Eagle. She asked him to make her husband stop his roaming. The only way the eagle could do this was to make La Cigarra ugly in the sight of the ladies, making his eyes pop out and turning his beautiful, colorful wings to an ugly gray. The next spring, when La Cigarra tried to make love to the butterflies and hummingbirds, they laughed at him and sent him on his way. Chagrined, he went home, but he constantly complained about his plight. Realizing she could never be happy with this ugly creature who did nothing but complain, the wife went to King Eagle again and asked him to make her like her husband. With her change, she became as fretful as he, and to this day you can hear them, the male complaining of his lost beauty in a shrill voice, and the female shrill but contented."

Morgan's lips twitched with amusement. "And we humans have to suffer because of his infidelity?"

"Yes, and let it be a lesson to you males," Jessie answered in a teasing voice.

Suddenly serious, Morgan said, "If I were your husband, Jess, I'd never be unfaithful. You're all the woman I'd ever want."

At Morgan's words Jessie was suddenly assailed with conflicting emotions. The thought of being Morgan's wife both thrilled and frightened her. It would be heaven and hell, for she would have to give up her dream and follow him. Terrified that he might propose and she wouldn't know how to answer, she tossed the bridle aside, rose to her feet, and muttered, "I have to check on the remuda," before rushing away.

Later that night Morgan and Pedro sat beside the campfire and talked in hushed tones. During a pause in the conversation Pedro studied the tall Texan thoughtfully, then asked, "Do you have plans for the future?"

"Not really," Morgan answered evasively. Without Jessie, there didn't seem to be much of a future, and yet he couldn't ask her to share it with him. He had nothing to offer her but the insecure life of a wanderer, and God knows, she'd had enough of that. Besides, she had her own plans, a bright, promising future on her ranch.

"I understand you were once a cowhand," Pedro commented after a long silence.

"That's right."

"Have you considered your own ranch?"

"I've toyed around with that idea off and on, but I never did anything about it. I guess I just wasn't ready to settle down."

Pedro gave Morgan a long, penetrating look across the fire, then gazed off into the darkness, saying, "You know, horse and cattle ranching are not so different."

Morgan laughed. "For me they are. I know a hell of a lot about cows, but very little about horses."

"But you have already learned much since you have joined us, and what you do not know, I would be happy to teach you."

Morgan shot Pedro a sharp look, suddenly realizing what the old *mesteñero* was suggesting. That he marry Jessie and become a rancher, a *horse* rancher. There could be a future with Jessie after all! For a brief moment Morgan's spirits soared, then plummeted when he remembered how Jessie had behaved that afternoon at the mention of marriage.

Since then she had gone out of her way to avoid him, finding things to do to keep her busy, then rushing off to the river, announcing she was going to bathe and didn't want to be disturbed by anyone. And that wasn't the first time Jessie had acted suddenly aloof at the mention of marriage. The subject seemed to upset her.

Pedro broke into Morgan's thoughts. "Forgive me, *amigo.* I was being presumptuous."

"No, I like the idea. It's Jessie I'm worried about. I've gotten the impression that she's not particularly interested in marriage, that she doesn't want to give up her independence. She has her own plans for the future, her own ranch. I don't think she'd agree to settle down with me on mine."

"Then why not settle on her ranch?"

At Morgan's frown, Pedro continued. "I know what is bothering you, *amigo.* You wish to be the provider. Otherwise you would not feel manly. But in my country it is not unusual for the land to come from the woman's side, at no loss of honor for the man. After the two are married, the man is still the provider."

"Jessie would *never* allow me to run her ranch."

"Ah, *amigo,* already you are making a mistake in your thinking. After you are married, it would not be her ranch. Nor would it be your ranch. It would be yours together. And that is how it must be run—together. As you said, she is very independent. She is not going to give up her say on the matter completely. Can you do this, *amigo*? Put aside your male pride, your urge to dominate, and meet her halfway?"

"I don't know," Morgan admitted truthfully. "I'd have to think about it. It would take some adjusting from both of us." He rose. "But no matter how it turns out, I want to thank you for your offer to teach me about horses."

Pedro averted his eyes and gazed off, saying, "When I told you the other day that I was content as long as I could work with the horses, I was not being completely honest with you, *amigo*. I have always regretted not having a son, someone to whom I could pass on my knowledge and skill. In my family, that was as much a legacy as inheriting the land. I would die much happier if I knew it was in the hands of a man I admire and respect, a man who would pass it down to his sons and grandsons. I would hate to have it die with me."

Morgan was deeply touched. His own father had been ashamed of him, had scorned him, had been more than happy to see him walk out of his life for good, and yet this proud old aristocrat was offering him a legacy that should have been his son's, a legacy that was priceless, skills and knowledge accumulated over hundreds of years by Pedro's ancestors. A lump formed in Morgan's throat, making it difficult for him to answer. "Thank you, Pedro, but I don't know if I could be worthy of your great gift."

There were tears in the old man's eyes when he turned his head back to face Morgan. "My gift to you is no more than the one you offered me. Your friendship. That is the greatest gift a man can offer another."

Pedro rose, saying, "And now, if you will excuse me, I have work to do."

Morgan knew that Pedro was only giving him an excuse to leave, but he didn't object. The moment was emotionally charged, both harboring deep feelings that had no outlet for expression because their cultures prohibited the display of such emotions between men. As a result, they felt awkward and uncomfortable.

After Pedro had left, Morgan walked down to the river. For a long while he strolled along its bank, deep in thought as he considered everything Pedro had said. Finally he turned and retraced his steps, a look of purpose on his face.

He found Jessie farther upstream, sitting on a blanket and drying her hair with a towel. In the moonlight, her wet, naked body glistened, her alabaster skin looking almost translucent. Morgan took a brief moment to savor her beauty, then approached her, saying softly, "Jessie?"

Startled, Jessie dropped the towel and looked up. "What are you doing here?" she asked sharply, feeling panic rising. "I said I didn't want to be disturbed."

Morgan crouched beside her and drew the blanket around her shoulders, not wanting to be distracted by her lovely body. Then he sat beside her, saying, "This can't wait. I need to talk to you."

Jessie felt as if a trap were closing in on her. Averting her eyes and pulling the blanket closer, she answered, "Not tonight, Morgan. I'm tired."

"Look at me, Jess," Morgan commanded softly.

Jessie turned her head farther away, knowing if she did look at Morgan, she would be lost. She could refuse him nothing when she gazed into those shimmering silver eyes.

Morgan took Jessie's chin between his thumb and forefinger and turned her head. "Do you love me, Jess?"

Jessie thought to lie, thinking if she told him no, he wouldn't ask the question that she both longed for and feared, but her answer came out a tortured sob. "Yes."

"And did you mean what you said the other night? That loving someone is sharing both the pain and the joy?"

"Yes, I meant it."

A smile came over Morgan's face, and his eyes glowed with emotion. Seeing them, Jessie knew that she had lost the battle to retain her fierce independence. He had captured her heart, enslaved her soul, and she would follow him to the ends of the earth if necessary.

"Does that include dreams, Jess? Do you love me enough to share your ranch, your future, your life?"

Her ranch? Jessie couldn't believe her ears. He would come with her, instead of expecting her to go with him? "What are you saying?" she asked in a breathless voice.

"I'm asking you to marry me, Jess. Let your dream for the biggest and best horse ranch in Texas become our dream, sharing responsibilities, decisions, rewards, everything."

Jessie knew that he was asking her to give up a part of her independence. There would be times when she would have to bow to *his* decisions, do things *his* way. It was the price she would have to pay for having him beside her for the rest of her life. Was the price too high? No, it was a small price to pay for such a great treasure.

Her happiness bubbled up and burst from her. "Oh, yes!" She threw herself into his arms, hugging him tightly, sobbing over and over, "Yes, yes, yes!"

Morgan embraced her fiercely, feeling a strange moisture in his eyes. He could never remember having cried. Even before he had been captured by the Comanches, he had been a stoic child. The tears threatening in his eyes horrified him. Hoping to distract himself from the intense emotionalism of the moment, he said in a shaky voice, "Now, how about telling me more about this place we'll be calling home?"

Home. A rush of warmth ran through Morgan at the

thought. It had been a long time since he had thought of anyplace as a home. Certainly the Indian camp had never been one, nor was the house to which he and his mother had returned. No, a home wasn't just someplace in which to escape the elements, a place to hang one's hat. It was meaningless unless there was someone there waiting for you, someone to welcome you with love and open arms. He hadn't realized how much he had hungered for a home, and now he'd have one with Jessie, a real home.

Jessie didn't need any further urging to tell Morgan about her ranch. It was her dream and therefore her favorite topic. She pushed away from Morgan and glanced around her. Spying a patch of moonlight on the ground a few feet away, she reached and picked up a twig lying there, saying, "I'll draw you a map."

Morgan watched as she drew a wavy line in the soft sand. "That's the San Saba River. The land I hope to buy for my ranch"—she flushed, then corrected herself— "our ranch lies on this side of the river, from this bend to that. The bank on that side isn't nearly as steep as the other side, and the ground isn't as rocky."

Jessie squirmed, hardly able to contain her excitement. "Oh, Morgan, I can't wait for you to see it. The grass is unbelievably lush and at least a foot tall, and there are huge oak and pecan trees scattered all over the ranch, where the horses can get out of the hot sun during the summer. Two creeks run through it, one here and another here." Jessie drew two more squiggly lines.

Morgan watched with an amused smile on his face as Jessie continued drawing, pointing out where she wanted to dig the wells, where the barn and outbuildings would sit, where the fence lines for the different pastures would be. Then she pointed the stick in the middle of her map, saying, "This is where I want to put the ranch house, on this rise. From there, you can see the whole ranch. And I want it to be two-storied, fashioned after the haciendas on the *ranchos* in Mexico, with thick adobe walls to keep it cool in the summers, and a red tile roof, and a courtyard with a fountain in the center."

Morgan chuckled. "And I bet you've even figured out how many bedrooms you want."

"Yes, I have," Jessie replied matter-of-factly. "I was thinking of four." Seeing Morgan's frown, she quickly said, "We'll need a guest room for the buyers to stay in when they visit. There isn't a town within twenty miles."

"I wasn't thinking four was too many. Just the opposite, particularly if we're going to have children." Morgan looked Jessie in the eye, asking, "You do want children, don't you?"

Jessie had never considered children. Until tonight, there hadn't even been a man in her future. She pictured Morgan as he must have been as a child, and her latent maternal instincts came rushing to the surface. "Oh, yes, I want children."

"Good. So do I. I think an even dozen would do nicely."

"A dozen? Children?" Jessie asked in a shocked voice. "My God! Do you expect to keep me perpetually pregnant?"

Morgan laughed, his eyes twinkling with mischief. "Well, maybe that is a few too many. How about half a dozen?"

Jessie laughed, realizing he had been teasing her. "That sounds much better."

Morgan gazed down at the map Jessie had drawn, then said, "It looks like it's a pretty big spread. Maybe we could run a few head of cattle too."

"Cattle?" Jessie gasped, a horrified look on her face. "On my ranch? Absolutely not! I won't have one of those dumb, clumsy creatures on the place." Then, seeing Morgan's lips twitching, she said, "Stop teasing me, Morgan. You scared me to death."

"How about a milch cow? With all those kids, we're going to need one. Unless you plan on giving them mare's milk."

"All right, one milch cow," Jessie conceded. "But only one! And you've got to promise to keep it hidden away in a back pasture."

Morgan threw his head back and laughed. Jessie ignored him, continuing with her plans for the ranch, this time outlining her breeding program. But Morgan wasn't listening. His gaze was riveted on one creamy breast that was peeking through the gaping blanket.

He placed his finger over Jessie's lips, saying in a husky voice, "That's enough."

Jessie's eyes widened. "But I thought you wanted to hear more about the ranch."

Morgan pushed the blanket back from her shoulders. "Later, maybe. But right now, I want to love you."

Seeing the smoldering look in his eyes, Jessie's disappointment at his sudden lack of interest in the ranch quickly disappeared; her heart quickened. When he laid her back on the blanket, she didn't object, her mouth parting as he lowered his head, her arms folding around his broad shoulders.

His kiss was agonizingly sweet and tender, beginning with just butterfly brushes of his lips against hers, then teasing her lips with the tip of his tongue, then her teeth. He slipped his tongue inside, slowly sliding it in and out, brushing the roof of her mouth and the insides of her cheeks, then tracing her small, serrated teeth before swirling around her tongue; tears came to Jessie's eyes at the sweet torture. She kissed him back, would have deepened the kiss and brought their passion to a quick, white-hot pitch, but Morgan wouldn't allow it. This would be no feast to be quickly and mindlessly devoured, but one to be slowly savored. Tonight was special. It was a celebration of their commitment to each other.

Morgan's tongue moved around hers, first as wild and tempestuous as a Gypsy dance, then as slow and gliding as a seductive waltz, then wild again, then slow, alternately exciting, then soothing, until Jessie was whimpering in frustration.

His mouth left hers to shower soft kisses over her face, and when Jessie tried to kiss him back again, he dropped his head to her throat, mouthing and tonguing the long, slender column, stopping to sup at the hollow of her throat, while his hands smoothed over her arms and caressed her breasts and the soft skin of her abdomen.

Jessie tangled her fingers in his dark hair, trying to pull his head back up, desperate for the feel of his lips on hers, but Morgan only slipped lower, kissing her breast in slowly decreasing circles, then laving it, then gently biting, until Jessie thought she would go out of her mind if he didn't take her nipple in his mouth. And when he finally did, rolling it around his tongue before he drew it into his mouth, Jessie cried out as a bolt of fire pierced her loins and spiraled outward, down her thighs, up her belly, leaving her quivering and gasping for breath.

Jessie reached for his shoulders, catching two fistfuls of material instead, which only frustrated her more. "Take off your clothes," she whimpered urgently, then gasped as Morgan tugged on the other nipple and a fresh bolt of fire went through her.

But Morgan either didn't hear, or wasn't ready to give up his feast at her breasts. Instead, he slipped his arms under her back and arched her to him, paying homage to one soft mound, then the other, his torrid mouth and hot tongue devouring her. Jessie was left gasping weakly as liquid fire raced through her veins and pounded in her ears, leaving in its wake tingling nerve endings and trembling muscles.

By the time Morgan rose and stripped off his clothes, Jessie had become like quivering jelly. She watched through dazed eyes as his masculine beauty was exposed to her eyes. First the broad, muscular chest with its mat of tight curls, then, as he skimmed down his pants, his lean hips, taut belly, and long legs. When he rose, Jessie's gaze locked on his arousal standing long and full before her. Her mouth went dry with anticipation and her nerves tingled with renewed excitement as she remembered only too well the pleasures that powerful instrument could bring her. Then, realizing that she was brazenly staring at him, she flushed and looked up at his face, seeing that his gaze on her was just as hungry.

As he sank to his knees beside her, Jessie caught his shoulders and pulled him down, raising her head to capture his lips, her tongue boldly entering his mouth and kissing him with wild abandon, ravishing him with the heat of her passion. She felt his groan, a rush of hot air in the back of her throat, and held his head in a firm grasp, fearing he'd break away and deny her of her turn to devour him.

Morgan reached up and pried Jessie's hands from his head. When he jerked his mouth from hers, Jessie muttered, "No!"

"Take it easy, sweetheart. There's no hurry. I'm not going anywhere."

"But I want you—now!" Jessie sobbed.

Morgan smiled down at her, a smile that promised heaven and more. "Not yet, sweetheart. I want this loving to be something you never forget!"

Then he was kissing and caressing her—all over, from the tip of her head to her toes, lingering at her breasts and again at her thighs. Jessie was consumed with a burning heat, her secret place throbbing and demanding release. She reached for him, but Morgan deflected her hand with his thigh, knowing that once she had him in that sweet vise, his passion would spiral out of control.

Morgan rose over her and positioned his knees between her thighs, slipping his hands under her buttocks. Thinking release was finally at hand, Jessie gave a cry of relief and arched her pelvis to meet his thrust. But there was no thrust. She looked up and saw the smile on his face, a smile that told her he wasn't through tormenting her yet. As he lowered his head she moaned, "You devil!"

She tried to close her legs, but it was too late. Morgan had already buried his face in her soft curls, his mouth and tongue teasing and tantalizing, driving her wild. And that tongue was artful. My God, where had he learned this agonizing, sweet torture, swirling, darting, laving—in and out—here, there, everywhere. Over and over he brought her to the shuddering brink, then retreated, soothing her, only to drive her half out of her mind when he resumed his erotic attack on her senses. Jessie was writhing, sobbing uncontrollably, burning with unfulfilled need. Her heart was pounding so fast and hard that she feared it would burst. She'd die from this exquisite torture.

"Stop, Morgan. I can't stand any more. You're killing me."

Morgan chuckled and lifted his head. Looking up at her, he said softly, "No, sweetheart. Maybe a little death or two, but nothing you won't survive."

"Why are you torturing me like this?" Jessie sobbed.

"Because I love you. But if you don't want me to do that anymore, I won't."

Jessie gasped as she felt the moist, hot tip of him against her. "Yes! That's what I want," she cried out.

But to her utter dismay, she discovered that Morgan had only found another method of delicious torment, that hot male flesh searing her, circling, tantalizing, so close, yet not where she wanted him. It was maddening. He would drive her insane!

Several times she lunged, trying to impale herself on him, but Morgan held her hips firmly, and each effort was thwarted, only increasing her frenzy. She thrashed wildly, her head twisting from side to side. Every nerve in her body screamed for release, her breath rasping in her throat, her heart threatening to burst from her chest.

Unknown to Jessie, what Morgan was doing to her was an agony for him, too, as it had been when he had made love to her with his mouth. Her honeyed nectar had intoxicated him, her scent a powerful aphrodisiac. Only by supreme will had he been able to maintain control, wanting to make this loving as pleasurable as possible for her, but now his steely control broke, and he drove into her.

His sudden entry made sparks dance up Jessie's spine and seared her brain. She convulsed among exploding stars. Dazed, she opened her eyes to see Morgan hovering over her. Then, becoming aware of him deep inside her, his rigid heat completely filling her, she realized what had happened. Her release had come as suddenly as his plunge.

Guessing her thoughts, Morgan whispered, "That was just a preview, sweetheart. The best is still to come."

As Morgan began his movements, slow, sensuous strokes that rekindled her smoldering fires, Jessie wrapped her legs around him. When he bent his head to kiss her, Jessie tasted herself, which both shocked and excited her even more. Soon she was drowning in a tempestuous flood tide of fresh sensations, growing more and more frenzied as Morgan carried her to the summit, bringing her to a bursting, explosive release over and over, before he finally allowed himself his own shattering firestorm.

Later, Jessie lay snuggled against Morgan as he slept, feeling completely drained and totally satiated. She remembered what Morgan had said about making their lovemaking unforgettable. She smiled, muttering to herself, "Yes, it certainly has been. That and much more."

She snuggled closer, purring with contentment.

Neither Jessie or Morgan told anyone the next morning that he had proposed and she had accepted. But then, they didn't have to. There was a sparkle in Jessie's eyes, a radiant glow on her face, and a lightness to her

step that told all. She laughed at everything, no matter
how inconsequential, unable to contain her happiness,
and she couldn't keep her eyes off Morgan.

The change in Morgan, although more subdued, was
just as noticeable. The haunted look was gone from his
eyes and the lines of tension from his face. An aura of
deep contentment surrounded him, the satisfaction of a
man who had found what he was searching for in life
and whose soul was at peace.

The *mesteñeros* were pleased with the newest development, one and all. More than once Morgan had given
them reason to admire his courage and strength, and his
leadership and coolness under fire the night the raiders
attacked had gained the Mexicans' deep respect. He
was a man worthy of their fierce, fiery *patrona,* to
whom they had given all their loyalty, and now that
loyalty would extend to Morgan.

Four days later they were awakened at dawn with the
news that the White Steed was crossing the river. In a
flurry of activity, the camp was broken and everyone
mounted to follow. Fifteen minutes later they had
crossed the Nueces and saw the white mustang still
following it upriver.

"Now, why did he do that?" Jessie asked in an irritated voice. "I thought he was going to take off cross-
country again. If we had known that he was going stay
on his same course, we could have had breakfast before
we broke camp."

Morgan, riding beside her, shrugged. "Maybe he likes
the scenery on this side of the river better."

"Well, as far as I can see, it isn't any different," Jessie
replied in a disgusted voice, her empty stomach protesting its plight with a low growl.

"You know, I can't believe his endurance," Morgan

said, gazing off at the stallion in the distance. "We've been chasing him all day and keeping him awake all night, and yet he still finds the strength to flee."

"Ah, *amigo*," Pedro said from the other side of Jessie, "his beauty, speed, grace, and intelligence are exceeded only by his passion for freedom. That is the wellspring from which he finds the strength still to flee."

"Patrona!"

Jessie, Morgan, and Pedro reined in and turned at the urgent, sharp cry. Seeing the *mesteñero* who had called pointing to the east, their eyes swiveled in that direction. A large band of riders was coming like the wind. With the plain shimmering in the light of the newly risen sun, they seemed to be emerging from the bright glow. Jessie saw the glitter of bronze and silver ornaments, the flutter of feathers, and then the copper color of their half-naked bodies.

"Indians?" she muttered in disbelief. "But what are they doing off the reservation?"

"They're probably a hunting party," Morgan answered. "They pretty much come and go at will. Usually they're back on the reservation before the Indian agent or the army at Fort Sill even knows they're gone."

"But why come way out here to hunt?" Jessie asked. "The reservation is in the Indian Territory, hundreds of miles away."

"Those are from the Penateka band of Comanches, the Honey Eaters," Morgan replied. "Their territory ranged from the Nueces to the Llano rivers. It's only natural that they come back to their old hunting grounds."

When Morgan identified the Indians as Comanches, every *mesteñero* reached for his Winchester in his saddle holster. Seeing them, Morgan commanded sharply, "Don't draw your weapons! They're only a hunting party."

Pedro's dark eyes glittered with hatred. "The Comanches are our ancient enemies, *amigo*."

"I know, but these come in peace. Their leader is signaling for a parley."

"The Comanches are *never* peaceable," Pedro countered. "I do not trust them."

"Then trust me," Morgan said in a firm voice. "Now, put away your guns, before we're all massacred."

Reluctantly the *mesteñeros* replaced their half-drawn rifles, their hatred for the Comanches seething just below the surface. As Pedro had said, of all the Indians in the Southwest and northern Mexico, the Mexicans feared and hated the Comanches the most. Bad feelings were just as strong on the Comanches' side. Both had good reason.

Unlike the other Texas Indians, the Comanches—the "Cossacks of the Plains"—had not limited their forays to Texas. For hundreds of years they had swept down into Mexico, sometimes as far south as Mexico City, killing, raping, looting, and burning. Neither the Spanish government, nor the Mexican one that had followed it, had been able to deal with these lordly, dark-eyed hunter-killers. The Spanish government ransomed the captives the Comanches had taken, an act of mercy that the Indians interpreted as tribute. Soon they came to expect tribute at every encounter. Hoping to eradicate them, the Spanish had lured them again and again with promises of gifts and peace parleys, then ambushed them or fed them poisoned food. The Comanches retaliated to that treachery with even more bloody raids into Mexico. The Mexican government handled *Indio* problems no better than the Spanish had. They put a bounty on Comanche and Apache scalps, hoping the bounty hunters would kill them off. Hunted like animals, the Comanches' hatred only grew, and the raids became more and more frequent.

"Stay here while I ride out and see what they want," Morgan said. "And for God's sake, keep your hands off those guns."

Jessie and the others watched as Morgan rode out to meet the spokesman from the Comanches. The two met halfway between the two groups and reined in.

As Morgan and the Comanche spoke, Pedro muttered, "They want something from us, *patrona*. They are always wanting something."

When the Comanche spokesman whirled his pinto and raced back to the others, Jessie tensed and, despite Morgan's warning, reached for her Winchester, expecting to see the Indians come tearing at them, howling and with all guns blazing. But to everyone's surprise the Comanches turned and rode back in the direction they had come, disappearing into the dazzling glow they had emerged from, a whirling cloud of dust on the plain the only evidence of their short, unexpected visit.

"They're gone," Jessie uttered in disbelief.

"Still, they want something, *patrona*," Pedro said in a bitter voice. "It is their way. You will see."

Morgan waited until the Comanches had ridden completely away before he turned his mount and rode back, a grim look on his face. Reining in beside Jessie, he said in a low voice, "We need to talk, Jess. Privately."

Alarmed by his ominous tone, Jessie turned her horse and followed Morgan as he rode away, saying over her shoulder to Pedro, "You go on ahead. We'll catch up."

Morgan stopped near an outcrop of boulders, dismounted, and turned to help Jessie from her horse.

As soon as her feet hit the ground, Jessie asked anxiously, "What did they want?"

"They want us to leave the White Steed alone. To stop trying to capture him."

Jessie's eyes narrowed. "They're crazy if they think I'll do that! I hope you told them to go to hell."

"No, Jess. I told them we'd give it serious consideration."

"You what?" Jessie shrieked.

"Calm down, Jess," Morgan said in a soothing voice.

"No! I won't calm down. And there's nothing to consider. It's out of the question!"

"Jess, the Comanches have a special reverence for the Ghost Horse of the Plains. They think he's supernatural. To the Comanche, the stallion is the living spirit of all free things, and to capture that spirit would be a grievous offense to the Great Spirit, who sent the ghost horse to them."

"I don't give a damn about the Comanches' silly superstitions. I want the White Steed—and I intend to have him!"

"Jess, it wasn't a request. It was a demand."

"To hell with them and their demands! That's why the Comanches got so arrogant in the first place. Everyone gave in to them, paying them tribute, making them think they were the lords of the land. Well, I'm not going to bow to them. If they try to stop us from capturing the White Steed—we'll fight them!"

"Jess, you're just upset. You're not thinking straight. There were at least a hundred warriors in that party, and there's only nine of us. We can't possibly survive odds like that. They'll massacre us."

"We fought off Gibbons's hired guns, and we were outnumbered then, too."

"Not ten to one. And we were well fortified. Out here, we're in the open, and the Comanches are masters at fighting that kind of warfare." Morgan put his hands on her shoulders. "I know its going to be hard for you to give up the stallion. A great disappointment. But, Jess, you've *got* to do it," he said gently.

For Jessie, what Morgan was asking of her wasn't just hard; it was impossible. Her dream of capturing and owning the White Steed had been with her so long, it would be easier to give up an arm or a leg than a part of her soul.

She jerked her shoulders from Morgan's hands. "No! I won't give him up! Never!"

Morgan had known Jessie was going to take the news badly, but he had never dreamed she would be this hysterical and irrational. "Jess, you can't do that. If you won't think of yourself, at least think of your men. You can't endanger their lives that way."

"A bunch of scraggly Indians aren't going to scare off my men. They're not afraid of those Comanches. You saw how they were ready to fight."

"Jess, it isn't your men's decision. It's yours. You're their *patrona*, their employer and protector. You have a responsibility to them to make a wise decision. Their lives are in your hands. And this time, they wouldn't have a fighting chance. They'd be slaughtered."

"You don't know that they'd attack us. They might just be threatening us," Jessie said, taking a different approach. "They left, didn't they?"

"The Indians left because I asked them to give us some time to consider it. And the Comanches don't make empty threats, Jess. Believe me, I know. They'll be back."

Jessie acted as if she hadn't heard a word Morgan had said. She rushed on, saying, "The army is probably hot on their trail. Why, they might be rounding up those renegades this very minute, and we're worrying ourselves over something that won't even happen."

Morgan's patience was at an end. He caught Jessie's shoulders and shook her, desperate to get through to her somehow. "Dammit, Jess, you haven't listened to anything I've said. I told you they probably haven't even missed them at Fort Sill. There are thousands of Indians in the Indian Territory, and not just Comanches. It's impossible for the army to keep an eye on all of them at one time. No one could."

"All right! So the army isn't anywhere nearby. But that doesn't change anything. I'm still going after the White Steed."

A hard look came over Morgan's face. "You place that damned stallion over everything and everyone, don't you, Jess? No price is too high to pay for him. You'd sacrifice everything for him. Yourself. Your men. Me."

There was something in Morgan's voice that gave Jessie pause. She searched his face, but his expression was unreadable. "What are you saying?"

"I'm telling you that you've got to decide which is more important to you. Me—or that stallion."

Jessie's face paled. "You're giving me an ultimatum?" she asked in disbelief. "You're forcing me to chose between you?"

"Yes."

"But why?" Jessie cried in an anguished voice.

"In the first place, I'm hoping it will bring you to your senses. In the second, I have to know where I really stand with you." A warning tone came into Morgan's voice. "Hear me, Jess. I won't take second place in your life to anything or anyone—and certainly not to a goddamned horse!"

"You don't understand, Morgan. I'm not just being stubborn. I can't give him up. I've dreamed of owning him ever since I was a child."

"A dream bought with the lives of others isn't a dream, Jess. It's an obsession. Now, which is it going to be? Him or me?"

Tears glittered in Jessie's eyes. "Why are you doing this, Morgan? Tearing me apart like this? You can't love me, or you wouldn't force me to make an impossible choice."

Morgan stiffened, his fingers biting into the soft flesh of her shoulders. Then he released her and stepped back, saying in a bitter voice, "I guess I got my answer."

Jessie shook her head, completely taken aback by his hard words, saying, "No . . . no, I didn't give you an answer. I said—"

"Yes, you did, Jess," Morgan interjected. "You told me all I need to know. If you loved me, the choice wouldn't be impossible."

Morgan turned and walked to his horse.

"You're leaving?" Jessie gasped, her face draining of all color.

Morgan swung into his saddle and looked down at her, saying in a tight voice, "Don't worry, Jess. I'm not running out on you. I made a vow, a promise to myself, and I intend to keep it."

"What vow?"

To protect you, even if it killed me, Morgan thought. "Something that wouldn't interest you. No, Jess, I'll stick it out to the bitter end. Then, if we're still alive, I'll leave and you can have your precious stallion."

What was wrong with him? Jessie thought frantically. Why was he being so unreasonable? She stepped up to him, placing her hand on his thigh, saying in a pleading voice, "Please, Morgan, try to understand. I do love you, but—"

"No buts, Jess."

"All right!" Jessie retorted angrily, jerking her hand back. "Be stubborn about it! I guess it's a good thing I found out now what you're really like. The first time I don't do what you want, you start issuing ultimatums. You're just like all men, domineering and overbearing. Except you're worse. You use my love like a weapon against me, trying to force me to your will. It would have never worked out between us. It's just as well it's over."

When Morgan made no comment, his face looking as if it were made of stone, Jessie whirled, caught La Duquesa's reins, and swiftly mounted. Without another glance in his direction, she rode away, and Morgan didn't see the anguished tears streaming down her face. Not until she had almost disappeared in the distance did Morgan follow. It might be over between them, but he still had his vow to keep.

Chapter 22

BY THE TIME JESSIE CAUGHT UP WITH THE *MES-teñeros,* she had managed to bring her tears under control—but not her emotions. They roiled inside her, a boiling cauldron of mixed feelings, and the foremost was a seething, blind anger.

The Mexicans had only to look at Jessie to know something had happened between her and Morgan. Her eyes were red-rimmed and glittering with anger, her small body rigid with outrage. When Morgan rode up a few minutes later and fell in beside Jessie, the determined set of his jaw and the hard look in his eyes confirmed the men's suspicions. The two had just had a disagreement, and it had been no silly lover's quarrel.

The uncomfortable silence hung over the group of riders like a heavy shroud, the only sounds the steady clip-clop of the horses' hooves on the ground, the swish of their tails, the squeak of a saddle. The *mesteñeros* sensed that the tension between Jessie and Morgan had something to do with them and the Comanches, and that knowledge made them even more uneasy. Patiently, the men held their silence, not even daring to glance at the man riding next to them, their nerves crawling.

Finally, Jessie whirled her bay and reined in. The *mesteñeros* brought their horses to a halt, their expressions anxious.

"The Comanches have demanded that we leave the White Steed alone," Jessie informed the men. "It seems they have some silly superstition that he's supernatural, a spirit sent from their god. Señor West thinks we should give up the chase, that the Comanches will return, and if we haven't, will attack us. If any one of you wants to turn around and go back, you have my permission to do so. You can wait with Gabe and the others at the Rodriguez *rancho*." Jessie slashed Morgan with a defiant look, then said, "But I'm going on. If it's the last thing I do—I'm going to capture that stallion!"

Jessie turned her horse and rode off. Wordlessly, every one of the *mesteñeros* followed her.

As Morgan sidled his horse up to hers, Jessie hissed beneath her breath, "See? I told you they wouldn't go back. They're just as anxious as I am to capture that stallion, and they're *not* afraid of the Comanches."

Morgan thought that the *mesteñeros* were continuing more from loyalty to Jessie than the reasons she had given him, but he didn't comment. He knew it would be a waste of his breath to argue with her. That unholy gleam was back in her eyes. She was being driven by her obsession, the devil once again riding her back. There would be no turning back.

The next day they followed the White Steed upriver into the Cañón de Ugalde. Morgan glanced up uneasily at the high cliffs on both sides of him, thinking that this would be an excellent spot for an ambush. Below the steep walls the river flowed through a narrow, rocky gorge that was devoid of all vegetation—and protection —except for an occasional tuft of grass or clump of cactus.

When the Comanches had not attacked them either at sunset or at dawn—the Indians' preferred time to hit their enemies—the *mesteñeros* visibly relaxed, mistakenly thinking that the danger had passed. But Morgan knew that the Comanches never attacked when or where you expected them to. That had been part of the secret of their success in waging war, that and their remarkable horsemanship. They had been defiant to the bitter end, the last of the Texas tribes to be put on a reservation, and then, only after their defeat at the battle of Palo Alto Canyon several years before. Ironically, the chief to hold out the longest had been Quanah Parker, a half-breed, the son of an Anglo woman who had been taken captive by the Comanches as a child. The greatest and most powerful chief the Comanche nation had ever known had been not a full-blooded Comanche but half white.

As the sun rose higher and higher in the sky and beat down on them, the heat was reflected from the canyon's walls, making them feel as if they were riding in an oven. The sweat streamed from them and their mounts, and there wasn't a breath of air.

Early that afternoon the White Steed turned in to a side canyon, surprising them all, for this was the first time he had left the river. When Jessie recognized the entrance to the canyon, she cried out excitedly, "This canyon ends in a cul-de-sac. We've got him! He's trapped!"

"Ah, *patrona,* he must be so exhausted that he doesn't even realize where he is going," Pedro said. "Surely, he knows these side canyons and that this one is a dead end. He would never allow himself to fall into that trap under normal circumstances."

"Yes, our hounding him day and night has finally paid off," Jessie answered. She glanced over her shoulder at the *mesteñeros* who were lagging behind from the heat. "Get the men up here, Pedro. Quickly! So we can block that entrance before the White Steed realizes his mistake."

As Pedro rode off to joggle the *mesteñeros* out of their heat-induced stupor, Morgan asked Jessie, "Do you know the history of that cul-de-sac? That's where the Spanish general Ugalde and his lancers, along with a powerful horde of Comanches and Wichitas, trapped a major band of Lipan Apaches over a hundred years ago. Hundreds of Apaches were slaughtered there."

"Keep your voice down," Jessie hissed. "You know how superstitious the *mesteñeros* are. And don't you dare say anything to them. We're going in after that stallion, and I want them to keep their minds on their work and not be looking for ghosts."

"I wasn't about to say anything. They can see for themselves. That whole canyon is littered with bones bleaching in the sun. That's what I'm trying to tell you. This canyon is bad enough, but at least we have two ways to run if we have to. But that side canyon is a trap, not just for the White Steed, but for us too."

"Are you still worried about the Comanches?" Jessie asked in biting voice. "If they were going to attack, they would have done so by now."

"Jess—"

"No!" Jessie interjected angrily. "I won't listen to any more of your silly arguments. You're just as bad as the *mesteñeros,* seeing ghosts in every shadow. No, we're going in there. I'll never get another opportunity like this one to catch that stallion. If you're afraid, you can stay out here."

Jessie whirled her horse and rode into the small side canyon. Morgan glared at her back, infuriated at both her blind stubbornness and her insinuation that he was afraid for himself. He was tempted to ride off and leave her to her fate, but he couldn't. He still loved her. He shook his head in dismay, thinking that love could be a trap too. Perhaps the biggest trap of all.

When the last *mesteñero* trotted his horse into the side canyon, Morgan followed, a grim look on his face.

There was an eeriness about the place that made the hair on the backs of their necks stand on end. The silence was oppressive, and despite the hot sun beating down on them, there was a chill in the air. A musty odor permeated everything—the rocky walls, the sand, the air. It was like riding into a tomb in broad daylight.

Seeing a bleached skull on the canyon floor, one *mesteñero*'s eyes widened, and his face drained of all color. *"Madre de Dios,"* he muttered.

As more skeletons appeared, several of the Mexicans crossed themselves, while others muttered prayers beneath their breath, casting frightened glances around them. Even the horses were jittery, sensing that this was a place of death.

When the canyon made a sharp turn, they came to a dead halt, seeing the White Steed standing several hundred feet away. Behind him rose a solid wall of rock.

On reaching the end of the canyon the stallion had turned and then, utterly exhausted, had been unable to retrace his steps. Swaying on his feet, his head hanging low, he was sound asleep.

Jessie motioned for her *mesteñeros* to fan out and block the canyon. Then she and her men approached the stallion cautiously, their lariats ready, every muscle in their bodies tense with expectation.

Suddenly the stallion's head snapped up. When he saw them, a look of stunned surprise crossed his eyes. Then, as his powerful heart pumped adrenaline through his veins, the mustang came suddenly to life, revitalized. He reared on his hind legs, his front hooves pawing the air, his dark eyes spitting defiance. A shrill, angry trumpet rent the air, the loud sound bouncing off the canyon walls and echoing down its entire length.

"Now!" Jessie cried, and she and the Mexicans rushed forward, lariats whirling over their heads. The stallion came down on his front hooves at the same time and lunged, speeding toward them, determined to make one last desperate bid for freedom.

Seeing the wild-eyed mustang bearing down on them, two of the *mesteñeros* veered their horses to avoid a head-on collision, and the white stallion raced through the narrow opening as ropes flew everywhere through the air.

One loop, then another and another, fell over the stallion's head, and then, suddenly tightening, snapped the horse's neck and flipped him backward. The White

Steed fell on his side, the impact shaking the ground and raising a cloud of dust. Everyone held their breath, fearing that the magnificent animal's neck had been broken.

Seeing the stallion lying so deathly still, tears sprang to Jessie's eyes as she muttered, "Oh, my God, no. Please, no!"

Morgan, watching from the sidelines, felt sick at heart. His gaze swept over Jessie and the *mesteñeros,* all paralyzed with dread, their faces ashen, a look of horror in their eyes. Grim-lipped, Morgan dismounted and walked to the stallion. Then, bending over the mustang, he called, "He's breathing! He's just stunned!"

Jessie was off her horse in a flash, calling to Morgan as she ran, "Loosen the ropes on his neck a little."

Morgan crouched beside the stallion and loosened the ropes, then rose and stepped back. As Jessie rushed up he caught her arm, pulling her back, saying sharply, "Be careful! He's trying to get up."

The stallion stumbled to his feet and shook his head, still dazed. The loops of rope dangled from his neck. The *mesteñeros* clutched the ends of their lariats, their eyes watchful, ready to tighten them if the horse made another break for freedom. But the White Steed made no effort to move. He had expended the last of his strength on his unsuccessful attempt to escape.

Morgan's eyes filled with compassion as he looked at the stallion, standing with his proud head bowed and his powerful muscles trembling from sheer exhaustion. But strangely, even in defeat there was something regal about the horse. He had fought the battle for his freedom valiantly, with all his strength and all his cunning, and there was no shame or fear in those dark, velvety eyes, as if he knew there was no dishonor in losing if one fought well and courageously. Instead, there was a quiet resignation, and Morgan found himself admiring the noble animal even more for his dignity in defeat.

"*Patrona!*"

The cry was barely more than a whisper, but the urgency in it snapped Morgan's attention from the stallion to the man who had uttered it. The *mesteñero* was staring over Morgan and Jessie's heads, his face ashen.

Both Jessie and Morgan whirled around. Frank Gibbons and his five gunslingers sat on their horses where the canyon made its sharp turn, and each gunman with a six-shooter in his hand. Morgan silently cursed himself for every kind of fool. Instead of paying attention and covering their rear, he had allowed himself to get caught up in the drama of the capture, and now they were in the same situation as the white mustang, trapped, with no avenue of escape.

Gibbons trotted his horse to where Jessie and Morgan stood, a sickening smirk on his face. Morgan noted that the rancher's complexion was even more flushed than the last time he had seen him, and that the man's eyes were bloodshot and his face puffy, all testimony to Gibbons's advancing alcoholism.

Reining in before Jessie, Gibbons asked, "Why do you look so surprised, gal? I told you I'd never let you take that stallion."

Recovering from her shock, Jessie glared at Gibbons, saying hotly, "You can't get away with this!"

Gibbons sneered. "Can't I? Who's gonna stop me?" He gave a harsh, ugly laugh before continuing. "Nobody cares what happens to a bunch of greasy Mexicans. And even if they did, they'd never come looking here. Everyone's scared of this place. They say it's haunted.

In a few years no one will be able to tell the difference between those Apaches' bones and yours."

"Is that why you waited all this time, instead of attacking us when we were in the open?" Jessie asked, too angry to be afraid. "Were you waiting for someplace where you could hide the evidence?"

Gibbons's eyes flashed. Bitch! he thought angrily. She had caused him nothing but trouble ever since he had laid eyes on her and, by the time this was over, a small fortune too. He'd be glad to see her dead, her and that treacherous bastard standing by her side, but he'd hoped to see her beg and plead first. Instead, she was just as defiant as ever—damn her!

"I could have wiped you out anytime out there in the open," Gibbons answered in a tight voice. "But when I saw what a chase that stallion was giving you, I decided to let you do all the work and catch him for me. I was just lucky the White Steed led you in here. It couldn't have worked out better if I'd planned it myself."

Jessie felt sick with self-recrimination. Morgan had warned her about following the White Steed into this canyon, but she had refused to listen. Now they'd all die because of her stubbornness.

Gibbons dismounted awkwardly with his one arm and then pulled his gun. Staring at the stallion as he walked toward him, with that fanatical gleam in his eyes and his face distorted with fury, he looked exactly like what he was—a madman.

As Gibbons came closer Jessie and Morgan heard him muttering to himself, "I'm gonna kill that bastard. Shoot him one leg at a time, then skin the hide off him just like the Indians do. He's gonna pay for what he did to me. He's gonna suffer just like I did."

Horrified, Jessie jumped in front of the stallion,

shielding him with her body and crying, "No! I won't let you do it!"

"Get out of my way, you goddamned bitch!" Gibbons yelled, shoving Jessie aside so violently that she stumbled and fell to her knees.

Gibbons's loud curse caught the White Steed's attention. Exhausted, he had been dozing, oblivious to all around him. He looked up and saw Gibbons standing before him. A brief flicker of recognition came into the stallion's eyes, to be quickly replaced with a look of unadulterated hatred. Enraged, the steed issued a bloodcurdling scream that shook the walls of the canyon and sent ice water flowing through the veins of the observers. He reared on his hind legs, his lips drawn back over his teeth, his nostrils flaring.

When Gibbons shoved Jessie aside, he had lost his balance, a balance that had been precarious ever since the loss of his arm. The moment it took him to regain it and look up at the stallion cost him his life. He raised his gun and fired, but the shot missed, going over the stallion's shoulder. The last thing Gibbons saw was those massive, razor-sharp hooves descending on him before his skull was split open.

Even after Gibbons had fallen to the ground, the white mustang kept pounding on the rancher's inert body with his hooves, battering and ripping open the dead man's flesh in a frenzy of hate. Those watching the violent scene were both shocked and mesmerized, temporarily paralyzed by the animal's sudden eruption. All except Morgan. He took the opportunity to whip his gun from his holster while the gunfighters were occupied with watching the gory scene.

When the white stallion finally stood still over his victim, his chest heaving from his exertions and his eyes gleaming in triumph, one of the gunslingers muttered, "Jesus Christ! What in the hell got into that stallion?"

"He and Gibbons have met before," Morgan informed the man. "Gibbons claimed the stallion cost him his arm. He creased the horse, something I understand can be quite painful if it's not done correctly. That's why the mustang attacked him, and that's why he remembered Gibbons after all these years."

When Morgan spoke up, the gunfighters' eyes swiveled from the stallion to him. Seeing the gun he was pointing at them, they stiffened in their saddles.

"Don't shoot!" Morgan warned in a low, menacing voice.

One of the gunslingers' eyes narrowed. Then he scoffed, saying, "You're crazy. There are five of us. We'll riddle you."

"Yes, but I can take two, maybe three of you with me before I die," Morgan reminded him. "And you don't know which of you it's going to be. Besides, there's no need for this to go any further. Gibbons is dead. There's nothing in it for you, unless you just like gambling with your life."

"He's right, Sam," another gunslinger said to the man who had laughed at Morgan. "We ain't gonna get paid. After all we've gone through, we ain't gonna get a lousy cent out of it. Why risk our necks for nothing? It was Gibbons's fight."

"It ain't gonna be for nothing, Willie," Sam answered, his eyes boring into Morgan. "Didn't you hear what Gibbons called that stallion? The White Steed! There are people who'd pay a fortune for that horse."

Willie looked back at the stallion in amazement and then down at Gibbons's battered body at his feet. A shiver ran through the gunfighter. "Not me. I ain't getting nowhere near that man-killer. I'm getting out of here."

Willie turned his horse and rode off. Another gun-slinger peeled off from the others and followed him.

"Cowards," Sam muttered under his breath, and then turned back to face Morgan, saying in a hard voice, "You've got a choice, mister. You can give us that stallion, and we'll ride out of here real peaceful-like—or we can kill you for him!"

The gunfighter completely discounted any of the others, knowing he and his cohorts could quickly outgun them before their Winchesters could even clear leather. No, the hard-eyed man in front of him was the only thing standing between him and a fortune.

Morgan walked away from the White Steed, and Sam smirked, thinking that Morgan was backing down. Then, when Morgan stopped, his gun still aimed at the gunfighters with deadly intent, Sam realized that he had only moved to put the girl and the horse out of the line of fire.

"You're going to have to kill me if you want that horse," Morgan said in a steely voice.

Jessie gasped at Morgan's words, terror welling up in her. Once before he had faced three gunfighters, but their guns hadn't already been aimed at him. He had killed those men because he was faster on the draw. He'd die, and all because of her. He had given her a choice, and she had made the wrong one. She must have been insane at the time. Life without Morgan would be meaningless, an empty stretch of time, and nothing on earth could fill that emptiness—nothing! Oh, God, if she only had it to do all over.

Jessie jumped to her feet, crying out, "No, Morgan! Let them have the stallion!"

Morgan glanced toward Jessie at her sudden, surprising cry. Thinking that he was distracted, the three gunfighters squeezed their triggers. But Morgan had seen the intent in their eyes and threw himself to the side, hitting the ground and rolling as his gun roared in rapid succession.

Two men went flying from their saddles as the impact of Morgan's bullets hit them, one dead before he even hit the ground, the other mortally wounded. Only Sam was left, and he cursed his horse, made skittish by the bullets flying all around him and keeping the gunslinger from getting a clear shot at Morgan. Then, realizing that Morgan's gun was empty, Sam laughed, carefully aimed his six-shooter, and yelled triumphantly, "I've got you now, you bastard!"

The sharp crack of a rifle shot reverberated through the small canyon, and a surprised look came over Sam's face. He sat for a moment, frozen in that position, his hand still holding the gun that was pointed at Morgan. But the message to squeeze the trigger never got from his brain to his finger. A bloodstain slowly spread over his shirt front, and he toppled from his horse and into the dust.

Morgan glanced over his shoulder and saw Pedro sitting on his horse, his Winchester still smoking. He grinned and said, *"Gracias, amigo."*

"De nada, amigo," Pedro answered, grinning back.

Morgan got to his feet and looked around him, quickly assessing the situation. Then he turned his attention to reloading his gun.

Jessie rushed up to him, asking anxiously, "Are you hurt?"

"No, amazingly," Morgan replied, rotating the cylinder on his gun and slipping another bullet into the chamber.

How can he be so cool and calm? Jessie wondered. Didn't anything unnerve him? Then, remembering the promise she had made herself, she turned to the *mesteñeros* and said, "Release the stallion."

Morgan's head snapped up. The Mexicans stared at her as if she had lost her mind.

"I said, let him go," Jessie repeated in a firm voice to the stunned *mesteñeros*.

Morgan slipped his gun in his holster and took her arm, turning her to face him. "Do you know what you're saying?"

"Yes, I do."

Morgan's eyes searched her face. Then he asked, "Why, Jess? Why are you doing this?"

Tears shimmered in Jessie's eyes, and her lips trembled. Her voice was choked with emotion as she said, "Oh, Morgan, I was terrified when you faced those gunmen. I knew then that I had made a terrible mistake. The White Steed means nothing to me compared to you. I'm only doing what I should have done yesterday, what I promised myself I'd do if you somehow survived that hail of bullets. I'm giving him back his freedom."

Jessie turned and nodded to the *mesteñeros*. The Mexicans obeyed her silent command and slipped the ropes from the stallion's neck. The White Steed stood perfectly still, as if he didn't know what was expected of him.

Jessie walked up to the mustang and patted his sleek neck, saying, "You're free, boy. Go on now."

Finally realizing that this was no trick, that he was actually free, the stallion gave a joyful snort and paced off. Jessie watched as he rounded the bend in the canyon, gliding like a sailing ship over smooth waters, and tears came to her eyes at the beauty of his graceful motion, thinking that there would never be another horse to equal him.

Seeing the expression on her face, Morgan took her shoulder and turned her to face him. "I would have liked to let you keep him, Jess, but I didn't dare. Look up there." His eyes rose to the top of the canyon.

Jessie glanced up and gasped, seeing the Comanches sitting on their horses at the top of the canyon. They lined both walls and the end of the cul-de-sac, almost completely surrounding them. It was obvious that this was no longer a hunting party. Their bronze faces were slashed with black paint—the color of death—and their mounts were splattered with the rich colors of vermilion and ocher. Bright feathers dangled from the manes and tails of the horses and fluttered in the Indian's scalp locks and on their long lances, weapons that could be just as lethal as the drawn rifles that were flashing in the sunlight.

Jessie's face was deathly pale as she asked in a weak voice, "How long have they been there?"

"I don't honestly know," Morgan answered. "I noticed them when I glanced over your shoulder, when you were explaining why you were releasing the stallion. That's why I didn't object to your letting him go. I knew it had to be done. Right then."

"Maybe . . . maybe it's already too late," Jessie said, her voice trembling with fear.

"No, I don't think so, or they would have already attacked." Then, hearing the excited murmur of the *mesteñeros* behind him, Morgan realized that they, too, had spied the Comanches. He turned to the men, saying in a firm voice, "Don't make one move toward your guns, or it's all over. I don't think they're going to attack now that we've freed the stallion."

Pedro scanned the rim of the canyon, asking nervously, "If they are not going to attack, then what are they waiting for?"

"I guess they just want to make us sweat a little."

Waiting in the hot sun, with the Comanches' guns pointed down at them, seemed an eternity. When the leader of the Indians raised his arm, Jessie sucked in her breath, thinking that he was signaling to fire. Then, to her surprise and utter relief, the Comanches backed their horses away from the rim of the canyon, whirled them around, and rode off, disappearing as suddenly and silently as they had appeared.

An hour later Jessie, Morgan, and the *mesteñeros* rode out of the cul-de-sac, having buried Gibbons and the three dead gunfighters. The Mexicans rode ahead of Morgan and Jessie, anxious to be out of the canyon that had known so much violence and death.

As they rode side by side, Morgan noticed that Jessie was quiet and withdrawn. Finally he asked, "What are you thinking about? Gibbons and those other men?"

"No, I was wondering what we're going to do for a master stallion, now that we don't have the White Steed. I guess we'll have to buy a Thoroughbred, but they're so expensive. I hate to put that much money out for a stallion. It will mean we'll have to settle for less land."

Reaching out and catching Jessie's reins, Morgan brought both their horses to a halt. Jessie looked at him in surprise at his abrupt action.

"What in the hell are you going to buy a stallion for?" Morgan asked.

"I should think that would be obvious," Jessie retorted. "You can't breed horses without a stallion."

"But we've already got a master stallion. Right here," Morgan countered, patting El Dragón's neck proudly.

"El Dragón?" Jessie asked in disbelief.

"Dammit, Jess, will you look at him! For once, *really* look at him. You've been so blinded by the White Steed that you've never even noticed that El Dragón is just as powerfully built and beautiful as he is. And El Dragón is fast, too. Not as fast as the White Steed, but almost. True, El Dragón isn't a pacer, but he's got something that's almost as prized. His irises. And he's a strong herd stallion, strong enough to be anyone's master stallion. It's in his blood. You admitted that much yourself."

Jessie had admired El Dragón as fine horseflesh, but she had never considered him—or any other stallion— as a substitute for the White Steed. For the first time she really looked at the horse with a critical, professional eye and realized that everything Morgan had said was true.

"Oh, he doesn't have the notoriety that the White Steed has," Morgan admitted as Jessie continued to study El Dragón thoughtfully, "but he has one big advantage over the white stallion. El Dragón is much younger. He'll have years and years of siring foals. And Jess, can't you just see the foals that he and your mares will produce? Colts of every color of horseflesh, with his beautiful irises."

Jessie's eyes lit up at the thought, and then she frowned. "No, Morgan, I can't take El Dragón for our master stallion. He's *your* horse. Your personal mount. You captured and saddle-broke him for that purpose, at considerable time and effort on your part. It wouldn't be fair to you."

"Jess," Morgan said in exasperation, "our ranch is going to be a joint venture, remember? Just consider El Dragón my contribution to the breeding stock." Then Morgan grinned ruefully. "Besides, you were right when you said master herd stallions didn't make good mounts. He's much too independent. Every time I ride him, it's a contest between us over who is going to dominate who. That kind of challenge is exciting and stimulating every now and then, but on an everyday basis it could become irritating and tiring. No, I have my trusty old gelding for a dependable mount."

"You're sure you won't regret it?" Jessie asked, still doubtful.

"No, Jess, I won't regret it," Morgan answered firmly. "El Dragón wasn't meant to be a saddle horse. As our master stallion, he'll be doing what he's meant to do, what's in his blood." He patted the stallion's neck fondly, saying, "And maybe you'll let me ride you every now and then, huh, boy? When we're both in the mood for a good hard run and have a need to get away from the ladies for a while?"

Jessie laughed. "Get away from the ladies? That's a fine thing to say! Maybe I can see El Dragón needing a respite from the demands of his duties—but you? After all, you'll have only one female to keep contented, while he'll have over a hundred."

Morgan thought that Jessie was going to be just as much a handful for him as El Dragón's entire *manada* would be for the stallion—or more so. The stallion's mares knew who was lord and master and accepted it, while Morgan had a very independent little lady on his hands, a woman who would never accept any man as her master. But then Morgan wouldn't have it any other way. That's what made his Jess so special.

As they retraced their steps through the winding Cañón de Ugalde, Morgan and Jessie talked in low voices, laying their plans for their exciting future. The *mesteñeros* rode at a respectful distance ahead of them, pleased with how things had turned out. They may have lost the White Steed, but they had gained a *patrón*, a strong leader who would see to their future just as he would the small woman riding beside him. Yes, the future looked very promising for everyone.

When they emerged from the canyon, Jessie's gaze swept over the landscape. Here the ground dipped and swelled in narrow valleys covered with lush grass and steep, rocky hills where there was very little vegetation, except for an occasional cedar brake, a clump of cactus, or a lone, squatty mesquite. Above them the sun dipped in and out behind low-hung, fluffy clouds, and the entire landscape was covered with patches of moving light and shadow, the subdued light turning the valleys to a deep purple.

Seeing something in one of the shadows in the distance, Jessie looked closer. Then, as it emerged into the bright light, Jessie cried softly, "Look, it's the White Steed!"

"My God, how could he recuperate so fast?" Morgan said in amazement. "He couldn't have rested for long, and yet to see him now you'd never guess he was too exhausted even to move a few hours ago."

The stallion *had* amazingly returned to his former magnificence, tirelessly flying up and over the crest of one hill, then disappearing into a purple valley, then up another hill, dipping in and out of the landscape, his long mane spread out like huge white wings.

Seeing the wistful expression on Jessie's face, Morgan asked softly, "Are you having regrets?"

"No, I'm glad I turned him loose," Jessie answered, her eyes still on the stallion in the distance. "He belongs out there in the open, wild and free. That's his domain, his kingdom." A look of sadness came into her eyes. "I wish it could be true what the Indians say about him, that he's immortal, that he'll never die."

"Why?" Morgan asked curiously.

"Look at this land, Morgan. How empty it is. At one time, herds of buffalo, longhorns, mustangs, even bands of Indians roamed here. All the wild ones are slowly disappearing, and this country will never be the same without them. But as long as the White Steed lives and roams at will, their wild, free spirit will live on, a beautiful reminder of what this land was once like."

Morgan and Jessie watched as the White Steed streaked over the horizon, both feeling a sadness at knowing this was the last time they would see the beautiful, graceful stallion. And even then they sat silently staring off into the distance, perhaps hoping they might get just one more fleeting glimpse of the famous mustang.

Then, when the shadows of dusk were falling all around them, Morgan touched Jessie's arm and said softly, "Let's go, sweetheart. Let's go home."

Epilogue

JESSIE SLIPPED FROM BENEATH THE COVERS AND stood beside the bed, smiling down at her sleeping husband. The sun was rising, and she knew she should wake him, but she decided to let Morgan sleep a little longer. He needed his rest after their long siege of lovemaking the night before.

Jessie put on her wrapper and padded to the window, wondering what their grandchildren, sleeping in the room down the hall, would think if they knew that she and Morgan still made love. Undoubtedly they would be shocked. Young people seemed to think that sex was an intimate pleasure reserved for them alone, and certainly not something she and Morgan should be doing at their advanced age. But the passion she and Morgan felt for each other had never diminished. Like their love, it had only grown.

Jessie pushed back the curtain and looked down on the lush, gently rolling land before her, the dewdrops on the grass glistening in the early morning sun. Each fenced-in pasture held a different stallion and his *manada*, the mares quietly grazing while their colts frisked playfully around them. Noting that many of the horses had irises that changed color when they moved, she smiled, pleased to see that so many carried the mark of the proud stallion that had been their ancestor.

She leaned against the windowsill, her mind going back over the years she and Morgan had shared. To Jessie's surprise and delight, Morgan had bought the spread of land lying next to hers with his savings, making their ranch twice as big as she had ever dreamed. Their ranch had been a success almost from the very beginning, because their reputation for producing horseflesh of the finest quality had quickly spread all over Texas and the Southwest. Several of their colts had gone on to become great racehorses, two even winning the Kentucky Derby, much to Morgan's and her delight.

Of course, she and Morgan had clashed over the years. With their strong wills disagreements had been inevitable, but none had been serious or lasted very long before they had compromised. Instead of weakening the marriage, the clashes of will had given it added spark. No, their union had never been dull, had never slipped into that boring monotony that seemed to smother so many marriages.

But all had not been smooth sailing. They'd had their trials and tribulations with their ranch, too. But in weathering them, they had emerged even stronger. Over the years several droughts had dried up the San Saba, and the grass had turned brown, the wells run dry. They had been forced to sell the majority of their horses for a pittance, rather than see them die. Then there had been the year they'd had that unusually hard freeze, and many of their horses had frozen to death, followed by the horrible anthrax epidemic a few years later. Surviving all these natural disasters, they had been faced with yet another crisis, this time man-made. The horseless carriage. As more and more of the ugly, noisy monsters had taken to the roads, Morgan and Jessie had feared their ranch would go under. But their reputation as breeders of fine horses with exceptionally good footing had stood them in good steed. In the West, reliable horses were still needed on ranches and in remote areas where the terrain was too rugged for automobiles to travel.

Now, even as the world became more and more automated, Jessie thought that there would always be a place for the horse. Even if cattle ranching itself somehow became obsolete, and man figured out some ungodly machine to get into remote areas, there would always be a demand for the animals on the western scene, where the horse had played such an important role in its development, for the sheer pleasure of riding the noble animal, if not for practical reasons.

There had been personal tragedies in her and Morgan's life, too, just as there are in everyone's lives. The deaths of Pedro and Gabe, although they had both lived to ripe old ages, had deeply saddened them, and the loss of one of their sons to diphtheria had broken their hearts. Even the death of El Dragón had hit them hard, for the stallion had served them well for many, many years. But they had so much to be thankful for, the success of their ranch and the beautiful family they had been blessed with, a family that had grown from three sons and two daughters to sixteen grandchildren and two great-grandchildren so far. Yes, all and all, it had been a rich, full life, sharing the good and the bad.

Jessie's eyes caught a glimpse of white. She turned
her attention to the stallion in the distance. He was one
of her favorites, reminding her so much of the White
Steed. She still heard stories of a wild white stallion that
was reputed to roam in remote areas all over the Southwest. The stories all proclaimed the stallion as being
unusually beautiful, graceful, spirited, and endowed
with a remarkable speed. Jessie knew that it couldn't be
the White Steed, for the famous mustang had been
even older than El Dragón and was bound to have died
years ago. But as long as men hungered for freedom and
admired beauty and grace, the white stallion would
live, in their imaginations if nothing else, the symbol of
the beautiful wild ones that had vanished from the
earth but whose spirits would live forever in men's
minds.

"Jess?" Morgan called softly from the bed.

Jessie turned to Morgan, her gaze sweeping over him
admiringly. His hair was still thick, but silver now, picking up the unusual color of his eyes and giving him a
distinguished air. His body was just as lean and powerfully muscled as it had been the day she had met him,
and Jessie knew he had lost none of his virility.

"What are you doing over there by the window?"
Morgan asked.

"Just admiring our ranch."

"Come back to bed, sweetheart. It's cold out there,"
Morgan said, sweeping back the covers. His voice
dropped to a husky timbre. "Let me warm you up."

A shiver of anticipation ran through Jessie at the sensual delights Morgan's words and warm gaze were
promising her. Yes, he was the warmth of her life, both
in bed and out, the strong, steady rock from which she
drew her strength, the man who had enslaved her heart

but never mastered her spirit. He was all things to her: her helpmate, her sensuous lover, her comforter, her exciting adversary—her man, and oh, God, how she loved him.

For a moment Jessie lingered at the window, just to prove that she retained some of her fierce independence. Then she smiled and walked to him, saying, "Coming, my love."

Don't miss best-selling author Virginia Henley's new historical romance, THE HAWK AND THE DOVE, available from Dell next month.

Cheltenham, 1586

Spring had not yet arrived. Icicles hung by the river and the horses' breath formed frosty clouds upon the air as the two young riders playfully raced the last hundred yards before reaching the stables.

Inside, the warmth enveloped them and the tang of horse, leather, and hay heightened all their senses in a most disturbing fashion. The young man, so fair, took both hands of the vibrant beauty into his own and drew her toward him. He knew he must taste her or go mad. "Sara," he breathed her name raggedly against her lips, before covering them in the kiss they had both been anticipating for weeks.

Now that they were finally fused, they had no strength to pull apart. Her arms were lovingly entwined about his neck and his hands caressed her back and slowly moved to cup and fondle her breasts. He moaned low in his throat and sank down into the hay, pulling his beautiful tormentor with him.

Sara was tempted, tempted badly. She had never felt like this before. It was as if her bones wanted to melt with the delicious languor that was stealing over her. "Andrew, no, we cannot."

"Please, Sara, please. I'm going to offer for you." And once more he covered her protesting mouth and fumbled with the buttons of her riding dress. He had managed to undo three before she found the strength to tear herself away from him.

It wasn't that she didn't believe him. She knew he was as good as his word and that he would certainly offer for her. But others had offered for her and nothing had ever come of it. Now she held his hands firmly to keep them in check. She laughed up at him lovingly. "You haven't even proposed to me yet!"

"Sara, darling, will you marry me?"

She heard the words echoing in her mind, then the scene dissolved in a shimmer as she gazed through the window, unseeing. She forced back unshed, unwanted tears before anyone ever suspected she was crying. She would rather die!

"Witches!" thought Sara Bishop, barely hanging on to her infamous temper. She set her teeth and faced her four half sisters in the beautifully appointed family room. The two older ones from her mother's first marriage were dark, sleek, almost smug from their secure position in the family hierarchy. The pair younger than herself, from her mother's third and present marriage, were pretty and blond, spoiled and selfish to the core.

They had gathered to organize the details of the upcoming wedding—to make lists of potential guests, to word the actual invitations, and to choose material for their gowns. Their gently bred mother, Mary Bishop, had already retired with a headache; never had she been capable of coping with her daughters en masse.

" 'Tis a conspiracy!" Sara stormed and her hair flew about her shoulders the color of pale molten copper. "You know damned well that deep rose-pink makes me look hideous, and 'tis precisely why you always choose it."

"Sabre Wilde, stop that swearing instantly," hissed Jane, who at twenty-two was the eldest.

"Don't you dare to call me Sabre Wilde! You lot are enough to make a saint swear," shouted Sara in exasperation.

"Saint?" they hooted with laughter.

"Saint?" echoed Jane. "Devil's spawn more likely, Sabre Wilde." She emphasized the name derisively.

"You earned the nickname for yourself," smirked Ann, the youngest. "Jane, is it true that when her father died she trailed his sabre about the house for weeks and even insisted on sleeping with it?"

" 'Tis true, and she was only four years old. She had such a dangerous temper, she ruled the household, terrorized poor mother, and was so willful, she attempted to wound the servants with that sabre."

"I'll go and fetch the bloody thing now if you don't shut up!" Sara threatened.

"If you swear again, I shall report you to Father," Jane threatened as she arose from the writing desk now littered with the forgotten lists.

The room seemed stifling to Sara. The spring weather had been unusually sticky and oppressive and now that her blood was up, her cheeks flushed and she tried to breathe deeply to calm herself. Her beautiful high, round breasts quivered with her great agitation and her older sister, Margaret, eyed them enviously and said with great malice, "The color of Sabre's hair screams so loudly she would be a disaster in any shade we chose. We all know 'tis not the color of the bridesmaids' dresses that has angered her, but the fact that sweet little Beth has received an offer of marriage and she has not."

" 'Tis not fair!" cried Sara. "Andrew was supposed to be my husband. After Jane and Margaret were married,

I was supposed to be next. I'm almost twenty years old! Beth is only fifteen."

The sisters were greatly amused at this. "You are living in a fantasy, Sabre Wilde. You will never receive an offer of marriage. Your Irish father left you without a dowry and everyone for miles about knows you for an *eccentric*," Jane pointed out.

Reverend Bishop threw open the door of his study, where he had been trying to compose a biting sermon for next Sunday. The girl was causing trouble again. She had been the only thorn in his side in an otherwise perfect marriage. His tall shadow fell across the doorway just as Sara shouted, "My Irish father, let me point out, was the only one of her husbands my mother married for love! The first she married for money, the last she married for respectability. You are four jealous witches!"

The girls' father issued a one-word command. "Apologize!"

Sara spun about with fear in her eyes. Then, determined to defy him, she drew herself up to her full height and said softly, "I'm sorry . . . I'm sorry they are jealous witches."

His mouth curved downward cruelly and he issued his orders without hesitation. "Fetch her in here. Put her across the table."

She was livid to be handled so and would have successfully fought off her two older sisters, but their father cruelly clamped a hand to the back of her neck and reached for his cane. They held her down gleefully to receive the beating they had never had to endure. The thin cotton of Sara's gown and petticoat was scant protection against the sting of the cane wielded so heavily by the Reverend. She felt the blood rush to her head, but she would be damned if she'd give them the satisfaction of seeing her faint.

"Go to your room, mistress," the Reverend finally ordered. "She has the Devil's mark upon her." The words followed Sara up the stairs and were like a spark to gunpowder as her temper exploded and she swore to be even with them all.

Sara slammed her chamber door and without stopping opened her window, climbed down the huge hawthorn tree, and ran for the stables. She grabbed a bridle, didn't waste time with a saddle but mounted Sabbath and, bending low over her palfrey's neck to protect her sore bottom, rode off toward the beautiful Cotswolds like the wind. She usually took great pleasure in the flowering trees and gamboling spring lambs, but today tears blinded her to the beauties of the countryside.

She rode a direct path through the woods, which were carpeted with bluebells, to the edge of the small, secluded lake. Slipping down from its back, she tethered her horse where it could reach the sweet green grass and stroked its muzzle lovingly. It had pleased her stepfather when she had called the colt "Sabbath." The corners of her mouth went up in a secret smile. How furious he would be if he knew the animal's full name was "Black Sabbath."

As she knelt by the edge of the lake and bent down to cup a handful of cooling water to bathe her face, she caught sight of her reflection. "I'm not ugly," she said defiantly, then sighed as she thought of her half sisters' beauty.

In reality she was far more fair of face and figure than they, but years of being disparaged had taken their toll. While her sisters were attractive, by comparison she was exquisite. Her hair was all molten flames and fire, her mouth voluptuously curved, and her green eyes were highlighted by dark brows and long dark lashes. Beside her left eye on the very tip of her cheekbone was a beauty spot. Tentatively she put her finger on the tiny black mole her family referred to as the mark of the Devil, then, obeying an impulse that was as old as Eve, she undressed quickly and slipped naked into the cool, soothing water.

She smiled as a pair of ducks paddled madly away to the safety of the reeds, and as her body and temper cooled and relaxed, her attention was caught by the iridescent colors of the hovering dragonflies. Mayhap she was wicked, she mused. Hadn't she forged a letter in her mother's hand to Lady Katherine Ashford at the Queen's Court? Kate was sister to her mother's first husband. She had made a brilliant marriage with Lord Ashford ten years ago and now held the lofty title of Mistress of the Queen's Robes. She moved in heady circles indeed! Sara, pretending to be her mother, had written reminding Kate that she was the mother of five lovely daughters and was begging for a position at court for one of them, no matter how lowly. She intimated at how difficult it was to find suitable husbands for them all and hinted that surely amongst Elizabeth's Court of sixteen hundred gentlemen a husband might be found for just one of her sweet, pretty-mannered girls.

It had been over two months since Sara had sent off the letter and she would have to keep a sharp watch to intercept an answering message from Lady Ashford.

Her imagination soared deliciously as she floated in the water. She saw herself dressed in a pale green ball gown fluttering a jeweled fan at a gentleman who would not quite behave himself. The brilliant room was lit with a thousand candles as she watched herself go into the man's arms for the dance.

Suddenly a shot rang out and she cried out in alarm for the poor duck that rose up from the lake then dropped back to the water stone-dead. The man heard her and came to the water's edge. It was Margaret's husband, John.

"Sabre! God's bones, you're naked!" He licked his lips and felt himself harden in response to his delicious sister-in-law.

"Bugger off!" she swore.

His retriever swam after the downed water fowl, but John only had eyes for the nymph before him. He was a handsome young man and he smiled slyly as he realized the compromising situation of his quarry. "There's one way of making sure my lips are sealed, sweetheart."

"Go home to your wife!" she said coldly.

"You should have been my wife, Sabre. I offered for you first."

"Piffle! You soon grabbed Margaret when you found out I was penniless, but she was mistress moneybags."

"Our parents arranged it; I had little choice in the matter. Be kind to me, Sabre, you know you broke my heart."

"I'd like to break your head, you lecher!" she cried.

"I'm coming in." He grinned wickedly and bent to remove his boots.

Though fear gripped her and her heart pounded frantically inside her breast, she would not let him see her fear. "John Thatcher, my lips will not be sealed if you make one more move toward me!"

He hesitated for only a second. "You wouldn't dare let the worthy Reverend know you'd been cavorting naked in the woods."

"What could he do to me? Thrash me? I've already had one beating today," she retorted bravely.

He finished disrobing and plunged into the lake. Sabre quickly ducked beneath the surface and swam underwater, not surfacing until she reached the grassy bank some thirty feet away. She flung on her petticoat and dress and was in the saddle almost before he spotted her.

"Sabre, help! My legs are tangled in the weeds," he called, and she could hear the irritation in his voice.

She laughed as she dug her heels into Black Sabbath's haunches. "I hope you never untangle them!"

Sara thought she had gotten away with her escapade when three days had passed and the Wrath of God had not descended upon her. The seamstresses for the wedding clothes were coming to Cheltenham all the way from Gloucester, and Sara grabbed the opportunity to go with the coach so that she could collect the mail for the Church and priory. Her mother and Beth, the bride-to-be, traveled into the city of Gloucester to select bed linen and deliver the wedding invitations to the aunts and uncles and cousins related to them through Mrs. Bishop's three marriages.

The Swan Inn was the posting house where the coaches brought the mail up from London. Sara quickly sorted through the papers that were addressed to the rectory and church and her heart skipped a beat as her fingers closed about the long-awaited reply from Lady Katherine Ashford in London. She stuffed it down the neck of her gown and wriggled it inside her busk, where the long-anticipated message it might hold almost burned her breasts. She then took the rest out to the coach and turned it all over to her mother.

Her heart was singing with such joy that even a

dreaded visit with the cousins could not quell her happiness. She closed her ears to the incessant chatter of weddings. Beth was wearing a pale blue silk afternoon dress with a fetching little pelisse in the same shade. Her blue satin slippers also matched and she sat crossing her ankles so that her pale blue silk stockings could be glimpsed by all.

Sara's thoughts were diverted from the letter when one of her cousins said, "That dark wine gown doesn't become your odd coloring, Sabre. It looked much prettier on Margaret before it was handed down to you."

Beth and her cousins all giggled.

Sara answered sweetly, "But I fill the bodice out better, don't you think?" Then she pointedly looked at each girl's small breasts.

The name of the game was spite as her cousin asked, "You must be very upset because Beth has had a proposal. Before we know it Ann, too, will be betrothed and you will be left a spinster."

God, how she hated them all. Her cheeks flushed and she said loftily, "I'm not in the least upset for I shall very likely be going to Court shortly." She could have bitten her tongue the moment the words were out, but she had such a habit of saying the first thing that came into her head and it usually landed her in hot water.

Beth laughed and said, "Why, Sabre, that's an outright lie."

Her cousin, instantly jealous that there might be a grain of truth in Sabre's remark, said to Beth, "I'm afraid Sabre suffers from delusions of grandeur. There are many locked up in the Gloucester Asylum with such afflictions."

"Is it your habit to visit asylums? Amazing they don't

mistake you for an inmate and detain you," replied Sara lightly.

"If you don't watch your tongue, Sabre Wilde, I'll get Daddy to give you another beating," threatened Beth.

"Beating?" asked her cousin breathlessly.

"We held her down across the table while Daddy took his cane to her bottom!"

Somehow Sara's teacup slipped through her fingers and its contents ruined not only Beth's blue silk, but the afternoon visit as well. Everyone watching would have sworn it was an accident, yet they knew better. Beth was in tears, incoherent, then hysterical, and there was nothing Mrs. Bishop could do but gather her two daughters and depart quickly amid a flurry of apologies for the disastrous turn of events.

Mary Bishop leaned her head back onto the velvet squabs of the coach and closed her eyes. Sara felt guilty for she knew her mother had a delicate constitution. Beth was carrying on ridiculously, so Sara had no alternative but to fix her with a penetrating look. "If you don't shut up instantly, I'll thump you." Beth sat back quietly and sniffled, for without the backing of her cousins or sisters, she was gutless.

When the coach arrived back at Cheltenham priory, Mrs. Bishop ushered Beth into the house to repair the damage to the blue silk and Sara stayed with the coach as it was taken to the stables. She reached into her busk and drew forth the treasured letter.

With eager eyes she scanned the contents, skipping over the flowery salutations and small talk. Ah, here it was . . . "As mistress of Her Majesty's wardrobe I do indeed have need of many assistants and I would be pleased to take one of your gentle daughters under my wing, should you decide to send her to Court. I know that you will appreciate this great opportunity I am offering and assure you that a gentlewoman with manners and breeding may receive many offers of marriage which would be otherwise closed to her. We are at Greenwich until the hot summer months make London an unhealthy place, at which time we go on progress, so I urge you to hasten your daughter's departure and rest assured I shall welcome any child of yours wholeheartedly. All I ask, dearest Mary, is that you do not saddle me with the little redhead of the volatile temper. I need a girl who is both amenable and biddable, and we both know that the 'Wilde' one is neither."

Sara let the letter fall from her fingers and a single tear slipped down her cheek; all her fine dreams and schemes reduced to ashes. It was almost an hour before she gradually became aware of her surroundings. The smell of leather and horses teased her nostrils and she stirred herself, sighing deeply for what might have been, and walked slowly to the house. As she passed her stepfather's study, his cold command reached her ears. "Come in here!"

She pushed open the doors and met his eyes. Suddenly she knew the reprieve of three days standing was over. He knew that she had swum naked. She stood motionless through the endless sermon, only longing to know her punishment and to get it over with. She was the scandal of the neighborhood. Her behavior was wanton, wicked, eccentric. She was an instrument of the Devil. Her Wilde Irish blood was tainted and she responded neither to chastisement nor punishment; she neither regretted nor repented. She heard him list her long catalogue of sins and waited for his verdict. When it came it was totally unexpected. It was said quietly without anger, yet it was more terrible for her than any beating.

"From now on you will be deprived of your privileges beginning with your riding. To ensure your obedience, I sold your horse today."

"No," she whispered, stunned. "Who did you sell her to?" Her mind screamed its denial.

"Silence!" he ordered.

Her pale green eyes narrowed. She dipped him an insolent little curtsey and departed with dignity.

Cheltenham was a small enough town that she soon discovered where Sabbath had gone. At the moment she was helpless to do anything about losing her, but she resolved to get her horse back come hell or high water when it was possible, and until that time she accepted the fact that she could only visit her occasionally and then only after a two-mile walk in each direction.

The wedding of Beth was imminent. Such loving attention had been given to each detail of the lavish affair that Sara was sick to death of it all and wished the ordeal was over and done with. She dreaded the wedding ceremony itself with her stepfather officiating at the marriage of his own daughter. Jane's husband was to walk Beth down the aisle of the English church, which would be packed with all their relatives from Gloucester and all her father's regular congregation from Cheltenham. The church would echo to the rafters with whispers about why she was not being married. After all, it was her turn and Beth was almost five years her junior. In Tudor England girls married before the age of sixteen or were considered to be left on the shelf—unsuitable, unmarriageable, unwanted.

Damn, I'd like to give them something to talk about,

she thought unhappily. She sat in the orchard, thinking up one scheme after another, rejecting her ideas almost as quickly as she thought of them.

The deep pink bridesmaid gown, which she hated, was finished and hanging in her room. She felt depressed every time she looked at it. Ah well, in two days time it would all be over but the shouting, and then she would have the attentions of three brothers-in-law to dodge instead of just two, for the bridegroom had already caught her alone a couple of times and tried to steal kisses from her.

As she walked past the washhouse she saw one of the servants busy over a large washtub. "What are you doing, Mrs. Pringle?"

"Ah, lovey, I'm busy dyeing the choirboys' cassocks. The Reverend sets great store by a grand show in the church. These cassocks are to be scarlet, do ye see. With the white lace surplices over the scarlet cassocks it will be like a pageant!"

"Do you need any help, Mrs. Pringle?"

"Well, now, lovey, ye know how sore me old back gets. While I'm taking these cassocks out to the orchard to dry, you can empty the tub with yon bucket. But be careful to let it cool down first so ye don't go scaldin' yerself."

As Sara watched the scarlet dye bubble, her own wicked juices began to stir. Did she dare? Why not? The only color that would make her look worse than deep pink would be scarlet! She wasted no time in smuggling her pink bridesmaid's gown down to the washhouse.

The wedding day dawned and none had time to give Sara Bishop a passing thought. She would keep her cloak on until the last possible moment, then she would throw it off as she walked down the aisle and everyone would recognize that Sara's alter ego, Sabre Wilde, had turned up.

Every pew of the church was packed. Her mother was escorted to the front row, while the bridegroom and the Reverend Bishop stood at the altar. Fourteen-year-old Ann was to go first in the procession scattering rose petals, then the lovely dark-haired Margaret and Jane, so alike, were paired to walk hand in hand. The bride on her brother-in-law's arm was to be followed by Sara, who would carry her train.

Beth was far too concerned over her own wedding attire to pay heed to eccentric Sara, who had insisted upon wearing her cloak until the last possible moment. The notes of the virginal rang out and the choirboys' sweet voices rose like the sound of angels. Then the solemn little procession started down the aisle and an expectant hush fell over the congregation.

Suddenly the musician struck a discordant note, the choirboys forgot the words to the hymn, and the assembled congregation gasped in unison. The girl was in bright red! The color screamed aloud its shocking unsuitability for a nuptial ceremony, especially inside a church, a hallowed place of God.

Sara had her revenge, upsetting the smug propriety of her half sister's wedding day, and at the same time reducing the Reverend Bishop's sacrament to the level of farce. The wedding would be talked about for months, and after the first shock waves wore off, people could not hide their laughter. That Sabre was a red-headed virago who had a penchant for scandalous behavior and they would never tame her!

Experience the Passion and the Ecstasy

☐ **AVENGING ANGEL** by Lori Copeland
Jilted by her thieving fiancé, Wynne Elliot rides
west seeking revenge...only to wind up in the
arm's of her enemy's brother.
10374-6 $3.95

☐ **DESIRE'S MASQUERADE** by Kathryn Kramer
Passion turns to treachery in Europe's Middle
Ages as Lady Madrigal and Stephan Valentine
are lost in a web of deception and desire.
11876-X $3.95

☐ **THE WINDFLOWER** by Laura London
Kidnapped by a handsome pirate, Merry
Wilding dreams of revenge on the high seas—
until she becomes a prisoner of her own
reckless longing.   19534-9 $3.95

At your local bookstore or use this handy coupon for ordering:

DELL READERS SERVICE, DEPT. DFH
P.O. Box 5057, Des Plaines, IL . 60017-5057
Please send me the above title(s). I am enclosing $_____
(Please add $2.00 per order to cover shipping and handling.) Send
check or money order—no cash or C.O.D.s please.

Ms./Mrs./Mr._____

Address _____

City/State _____ Zip _____

DFH - 7/88
Prices and availability subject to change without notice. Please allow four to six
weeks for delivery. This offer expires 1/89.

Extraordinary Books about Extraordinary Women

—**GRACE: The Secret Lives of a Princess** by James Spada
The national bestselling biography of Grace Kelly that
exposes the not-so-fairy-tale life behind the elegant
superstar image of America's favorite princess.

20107-1 $4.95

—**LADY OF HAY** by Barbara Erskine
The timeless human drama of a contemporary woman's
flight back through time where she discovers her past
life as a twelfth-century noblewoman. "...impossible to
put down."—*Philadelphia Inquirer.*

20005-9 $4.95

—**UNDER GYPSY SKIES** by Kathryn Kramer
The lush, sensual romance of a wild, impetuous gypsy
girl and a handsome nobleman, whose star-crossed
love affair triumphs amid the troubled years of the
Spanish Inquisition.

20008-3 $3.95

At your local bookstore or use this handy coupon for ordering:

DELL READERS SERVICE, DEPT. DLM
P.O. Box 5057, Des Plaines, IL . 60017-5057

Please send me the above title(s). I am enclosing $_____.
(Please add $2.00 per order to cover shipping and handling.) Send
check or money order—no cash or C.O.D.s please.

Ms./Mrs./Mr. _____

Address _____

City/State _____ Zip _____

DLM - 7/88
Prices and availability subject to change without notice. Please allow four to six
weeks for delivery. This offer expires 1/89.

A magnificent array of tempestuous, passionate historical romances— from the pageantry of Renaissance England and Venice to the harsh beauty of the Texas frontier.

☐ **THE RAVEN AND THE ROSE**
by Virginia Henley   17161-X $3.95

☐ **TO LOVE AN EAGLE**
by Joanne Redd   18982-9 $3.95

☐ **DESIRE'S MASQUERADE**
by Kathryn Kramer   11876-X $3.95

At your local bookstore or use this handy coupon for ordering:

DELL READERS SERVICE, DEPT. DHR
P.O. Box 5057, Des Plaines, IL . 60017-5057

Please send me the above title(s). I am enclosing $_____.
(Please add $2.00 per order to cover shipping and handling.) Send
check or money order—no cash or C.O.D.s please.

Ms./Mrs./Mr._____

Address _____

City/State _____ Zip _____

DHR-7/88

Prices and availability subject to change without notice. Please allow four to six
weeks for delivery. This offer expires 1/89.